THE BEST OF
KIM STANLEY
ROBINSON

THE BEST OF
KIM STANLEY
ROBINSON

EDITED BY
JONATHAN STRAHAN

NIGHT SHADE BOOKS
SAN FRANCISCO

First Edition

ISBN: 978-1-59780-184-3

Night Shade Books
Please visit us on the web at
http://www.nightshadebooks.com

CONTENTS

VENICE DROWNED

By the time Carlo Tafur struggled out of sleep, the baby was squalling, the teapot whistled, the smell of stove smoke filled the air. Wavelets slapped the walls of the floor below. It was just dawn. Reluctantly he untangled himself from the bedsheets and got up. He padded through the other room of his home, ignoring his wife and child, and walked out the door onto the roof.

Venice looked best at dawn, Carlo thought as he pissed into the canal. In the dim mauve light it was possible to imagine that the city was just as it always had been, that hordes of visitors would come flooding down the Grand Canal on this fine summer morning.... Of course, one had to ignore the patchwork constructions built on the roofs of the neighborhood to indulge the fancy. Around the church—San Giacomo du Rialto—all the buildings had even their top floors awash, and so it had been necessary to break up the tile roofs, and erect shacks on the roof beams made of materials fished up from below: wood, brick lath, stone, metal, glass. Carlo's home was one of these shacks, made of a crazy combination of wood beams, stained glass from San Giacometta, and drainpipes beaten flat. He looked back at it and sighed. It was best to look off over the Rialto, where the red sun blazed over the bulbous domes of San Marco.

"You have to meet those Japanese today," Carlo's wife, Luisa, said from inside.

"I know." Visitors still came to Venice, that was certain.

"And don't go insulting them and rowing off without your pay," she went on, her voice sounding clearly out of the doorway, "like you did with those Hungarians. It really doesn't matter what they take from under the water, you know. That's the past. That old stuff isn't doing anyone any good under there, anyway."

1

"Shut up," he said wearily. "I know."

"I have to buy stovewood and vegetables and toilet paper and socks for the baby," she said. "The Japanese are the best customers you've got; you'd better treat them well."

Carlo reentered the shack and walked into the bedroom to dress. Between putting on one boot and the next he stopped to smoke a cigarette, the last one in the house. While smoking he stared at his pile of books on the floor, his library as Luisa sardonically called the collection; all books about Venice. They were tattered, dog-eared, mildewed, so warped by the damp that none of them would close properly, and each moldy page was as wavy as the Lagoon on a windy day. They were a miserable sight, and Carlo gave the closest stack a light kick with his cold boot as he returned to the other room.

"I'm off," he said, giving his baby and then Luisa a kiss. "I'll be back late—they want to go to Torcello."

"What could they want up there?"

He shrugged. "Maybe just to see it." He ducked out the door.

Below the roof was a small square where the boats of the neighborhood were moored. Carlo slipped off the tile onto the narrow floating dock he and the neighbors had built, and crossed to his boat, a wide-beamed sailboat with a canvas deck. He stepped in, unmoored it, and rowed out of the square onto the Grand Canal.

Once on the Grand Canal he tipped the oars out of the water and let the boat drift downstream. The big canal had always been the natural course of the channel through the mudflats of the Lagoon; for a while it had been tamed, but now it was a river again, its banks made of tile rooftops and stone palaces, with hundreds of tributaries flowing into it. Men were working on roof-houses in the early-morning light; those who knew Carlo waved, hammers or rope in hand, and shouted hello. Carlo wiggled an oar perfunctorily before he was swept past. It was foolish to build so close to the Grand Canal, which now had the strength to knock the old structures down, and often did. But that was their business. In Venice they were all fools, if one thought about it.

Then he was in the Basin of San Marco, and he rowed through the Piazzetta beside the Doge's Palace, which was still imposing at two stories high, to the Piazza. Traffic was heavy as usual. It was the only place in Venice that still had the crowds of old, and Carlo enjoyed it for that reason, though he shouted curses as loudly as anyone when gondolas streaked in front of him. He jockeyed his way to the basilica window and rowed in.

Under the brilliant blue and gold of the domes it was noisy. Most of the water in the rooms had been covered with a floating dock. Carlo moored his boat to it, heaved his four scuba tanks on, and clambered up after them. Carrying two tanks in each hand he crossed the dock, on which the fish market was in full swing. Displayed for sale were flats of mullet, lagoon sharks, tunny, skates, and flatfish. Clams were piled in trays, their shells gleaming in the shaft of sunlight from the stained-glass east window; men and women pulled live crabs out of holes in the dock, risking fingers in the crab-jammed traps below; octopuses inked their buckets of water, sponges oozed foam; fishermen bawled out prices, and insulted the freshness of their neighbors' product.

In the middle of the fish market, Ludovico Salerno, one of Carlo's best friends, had his stalls of scuba gear. Carlo's two Japanese customers were there. He greeted them and handed his tanks to Salerno, who began refilling them from his machine. They conversed in quick, slangy Italian while the tanks filled. When they were done, Carlo paid him and led the Japanese back to his boat. They got in and stowed their backpacks under the canvas decking, while Carlo pulled the scuba tanks on board.

"We are ready to voyage at Torcello?" one asked, and the other smiled and repeated the question. Their names were Hamada and Taku. They had made a few jokes concerning the latter name's similarity to Carlo's own, but Taku was the one with less Italian, so the sallies hadn't gone on for long. They had hired him four days before, at Salerno's stall.

"Yes," Carlo said. He rowed out of the Piazza and up back canals past Campo San Maria Formosa, which was nearly as crowded as the Piazza. Beyond that the canals were empty, and only an occasional roof-house marred the look of flooded tranquillity.

"That part of city Venice here not many people live," Hamada observed. "Not houses on houses."

"That's true," Carlo replied. As he rowed past San Zanipolo and the hospital, he explained, "It's too close to the hospital here, where many diseases were contained. Sicknesses, you know."

"Ah, the hospital!" Hamada nodded, as did Taku. "We have swam hospital in our Venice voyage previous to that one here. Salvage many fine statues from lowest rooms."

"Stone lions," Taku added. "Many stone lions with wings in room below Twenty-forty waterline."

"Is that right," Carlo said. Stone lions, he thought, set up in the entryway of some Japanese businessman's expensive home around the world.... He tried to divert his thoughts by watching the brilliantly healthy, masklike faces of his two passengers as they laughed over their reminiscences.

Then they were over the Fondamente Nuova, the northern limit of the city, and on the Lagoon. There was a small swell from the north. Carlo rowed out a way and then stepped forward to raise the boat's single sail. The wind was from the east, so they would make good time north to Torcello. Behind them, Venice looked beautiful in the morning light, as if they were miles away, and a watery horizon blocked their full view of it.

The two Japanese had stopped talking and were looking over the side. They were over the cemetery of San Michele, Carlo realized. Below them lay the island that had been the city's chief cemetery for centuries; they sailed over a field of tombs, mausoleums, gravestones, obelisks that at low tide could be a navigational hazard.... Just enough of the bizarre white blocks could be seen to convince one that they were the result of the architectural thinking of fishes. Carlo crossed himself quickly to impress his customers, and sat back down at the tiller. He pulled the sail tight and they heeled over slightly, slapped into the waves.

In no more than forty minutes they were east of Murano, skirting its edge. Murano, like Venice an island city crossed with canals, had been a quaint little town before the flood. But it didn't have as many tall buildings as Venice, and it was said that an underwater river had undercut its islands; in any case, it was a wreck. The two Japanese chattered with excitement.

"Can we visit to that city here, Carlo?" asked Hamada.

"It's too dangerous," Carlo answered. "Buildings have fallen into the canals."

They nodded, smiling. "Are people live here?" Taku asked.

"A few, yes. They live in the highest buildings on the floors still above water, and work in Venice. That way they avoid having to build a roof-house in the city."

The faces of his two companions expressed incomprehension.

"They avoid the housing shortage in Venice," Carlo said. "There's a certain housing shortage in Venice, as you may have noticed." His listeners caught the joke this time and laughed uproariously.

"Could live on floors below if owning scuba such as that here," Hamada said, gesturing at Carlo's equipment.

"Yes," he replied. "Or we could grow gills." He bugged his eyes out and waved his fingers at his neck to indicate gills. The Japanese loved it.

Past Murano, the Lagoon was clear for a few miles, a sunbeaten blue covered with choppy waves. The boat tipped up and down, the wind tugged at the sail cord in Carlo's hand. He began to enjoy himself. "Storm coming," he volunteered to the others and pointed at the black line over the horizon to the north. It was a common sight; short, violent storms swept over Brenner Pass from the Austrian Alps, dumping on the Po Valley and the Lagoon before dissipating in the Adriatic... once a week, or more, even in the summer. That was one reason the fish market was held under the domes of San Marco; everyone had gotten sick of trading in the rain.

Even the Japanese recognized the clouds. "Many rain fall soon here," Taku said.

Hamada grinned and said, "Taku and Tafur, weather prophets no doubt, make big company!"

They laughed. "Does he do this in Japan, too?" Carlo asked.

"Yes indeed, surely. In Japan rains every day—Taku says, 'It rains tomorrow for surely.' Weather prophet!"

After the laughter receded, Carlo said, "Hasn't all the rain drowned some of your cities too?"

"What's that here?"

"Don't you have some Venices in Japan?"

But they didn't want to talk about that. "I don't understand… No, no Venice in Japan," Hamada said easily, but neither laughed as they had before. They sailed on. Venice was out of sight under the horizon, as was Murano. Soon they would reach Burano. Carlo guided the boat over the waves and listened to his companions converse in their improbable language, or mangle Italian in a way that alternately made him want to burst with hilarity or bite the gunwale with frustration.

Gradually, Burano bounced over the horizon, the campanile first, followed by the few buildings still above water. Murano still had inhabitants, a tiny market, even a midsummer festival; Burano was empty. Its campanile stood at a distinct angle, like the mast of a foundered ship. It had been an island town, before 2040; now it had "canals" between every rooftop. Carlo disliked the town intensely and gave it a wide berth. His companions discussed it quietly in Japanese.

A mile beyond it was Torcello, another island ghost town. The campanile could be seen from Burano, tall and white against the black clouds to the north. They approached in silence. Carlo took down the sail, set Taku in the bow to look for snags, and rowed cautiously to the edge of town. They moved between rooftops and walls that stuck up like reefs or like old foundations out of the earth. Many of the roof tiles and beams had been taken for use in construction back in Venice. This had happened to Torcello before; during the Renaissance it had been a little rival of Venice, boasting a population of twenty thousand, but during the sixteenth and seventeenth centuries it had been entirely deserted. Builders from Venice had come looking in the ruins for good marble or a staircase of the right dimensions…. Briefly a tiny population had returned, to make lace and host those tourists who wanted to be melancholy; but the waters rose, and Torcello died for good. Carlo pushed off a wall with his oar, and a big section of it tilted over and sank. He tried not to notice.

He rowed them to the open patch of water that had been the Piazza. Around them stood a few intact rooftops, no taller than the mast of their boat; broken walls of stone or rounded brick; the shadowy suggestion of walls just underwater. It was hard to tell what the street plan of the town would have been. On one side of the Piazza was the cathedral of Santa Maria Assunta, however, still holding fast, still supporting the white campanile that stood square and solid, as if over a living community.

"That here is the church we desire to dive," Hamada said.

Carlo nodded. The amusement he had felt during the sail was entirely gone. He rowed around the Piazza looking for a flat spot where they could stand and put the scuba gear on. The church outbuildings—it had been an extensive structure—were all underwater. At one point the boat's keel scraped the ridge of a roof. They rowed down the length of the barnlike nave, looked in the high windows: floored with water. No surprise. One of the small windows in the side of the campanile had been widened with sledgehammers; directly inside it was the stone staircase and, a few steps up, a stone floor. They hooked the boat to the wall and moved their gear up to the floor. In the dim midday light the stone of the interior was pocked with shadows. It had a rough-hewn look. The citizens of Torcello had built the campanile in a hurry, thinking that the world would end at the millennium, the year 1000. Carlo smiled to think how much longer they had had than that. They climbed the steps of the staircase, up to the sudden sunlight of the bell chamber, to look around; viewed Burano, Venice in the distance… to the north, the shallows of the Lagoon, and the coast of Italy. Beyond that the black line of clouds was like a wall nearly submerged under the horizon, but it was rising; the storm would come.

They descended, put on the scuba gear, and flopped into the water beside the campanile. They were above the complex of church buildings, and it was dark; Carlo slowly led the two Japanese back into the Piazza and swam down. The ground was silted, and Carlo was careful not to step on it. His charges saw the great stone chair in the center of the Piazza (it had been called the Throne of Attila, Carlo remembered from one of his moldy books, and no one had known why), and waving to each other they swam to it. One of them made ludicrous attempts to stand on the bottom and walk around in his fins; he threw up clouds of silt. The other joined him. They each sat in the stone chair, columns of bubbles rising from them, and snapped pictures of each other with their underwater cameras. The silt would ruin the shots, Carlo thought. While they cavorted, he wondered sourly what they wanted in the church.

Eventually, Hamada swam up to him and gestured at the church. Behind the mask his eyes were excited. Carlo pumped his fins up and down slowly and led them around to the big entrance at the front. The doors were gone. They swam into the church.

Inside it was dark, and all three of them unhooked their big flashlights and turned them on. Cones of murky water turned to crystal as the beams swept about. The interior of the church was undistinguished, the floor thick with mud. Carlo watched his two customers swim about and let his flashlight beam rove the walls. Some of the underwater windows were still intact, an odd sight. Occasionally the beam caught a column of bubbles, transmuting them to silver.

Quickly enough the Japanese went to the picture at the west end of the nave, a tile mosaic. Taku (Carlo guessed) rubbed the slime off the tiles, vastly improving their color. They had gone to the big one first, the one portraying the Crucifixion, the Resurrection of the Dead, and the Day of Judgment: a busy mural. Carlo swam over to have a better look. But no sooner had the Japanese wiped the wall clean than they were off to the other end of the church, where above the stalls of the apse was another mosaic. Carlo followed.

It didn't take long to rub this one clean; and when the water had cleared, the three of them floated there, their flashlight beams converged on the picture revealed.

It was the Teotaca Madonna, the God-bearer. She stood against a dull gold background, holding the Child in her arms, staring out at the world with a sad and knowing gaze. Carlo pumped his legs to get above the Japanese, holding his light steady on the Madonna's face. She looked as though she could see all of the future, up to this moment and beyond; all of her child's short life, all the terror and calamity after that. There were mosaic tears on her cheeks. At the sight of them Carlo could barely check tears of his own from joining the general wetness on his face. He felt that he had suddenly been transposed to a church on the deepest floor of the ocean; the pressure of his feelings threatened to implode him, he could scarcely hold them off. The water was freezing, he was shivering, sending up a thick, nearly continuous column of bubbles… and the Madonna watched. With a kick he turned and swam away. Like startled fish his two companions followed him. Carlo led them out of the church into murky light, then up to the surface, to the boat and the window casement.

Fins off, Carlo sat on the staircase and dripped. Taku and Hamada scrambled through the window and joined him. They conversed for a moment in Japanese, clearly excited. Carlo stared at them blackly.

Hamada turned to him. "That here is the picture we desire," he said. "The Madonna with child."

"What?" Carlo cried.

Hamada raised his eyebrows. "We desire taking home that here picture to Japan."

"But it's impossible! The picture is made of little tiles stuck to the wall—there's no way to get them off!"

"Italy government permits," Taku said, but Hamada silenced him with a gesture.

"Mosaic, yes. We use instruments we take here—water torch. Archaeology method, you understand. Cut blocks out of wall, bricks, number them—construct on new place in Japan. Above water." He flashed his pearly smile.

"You can't do that," Carlo stated, deeply affronted.

"I don't understand," Hamada said. But he did. "Italian government permits us that."

"This isn't Italy," Carlo said savagely, and in his anger stood up. What good would a Madonna do in Japan, anyway? They weren't even Christian. "Italy is over there," he said, in his excitement mistakenly waving to the southeast, no doubt confusing his listeners even more. "This has never been Italy! This is Venice! The Republic!"

"I don't understand." He had that phrase down pat. "Italian government has giving permit us."

"Christ," Carlo said. After a disgusted pause: "Just how long will this take?"

"Time? We work that afternoon, tomorrow: place the bricks here, go hire Venice barge to carry bricks to Venice—"

"Stay here overnight? I'm not going to stay here overnight, God damn it!"

"We bring sleeping bag for you—"

"No!" Carlo was furious. "I'm not staying, you miserable heathen hyenas—" He pulled off his scuba gear.

"I don't understand."

Carlo dried off, got dressed. "I'll let you keep your scuba tanks, and I'll be back for you tomorrow afternoon, late. *Understand?*"

"Yes," Hamada said, staring at him steadily, without expression. "Bring barge?"

"What?—yes, yes, I'll bring your barge, you miserable slime-eating catfish. Vultures…" He went on for a while, getting the boat out of the window.

"Storm coming!" Taku said brightly, pointing to the north.

"To hell with you!" Carlo said, pushing off and beginning to row. "Understand?"

He rowed out of Torcello and back into the Lagoon. Indeed, a storm was coming: he would have to hurry. He put up the sail and pulled the canvas decking back until it covered everything but the seat he was sitting on. The wind was from the north now, strong but fitful. It pulled the sail taut: the boat bucked over the choppy waves, leaving behind a wake that was bright white against the black of the sky. The clouds were drawing over the sky like a curtain, covering half of it: half black, half colorless blue, and the line of the edge was solid. It resembled that first great storm of 2040, Carlo guessed, that had pulled over Venice like a black wool blanket and dumped water for forty days. And it had never been the same again, not anywhere in the world.

Now he was beside the wreck of Burano. Against the black sky he could see only the drunken campanile, and suddenly he realized why he hated the sight of this abandoned town: it was a vision of the Venice to come, a cruel model of the future. If the water level rose even three meters, Venice would become nothing but a big Burano. Even if the water didn't rise, more people were leaving Venice every year. One day it would be empty. Once again the sadness he had felt looking at the Teotaca filled him, a sadness become a bottomless despair. "God damn it," he said, staring at the crippled campanile: but that wasn't enough. He didn't know words that were enough. "God *damn* it."

Just beyond Burano the squall hit. It almost blew the sail out of his hand; he had to hold on with a fierce clench, tie it to the stern, tie the tiller in place, and scramble over the pitching canvas deck to lower the sail, cursing all the while. He brought the sail down to its last reefing, which left a handkerchief-sized patch exposed to the wind. Even so, the boat yanked over the waves and the mast creaked as if it would tear loose.... The choppy waves had become whitecaps: in the screaming wind their tops were tearing loose and flying through the air, white foam in the blackness....

Best to head for Murano for refuge, Carlo thought. Then the rain started. It was colder than the Lagoon water and fell almost horizontally. The wind was still picking up: his handkerchief sail was going to pull the mast out.... "Jesus," he said. He got onto the decking again, slid up to the mast, took down the sail with cold and disobedient fingers. He crawled back to his hole in the deck, hanging on desperately as the boat yawed. It was almost broadside to the waves and hastily he grabbed the tiller and pulled it around, just in time to meet a large wave stern-on. He shuddered with relief. Each wave seemed bigger than the last: they picked up quickly on the Lagoon. Well, he thought, what now? Get out the oars? No, that wouldn't do; he had to keep stern-on to the waves, and besides, he couldn't row effectively in this chop. He had to go where the waves were going, he realized; and if they missed Murano and Venice, that meant the Adriatic.

As the waves lifted and dropped him, he grimly contemplated the thought.

His mast alone acted like a sail in a wind of this force; and the wind seemed to be blowing from a bit to the west of north. The waves—the biggest he had ever seen on the Lagoon, perhaps the biggest *ever* on the Lagoon—pushed in about the same direction as the wind, naturally. Well, that meant he would miss Venice, which was directly south, maybe even a touch west of south. Damn, he thought. And all because he had been angered by those two Japanese and the Teotaca. What did he care what happened to a sunken mosaic from Torcello? He had helped foreigners find and cart off the one bronze horse of San Marco that had fallen… more than one of the stone lions of Venice, symbol of the city… the entire Bridge of Sighs, for Christ's sake! What had come over him? Why should he have cared about a forgotten mosaic?

Well, he had done it; and here he was. No altering it. Each wave lifted his boat stern first and slid under it until he could look down in the trough, if he cared to, and see his mast nearly horizontal, until he rose over the broken, foaming crest, each one of which seemed to want to break down his little hole in the decking and swamp him—for a second he was in midair, the tiller free and useless until he crashed into the next trough. Every time at the top he thought, this wave will catch us, and so even though he was wet and the wind and rain were cold, the repeated spurts of fear adrenaline and his thick wool coat kept him warm. A hundred waves or so served to convince him that the next one would probably slide under him as safely as the last, and he relaxed a bit. Nothing to do but wait it out, keep the boat exactly stern-on to the swell… and he would be all right. Sure, he thought, he would just ride these waves across the Adriatic to Trieste or Rijeka, one of those two tawdry towns that had replaced Venice as Queen of the Adriatic… the princesses of the Adriatic, so to speak, and two little sluts they were, too…. Or ride the storm out, turn around, and sail back in, better yet.

On the other hand the Lido had become a sort of reef in most places, and waves of this size would break over it, capsizing him for sure. And, to be realistic, the top of the Adriatic was wide; just one mistake on these waves (and he couldn't go on forever) and he would be broached, capsized, and rolled down to join all the other Venetians who had ended up on the bottom of the Adriatic. And all because of that damn Madonna. Carlo sat crouched in the stern, adjusting the tiller for the particulars of each wave, ignoring all else in the howling black chaos of water and air around him, pleased in a grim way that he was sailing to his death with such perfect seamanship. But he kept the Lido out of mind.

And so he sailed on, losing track of time as one does when there is no spatial referent. Wave after wave after wave. A little water collected at the bottom of his boat, and his spirits sank; that was no way to go, to have the boat sink by degrees under him.

Then the high-pitched, airy howl of the wind was joined by a low booming, a bass roar. He looked behind him in the direction he was being driven and saw a white line, stretching from left to right; his heart jumped, fear exploded through him. This was it. The Lido, now a barrier reef tripping the waves. They were smashing down on it; he could see white sheets bouncing skyward and blowing to nothing. He was terrifically frightened. It would have been so much easier to founder at sea.

But there—among the white breakers, off to the right—a gray finger pointing up at the black—

A campanile. Carlo was forced to look back at the wave he was under, to straighten the boat; but when he looked back it was still there. A campanile, standing there like a dead lighthouse. "Jesus," he said aloud. It looked as if the waves were pushing him a couple hundred meters to the east of it. As each wave lifted him he had a moment when the boat was sliding down the face of the wave as fast as it was moving under him; during these moments he shifted the tiller a bit and the boat turned and surfed across the face, to the west, until the wave rose up under him to the crest and he had to straighten it out. He repeated the delicate operation time after time, sometimes nearly broaching the boat in his impatience. But that wouldn't do—just take as much from each wave as it will give you, he thought. And pray it will add up to enough.

The Lido got closer, and it looked as if he was directly upwind of the campanile. It was the one at the Lido channel entrance or perhaps the one at Pellestrina, he had no way of knowing. He was just happy that his ancestors had seen fit to construct such solid bell towers. In between waves he reached under the decking and by touch found his boathook and the length of rope he carried. It was going to be a problem, actually, when he got to the campanile—it would not do to pass it helplessly by a few meters; on the other hand he couldn't smash into it and expect to survive either, not in these waves. In fact the more he considered it the more exact and difficult he realized the approach would have to be, and fearfully he stopped thinking about it and concentrated on the waves.

The last one was the biggest. As the boat slid down its face, the face got steeper, until it seemed they would be swept on by this wave forever. The campanile loomed ahead, big and black. Around it waves pitched over and broke with sharp, deadly booms; from behind Carlo could see the water sucked over the breaks, as if over short but infinitely broad waterfalls. The noise was tremendous. At the top of the wave it appeared he could jump in the campanile's top window—he got out the boathook, shifted the tiller a touch, took three deep breaths. Amid the roaring, the wave swept him just past the stone tower, smacking against it and splashing him; he pulled the tiller over hard, the boat shot into the wake of the campanile—he stood and swung the boathook over a window casement above him. It caught, and he held on hard.

He was in the lee of the tower. Broken water rose and dropped under the boat, hissing, but without violence, and he held. One-handed, he wrapped the end of his rope around the sail-cord bolt in the stern, tied the other end to the boathook. The hook held pretty well; he took a risk and reached down to tie the rope firmly to the bolt. Then another risk: when the boiling soupy water of another broken wave raised the boat, he leaped off his seat, grabbed the stone windowsill, which was too thick to get his fingers over—for a moment he hung by his fingertips. With desperate strength he pulled himself up, reached in with one hand and got a grasp on the inside of the sill, and pulled himself in and over. The stone floor was about four feet below the window. Quickly he pulled the boathook in and put it on the floor, and took up the slack in the rope.

He looked out the window. His boat rose and fell, rose and fell. Well, it would sink or it wouldn't. Meanwhile, he was safe. Realizing this, he breathed deeply, let out a shout. He remembered shooting past the side of the tower, face no more than two meters from it—getting drenched by the wave slapping the front of it—why, he had done it perfectly! He couldn't do it again like that in a million tries. Triumphant laughs burst out of him, short and sharp: "Ha! Ha! Ha! Jesus Christ! Wow!"

"Whoooo's theeeerre?" called a high scratchy voice, floating down the staircase from the floor above. "Whooooooo's there?…"

Carlo froze. He stepped lightly to the base of the stone staircase and peered up; through the hole to the next floor flickered a faint light. To put it better, it was less dark up there than anywhere else. More surprised than fearful (though he was afraid), Carlo opened his eyes as wide as he could—

"Whooooooo's theeeeeerrrrrrrre?…"

Quickly he went to the boathook, untied the rope, felt around on the wet floor until he found a block of stone that would serve as anchor for his boat. He looked out the window: boat still there; on both sides, white breakers crashed over the Lido. Taking up the boathook, Carlo stepped slowly up the stairs, feeling that after what he had been through he could slash any ghost in the ether to ribbons.

It was a candle lantern, flickering in the disturbed air—a room filled with junk—

"Eeek! Eeek!"

"Jesus!"

"Devil! Death, away!" A small black shape rushed at him, brandishing sharp metal points.

"Jesus!" Carlo repeated, holding the boathook out to defend himself. The figure stopped.

"Death comes for me at last," it said. It was an old woman, he saw, holding lace needles in each hand.

"Not at all," Carlo said, feeling his pulse slow back down. "Swear to God, Grandmother, I'm just a sailor, blown here by the storm."

The woman pulled back the hood of her black cape, revealing braided white hair, and squinted at him.

"You've got the scythe," she said suspiciously. A few wrinkles left her face as she unfocused her gaze.

"A boathook only," Carlo said, holding it out for her inspection. She stepped back and raised the lace needles threateningly. "Just a boathook, I swear to God. To God and Mary and Jesus and all the saints, Grandmother. I'm just a sailor, blown here by the storm from Venice." Part of him felt like laughing.

"Aye?" she said. "Aye, well then, you've found shelter. I don't see so well anymore, you know. Come in, then, sit down." She turned around and led him into the room. "I was just doing some lace for penance, you see... though there's scarcely enough light." She lifted a tombolo with the lace pinned to it; Carlo noticed big gaps in the pattern, as in the webs of an injured spider. "A little more light," she said and, picking up a candle, held it to the lit one. When it was fired, she carried it around the chamber and lit three more candles in lanterns that stood on tables, boxes, a wardrobe. She motioned for him to sit in a heavy chair by her table, and he did so.

As she sat down across from him, he looked around the chamber. A bed piled high with blankets, boxes and tables covered with objects... the stone walls around, and another staircase leading up to the next floor of the campanile. There was a draft. "Take off your coat," the woman said. She arranged the little pillow on the arm of her chair and began to poke a needle in and out of it, pulling the thread slowly.

Carlo sat back and watched her. "Do you live here alone?"

"Always alone," she replied. "I don't want it otherwise." With the candle before her face, she resembled Carlo's mother or someone else he knew. It seemed very peaceful in the room after the storm. The old woman bent in her chair until her face was just above her tombolo; still, Carlo couldn't help noticing that her needle hit far outside the apparent pattern of lace, striking here and there randomly. She might as well have been blind. At regular intervals Carlo shuddered with excitement and tension; it was hard to believe he was out of danger. More infrequently they broke the silence with a short burst of conversation, then sat in the candlelight absorbed in their own thoughts, as if they were old friends.

"How do you get food?" Carlo asked, after one of these silences had stretched out. "Or candles?"

"I trap lobsters down below. And fishermen come by and trade food for lace. They get a good bargain, never fear. I've never given less, despite what he said—" Anguish twisted her face as the squinting had, and she stopped. She needled furiously, and Carlo looked away. Despite the draft, he was warming up (he hadn't removed his coat, which was wool, after all), and he was beginning to feel drowsy....

"He was my spirit's mate, do you comprehend me?"

Carlo jerked upright. The old woman was still looking at her tombolo.

"And—and he left me here, here in this desolation when the floods began, with words that I'll remember forever and ever and ever. Until death comes.... I wish you had been death!" she cried. "I wish you had."

Carlo remembered her brandishing the needles. "What is this place?" he asked gently.

"What?"

"Is this Pellestrina? San Lazzaro?"

"This is Venice," she said.

Carlo shivered convulsively, stood up.

"I'm the last of them," the woman said. "The waters rise, the heavens howl, love's pledges crack and lead to misery. I—I live to show what a person can bear and not die. I'll live till the deluge drowns the world as Venice is drowned, I'll live till all else living is dead; I'll live..." Her voice trailed off; she looked up at Carlo curiously. "Who are you, really? Oh, I know. I know. A sailor."

"Are there floors above?" he asked, to change the subject.

She squinted at him. Finally she spoke. "Words are vain. I thought I'd never speak again, not even to my own heart, and here I am, doing it again. Yes, there's a floor above intact; but above that, ruins. Lightning blasted the bell chamber apart, while I lay in that very bed." She pointed at her bed, stood up. "Come on, I'll show you." Under her cape she was tiny.

She picked up the candle lantern beside her, and Carlo followed her up the stairs, stepping carefully in the shifting shadows.

On the floor above, the wind swirled, and through the stairway to the floor above that, he could distinguish black clouds. The woman put the lantern on the floor, started up the stairs. "Come up and see," she said.

Once through the hole they were in the wind, out under the sky. The rain had stopped. Great blocks of stone lay about the floor, and the walls broke off unevenly.

"I thought the whole campanile would fall," she shouted at him over the whistle of the wind. He nodded, and walked over to the west wall, which stood chest high. Looking over it, he could see the waves approaching, rising up, smashing against the stone below, spraying back and up at him. He could feel the blows in his feet. Their force frightened him; it was hard to believe he had survived them and was now out of danger. He shook his head violently. To his right and left, the white lines of crumbled waves marked the Lido, a broad swath of them against the black. The old woman was speaking, he could see; he walked back to her side to listen.

"The waters yet rise," she shouted. "See? And the lightning... you can see the lightning breaking the Alps to dust. It's the end, child. Every island fled away, and the mountains were not found... the second angel poured out his vial upon the sea, and it became as the blood of a dead man: and every living thing died in the sea." On and on she spoke, her voice mingling with the sound of the gale and the boom of the waves, just carrying over it all... until Carlo, cold and tired, filled with pity and a black anguish like the clouds rolling over them, put his arm around her thin shoulders and turned her around. They descended to the floor below, picked up the extinguished lantern, and descended to her chamber, which was still lit. It seemed warm, a refuge. He could hear her still speaking. He was shivering without pause.

"You must be cold," she said in a practical tone. She pulled a few blankets from her bed. "Here, take these." He sat down in the big heavy chair, put the blankets around his legs, put his head back. He was tired. The old woman sat in her chair and wound thread onto a spool. After a few minutes of silence she began talking again; and as Carlo dozed and shifted position and nodded off again, she talked and talked, of storms, and drownings, and the world's end, and lost love....

In the morning when he woke up, she wasn't there. Her room stood revealed in the dim morning light: shabby, the furniture battered, the blankets worn, the knickknacks of Venetian glass ugly, as Venetian glass always was. But it was clean. Carlo got up and stretched his stiff muscles. He went up to the roof; she wasn't there. It was a sunny morning. Over the east wall he saw that his boat was still there, still floating. He grinned—the first one in a few days, he could feel that in his face.

The woman was not in the floors below, either. The lowest one served as her boathouse, he could see. In it were a pair of decrepit rowboats and some lobster pots. The biggest "boatslip" was empty; she was probably out checking pots. Or perhaps she hadn't wanted to talk with him in the light of day.

From the boathouse he could walk around to his craft, through water only knee deep. He sat in the stern, reliving the previous afternoon, and grinned again at being alive.

He took off the decking and bailed out the water on the keel with his bailing can, keeping an eye out for the old woman. Then he remembered the boathook and went back upstairs for it. When he returned there was still no sight of her. He shrugged; he'd come back and say good-bye another time. He rowed around the campanile and off the Lido, pulled up the sail, and headed northwest, where he presumed Venice was.

The Lagoon was as flat as a pond this morning, the sky cloudless, like the blue dome of a great basilica. It was amazing, but Carlo was not surprised. The weather was like that these days. Last night's storm, however, had been something else. That was the mother of all squalls; those were the biggest waves in the Lagoon ever, without a doubt. He began rehearsing his tale in his mind, for wife and friends.

Venice appeared over the horizon right off his bow, just where he thought it would be: first the great campanile, then San Marco and the other spires. The campanile… Thank God his ancestors had wanted to get up there so close to God—or so far off the water—the urge had saved his life. In the rain-washed air the sea approach to the city was more beautiful than ever, and it didn't even bother him as it usually did that no matter how close you got to it, it still seemed to be over the horizon. That was just the way it was, now. The Serenissima. He was happy to see it.

He was hungry, and still very tired. When he pulled into the Grand Canal and took down the sail, he found he could barely row. The rain was pouring off the land into the Lagoon, and the Grand Canal was running like a mountain river. It was tough going. At the fire station where the canal bent back, some of his friends working on a new roof-house waved at him, looking surprised to see him going upstream so early in the morning. "You're going the wrong way!" one shouted.

Carlo waved an oar weakly before plopping it back in. "Don't I know it!" he replied.

Over the Rialto, back into the little courtyard of San Giacometta. Onto the sturdy dock he and his neighbors had built, staggering a bit—careful there, Carlo.

"Carlo!" his wife shrieked from above. "Carlo, Carlo, Carlo!" She flew down the ladder from the roof.

He stood on the dock. He was home.

"Carlo, Carlo, Carlo!" his wife cried as she ran onto the dock.

"Jesus," he pleaded, "shut up." And pulled her into a rough hug.

"Where have you been, I was so worried about you because of the storm, you said you'd be back yesterday, oh, Carlo, I'm so glad to see you…." She tried to help him up the ladder. The baby was crying. Carlo sat down in the kitchen chair and looked around the little makeshift room with satisfaction. In between chewing down bites of a loaf of bread, he told Luisa of his adventure: the two Japanese and their vandalism, the wild ride across the Lagoon, the madwoman on the campanile. When he had finished the story and the loaf of bread, he began to fall asleep.

"But, Carlo, you have to go back and pick up those Japanese."

"To hell with them," he said slurrily. "Creepy little bastards…. They're tearing the Madonna apart, didn't I tell you? They'll take everything in Venice, every last painting and statue and carving and mosaic and all…. I can't stand it."

"Oh, Carlo. It's all right. They take those things all over the world and put them up and say this is from Venice, the greatest city in the world."

"They should be here."

"Here, here, come in and lie down for a few hours. I'll go see if Giuseppe will go to Torcello with you to bring back those bricks." She arranged him on their bed. "Let them have what's under the water, Carlo. Let them have it." He slept.

He sat up struggling, his arm shaken by his wife.

"Wake up, it's late. You've got to go to Torcello to get those men. Besides, they've got your scuba gear."

Carlo groaned.

"Maria says Giuseppe will go with you; he'll meet you with his boat on the Fondamente."

"Damn."

"Come on, Carlo, we need that money."

"All right, all right." The baby was squalling. He collapsed back on the bed. "I'll do it; don't pester me."

He got up and drank her soup. Stiffly he descended the ladder, ignoring Luisa's good-byes and warnings, and got back in his boat. He untied it, pushed off, let it float out of the courtyard to the wall of San Giacometta. He stared at the wall.

Once, he remembered, he had put on his scuba gear and swum down into the church. He had sat down in one of the stone pews in front of the altar, adjusting his weight belts and tank to do so, and had tried to pray through his mouthpiece and the facemask. The silver bubbles of his breath had floated up through the water toward heaven; whether his prayers had gone with them, he had no idea. After a while, feeling somewhat foolish—but not entirely—he had swum out the door. Over it he had noticed an inscription and stopped to read it, facemask centimeters from the stone. *Around This Temple Let the Merchant's Law Be Just, His Weight True, and His Covenants*

Faithful. It was an admonition to the old usurers of the Rialto, but he could make it his, he thought; the true weight could refer to the diving belts, not to overload his clients and sink them to the bottom....

The memory passed and he was on the surface again, with a job to do. He took in a deep breath and let it out, put the oars in the oarlocks and started to row.

Let them have what was under the water. What lived in Venice was still afloat.

RIDGE RUNNING

Three men sit on a rock. The rock is wet granite, a bouldertop surrounded by snow that has melted just enough to reveal it. Snow extends away from the rock in every direction. To the east it drops to treeline, to the west it rises to a rock wall that points up and ends at sky. The boulder the three men are on is the only break in the snow from the treeline to rock wall. Snowshoe tracks lead to the rock, coming from the north on a traverse across the slope. The men sit sunning like marmots.

One man chews snow. He is short and broad-chested, with thick arms and legs. He adjusts blue nylon gaiters that cover his boots and lower legs. His thighs are bare, he wears gray gym shorts. He leans over to strap a boot into an orange plastic snowshoe.

The man sitting beside him says, "Brian, I thought we were going to eat lunch." This second man is big, and he wears sunglasses that clip onto prescription wire-rims.

"Pe-ter," Brian drawls. "We can't eat here comfortably, there's barely room to sit. As soon as we get around that shoulder"—he points south—"the traverse will be done and we'll be at the pass."

Peter takes in a deep breath, lets it out. "I need to rest."

"O.K.," Brian says, "do it. I'm just going to go around to the pass, I'm tired of sitting." He picks up the other orange snowshoe, sticks his boot in the binding.

The third man, who is medium height and very thin, has been staring at the snow granules on his boot. Now he picks up a yellow snowshoe and kicks into it. Peter sees him do it, sighs, bends over to yank his aluminum-and-cord snowshoes out of the snow they are stuck in.

"Look at that hummingbird," the third man says with pleasure and points.

He is pointing at blank snow. His two companions look where he is pointing, then glance at each other uncomfortably. Peter shakes his head, looks at his boots.

"I didn't know there were hummingbirds in the Sierras," the third man says. "What a beauty!" He looks at Brian uncertainly. "*Are* there hummingbirds in the Sierras?"

"Well," Brian says, "actually, I think there are. But…"

"But not this time, Joe," Peter finishes.

"Ah," Joe says, and stares at the spot in the snow. "I could have sworn…" Peter looks at Brian, his face squinched up in distress. "Maybe the light breaking on that clump of snow," Joe says, mystified. "Oh, well."

Brian stands and hoists a compact blue pack onto his shoulders, and steps off the boulder onto the snow. He leans over to adjust a binding. "Let's get going, Joe," he says. "Don't worry about it." And to Peter: "This spring snow is great."

"If you're a goddamn polar bear," Peter says.

Brian shakes his head, and his silvered sunglasses flash reflections of snow and Peter. "This is the best time to be up here. If you would ever come with us in January or February you'd know that."

"Summer!" Peter says as he picks up his long frame pack. "Summer's what I like—catch the rays, see the flowers, walk around without these damn flippers on—" He swings his pack onto his back, steps back quickly (clatter of aluminum on granite) to keep his balance. He buckles his waistbelt awkwardly, looks at the sun. It is near midday. He wipes his forehead.

"You don't even come up with us in the summer anymore," Brian points out. "What has it been, four years?"

"Time," Peter says. "I don't have any time, and that's a fact."

"Just all your life," Brian scoffs. Peter shakes off the remark with an irritated scowl, and steps onto the snow.

They turn to look at Joe, who is still inspecting the snow with a fierce squint.

"Hey, Joe!" Brian says.

Joe starts and looks up.

"Time to hike, remember?"

"Oh, yeah, just a second." Joe readies himself.

Three men snowshoeing.

Brian leads. He sinks about a foot into the snow with every step. Joe follows, placing his yellow snowshoes carefully in the prints of Brian's, so that he sinks hardly at all. Peter pays no attention to prints, and his snowshoes crash into and across the holes. His snowshoes slide left, downhill, and he slips frequently.

The slope steepens. The three men sweat. Brian slips left one time too often and stops to remove his snowshoes. They can no longer see the rock wall above them, the slope is so steep. Brian ties his snowshoes to his pack, puts the pack back on. He puts a glove on his right hand and walks canted over so he can punch into the slope with his fist.

Joe and Peter stop where Brian stops, to make the same changes. Joe points ahead to Brian, who is now crossing a section of slope steeper than forty-five degrees.

"Strange three-legged hill animal," says Joe, and laughs. "Snoweater."

Peter looks in his pack for his glove. "Why don't we go down into the trees and avoid this damn traverse?"

"The view isn't as good."

Peter sighs. Joe waits, scuffs snow, looks at Peter curiously. Pete has put suntan oil on his face, and the sweat has poured from his forehead, so that his stubbled cheeks shine with reflected light. He says, "Am I imagining this, or are we working really hard?"

"We're working very hard," Joe says. "Traverses are difficult."

They watch Brian, who is near the middle of the steepest section. "You guys do this snow stuff for *fun?*" Peter says.

After a moment Joe starts. "I'm sorry," he says. "What were we talking about?"

Peter shrugs, examines Joe closely. "You O.K.?" he asks, putting his gloved hand to Joe's arm.

"Yeah, yeah. I just… *forgot.* Again!"

"Everyone forgets sometimes."

"I know, I know." With a discouraged sigh Joe steps off into Brian's prints. Peter follows.

From above they appear little dots, the only moving objects in a sea of white and black. Snow blazes white and prisms flash from sunglasses. They wipe their foreheads, stop now and then to catch their breath. Brian pulls ahead, Pete falls behind. Joe steps out the traverse with care, talking to himself in undertones. Their gloves get wet, there are ice bracelets around their wrists. Below them solitary trees at treeline wave in a breeze, but on the slope it is windless and hot.

The slope lessens, and they are past the shoulder. Brian pulls off his pack and gets out his groundpad, sits on it. He roots in the pack. After a while Joe joins him. "Whew!" Joe says. "That was a hard traverse."

"Not really hard," Brian replies. "Just boring." He eats some M&M's, waves a handful up at the ridge above. "I'm tired of traversing, though, that's for sure. I'm going up to the ridge so I can walk down it to the pass."

Joe looks at the wall of snow leading up to the ridge. "Yeah, well, I think Pete and I will continue around the corner here and go past Lake Doris to the pass. It's almost level from here on."

"True. I'm going to go up there anyway."

"All right. We'll see you in the pass in a while." Brian looks at Joe. "You'll be all right?"

"Sure."

Brian gets his pack on, turns and begins walking up the slope, bending forward to take big slow strides. Watching him, Joe says to himself, "Humped splayfoot pack beast, yes. House-backed creature. Giant snow snail. Yo ho for the mountains. Rum de dum. Rum de dum de dum."

Peter appears around the shoulder, walking slowly and carelessly. He spreads his groundpad, sits beside Joe. After a time his breathing slows. "Where's Brian?"

"He went up there."

"Is that where we're going?"

"I thought we might go around to the pass the way the trail goes."

"Thank God."

"We'll get to go by Lake Doris."

"The renowned Lake Doris," Peter scoffs.

Joe waves a finger to scold. "It is nice, you know."

Joe and Peter walk. Soon their breathing hits a regular rhythm. They cross a meadow tucked into the side of the range like a terrace. It is covered with suncones, small melt depressions in the snow, and the walking is uneven.

"My feet are freezing," Pete says from several yards behind Joe.

Joe looks back to reply. "It's a cooling system. Most of my blood is hot—so hot I can hold snow in my hand and my hand won't get cold. But my feet are chilled. It cools the blood. I figure there's a spot around my knees that's perfect. My knees feel great. I live there and everything's comfortable."

"My knees hurt."

"Hmm," Joe says. "Now that is a problem."

After a silence filled by the squeak of snow and the crick of boot against snowshoe, Pete says, "I don't understand why I'm getting so tired. I've been playing full-court basketball all winter."

"Mountains aren't as flat as basketball courts."

Joe's pace is a bit faster than Pete's, and slowly he pulls ahead. He looks left, to the tree-filled valley, but slips a few times and turns his gaze back to the snow in front of him. His breaths rasp in his throat. He wipes sweat from an eyebrow. He hums unmusically, then starts a breath-chant, muttering a word for each step: *animal, animal, animal, animal, animal.* He watches his snowshoes crush patterns onto the points and ridges of the pocked, glaring snow. White light blasts around the sides of his sunglasses. He stops to tighten a binding, looks up when he is done. There is a tree a few score yards ahead—he adjusts his course for it, and walks again.

After a while he reaches the tree. He looks at it; a gnarled old Sierra juniper, thick and not very tall. Around it hundreds of black pine needles are scattered, each sunk in its own tiny pocket in the snow. Joe opens his mouth several times, says "Lugwump?" He shakes his head, walks up to the tree, puts a hand on it. "I don't know who you are?" He leans in, his nose is inches from bark. The bark peels away from the tree like papery sheets of filo dough. He puts his arms out, hugs the trunk. "Tr-eeee," he says. "Tr-eeeeeeee."

He is still saying it when Peter, puffing hard, joins him. Joe steps around the tree, gestures at a drop beyond the tree, a small bowl notched high in the side of the range.

"That's Lake Doris," he says, and laughs.

Blankly Peter looks at the small circle of flat snow in the center of the bowl. "Mostly a summer phenomenon," Joe says. Peter purses his lips and nods. "But not the pass," Joe adds, and points west.

West of the lake bowl the range—a row of black peaks emerging from the snow—drops a bit, in a deep, symmetrical U, an almost perfect semicircle, a glacier road filled with blue sky. Joe smiles. "That's Rockbound Pass. There's no way you could forget a sight like that. I think I see Brian up there. I'm going to go up and join him."

He takes off west, walking around the side of the lake until he can go straight up the slope rising from the lake to the pass. The snow thins on the slope, and his plastic snowshoes grate on stretches of exposed granite. He moves quickly, takes big steps and deep breaths. The slope levels and he can see the spine of the pass. Wind blows in his face, growing stronger with every stride. When he reaches the flat of the saddle in mid-pass it is a full gale. His shirt is blown cold against him, his eyes water. He can feel sweat drying on his face. Brian is higher in the pass, descending the north spine. His high shouts are blown past Joe. Joe takes off his pack and swings his arms around, stretches them out to the west. He is in the pass.

Below him to the west is the curving bowl of a cirque, one dug by the glacier that carved the pass. The cirque's walls are nearly free of snow, and great tiers of granite gleam in the sun. A string of lakes—flat white spots—mark the valley that extends westward out of the cirque. Lower ranges lie in rows out to the haze-fuzzed horizon.

Behind him Lake Doris's bowl blocks the view of the deep valley they have left behind. Joe looks back to the west; wind slams his face again. Brian hops down the saddle to him, and Joe whoops. "It's windy again," he calls.

"It's always windy in this pass," Brian says. He strips off his pack, whoops himself. He approaches Joe, looks around. "Man, for a while there about a year ago I thought we'd never be here again." He claps Joe on the back. "I'm sure glad you're here," he says, voice full.

Joe nods. "Me, too. Me, too."

Peter joins them. "Look at this," calls Brian, waving west. "Isn't this amazing?" Peter looks at the cirque for a moment and nods. He takes off his pack and sits behind a rock, out of the wind.

"It's cold," he says. His hands quiver as he opens his pack.

"Put on a sweatshirt," Brian says sharply. "Eat some food."

Joe removes his snowshoes, wanders around the pass away from Brian and Peter. The exposed rock is shattered tan granite, covered with splotches of lichen, red and black and green. Joe squats to inspect a crack, picks up a triangular plate of rock. He tosses it west. It falls in a long arc.

Brian and Peter eat lunch, leaning against a boulder that protects them from the wind. Where they are sitting it is fairly warm. Brian eats slices of cheese cut from a big block of it. Peter puts a tortilla in his lap, squeezes peanut butter out of a plastic tube onto it. He picks up a bottle of liquid butter and squirts a stream of it over the peanut butter.

Brian looks at the concoction and squints. "That looks like shit."

"Hey," Peter says. "Food is food. I thought you were the big pragmatist."

"Yeah, but..."

Pete wolfs down the tortilla, Brian works on the block of cheese.

"So how did you like the morning's hike?" Brian asks.

Pete says, "I read that snowshoes were invented by Plains Indians, for level places. In the mountains, those traverses"—he takes a bite—"those traverses were terrible."

"You used to love it up here."

"That was in the summers."

"It's better now, there's no one else up here. And you can go anywhere you want over snow."

"I've noticed you think so. But I don't like the snow. Too much work."

"Work," Brian scoffs. "The old law office is warping your conception of work, Peter."

Peter chomps irritably, looking offended. They continue to eat. One of Joe's nonsense songs floats by.

"Speaking of warped brains," Peter says.

"Yeah. You keeping an eye on him?"

"I guess so. I don't know what to do when he loses it, though."

Brian arches back and turns to look over the boulder. "Hey, Joe!" he shouts. "Come eat some lunch!" They both watch Joe jerk at the sound of Brian's voice. But after a moment's glance around, Joe returns to playing with the rocks.

"He's out again," says Brian.

"That," Peter says, "is one sick boy. Those doctors really did it to him."

"That *crash* did it to him. The doctors saved his life. You didn't see him at the hospital like I did. Man, ten or twenty years ago an injury like that would have left him a vegetable for sure. When I saw him I thought he was a goner."

"Yeah, I know, I know. The man who flew through his windshield."

"But you don't know what they *did* to him."

"So what did they do to him?"

"Well, they stimulated what they call axonal sprouting in the areas where neuronal connections were busted up—which means, basically, that they grew his brain back!"

"*Grew* it?"

"Yeah! Well some parts of it—the broken connections, you know. Like the arm of a starfish. You know?"

"No. But I'll take your word for it." Peter looks over the boulder at Joe. "I hope they grew back everything, yuk yuk. He might have one of his forgetting spells and walk over the edge there."

"Nah. He just forgets how to talk, as far as I can tell. Part of the reorganization, I think. It doesn't matter much up here." Brian arches up. "Hey, JOE! FOOD!"

"It does too matter," Peter says. "Say he forgets the word *cliff*. He forgets the concept, he says to himself I'm just going to step down to that lake there, and whoops, over the edge he goes."

"Nah," Brian says. "It doesn't work that way. Concepts don't need language."

"What?" Peter cries. "Concepts don't need language? Are you kidding? Man I thought Joe was the crazy one around here."

"No seriously," Brian says, shifting rapidly from his usual reserve to interested animation. "Sensory input is already a thought, and the way we field it is conceptual. Enough to keep you from walking off cliffs anyway." Despite this assertion he looks over his shoulder again. There stands Joe nodding as if in agreement with him.

"Yes, language is a contact lens," Joe says.

Peter and Brian look at each other.

"A contact lens at the back of the eyeball. Color filters into this lens, which is made of nameglass, and its reflected to the correct corner of the brain, tree corner or rock corner."

Peter and Brian chew that one over.

"So you lose your contact lenses?" Brian ventures.

"Yeah!" Joe looks at him with an appreciative glance. "Sort of."

"So what's in your mind then?"

Joe shrugs. "I wish I knew." After a while, struggling for expression: "I feel things. I feel that something's not right. Maybe I have another language then, but I'm not sure. Nothing looks right, it's all just… color. The names are gone. You know?"

Brian shakes his head, involuntarily grinning.

"Hmm," Peter says. "It sounds like you might have some trouble getting your driver's license renewed." All three of them laugh.

Brian stands, stuffs plastic bags into his pack. "Ready for some ridge running?" he says to the other two.

"Wait a second," Peter says, "we just got here. Why don't you kick back for a while? This pass is supposed to be the high point of the trip, and we've only been here half an hour."

"Longer than that," says Brian.

"Not long enough. I'm tired!"

"We've only hiked about four miles today," Brian replies impatiently. "All of us worked equally hard. Now we can walk down a ridge all afternoon, it'll be great!"

Peter sucks air between his teeth, holds it in, decides not to speak. He begins jamming bags into his pack.

They stand ready to leave the pass, packs and snowshoes on their backs. Brian makes a final adjustment to hipbelt—Pete looks up the spine they are about to ascend—Joe stares down at the huge bowl of rock and snow to the west. Afternoon sun glares. The shadow of a cloud hurries across the cirque toward them, jumps up the west side of the pass and they are in it, for a moment.

"Look!" Joe cries. He points at the south wall of the pass. Brian and Pete look—

A flash of brown. A pair of horns, blur of legs, the distant *clacks* of rock falling.

"A bighorn sheep!" says Brian. "Wow!" He hurries across the saddle of the pass to the south spine, looking up frequently. "There it is again! Come on!"

Joe and Pete hurry after him. "You guys will never catch that thing," says Peter.

The south wall is faulted and boulderish, and they zig and zag from one small shelf of snow to the next. They grab outcroppings and stick fists in cracks, and strain to push themselves up steps that are waist-high. The wind peels across the spine of the wall and keeps them cool. They breathe in gasps, stop frequently. Brian pulls ahead, Peter falls behind. Brian and Joe call to each other about the bighorn.

Brian and Joe top the spine, scramble up the decreasing slope. The ridge edge—a hump of shattered rock, twenty or twenty-five feet wide, like a high road—is nearly level, but still rises enough to block their view south. They hurry up to the point where the ridge levels, and suddenly they can see south for miles.

They stop to look. The range rises and falls in even swoops to a tall peak. Beyond the peak it drops abruptly and rises again, up and down and up, culminating in a huge knot of black peaks. To the east the steep snowy slope drops to the valley paralleling the range. To the west a series of spurs and cirques alternate, making a broken desert of rock and snow.

The range cuts down the middle of it all, high above everything else that can be seen. Joe taps his boot on solid rock. "Fossil backbone, primeval earth being," he says.

"I think I still see that sheep," says Brian, pointing. "Where's Peter?"

Peter appears, face haggard. He stumbles on a rock, steps quickly to keep his balance. When he reaches Brian and Joe he lets his pack thump to the ground.

"This is ridiculous," he says. "I have to rest."

"We can't exactly camp here," Brian says sarcastically, and gestures at the jumble of rock they are sitting on.

"I don't care," Peter says, and sits down.

"We've only been hiking an hour since lunch," Brian objects, "and we're trying to close in on that bighorn!"

"Tired," Peter says. "I have to rest."

"You get tired pretty fast these days!"

An angry silence.

Joe says in a mild voice. "You guys sure are bitching at each other a lot."

A long silence. Brian and Peter look in different directions.

Joe points down at the first dip in the ridge, where there is a small flat of granite slabs and corners filled with sand. "Why don't we camp there? Brian and I can drop our packs and go on up the ridge for a walk. Pete can rest and maybe start a fire later. If you can find wood."

Brian and Pete both agree to the plan, and they descend to the saddle campsite.

Two men ridge running. They make swift progress up the smooth rise, along the jumbled road at the top of the range. The bare rock they cross is smashed into fragments, splintered by ice and lightning. Breaking out of the blackish granite are knobs of tan rock, crushed into concentric rings of shards. They marvel at boulders which look like they have sat on the range since it began to rise. They jump from rock to rock, flexing freed shoulders. Brian points ahead and calls out when he sees the sheep. "Do you see it?"

"Sure do," Joe says, but without looking up. Brian notices this and snorts disgustedly.

Shadows of the range darken the valley to the east. Joe hops from foothold to foothold, babbling at Brian all the while from several yards behind him. "Name it, name it. You name it. Naammme. What an idea. I've got three blisters on my feet. I named the one on the left heel Amos." Pause to climb a shoulder-high slab of granite. "I named the one on the right heel Crouch. Then I've got one on the front of my right ankle, and I named that one Achilles. That way when I feel it it's not like pain, it's like a little joke. Twinges in my heel"—panting so he can talk—"are little hellos, hellos with every step. Amos here, hi, Joe; Crouch here, hi, Joe. It's amazing. The way I feel I probably don't need boots at all. I should take them off!"

"You'd probably better keep them on," Brian says seriously. Joe grins.

The incline becomes steeper and the edge of the ridge narrows. They slow down, step more carefully. The shattered rock gives way to great faulted blocks of solid mountain. They find themselves straddling the ridge on all fours, left feet on the east slope and right feet on the west. Both sides drop sharply away, especially the west. Sun gilds this steeper slope. Joe runs his hand down the edge of the range.

The ridge widens out, and they can walk again. The rock is shattered, all brittle plated angular splinters, covered with lichen. "Great granite," Joe says.

"This is actually diorite," Brian says. "Diorite or gabbro. Made of feldspar and darker stuff."

"Oh, don't give me that," Joe says. "I'm doing well just to remember granite. Besides, this stuff has been granite for a lot longer than geologists have been naming things. They can't go messing with a name like that." Still, he looks more closely at the rock. "Gabbro, gabbro... sounds like one of my words."

They wind between boulders, spring up escarpments. They come upon a knob of quartz that rises out of the black granite. The knob is infinitely cracked, as if struck on top by a giant sledgehammer. "Rose quartz," says Brian, and moves on. Joe stares at the knob, mouth open. He kneels to pick up chunks of the quartz, peers at them. He sees that Brian is moving on. Rising, he says to himself, "I wish I knew everything."

Suddenly they are at the top. Everything is below them. Beside Brian, Joe stops short. They stand silently, inches apart. Wind whips around them. To the south the range drops and rises yet again, to the giant knob of peaks they saw when they first topped the ridge. At every point of the compass mountains drop away, white folds crumpling to every horizon. Nothing moves but the wind. Brian says, "I wonder where that sheep went to."

Two men sitting on a mountaintop. Brian digs into a pile of rocks, pulls out a rusty tin box. "Aha," he says. "The sheep left us a clue." He takes a piece of paper from the box. "Here's its name—Diane Hunter."

"Oh, bullshit!" cries Joe. "That's no name. Let me see that." He grabs the box out of Brian's hand and the top falls off. A shower of paper, ten or twenty pieces of it, pops out of the box and floats down to the east, spun by the wind. Joe pulls out a piece still wedged in the box. He reads, "Robert Spencer, July 20th, 2014. It's a name box. It's for people who want to leave a record of their climb."

Brian laughs. "How could anyone get into something like that? Especially on a peak you can just walk right up to." He laughs again.

"I suppose I should try to recover as many as I can," Joe says dubiously, looking down the steep side of the peak.

"What for? It's not going to erase their experience."

"You never know," says Joe, laughing to himself. "It very well might. Just think, all over the United States the memory of this peak has popped right out of twenty people's heads." He waves to the east. "Bye-bye..."

They sit in silence. Wind blows. Clouds pass by. The sun closes on the horizon. Joe talks in short bursts, waves his arms. Brian listens, watches the clouds. At one point he says, "You're a new being, Joseph." Joe cocks his head at this.

Then they just sit and watch. It gets cold.

"Hawk," says Brian in a quiet voice. They watch the black dot soar on the updraft of the range.

"It's the sheep," says Joe. "It's a shapechanger."

"Nah. Doesn't even move the same."

"I say it is."

The dot turns in the wind and rises, circling higher and higher above the world, coasting along the updraft with minute wing adjustments, until it hovers over the giant, angular knotpeak. Suddenly it plummets toward the peaks, stooping faster than objects fall. It disappears behind the jagged black teeth. "Hawk," Joe breathes. "Hawuck divvve."

They look at each other.

Brian says, "That's where we'll go tomorrow."

Glissading down the snow expanse, skidding five or ten feet with each stiff-legged step, the two of them make rapid progress back to camp. The walking is dreamlike as they pump left… right… left… right down the slope.

"So what about that bighorn sheep?" says Joe. "I never did see any prints."

"Maybe we shared a hallucination," says Brian. "What do they call that?"

"A folie à deux."

"I don't like the sound of that." A pause while they skid down a steep bank of snow, straight-legged as if they are skiing. "I hope Pete got a fire going. Damn cold up here."

"A feature of the psychic landscape," Joe says, talking to himself again. "Sure, why not? It looks about like what I'd expect, I'll tell you that. No wonder I'm getting things confused. What you saw was probably a fugitive thought of mine, escaping off across the waste. Bighorn sheep, sure."

After a while they can see the saddle where they left Peter, far below them in the rocky expanse. There is a spark of yellow. They howl and shout. "Fire! FIRE!"

In the sandy camp, situated in a dip between slabs of granite, they greet Pete and root through their packs with the speed of hungry men. Joe takes his pot, jams it with snow, puts it on the fire. He sits down beside Peter.

"You guys were gone a long time," Peter says. "Did you find that sheep?"

Joe shakes his head. "It turned into a hawk." He moves his pot to a bigger flame. "Sure am glad you got this fire going," he says. "It must have been a bitch to start in this wind." He starts to pull off his boots.

"There wasn't much wood, either," Pete says. "But I found a dead tree down there a ways."

Joe prods a burning branch, frowns. "Juniper," he says with satisfaction. "Good wood."

Brian appears, dressed in down jacket, down pants, and down booties. Pete falls silent. Glancing at Pete, Joe notices this, and frowns again. He gets up stiffly to go to his pack and get his own down booties. He returns to the fire, finishes taking off his boots. His feet are white and wrinkled, with red blisters.

"Those look sore," says Pete.

"Nah." Joe gulps down the melted snow in his pot, starts melting more. He puts his booties on.

They watch the fire in silence.

Joe says, "Remember that time you guys wrestled in the living room of our apartment?"

"Yeah, we got all those carpet burns."

"And broke the lamp that never worked anyway—"

"And then you went berserk!" Brian laughs. "You went berserk and tried to bite my ear off!" They all laugh, and Pete nods, grinning with embarrassed pride.

"Pete won that one," Joe says.

"That's right," says Brian. "Put my shoulders to the mat, or to the carpet in that case. A victory for maniacs everywhere."

Ponderously Peter nods, imitating official approval. "But I couldn't beat you tonight," he admits. "I'm exhausted. I guess I'm not up to this snow camping."

"You were strong in those days," Brian tells him. "But you hiked a radical trail with us today, I'll tell you. I don't know too many people who would have come with us, actually."

"What about Joe here? He was on his back most of last year."

"Yeah, but he's crazy now."

"I was crazy before!" Joe protests, and they laugh.

Brian pours macaroni into his pot, shifts to a rock seat beside Peter so he can tend the pot better. They begin to talk about the days when they all lived together as students. Joe grins to hear them. He nearly overturns his pot, and they call out at him. Pete says, "The black thing is the pot, Joseph, the yellow stuff is fire—try to remember that." Joe grins. Steam rises from the pots and is whipped east by the evening breeze.

Three men sitting round a fire. Joe gets up, very slowly, and steps carefully to his pack. He unrolls his groundcloth, pulls out his sleeping bag.

He straightens up. The evening star hangs in the west. It's getting darker. Behind him his old friends laugh at something Pete has said.

In the east there are stars. Part of the sky is still a light velvet blue. The wind whistles softly. Joe picks up a rock, looks at it closely. "Rock," he says. He clenches the rock in his fist, shakes it at the evening star, lofts it skyward. "Rock!" He looks down the range: *black dragon back breaking out of blue-white*, like consciousness from chaos, an unbroken range of peaks—

"Hey, Joseph! You lamebrain!"

"Space case!"

"—come take care of your pot before it puts out the fire." Joe walks to the woodpile grinning, puts more wood on the fire, until it blazes up yellow in the dusk.

BEFORE I WAKE

Then he woke up, and it was all a dream.

In his dream Abernathy stood on a steep rock ridge. A talus slope dropped from the ridge to a glacial basin containing a small lake. The lake was cobalt in the middle, aquamarine around the edges. Here and there in the rock expanse patches of meadow grass gleamed, like the lawns of marmot estates. There were no trees. The cold air felt thin in his throat. He could see ranges many miles away, and though everything was perfectly still there was also an immense sweep in things, as if a gust of wind had caught the very fabric of being.

"Wake up, damn you," a voice said. He was shoved in the back, and he tumbled down the rockfall, starting a small avalanche.

He stood in a large white room. Glass boxes of various sizes were stacked everywhere, four and five to a pile, and in every box was a sleeping animal: monkey, rat, dog, cat, pig, dolphin, turtle. "No," he said, backing up. "Please, no."

A bearded man entered the room. "Come on, wake up," he said brusquely. "Time to get back to it, Fred. Our only hope is to work as hard as we can. You have to resist when you start slipping away!" He seized Abernathy by the arms and sat him down on a box of squirrels. "Now listen!" he cried. "We're asleep! We're dreaming!"

"Thank God," Abernathy said.

"Not so fast! We're awake as well."

"I don't believe you."

"Yes you do!" He slapped Abernathy in the chest with a large roll of graph paper, and it spilled loose and unrolled over the floor. Black squiggles smeared the graphs.

"It looks like a musical score," Abernathy said absently.

The bearded man shouted, "Yes! Yes! This is the symphony our brains play, very apt! Violins yammering away—that's what used to be ours, Fred; that was consciousness." He yanked hard on his beard with both hands, looking anguished. "Sudden drop to the basses, bowing and bowing, blessed sleep, yes, yes! And in the night the ghost instruments, horn and oboe and viola, spinning their little improvs over the ground bass, longer and longer till the violins start blasting again, yes, Fred, it's perfectly apt!"

"Thank you," Abernathy said. "But you don't have to yell. I'm right here."

"Then *wake up*," the man said viciously. "Can't, can you! Trapped, aren't you! Playing the new song like all the rest of us. Look at it there—REM sleep mixed indiscriminately with consciousness and deep sleep, turning us all into dreamwalkers. Into waking nightmares."

Looking into the depths of the man's beard, Abernathy saw that all his teeth were incisors. Abernathy edged toward the door, then broke for it and ran. The man leaped forward and tackled him, and they tumbled to the floor.

Abernathy woke up.

"Ah ha," the man said. It was Winston, administrator of the lab. "So now you believe me," he said sourly, rubbing an elbow. "I suppose we should write that down on the walls. If we all start slipping away we won't even remember what things used to be like. It'll all be over then."

"Where are we?" Abernathy asked.

"In the lab," Winston replied, voice filled with heavy patience. "We live here now, Fred. Remember?"

Abernathy looked around. The lab was large and well lit. Sheets of graph paper recording EEGs were scattered over the floor. Black countertops protruded from the walls, which were cluttered with machinery. In one corner were two rats in a cage.

Abernathy shook his head violently. It was all coming back. He was awake now, but the dream had been true. He groaned, walked to the room's little window, saw the smoke rising from the city below. "Where's Jill?"

Winston shrugged. They hurried through a door at the end of the lab, into a small room containing cots and blankets. No one there. "She's probably gone back to the house again," Abernathy said. Winston hissed with irritation and worry. "I'll check the grounds," he said. "You'd better go to the house. Be careful!"

Fred was already out the door.

In many places the streets were almost blocked by smashed cars, but little had changed since Abernathy's last venture home, and he made good time. The suburbs were choking in haze that smelled like incinerator smoke. A gas station attendant holding a pump handle stared in astonishment as he drove by, then waved. Abernathy didn't wave back. On one of these expeditions he had seen a knifing, and now he didn't like to look.

He stopped the car at the curb before his house. The remains of his house. It was charred almost to the ground. The blackened chimney was all that stood over chest high.

He got out of his old Cortina and slowly crossed the lawn, which was marked by black footprints. In the distance a dog barked insistently.

Jill stood in the kitchen, humming to herself and moving black things from here to there. She looked up as Abernathy stopped in the side yard before her. Her eyes twitched from side to side. "You're home," she said cheerily. "How was your day?"

"Jill, let's go out to dinner," Abernathy said.

"But I'm already cooking!"

"I can see that." He stepped over what had been the kitchen wall and took her arm. "Don't worry about that. Let's go anyway."

"My my," Jill said, brushing his face with a sooty hand. "Aren't you romantic this evening."

He stretched his lips wide. "You bet. Come on." He pulled her carefully out of the house and across the yard, and helped her into the Cortina. "Such chivalry," she remarked, eyes darting about in tandem.

Abernathy got in and started the engine. "But Fred," his wife said, "what about Jeff and Fran?"

Abernathy looked out his window. "They've got a babysitter," he finally said.

Jill frowned, nodded, sat back in her seat. Her broad face was smudged. "Ah," she said, "I do so like to dine out."

"Yes," Abernathy said, and yawned. He felt drowsy. "Oh no," he said. "No!" He bit his lip, pinched the back of the hand on the wheel. Yawned again. "No!" he cried. Jill jerked against her door in surprise. He swerved to avoid hitting an Oriental woman sitting in the middle of the road. "I must get to the lab," he shouted. He pulled down the Cortina's sun visor, took a pen from his coat pocket and scrawled *To The Lab*. Jill was staring at him. "It wasn't my fault," she whispered.

He drove them onto the freeway. All thirty lanes were clear, and he put his foot down on the accelerator. "To the lab," he sang, "to the lab, to the lab." A flying police vehicle landed on the highway ahead of them, folded its wings and sped off. Abernathy tried to follow it, but the freeway turned and narrowed, they were back on street level. He shouted with frustration, bit the flesh at the base of his thumb. Jill leaned back against her door, crying. Her eyes looked like small beings, a team trying to jerk its way free. "I couldn't help it," she said. "He loved me, you know. And I loved him."

Abernathy drove on. Some streets were burning. He wanted to go west, needed to go west. The car was behaving oddly. They were on a tree-lined avenue, out where there were few houses. A giant Boeing 747 lay across the road, its wings slewed forward. A high tunnel had been cut through it so traffic could pass. A cop with whistle and white gloves waved them through.

On the dashboard an emergency light blinked. *To The Lab.* Abernathy sobbed convulsively. "I don't know how!"

Jill, his sister, sat up straight. "Turn left," she said quietly. Abernathy threw the directional switch and their car rerouted itself onto the track that veered left. They came to other splits in the track, and each time Jill told him which way to go. The rear-view mirror bloomed with smoke.

Then he woke up. Winston was swabbing his arm with a wad of cotton, wiping off a droplet of blood.

"Amphetamines and pain," Winston whispered.

They were in the lab. About a dozen lab techs, postdocs, and grad students were in there at their countertops, working with great speed. "How's Jill?" Abernathy said.

"Fine, fine. She's sleeping right now. Listen, Fred. I've found a way to keep us awake for longer periods of time. Amphetamines and pain. Regular injections of benzedrine, plus a sharp burst of pain every hour or so, administered in whatever way you find most convenient. Metabolism stays too high for the mind to slip into the dreamwalking. I tried it and stayed fully awake and alert for six hours. Now we're all using the method."

Abernathy watched the lab techs dash about. "I can tell." He could feel his heart's rapid emphatic thumping.

"Well let's get to it," Winston said intently. "Let's make use of this time."

Abernathy stood. Winston called a little meeting. Feeling the gazes fixed on him, Abernathy collected his thoughts. "The mind consists of electrochemical action. Since we're all suffering the effects of this, it seems to me we can ignore the chemical and concentrate on the electrical. If the ambient fields have changed... Anyone know how many gauss the magnetic field is now? Or what the cosmic ray count is?"

They stared at him.

"We can tune in to the space station's monitor," he said. "And do the rest here."

So he worked, and they worked with him. Every hour a grinning Winston came around with hypodermics in hand, singing "Speed, speed, spee-ud!" He convinced Abernathy to let droplets of hydrochloric acid fall on the inside of his forearm.

It kept Abernathy awake better than it did the others. For a whole day, then two, he worked without pause, eating crackers and drinking water as he worked, giving himself the injections when Winston wasn't there.

After the first few hours his assistants began slipping back into dream-walking, despite the injections and acid splashings. Assignments he gave were never completed. One of his techs presented him with a successful experiment: the two rats, grafted together at the leg. Vainly Abernathy tried to pummel the man back to wakefulness.

In the end he did all the work himself. It took days. As his techs collapsed or wandered off he shifted from counter to counter, squinting sand-filled eyes to read oscilloscope and computer screen. He had never felt so exhausted in his life. It was like taking tests in a subject he didn't understand, in which he was severely retarded.

Still he kept working. The EEGs showed oscillation between wakefulness and REM sleep, in a pattern he had never seen. And there were correlations between the EEGs and fluctuations in the magnetic field.

Some of the men's flickering eyes were open, and they sat on the floors talking to each other or to him. Once he had to calm Winston, who was on the floor weeping and saying, "We'll never stop dreaming, Fred, we'll never stop." Abernathy gave him an injection, but it didn't have any effect.

He kept working. He sat at a crowded table at his high school reunion, and found he could work anyway. He gave himself an injection whenever he remembered. He got very, very tired.

Eventually he felt he understood as much as he was going to. Everyone else was lying in the cot room with Jill, or was slumped on the floors. Eyes and eyelids were twitching.

"We move through space filled with dust and gas and fields of force. Now all the constants have changed. The read-outs from the space station show that, show signs of a strong electromagnetic field we've apparently moved into. More dust, cosmic rays, gravitational flux. Perhaps it's the shockwave of a supernova, something nearby that we're just seeing now. Anyone looked up into the sky lately? Anyway. Something. The altered field has thrown the electrical patterns of our brains into something like what we call the REM state. Our brains rebel and struggle towards consciousness as much as they can, but this field forces them back. So we oscillate." He laughed weakly, and crawled up onto one of the countertops to get some sleep.

He woke and brushed the dust off his lab coat, which had served him as a blanket. The dirt road he had been sleeping on was empty. He walked. It was cloudy, and nearly dark.

He passed a small group of shacks, built in a tropical style with open walls and palm thatch roofs. They were empty. Dark light filled the sky.

Then he was at the sea's edge. Before him extended a low promontory, composed of thousands of wooden chairs, all crushed and piled together. At the point of the promontory there was a human figure, seated in a big chair that still had seat and back and one arm.

Abernathy stepped out carefully, onto slats and lathed cylinders of wood, from a chair arm to the plywood bottom of a chair seat. Around him the gray ocean was strangely calm; glassy swells rose and fell over the slick wood at waterline without a sound. Insubstantial clouds of fog, the lowest parts of a solid cloud cover, floated slowly onshore. The air was salty and wet. Abernathy shivered, stepped down to the next fragment of weathered gray wood.

The seated man turned to look at him. It was Winston. "Fred," he called, loud in the silence of the dawn. Abernathy approached him, picked up a chair back, placed it carefully, sat.

"How are you?" Winston said.

Abernathy nodded. "Okay." Down close to the water he could hear the small slaps and sucking of the sea's rise and fall. The swells looked a bit larger, and he could see thin smoky mist rising from them as they approached the shore.

"Winston," he croaked, and cleared his throat. "What's happened?"

"We're dreaming."

"But what does that mean?"

Winston laughed wildly. "Emergent stage one sleep, transitional sleep, rapid sleep, rhombencephalic sleep, pontine sleep, activated sleep, paradoxical sleep." He grinned ironically. "No one knows what it is."

"But all those studies."

"Yes, all those studies. And how I used to believe in them, how I used to work for them, all those sorry guesses ranging from the ridiculous to the absurd, we dream to organize experience into memory, to stimulate the senses in the dark, to prepare for the future, to give our depth perception exercise for God's sake! I mean we don't know, do we Fred. We don't know what dreaming is, we don't know what sleep is, you only have to think about it a bit to realize we didn't know what consciousness itself was, what it meant to be awake. Did we ever really know? We lived, we slept, we dreamed, and all three equal mysteries. Now that we're doing all three at once, is the mystery any deeper?"

Abernathy picked at the grain in the wood of a chair leg. "A lot of the time I feel normal," he said. "It's just that strange things keep happening."

"Your EEGs display an unusual pattern," Winston said, mimicking a scientific tone. "More alpha and beta waves than the rest of us. As if you're struggling hard to wake up."

"Yes. That's what it feels like."

They sat in silence for a time, watching swells lap at the wet chairs. The tide was falling. Offshore, near the limit of visibility, Abernathy saw a large cabin cruiser drifting in the current.

"So tell me what you've found," Winston said.

Abernathy described the data transmitted from the space station, then his own experiments.

Winston nodded. "So we're stuck here for good."

"Unless we pass through this field. Or—I've gotten an idea for a device you could wear around your head that might restore the old field."

"A solution seen in a dream?"

"Yes."

Winston laughed. "I used to believe in our rationality, Fred. Dreams as some sort of electrochemical manifestation of the nervous system, random activity, how reasonable it all sounded! Give the depth perception exercise! God, how small-minded it all was. Why shouldn't we have believed that dreams were great travels, to the future, to other universes, to a world more real than our own! They felt that way sometimes, in that last second before waking, as if we lived in a world so charged with meaning that it might burst... And now here we are. We're here, Fred, this is the moment and our only moment, no matter how we name it. *We're here.* From idea to symbol, perhaps. People will adapt. That's one of our talents."

"I don't like it," Abernathy said. "I never liked my dreams."

Winston merely laughed at him. "They say consciousness itself was a leap like this one, people were ambling around like dogs and then one day, maybe because the earth moved through the shockwave of some distant explosion, sure, one day one of them straightened up and looked around surprised, and said '*I am*.'"

"That would be a surprise," Abernathy said.

"And this time everyone woke up one morning still dreaming, and looked around and said '*What AM I?*'" Winston laughed. "Yes, we're stuck here. But I can adapt." He pointed. "Look, that boat out there is sinking."

They watched several people aboard the craft struggle to get a rubber raft over the side. After many dunkings they got it in the water and everyone inside it. Then they rowed away, offshore into the mist.

"I'm afraid," Abernathy said.

Then he woke up. He was back in the lab. It was in worse shape than ever. A couple of countertops had been swept clean to make room for chessboards, and several techs were playing blindfolded, arguing over which board was which.

He went to Winston's offices to get more benzedrine. There was no more. He grabbed one of his postdocs and said, "How long have I been asleep?" The man's eyes twitched, and he sang his reply: "Sixteen men on a dead man's chest, yo ho ho and a bottle of rum." Abernathy went to the cot room. Jill was there, naked except for light blue underwear, smoking a cigarette. One of the grad students was brushing her nipples with a feather. "Oh hi, Fred," she said, looking him straight in the eye. "Where have you been?"

"Talking to Winston," he said with difficulty. "Have you seen him?"

"Yes! I don't know when, though…"

He started to work alone again. No one wanted to help. He cleared a small room off the main lab, and dragged in the equipment he needed. He locked three large boxes of crackers in a cabinet, and tried to lock himself in his room whenever he felt drowsy. Once he spent six weeks in China, then he woke up. Sometimes he woke out in his old Cortina, hugging the steering wheel like his only friend. All his friends were lost. Each time he went back and started working again. He could stay awake for hours at a time. He got lots done. The magnets were working well, he was getting the fields he wanted. The device for placing the field around the head—an odd-looking wire helmet—was practicable.

He was tired. It hurt to blink. Every time he felt drowsy he applied more acid to his arm. It was covered with burns, but none of them hurt anymore. When he woke he felt as if he hadn't slept for days. Twice his grad students helped out, and he was grateful for that. Winston came by occasionally, but only laughed at him. He was too tired, everything he did was clumsy. He got on the lab phone once and tried to call his parents; all the lines were busy. The radio was filled with static, except for a station that played nothing but episodes of "The Lone Ranger." He went back to work. He ate crackers and worked. He worked and worked.

Late one afternoon he went out onto the lab's cafeteria terrace to take a break. The sun was low, and a chill breeze blew. He could see the air, filled with amber light, and he breathed it in violently. Below him the city smoked, and the wind blew, and he knew that he was alive, that he was aware he was alive, and that something important was pushing into the world, suffusing things…

Jill walked onto the terrace, still wearing nothing but the blue underwear. She stepped on the balls of her feet, smiled oddly. Abernathy could see goose-pimples sweep across her skin like cat's paws over water, and the power of her presence—distant, female, mysterious—filled him with fear.

They stood several feet apart and looked down at the city, where their house had been. The area was burning.

Jill gestured at it. "It's too bad we only had the courage to live our lives fully in dreams."

"I thought we were doing okay," Abernathy said. "I thought we engaged it the best we could, every waking moment."

She stared at him, again with the knowing smile. "You did think that, didn't you."

"Yes," he said fiercely, "I did. I did."

He went inside to work it off.

Then he woke up. He was in the mountains, in the high cirque again. He was higher now and could see two more lakes, tiny granite pools, above the cobalt-and-aquamarine one. He was climbing shattered granite, getting near the pass. Lichen mottled the rocks. The wind dried the sweat on his face, cooled him. It was quiet and still, so still, so quiet…

"Wake up!"

It was Winston. Abernathy was in his little room (high ranges in the distance, the dusty green of forests below), wedged in a corner. He got up, went to the crackers cabinet, pumped himself full of the benzedrine he had found in some syringes on the floor. (Snow and lichen.)

He went into the main lab and broke the fire alarm. That got everyone's attention. It took him a couple of minutes to stop the alarm. When he did his ears were ringing.

"The device is ready to try," he said to the group. There were about twenty of them. Some were as neat as if they were off to church, others were tattered and dirty. Jill stood to one side.

Winston crashed to the front of the group. "What's ready?" he shouted.

"The device to stop us dreaming," Abernathy said weakly. "It's ready to try."

Winston said slowly, "Well, let's try it then, okay, Fred?"

Abernathy carried helmets and equipment out of his room and into the lab. He arranged the transmitters and powered the magnets and the field generators. When it was all ready he stood up and wiped his brow.

"Is this it?" Winston asked. Abernathy nodded. Winston picked up one of the wire helmets.

"Well I don't like it!" he said, and struck the helmet against the wall.

Abernathy's mouth dropped open. One of the techs gave a shove to his electromagnets, and in a sudden fury Abernathy picked up a bat of wood and hit the man. Some of his assistants leaped to his aid, the rest pressed in and pulled at his equipment, tearing it down. A tremendous fight erupted. Abernathy swung his slab of wood with abandon, feeling great satisfaction each time it struck. There was blood in the air. His machines were being destroyed. Jill picked up one of the helmets and threw it at him, screaming, *"It's your fault, it's your fault!"* He knocked down a man near his magnets and had swung the slab back to kill him when suddenly he saw a bright glint in Winston's hand; it was a surgical knife, and with a swing like a sidearm pitcher's, Winston slammed the knife into Abernathy's diaphragm, burying it. Abernathy staggered back, tried to draw in a breath and found that he could, he was all right, he hadn't been stabbed. He turned and ran.

He dashed onto the terrace, closely pursued by Winston and Jill and the others, who tripped and fell even as he did. The patio was much higher than it used to be, far above the city, which burned and smoked. There was a long wide stairway descending into the heart of the city. Abernathy could hear screams, it was night and windy, he couldn't see any stars, he was at the edge of the terrace, he turned and the group was right behind him, faces twisted with fury. "No!" he cried, and then they rushed him, and he swung the wood slab and swung it and swung it, and turned to run down the stairs and then without knowing how he had done it he tripped and fell head over heels down the rocky staircase, falling falling falling.

Then he woke up. He was falling.

BLACK AIR

They sailed out of Lisbon harbor with the flags snapping and the brass culverins gleaming under a high white sun, priests proclaiming in sonorous Latin the blessing of the Pope, soldiers in armor jammed on the castles fore and aft, and sailors spiderlike in the rigging, waving at the citizens of the town who had left their work to come out on the hills and watch the ships crowd out the sunbeaten roads, for this was the Armada, the Most Fortunate Invincible Armada, off to subjugate the heretic English to the will of God. There would never be another departure like it.

Unfortunately, the wind blew out of the northeast for a month after they left without shifting even a point on the compass, and at the end of that month the Armada was no closer to England than Iberia itself. Not only that, but the hard-pressed coopers of Portugal had made many of the Armada's casks of green wood, and when the ship's cooks opened them the meat was rotten and the water stank. So they trailed into the port of Corunna, where several hundred soldiers and sailors swam to the shores of Spain and were never seen again. A few hundred more had already died of disease, so from his sickbed on the flagship, Don Alonso Perez de Guzman el Bueno, seventh Duke of Medina Sidonia and Admiral of the Armada, interrupted the composition of his daily complaint to Philip the Second to instruct his soldiers to go out into the countryside and collect peasants to help man the ships.

One squad of these soldiers stopped at a Franciscan monastery on the outskirts of Corunna, to impress all the boys who lived there and helped the monks, waiting to join the order themselves. Although they did not like it the monks could not object to the proposal, and off the boys went to join the fleet.

Among these boys, who were each taken to a different ship, was Manuel

Carlos Agadir Tetuan. He was seventeen years old; he had been born in Morocco, the son of West Africans who had been captured and enslaved by Arabs. In his short life he had already lived in the Moroccan coastal town of Tetuan, in Gibraltar, the Balearics, Sicily, and Lisbon. He had worked in fields and cleaned stables, he had helped make rope and later cloth, and he had served food in inns. After his mother died of the pox and his father drowned, he had begged in the streets and alleys of Corunna, the last port his father had sailed out of, until in his fifteenth year a Franciscan had tripped over him sleeping in an alley, inquired after him, and taken him to the refuge of the monastery.

Manuel was still weeping when the soldiers took him aboard *La Lavia*, a Levantine galleon of nearly a thousand tons. The sailing master of the ship, one Laeghr, took him in charge and led him below decks. Laeghr was an Irishman, who had left his country principally to practice his trade, but also out of hatred of the English who ruled Ireland. He was a huge man with a torso like a boar's, and arms as thick as the yardarms of the ship. When he saw Manuel's distress he showed that he was not without kindness; clapping a callused hand to the back of Manuel's neck he said, in accented but fluent Spanish, "Stop your snivelling, boy, we're off to conquer the damned English, and when we do your fathers at the monastery will make you their abbot. And before that happens a dozen English girls will fall at your feet and ask for the touch of those black hands, no doubt. Come on, stop it. I'll show you your berth first, and wait till we're at sea to show you your station. I'm going to put you in the main top, all our blacks are good topmen."

Laeghr slipped through a door half his height with the ease of a weasel ducking into one of its tiny holes in the earth. A hand half as wide as the doorway reemerged and pulled Manuel into the gloom. The terrified boy nearly fell down a broad-stepped ladder, but caught himself before falling onto Laeghr. Far below several soldiers laughed at him. Manuel had never been on anything larger than a Sicilian patache, and most of his fairly extensive seagoing experience was of coastal carracks, so the broad deck under him, cut by bands of yellow sunlight that flowed in at open ports big as church windows, crowded with barrels and bales of hay and tubs of rope, and a hundred busy men, was a marvel. "Saint Anna save me," he said, scarcely able to believe he was on a ship. Why, the monastery itself had no room as large as the one he descended into now. "Get down here," Laeghr said in an encouraging way.

Once on the deck of that giant room they descended again, to a stuffy chamber a quarter the size, illuminated by narrow fans of sunlight that were let in by ports that were mere slits in the hull. "Here's where you sleep," Laeghr said, pointing at a dark corner of the deck, against one massive oak wall of the ship. Forms there shifted, eyes appeared as lids lifted, a dull voice said, "Another one you'll never find again in this dark, eh master?"

"Shut up, Juan. See boy, there are beams dividing your berth from the rest, that will keep you from rolling around when we get to sea."

"Just like a coffin, with the lid up there."

"Shut up, Juan."

After the sailing master had made clear which slot in particular was Manuel's, Manuel collapsed in it and began to cry again. The slot was shorter than he was, and the dividing boards set in the deck were cracked and splintered. The men around him slept, or talked among themselves, ignoring Manuel's presence. His medallion cord choked him, and he shifted it on his neck and remembered to pray.

His guardian saint, the monks had decided, was Anne, mother of the Virgin Mary and grandmother of Jesus. He owned a small wooden medallion with her face painted on it, which Abbot Alonso had given to him. Now he took the medallion between his fingers, and looked in the tiny brown dots that were the face's eyes. "Please, Mother Anna," he prayed silently, "take me from this ship to my home. Take me home." He clenched the tag in his fist so tightly that the back of it, carved so that a cross of wood stood out from its surface, left an imprinted red cross in his palm. Many hours passed before he fell asleep.

Two days later the Most Fortunate Invincible Armada left Corunna, this time without the flags, or the crowds of spectators, or the clouds of priestly incense trailing downwind. This time God favored them with a westerly wind, and they sailed north at good speed. The ships were arranged in a formation devised by the soldiers, orderly phalanxes rising and falling on the swells: the galleasses in front, the supply hulks in the center, and the big galleons on either flank. The thousands of sails stacked on hundreds of masts made a grand and startling sight, like a copse of white trees on a broad blue plain.

Manuel was as impressed by the sight as the rest of the men. There were four hundred men on *La Lavia*, and only thirty were needed at any one time to sail the ship, so all of the three hundred soldiers stood on the sterncastle observing the fleet, and the sailors who were not on duty or sleeping did the same on the slightly lower forecastle.

Manuel's duties as a sailor were simple. He was stationed at the port midships taffrail, to which were tied the sheets for the port side of the mainmast's sails, and the sheets for the big lateen-rigged sail of the foremast. Manuel helped five other men pull these ropes in or let them out, following Laeghr's instructions; the other men took care of the belaying knots, so

Manuel's job came down to pulling on a rope when told to. It could have been more difficult, but Laeghr's plan to make him a topman like the other Africans aboard had come to grief. Not that Laeghr hadn't tried. "God made you Africans with a better head for heights, so you can climb trees to keep from being eaten by lions, isn't that right?" But when Manuel had followed a Moroccan named Habedeen up the halyard ladder to the main top, he found himself plunging about space, nearly scraping low foggy clouds, and the sea, embroidered with the wakes of the ships ahead, was more often than not *directly below him*. He had clamped, arms and legs, around a stanchion of the main top, and it had taken five men, laughing and cursing, to pry him loose and pull him down. With rich disgust, but no real physical force, Laeghr had pounded him with his cane and shoved him to the port taffrail. "You must be a Sicilian with a sunburn." And so he had been assigned his station.

Despite this incident he got on well with the rest of the crew. Not with the soldiers; they were rude and arrogant to the sailors, who stayed out of their way to avoid a curse or a blow. So three-quarters of the men aboard were of a different class, and remained strangers. The sailors therefore hung together. They were a mongrel lot, drawn from all over the Mediterranean, and Manuel was not unusual because of his recent arrival. They were united only in their dislike and resentment of the soldiers. "Those heroes wouldn't be able to conquer the Isle of Wight if we didn't sail them there," Juan said.

Manuel became acquainted first with the men at his post, and then with the men in his berth. As he spoke Spanish and Portuguese, and fair amounts of Arabic, Sicilian, Latin, and a Moroccan dialect, he could converse with everyone in his corner of the lower foredeck. Occasionally he was asked to translate for the Moroccans; more than once this meant he was the arbiter of a dispute, and he thought fast and mistranslated whenever it would help make peace. Juan, the one who had made the bitter comments to Laeghr on Manuel's arrival, was the only pure Spaniard in the berth. He loved to talk, and complained to Manuel and the others continuously. "I've fought *El Draco* before, in the Indies," he boasted. "We'll be lucky to get past that devil. You mark my words, we'll never do it."

Manuel's mates at the main taffrail were more cheerful, and he enjoyed his watches with them and the drills under Laeghr's demanding instruction. These men called him Topman or Climber, and made jokes about his knots around the belaying pins, which defied quick untying. This inability earned Manuel quite a few swats from Laeghr's cane, but there were worse sailors aboard, and the sailing master seemed to bear him no ill will.

A life of perpetual change had made Manuel adaptable, and shipboard routine became for him the natural course of existence. Laeghr or Pietro, the leader at Manuel's station, would wake him with a shout. Up to the gundeck, which was the domain of the soldiers, and from there up the big ladder that led to fresh air. Only then could Manuel be sure of the time of day. For the first week it was an inexpressible delight to get out of the gloom of the lower decks and under the sky, in the wind and clean salt air; but as they proceeded north, it began to get too cold for comfort. After their watches were over, Manuel and his mates would retire to the galley and be given their biscuits, water and wine. Sometimes the cooks killed some of the goats and chickens and made soup. Usually, though, it was just biscuits, biscuits that had not yet hardened in their barrels. The men complained grievously about this.

"The biscuits are best when they're hard as wood, and bored through by worms," Habedeen told Manuel.

"How do you eat it then?" Manuel asked.

"You bang pieces of biscuit against the table until the worms fall out. You eat the worms if you want." The men laughed, and Manuel assumed Habedeen was joking, but he wasn't certain.

"I despise this doughy shit," Pietro said in Portuguese. Manuel translated into Moroccan Arabic for the two silent Africans, and agreed in Spanish that it was hard to stomach. "The worst part," he offered, "is that some parts are stale while others are still fresh."

"The fresh part was never cooked."

"No, that's the worms."

As the voyage progressed, Manuel's berthmates became more intimate. Farther north the Moroccans suffered terribly from the cold. They came belowdecks after a watch with their dark skins completely goose-pimpled, like little fields of stubble after a harvest. Their lips and fingernails were blue, and they shivered an hour before falling asleep, teeth chattering like the castanets in a fiesta band. Not only that, but the swells of the Atlantic were getting bigger, and the men, since they were forced to wear every scrap of clothing they owned, rolled in their wooden berths unpadded and unprotected. So the Moroccans, and then everyone in the lower foredeck, slept three to a berth, taking turns in the middle, huddling together like spoons. Crowded together like that the pitching of the ship could press them against the beams, but it couldn't roll them around. Manuel's willingness to join these bundlings, and to lie against the beams, made him well-liked. Everyone agreed he made a good cushion.

Perhaps it was because of his hands that he fell ill. Though his spirit had been reconciled to the crusade north, his flesh was slower. Hauling on the coarse hemp ropes every day had ripped the skin from his palms, and salt, splinters, belaying pins and the odd boot had all left their marks as well, so that after the first week he had wrapped his hands in strips of cloth torn from the bottom of his shirt. When he became feverish, his hands pulsed painfully at every nudge from his heart, and he assumed that the fever had entered him through the wounds in his palms.

Then his stomach rebelled, and he could keep nothing down. The sight of biscuits or soup revolted him; his fever worsened, and he became parched and weak; he spent a lot of time in the head, wracked by dysentery. "You've been poisoned by the biscuits," Juan told him. "Just like I was in the Indies. That's what comes of boxing fresh biscuits. They might as well have put fresh dough in those barrels."

Manuel's berthmates told Laeghr of his condition, and Laeghr had him moved to the hospital, which was at the stern of the ship on a lower deck, in a wide room that the sick shared with the rudder post, a large smoothed tree trunk thrusting through floor and ceiling. All of the other men were gravely ill. Manuel was miserable as they laid him down on his pallet, wretched with nausea and in great fear of the hospital, which smelled of putrefaction. The man on the pallet next to him was insensible, and rolled with the sway of the ship. Three candle lanterns lit the low chamber and filled it with shadows. One of the Dominican friars, a Friar Lucien, gave him hot water and wiped his face. They talked for a while, and the friar heard Manuel's confession, which only a proper priest should have done. Neither of them cared. The priests on board avoided the hospital, and tended to serve only the officers and the soldiers. Friar Lucien was known to be willing to minister to the sailors, and he was popular among them.

Manuel's fever got worse, and he could not eat. Days passed, and when he woke up the men around him were not the same men who had been there when he fell asleep. He became convinced he was going to die, and once again he felt despair that he had been made a member of the Most Fortunate Invincible Armada. "Why are we here?" he demanded of the friar in a cracked voice. "Why shouldn't we let the English go to hell if they please?"

"The purpose of the Armada is not only to smite the heretic English," said Lucien. He held a candle closer to his book, which was not a Bible, but a slender little thing which he kept hidden in his robes. Shadows leaped on the blackened beams and planks over them, and the rudder post squeaked as it turned against the leather collar in the floor. "God also sent us as a test. Listen:

"'I assume the appearance of a refiner's fire, purging the dross of forms outworn. This is mine aspect of severity; I am as one who testeth gold in a furnace. Yet when thou hast been tried as by fire, the gold of thy soul shall be cleansed, and visible as fire: then the vision of thy Lord shall be granted unto thee, and seeing Him shall thou behold the shining one, who is thine own true self.'

"Remember that, and be strong. Drink this water here—come on, do you want to fail your God? This is part of the test."

Manuel drank, threw up. His body was no more than a tongue of flame contained by his skin, except where it burst out of his palms. He lost track of the days, and forgot the existence of anyone beyond himself and Friar Lucien. "I never wanted to leave the monastery," he told the friar, "yet I never thought I would stay there long. I've never stayed long any place yet. It was my home but I knew it wasn't. I haven't found my home yet. They say there is ice in England—I saw the snow in the Catalonian mountains once, Father, will we go home? I only want to return to the monastery and be a father like you."

"We will go home. What you will become, only God knows. He has a place for you. Sleep now. Sleep, now."

By the time his fever broke his ribs stood out from his chest as clearly as the fingers of a fist. He could barely walk. Lucien's narrow face appeared out of the gloom clear as a memory. "Try this soup. Apparently God has seen fit to keep you here."

"Thank you Saint Anna for your intercession," Manuel croaked. He drank the soup eagerly. "I want to return to my berth."

"Soon."

They took him up to the deck. Walking was like floating, as long as he held on to railings and stanchions. Laeghr greeted him with pleasure, as did his stationmates. The world was a riot of blues; waves hissed past, low clouds jostled together in their rush east, tumbling between them shafts of sunlight that spilled onto the water. He was excused from active duty, but he spent as many hours as he could at his station. He found it hard to believe that he had survived his illness. Of course he was not entirely recovered; he could not yet eat any solids, particularly biscuit, so that his diet consisted of soup and wine. He felt weak, and perpetually light-headed. But when he was on deck in the wind he was sure that he was getting better, so he stayed there as much as possible. He was on deck, in fact, when they first caught sight of England. The soldiers pointed and shouted in great excitement, as the point Laeghr called The Lizard bounced over the horizon. Manuel had grown so used to the sea that the low headland rising off their port bow seemed unnatural, an intrusion into a marine world, as if the deluge was just now receding and these drowned hillsides were just now shouldering up out of the waves, soaking wet and covered by green seaweed that had not yet died. And that was England.

A few days after that they met the first English ships—faster than the Spanish galleons, but much smaller. They could no more impede the progress of the Armada than flies could slow a herd of cows. The swells became steeper and followed each other more closely, and the changed pitching of *La Lavia* made it difficult for Manuel to stand. He banged his head once, and another time ripped away a palmful of scabs, trying to keep his balance in the violent yawing caused by the chop. Unable to stand one morning, he lay in the dark of his berth, and his mates brought him cups of soup. That went on for a long time. Again he worried that he was going to die. Finally Laeghr and Lucien came below together.

"You must get up now," Laeghr declared. "We fight within the hour, and you're needed. We've arranged easy work for you."

"You have only to provide the gunners with slow match," said Friar Lucien as he helped Manuel to his feet. "God will help you."

"God will have to help me," Manuel said. He could see the two men's souls flickering above their heads: little triple knots of transparent flame that flew up out of their hair and lit the features of their faces. "The gold of thy soul shall be cleansed, and visible as fire," Manuel recalled. "Hush," said Lucien with a frown, and Manuel realized that what Lucien had read to him was a secret.

Amidships Manuel noticed that now he was also able to see the air, which was tinged red. They were on the bottom of an ocean of red air, just as they were on top of an ocean of blue water. When they breathed they turned the air a darker red; men expelled plumes of air like horses breathing out clouds of steam on a frosty morning, only the steam was red. Manuel stared and stared, marveling at the new abilities God had given his sight.

"Here," Laeghr said, roughly directing him across the deck. "This tub of punk is yours. This is slow match, understand?" Against the bulkhead was a tub full of coils of closely braided cord. One end of the cord was hanging over the edge of the tub burning, fizzing the air around it to deep crimson. Manuel nodded: "Slow match."

"Here's your knife. Cut sections about this long, and light them with a piece of it that you keep beside you. Then give sections of it to the gunners who come by, or take it to them if they call for it. But don't give away all your lit pieces. Understand?"

Manuel nodded that he understood and sat down dizzily beside the tub. One of the largest cannon poked through a port in the bulkhead just a few feet from him. Its crew greeted him. Across the deck his stationmates stood at their taffrail. The soldiers were ranked on the fore- and sterncastles, shouting with excitement, gleaming like shellfish in the sun. Through the port Manuel could see some of the English coast.

Laeghr came over to see how he was doing. "Hey, don't you lop your fingers off there, boy. See out there? That's the Isle of Wight. We're going to circle and conquer it, I've no doubt, and use it as our base for our attack on the mainland. With these soldiers and ships they'll *never* get us off that island. It's a good plan."

But things did not progress according to Laeghr's plan. The Armada swung around the east shore of the Isle of Wight, in a large crescent made of five distinct phalanxes of ships. Rounding the island, however, the forward galleasses encountered the stiffest English resistance they had met so far. White puffs of smoke appeared out of the ships and were quickly stained red, and the noise was tremendous.

Then the ships of *El Draco* swept around the southern point of the island onto their flank, and suddenly *La Lavia* was in the action. The soldiers roared and shot off their arquebuses, and the big cannon beside Manuel leaped back in its truck with a bang that knocked him into the bulkhead. After that he could barely hear. His slow match was suddenly in demand; he cut the cord and held the lit tip to unlit tips, igniting them with his red breath. Cannonballs passing overhead left rippling wakes in the blood air. Grimy men snatched the slow match and dashed to their guns, dodging tackle blocks that thumped to the deck. Manuel could see the cannonballs, big as grapefruit, flying at them from the English ships and passing with a whistle. And he could see the transparent knots of flame, swirling higher than ever about the men's heads.

Then a cannonball burst through the porthole and knocked the cannon off its truck, the men to the deck. Manuel rose to his feet and noticed with horror that the knots of flame on the scattered gunners were gone; he could see their heads clearly now, and they were just men, just broken flesh draped over the plowed surface of the deck. He tried, sobbing, to lift a gunner who was bleeding only from the ears. Laeghr's cane lashed across his shoulders: "Keep cutting match! There's others to attend to these men!" So Manuel cut lengths of cord and lit them with desperate puffs and shaking hands, while the guns roared, and the exposed soldiers on the castles shrieked under a hail of iron, and the red air was ripped by passing shot.

The next few days saw several battles like that as the Armada was forced past the Isle of Wight and up the Channel. His fever kept him from sleeping, and at night Manuel helped the wounded on his deck, holding them down and wiping the sweat from their faces, nearly as delirious as they were.

At dawn he ate biscuits and drank his cup of wine and went to his tub of slow match to await the next engagement. *La Lavia*, being the largest ship on the left flank, always took the brunt of the English attack. It was on the third day that *La Lavia*'s mainmast topgallant yard fell on his old taffrail crew, crushing Hanan and Pietro. Manuel rushed across the deck to help them, shouting his anguish. He got a dazed Juan down to their berth and returned amidships. Around him men were being dashed to the deck, but he didn't care. He hopped through the red mist that nearly obscured his sight, carrying lengths of match to the gun crews, who were now so depleted that they couldn't afford to send men to him. He helped the wounded below to the hospital, which had truly become an antechamber of hell; he helped toss the dead over the side, croaking a short prayer in every case; he ministered to the soldiers hiding behind the bulwarks of the bulkheads, waiting vainly for the English to get within range of their arquebuses. Now the cry amidships was "Manuel, match here! Manuel, some water! Help, Manuel!" In a dry fever of energy Manuel hurried to their aid.

He was in such perpetual haste that in the middle of a furious engagement he nearly ran into his patroness, Saint Anna, who was suddenly standing there in the corner of his tub. He was startled to see her.

"Grandmother!" he cried. "You shouldn't be here, it's dangerous."

"As you have helped others, I am here to help you," she replied. She pointed across the purplish chop to one of the English ships. Manuel saw a puff of smoke appear from its side, and out of the puff came a cannonball, floating in an arc over the water. He could see it as clearly as he could have seen an olive tossed at him from across a room: a round black ball, spinning lazily, growing bigger as it got closer. Now Manuel could tell that it was coming at him, *directly* at him, so that its trajectory would intersect his heart. "Um, blessed Anna," he said, hoping to bring this to his saint's attention. But she had already seen it, and with a brief touch to his forehead she floated up into the maintop, among the unseeing soldiers. Manuel watched her, eyeing the approaching cannonball at the same time. At the touch of her hand a rigging block fell away from the end of the main yard; it intercepted the cannonball's flight, knocking the ball downward into the hull where it stuck, half embedded in the thick wood. Manuel stared at the black half sphere, mouth open. He waved up at Saint Anna, who waved back and flew up into the red clouds toward heaven. Manuel kneeled and said a prayer of thanks to her and to Jesus for sending her and went back to cutting match.

A night or two later—Manuel himself was not sure, as the passage of time had become for him something plastic and elusive and, more than anything else, meaningless—the Armada anchored at Calais Roads, just off the Flemish coast. For the first time since they had left Corunna *La Lavia* lay still, and listening at night Manuel realized how much the constant chorus of wooden squeaks and groans was the voice of the crew, and not of the ship. He drank his ration of wine and water quickly, and walked the length of the lower deck, talking with the wounded and helping when he could to remove splinters. Many of the men wanted him to touch them, for his safe passage through some of the worst scenes of carnage had not gone unnoticed. He touched them, and when they wanted, said a prayer. Afterwards he went up on deck. There was a fair breeze from the southwest, and the ship rocked ever so gently on the tide. For the first time in a week the air was not suffused red: Manuel could see stars, and distant bonfires on the Flemish shore, like stars that had fallen and now burnt out their life on the land.

Laeghr was limping up and down amidships, detouring from his usual path to avoid a bit of shattered decking.

"Are you hurt, Laeghr?" Manuel inquired.

For answer Laeghr growled. Manuel walked beside him. After a bit Laeghr stopped and said, "They're saying you're a holy man now because you were running all over the deck these last few days, acting like the shot we were taking was hail and never getting hit for it. But I say you're just too foolish to know any better. Fools dance where angels would hide. It's part of the curse laid on us. Those who learn the rules and play things right end up getting hurt—sometimes from doing just the things that will protect them the most. While the blind fools who wander right into the thick of things are never touched."

Manuel watched Laeghr's stride. "Your foot?"

Laeghr shrugged. "I don't know what will happen to it."

Under a lantern Manuel stopped and looked Laeghr in the eye. "Saint Anna appeared and plucked a cannonball that was heading for me right out of the sky. She saved my life for a purpose."

"No." Laeghr thumped his cane on the deck. "Your fever has made you mad, boy."

"I can show you the shot!" Manuel said. "It stuck in the hull!" Laeghr stumped away.

Manuel looked across the water at Flanders, distressed by Laeghr's words, and by his hobbled walk. He saw something he didn't comprehend.

"Laeghr?"

"What?" came Laeghr's voice from across midships.

"Something bright… the souls of all the English at once, maybe…" His voice shook.

"*What?*"

"Something coming at us. Come here, master."

Thump, thump, thump. Manuel heard the hiss of Laeghr's indrawn breath, the muttered curse.

"*Fireships*," Laeghr bellowed at the top of his lungs. "Fireships! Awake!"

In a minute the ship was bedlam, soldiers running everywhere. "Come with me," Laeghr told Manuel, who followed the sailing master to the forecastle, where the anchor hawser descended into the water. Somewhere along the way Laeghr had gotten a halberd, and he gave it to Manuel. "Cut the line."

"But master, we'll lose the anchor."

"Those fireships are too big to stop, and if they're hellburners they'll explode and kill us all. Cut it."

Manuel began chopping at the thick hawser, which was very like the trunk of a small tree. He chopped and chopped, but only one strand of the huge rope was cut when Laeghr seized the halberd and began chopping himself, awkwardly to avoid putting his weight on his bad foot. They heard the voice of the ship's captain— "Cut the anchor cable!" And Laeghr laughed.

The rope snapped, and they were floating free. But the fireships were right behind them. In the hellish light Manuel could see English sailors walking about on their burning decks, passing through the flames like salamanders or demons. No doubt they were devils. The fires towering above the eight fireships shared the demonic life of the English; each tongue of yellow flame contained an English demon eye looking for the Armada, and some of these leaped free of the blaze that twisted above the fireships, in vain attempts to float onto *La Lavia* and incinerate it. Manuel held off these embers with his wooden medallion, and the gesture that in his boyhood in Sicily had warded off the evil eye. Meanwhile, the ships of the fleet were cut loose and drifting on the tide, colliding in the rush to avoid the fireships. Captains and officers screamed furiously at their colleagues on other ships, but to no avail. In the dark and without anchors the ships could not be regathered, and as the night progressed most were blown out into the North Sea. For the first time the neat phalanxes of the Armada were broken, and they were never to be reformed again.

When it was all over *La Lavia* held its position in the North Sea by sail, while the officers attempted to identify the ships around them, and find out what Medina Sidonia's orders were. Manuel and Juan stood amidships with the rest of their berthmates. Juan shook his head. "I used to make corks in Portugal. We were like a cork back there in the Channel, being pushed into the neck of a bottle. As long as we were stuck in the neck we were all right—the neck got narrower and narrower, and they might never have gotten us out. Now the English have pushed us right down into the bottle itself. We're floating about in our own dregs. And we'll never get out of the bottle again."

"Not through the neck, anyway," one of the others agreed.

"Not any way."

"God will see us home," Manuel said.

Juan shook his head.

Rather than try to force the Channel, Admiral Medina Sidonia decided that the Armada should sail around Scotland, and then home. Laeghr was taken to the flagship for a day to help chart a course, for he was familiar with the north as none of the Spanish pilots were.

The battered fleet headed away from the sun, ever higher into the cold North Sea. After the night of the fireships Medina Sidonia had restored discipline with a vengeance. One day the survivors of the many Channel battles were witness to the hanging from the yardarm of a captain who had let his ship get ahead of the Admiral's flagship, a position which was now forbidden. A carrack sailed through the fleet again and again so every crew could see the corpse of the disobedient captain, swinging freely from its spar.

Manuel observed the sight with distaste. Once dead, a man was only a bag of bones; nowhere in the clouds overhead could he spot the captain's soul. Perhaps it had plummeted into the sea, on its way to hell. It was an odd transition, death. Curious that God did not make more explicit the aftermath.

So *La Lavia* faithfully trailed the Admiral's flagship, as did the rest of the fleet. They were led farther and farther north, into the domain of cold. Some mornings when they came on deck in the raw yellow of the dawn the riggings would be rimed with icicles, so that they seemed strings of diamonds. Some days it seemed they sailed across a sea of milk, under a silver sky. Other days the ocean was the color of a bruise, and the sky a fresh pale blue so clear that Manuel gasped with the desire to survive this voyage and live. Yet he was as cold as death. He remembered the burning nights of his fever as fondly as if he were remembering his first home on the coast of North Africa.

All the men were suffering from the cold. The livestock were dead, so the galley closed down: no hot soup. The Admiral imposed rationing on everyone, including himself; the deprivation kept him in his bed for the rest of the voyage. For the sailors, who had to haul wet or frozen rope, it was worse. Manuel watched the grim faces, in line for their two biscuits and one large cup of wine and water—their daily ration—and concluded that they would continue sailing north until the sun was under the horizon and they were in the icy realm of death, the north pole where God's dominion was weak, and there they would give up and die all at once. Indeed, the winds drove them nearly to Norway, and it was with great difficulty that they brought the shot-peppered hulks around to a westerly heading.

When they did, they discovered a score of new leaks in *La Lavia's* hull, and the men, already exhausted by the effort of bringing the ship about, were forced to man the pumps around the clock. A pint of wine and a pint of water a day were not enough. Men died. Dysentery, colds, the slightest injury; all were quickly fatal.

Once again Manuel could see the air. Now it was a thick blue, distinctly darker where men breathed it out, so that they all were shrouded in dark blue air that obscured the burning crowns of their souls. All of the wounded men in the hospital had died. Many of them had called for Manuel in their last moments; he had held their hands or touched their foreheads, and as their souls had flickered away from their heads like the last pops of flame out of the coals of a dying fire, he had prayed for them. Now other men too weak to leave their berths called for him, and he went and stood by them in their distress. Two of these men recovered from dysentery, so his presence was requested even more frequently. The captain himself asked for Manuel's touch when he fell sick; but he died anyway, like most of the rest.

One morning Manuel was standing with Laeghr at the midships bulkhead. It was chill and cloudy, the sea was the color of flint. The soldiers were bringing their horses up and forcing them over the side, to save water.

"That should have been done as soon as we were forced out of the Sleeve," Laeghr said. "Waste of water."

"I didn't even know we had horses aboard," Manuel said.

Laeghr laughed briefly. "Boy, you are a prize of a fool. One surprise after another."

They watched the horses' awkward falls, their rolling eyes, their flared nostrils expelling clouds of blue air. Their brief attempts to swim.

"On the other hand, we should probably be eating some of those," Laeghr said.

"Horse meat?"

"It can't be that bad."

The horses all disappeared, exchanging blue air for flint water. "It's cruel," Manuel said.

"In the horse latitudes they swim for an hour," Laeghr said. "This is better." He pointed to the west. "See those tall clouds?"

"Yes."

"They stand over the Orkneys. The Orkneys or the Shetlands, I can't be sure anymore. It will be interesting to see if these fools can get this wreck through the islands safely." Looking around, Manuel could only spot a dozen or so ships; presumably the rest of the Armada lay over the horizon ahead of them. He stopped to wonder about what Laeghr had just said, for it would naturally be Laeghr's task to navigate them through the northernmost of the British Isles; at that very moment Laeghr's eyes rolled like the horses' had, and he collapsed on the deck. Manuel and some other sailors carried him down to the hospital.

"It's his foot," said Friar Lucien. "His foot is crushed and his leg has putrefied. He should have let me amputate."

Around noon Laeghr regained consciousness. Manuel, who had not left his side, held his hand, but Laeghr frowned and pulled it away.

"Listen," Laeghr said with difficulty. His soul was no more than a blue cap covering his tangled salt-and-pepper hair. "I'm going to teach you some words that may be useful to you later." Slowly he said, "*Tor conaloc an dhia*," and Manuel repeated it. "Say it again." Manuel repeated the syllables over and over, like a Latin prayer. Laeghr nodded. "*Tor conaloc an naom dhia*. Good. Remember the words always." After that he stared at the deckbeams above, and would answer none of Manuel's questions. Emotions played over his face like shadows, one after another. Finally he took his gaze from the infinite and looked at Manuel. "Touch me, boy."

Manuel touched his forehead, and with a sardonic smile Laeghr closed his eyes: his blue crown of flame flickered up through the deck above and disappeared.

They buried him that evening, in a smoky, hellish brown sunset. Friar Lucien said the shortened Mass, mumbling in a voice that no one could hear, and Manuel pressed the back of his medallion against the cold flesh of Laeghr's arm, until the impression of the cross remained. Then they tossed him overboard. Manuel watched with a serenity that surprised him. Just weeks ago he had shouted with rage and pain as his companions had been torn apart; now he watched with a peace he did not understand as the man who had taught him and protected him sank into the iron water and disappeared.

A couple of nights after that Manuel sat apart from his remaining berthmates, who slept in one pile like a litter of kittens. He watched the blue flames wandering over the exhausted flesh, watched without reason or feeling. He was tired.

Friar Lucien looked in the narrow doorway and hissed. "Manuel! Are you there?"

"I'm here."

"Come with me."

Manuel got up and followed him. "Where are we going?"

Friar Lucien shook his head. "It's time." Everything else he said was in Greek. He had a little candle lantern with three sides shuttered, and by its illumination they made their way to the hatch that led to the lower decks.

Manuel's berth, though it was below the gun deck, was not on the lowest deck of the ship. *La Lavia* was very much bigger than that. Below the berth deck were three more decks that had no ports, as they were beneath the waterline. Here in perpetual gloom were stored the barrels of water and biscuit, the cannonballs and rope and other supplies. They passed by the powder room, where the armorer wore felt slippers so that a spark from his boots might not blow up the ship. They found a hatchway that held a ladder leading to an even lower deck. At each level the passages became narrower, and they were forced to stoop. Manuel was astounded when they descended yet again, for he would have imagined them already on the keel, or in some strange chamber suspended beneath it; but Lucien knew better. Down they went, through a labyrinth of dank black wooden passageways. Manuel was long lost, and held Lucien's arm for fear of being separated from him and becoming hopelessly trapped in the bowels of the ship. Finally they came to a door that made their narrow hallway a dead end. Lucien rapped on the door and hissed something, and the door opened, letting out enough light to dazzle Manuel.

After the passageways, the chamber they entered seemed very large. It was the cable tier, located in the bow of the ship just over the keel. Since the encounter with the fireships, *La Lavia* had little cable, and what was left lay in the corners of the room. Now it was lit by candles set in small iron candelabra that had been nailed to the side beams. The floor was covered by an inch of water, which reflected each of the candle flames as a small spot of white light. The curving walls dripped and gleamed. In the center of the room a box had been set on end and covered with a bit of cloth. Around the box stood several men: a soldier, one of the petty officers, and some sailors Manuel knew only by sight. The transparent knots of cobalt flame on their heads added a bluish cast to the light in the room.

"We're ready, Father," one of the men said to Lucien. The friar led Manuel to a spot near the upturned box, and the others arranged themselves in a circle around him. Against the aft wall, near gaps where floor met wall imperfectly, Manuel spotted two big rats with shiny brown fur, all ablink and twitch-whiskered at the unusual activity. Manuel frowned and one of the rats plopped into the water covering the floor and swam under the wall, its tail swishing back and forth like a small snake, revealing to Manuel its true nature. The other rat stood its ground and blinked its bright little round eyes as it brazenly returned Manuel's unwelcoming gaze.

From behind the box Lucien looked at each man in turn, and read in Latin. Manuel understood the first part: "I believe in God the Father Almighty, Maker of Heaven and Earth, and of all things visible and invisible…" From there Lucien read on, in a voice powerful yet soothing, entreatful yet proud. After finishing the creed he took up another book, the little one he always carried with him, and read in Spanish:

"'Know ye, O Israel, that what men call life and death are as beads of white and black strung upon a thread; and this thread of perpetual change is mine own changeless life, which bindeth together the unending string of little lives and little deaths.

"'The wind turns a ship from its course upon the deep: the wandering winds of the senses cast man's mind adrift on the deep.

"'But lo! That day shall come when the light that *is* shall still all winds, and bind every hideous liquid darkness; and all thy habitations shall be blest by the white brilliance which descendeth from the crown.'"

While Lucien read this, the soldier moved slowly about the chamber. First he set on the top of the box a plate of sliced biscuit; the bread was hard, as it became after months at sea, and someone had taken the trouble to cut slices, and then polish them into wafers so thin that they were translucent, and the color of honey. Occasional wormholes gave them the look of old coins, that had been beaten flat and holed for use as jewelry.

Next the soldier brought forth from behind the box an empty glass bottle with its top cut off so that it was a sort of bowl. Taking a flask in his other hand, he filled the bowl to the midway point with *La Lavia*'s awful wine. Putting the flask down, he circled the group while the friar finished reading. Every man there had cuts on his hands that more or less continuously leaked blood, and each man pulled a cut open over the bottle held to him, allowing a drop to splash in, until the wine was so dark that to Manuel, aware of the blue light, it was a deep violet.

The soldier replaced the bottle beside the plate of wafers on the box. Friar Lucien finished his reading, looked at the box, and recited one final sentence: "O lamps of fire! Make bright the deep caverns of sense; with strange brightness give heat and light together to your beloved, that we may be one with you." Taking the plate in hand, he circled the chamber, putting a wafer in the mouths of the men. "The body of Christ, given for you. The body of Christ, given for you."

Manuel snapped the wafer of biscuit between his teeth and chewed it. At last he understood what they were doing. This was a communion for the dead: a service for Laeghr, a service for all of them, for they were all doomed. Beyond the damp curved wall of their chamber was the deep sea, pressing against the timbers, pressing in on them. Eventually they would all be swallowed, and would sink down to become food for the fishes, after which their bones would decorate the floor of the ocean, where God seldom visited. Manuel could scarcely get the chewed biscuit past the lump in his throat. When Friar Lucien lifted the half bottle and put it to his lips, saying first, "The blood of Christ, shed for you," Manuel stopped him. He took the bottle from the friar's hand. The soldier stepped forward, but Lucien waved him away. Then the friar kneeled before Manuel and crossed himself, but backwards as Greeks did, left to right rather than the proper way. Manuel said, "You are the blood of Christ," and held the half bottle to Lucien's lips, tilting it so he could drink.

He did the same for each of the men, the soldier included. "You are the Christ." This was the first time any of them had partaken of this part of the communion, and some of them could barely swallow. When they had all drunk, Manuel put the bottle to his lips and drained it to the dregs. "Friar Lucien's book says, all thy habitations shall be blest by the white brilliance that is the crown of fire, and we shall all be made the Christ. And so it is. We drank, and now we are the Christ. See"—he pointed at the remaining rat, which was now on its hind legs, washing its forepaws so that it appeared to pray, its bright round eyes fixed on Manuel—"even the beasts know it." He broke off a piece of biscuit wafer, and leaned down to offer it to the rat. The rat accepted the fragment in its paws and ate it. It submitted to Manuel's touch. Standing back up, Manuel felt the blood rush to his head. The crowns of fire blazed on every head, reaching far above them to lick the beams of the ceiling, filling the room with light— "He is here!" Manuel cried, "He has touched us with light, see it!" He touched each of their foreheads in turn, and saw their eyes widen as they perceived the others' burning souls in wonder, pointing at each other's heads; then they were all embracing in the clear white light, hugging one another with the tears running down their cheeks and giant grins splitting their beards. Reflected candlelight danced in a thousand parts on the watery floor. The rat, startled, splashed under the gap in the wall, and they laughed and laughed and laughed.

Manuel put his arm around the friar, whose eyes shone with joy. "It is good," Manuel said when they were all quiet again. "God will see us home."

They made their way back to the upper decks like boys playing in a cave they know very well.

The Armada made it through the Orkneys without Laeghr, though it was a close thing for some ships. Then they were out in the North Atlantic, where the swells were broader, their troughs deeper, and their tops as high as the castles of *La Lavia*, and then higher than that.

Winds came out of the southwest, bitter gales that never ceased, and three weeks later they were no closer to Spain than they had been when they slipped through the Orkneys. The situation on *La Lavia* was desperate, as it was all through the fleet. Men on *La Lavia* died every day, and were thrown overboard with no ceremony except the impression of Manuel's medallion into their arms. The deaths made the food and water shortage less acute, but it was still serious. *La Lavia* was now manned by a ghost crew, composed mostly of soldiers. There weren't enough of them to properly man the pumps, and the Atlantic was springing new leaks every day in the already broken hull. The ship began taking on water in such quantities that the acting captain of the ship—who had started the voyage as third mate—decided that they must make straight for Spain, making no spare leeway for the imperfectly known west coast of Ireland. This decision was shared by the captains of several other damaged ships, and they conveyed their decision to the main body of the fleet, which was reaching farther west before turning south to Spain. From his sickbed Medina Sidonia gave his consent, and *La Lavia* sailed due south.

Unfortunately, a storm struck from just north of west soon after they had turned homeward. They were helpless before it. *La Lavia* wallowed in the troughs and was slammed by crest after crest, until the poor hulk lay just off the lee shore, Ireland.

It was the end, and everyone knew it. Manuel knew it because the air had turned black. The clouds were like thousands of black English cannonballs, rolling ten deep over a clear floor set just above the masts, and spitting lightning into the sea whenever two of them banged together hard enough. The air beneath them was black as well, just less thick: the wind as tangible as the waves, and swirling around the masts with smoky fury. Other men caught glimpses of the lee shore, but Manuel couldn't see it for the blackness. These men called out in fear; apparently the western coast of Ireland was sheer cliff. It was the end.

Manuel had nothing but admiration for the third-mate-now-captain, who took the helm and shouted to the lookout in the top to find a bay in the cliffs they were drifting toward. But Manuel, like many of the men, ignored the mate's commands to stay at post, as they were clearly pointless. Men embraced each other on the castles, saying their farewells; others cowered in fear against the bulkheads. Many of them approached Manuel and asked for a touch, and Manuel brushed their foreheads as he angrily marched about the forecastle. As soon as Manuel touched them, some of the men flew directly up toward heaven while others dove over the side of the ship and became porpoises the moment they struck the water, but Manuel scarcely noticed these occurrences, as he was busy praying, praying at the top of his lungs.

"*Why* this storm, Lord, *why?* First there were winds from the north holding us back, which is the only reason I'm here in the first place. So you wanted me here, but why why why? Juan is dead and Laeghr is dead and Pietro is dead and Habedeen is dead and soon we will all be dead, and why? It isn't just. You promised you would take us home." In a fury he took his slow match knife, climbed down to the swamped midships, and went to the mainmast. He thrust the knife deep into the wood, stabbing with the grain. "There! I say *that* to your storm!"

"Now, that's blasphemy," Laeghr said as he pulled the knife from the mast and threw it over the side. "You know what stabbing the mast means. To do it in a storm like this—you'll offend gods a lot older than Jesus, and more powerful, too."

"Talk about blasphemy," Manuel replied. "And you wonder why you're still wandering the seas a ghost, when you say things like that. You should take more care." He looked up and saw Saint Anna, in the maintop giving directions to the third mate. "Did you hear what Laeghr said?" he shouted up to her. She didn't hear him.

"Do you remember the words I taught you?" Laeghr inquired.

"Of course. Don't bother me now, Laeghr, I'll be a ghost with you soon enough." Laeghr stepped back, but Manuel changed his mind, and said, "Laeghr, why are we being punished like this? We were on a crusade for God, weren't we? I don't understand."

Laeghr smiled and turned around, and Manuel saw then that he had wings, wings with feathers intensely white in the black murk of the air. He clasped Manuel's arm. "You know all that I know." With some hard flaps he was off, tumbling east swiftly in the black air, like a gull.

With the help of Saint Anna the third mate had actually found a break in the cliffs, a quite considerable bay. Other ships of the Armada had found it as well, and they were already breaking up on a wide beach as *La Lavia* limped nearer shore. The keel grounded and immediately things began breaking. Soupy waves crashed over the canted midships, and Manuel leaped up the ladder to the forecastle, which was now under a tangle of rigging from the broken foremast. The mainmast went over the side, and the lee flank of the ship splintered like a match tub and flooded, right before their eyes. Among the floating timbers Manuel saw one that held a black cannonball embedded in it, undoubtedly the very one that Saint Anna had deflected from its course toward him. Reminded that she had saved his life before,

Manuel grew calmer and waited for her to appear. The beach was only a few shiplengths away, scarcely visible in the thick air; like most of the men, Manuel could not swim, and he was searching with some urgency for a sight of Saint Anna when Friar Lucien appeared at his side, in his black robes. Over the shriek of the dark wind Lucien shouted, "If we hold on to a plank we'll float ashore."

"You go ahead," Manuel shouted back. "I'm waiting for Saint Anna." The friar shrugged. The wind caught his robes and Manuel saw that Lucien was attempting to save the ship's liturgical gold, which was in the form of chains that were now wrapped around the friar's middle. Lucien made his way to the rail and jumped over it, onto a spar that a wave was carrying away from the ship. He missed his hold on the rounded spar, however, and sank instantly.

The forecastle was now awash, and soon the foaming breakers would tear it loose from the keel. Most of the men had already left the wreck, trusting to one bit of flotsam or other. But Manuel still waited. Just as he was beginning to worry he saw the blessed grandmother of God, standing among figures on the beach that he perceived but dimly, gesturing to him. She walked out onto the white water, and he understood. "We are the Christ, of course! I will walk to shore as He once did." He tested the surface with one shoe; it seemed a little, well, infirm, but surely it would serve—it would be like the floor of their now-demolished chapel, a sheet of water covering one of God's good solids. So Manuel walked out onto the next wave that passed at the level of the forecastle, and plunged deep into the brine.

"Hey!" he spluttered as he struggled back to the surface. "Hey!" No answer from Saint Anna this time; just cold salt water. He began the laborious process of drowning, remembering as he struggled a time when he was a child, and his father had taken him down to the beach in Morocco, to see the galley of the pilgrims to Mecca rowing away. Nothing could have been less like the Irish coast than that serene, hot, tawny beach, and he and his father had gone out into the shallows to splash around in the warm water, chasing lemons. His father would toss the lemons out into the deeper water, where they bobbed just under the surface, and then Manuel would paddle out to retrieve them, laughing and choking on water.

Manuel could picture those lemons perfectly, as he snorted and coughed and thrashed to get his head back above the freezing soup one more time. Lemons bobbing in the green sea, lemons oblong and bumpy, the color of the sun when the sun is its own width above the horizon at dawn… bobbing gently just under the surface, with a knob showing here or there. Manuel pretended he was a lemon, at the same time that he tried to remember the primitive dog paddle that had gotten him around in the shallows. Arms, pushing downward. It wasn't working. Waves tumbled him, lemonlike, in toward the strand. He bumped on the bottom and stood up. The water was only waist deep. Another wave smashed him from behind and he couldn't find the bottom again. Not fair! he thought. His elbow ran into sand, and he twisted around and stood. Knee deep, this time. He kept an eye on the treacherous waves as they came out of the black, and trudged through them up to a beach made of coarse sand, covered by a mat of loose seaweed.

Down on the beach a distance were sailors, companions, survivors of the wrecks offshore. But there among them—soldiers on horses. English soldiers, on horses and on foot—Manuel groaned to see it—wielding swords and clubs on the exhausted men strewn across the seaweed. "No!" Manuel cried, "No!" But it was true. "Ah, God," he said, and sank till he was sitting. Down the strand soldiers clubbed his brothers, splitting their fragile eggshell skulls so that the yolk of their brains ran into the kelp. Manuel beat his insensible fists against the sand. Filled with horror at the sight, he watched horses rear in the murk, giant and shadowy. They were coming down the beach toward him. "I'll make myself invisible," he decided. "Saint Anna will make me invisible." But remembering his plan to walk on the water, he determined to help the miracle by staggering up the beach and burrowing under a particularly tall pile of seaweed. He was invisible without it, of course, but the cover of kelp would help keep him warm. Thinking such thoughts, he shivered and shivered and on the still land fell insensible as his hands.

When he woke up, the soldiers were gone. His fellows lay up and down the beach like white driftwood; ravens and wolves already converged on them. He couldn't move very well. It took him half an hour to move his head to survey the beach, and another half hour to free himself from his pile of seaweed. And then he had to lie down again.

When he regained consciousness, he found himself behind a large log, an old piece of driftwood that had been polished silver by its years of rolling in sand. The air was clear again. He could feel it filling him and leaving him, but he could no longer see it. The sun was out; it was morning, and the storm was over. Each movement of Manuel's body was a complete effort, a complete experience. He could see quite deeply into his skin, which appeared pickled. He had lost all of his clothes, except for a tattered shred of trousers around his middle. With all his will he made his arm move his hand, and with his stiff forefinger he touched the driftwood. He could feel it. He was still alive.

His hand fell away in the sand. The wood touched by his finger was changing, becoming a bright green spot in the surrounding silver. A thin green sprig bulged from the spot, and grew up toward the sun; leaves unfolded from this sprout as it thickened, and beneath Manuel's fascinated gaze a bud appeared and burst open: a white rose, gleaming wetly in the white morning light.

He had managed to stand, and cover himself with kelp, and walk a full quarter of a mile inland, when he came upon people. Three of them to be exact, two men and a woman. Wilder looking people Manuel couldn't imagine: the men had beards that had never been cut, and arms like Laeghr's. The woman looked exactly like his miniature portrait of Saint Anna, until she got closer and he saw that she was dirty and her teeth were broken and her skin was brindled like a dog's belly. He had never seen such freckling before, and he stared at it, and her, every bit as much as she and her companions stared at him. He was afraid of them.

"Hide me from the English, please," he said. At the word *English* the men frowned and cocked their heads. They jabbered at him in a tongue he did not know. "Help me," he said. "I don't know what you're saying. Help me." He tried Spanish and Portuguese and Sicilian and Arabic. The men were looking angry. He tried Latin, and they stepped back. "I believe in God the Father Almighty, Maker of Heaven and Earth, and in all things visible and invisible." He laughed, a bit hysterically. "Especially invisible." He grabbed his medallion and showed them the cross. They studied him, clearly at a loss.

"*Tor conaloc an dhia*," he said without thinking. All four of them jumped. Then the two men moved to his sides to hold him steady. They chattered at him, waving their free arms. The woman smiled, and Manuel saw that she was young. He said the syllables again, and they chattered at him some more. "Thank you, Laeghr," he said. "Thank you, Anna. Anna," he said to the girl, and reached for her. She squealed and stepped back. He said the phrase again. The men lifted him, for he could no longer walk, and carried him across the heather. He smiled and kissed both men on the cheek, which made them laugh, and he said the magic phrase again and started to fall asleep and smiled and said the phrase. *Tor conaloc an dhia*. The girl brushed his wet hair out of his eyes; Manuel recognized the touch, and he could feel the flowering begin inside him.

—*give mercy for God's sake*—

THE LUCKY STRIKE

War breeds strange pastimes. In July of 1945 on Tinian Island in the North Pacific, Captain Frank January had taken to piling pebble cairns on the crown of Mount Lasso—one pebble for each B-29 takeoff, one cairn for each mission. The largest cairn had four hundred stones in it. It was a mindless pastime, but so was poker. The men of the 509th had played a million hands of poker, sitting in the shade of a palm around an upturned crate sweating in their skivvies, swearing and betting all their pay and cigarettes, playing hand after hand after hand, until the cards got so soft and dog-eared you could have used them for toilet paper. Captain January had gotten sick of it, and after he lit out for the hilltop a few times some of his crewmates started trailing him. When their pilot Jim Fitch joined them it became an official pastime, like throwing flares into the compound or going hunting for stray Japs. What Captain January thought of the development he didn't say. The others grouped near Captain Fitch, who passed around his battered flask. "Hey, January," Fitch called. "Come have a shot."

January wandered over and took the flask. Fitch laughed at his pebble. "Practicing your bombing up here, eh, Professor?"

"Yah," January said sullenly. Anyone who read more than the funnies was Professor to Fitch. Thirstily January knocked back some rum. He could drink it any way he pleased up here, out from under the eye of the group psychiatrist. He passed the flask on to Lieutenant Matthews, their navigator.

"That's why he's the best," Matthews joked. "Always practicing."

Fitch laughed. "He's best because I make him be best, right, Professor?"

January frowned. Fitch was a bulky youth, thick-featured, pig-eyed—a thug, in January's opinion. The rest of the crew were all in their

67

mid-twenties like Fitch, and they liked the captain's bossy roughhouse style. January, who was thirty-seven, didn't go for it. He wandered away, back to the cairn he had been building. From Mount Lasso they had an overview of the whole island, from the harbor at Wall Street to the north field in Harlem. January had observed hundreds of B-29s roar off the four parallel runways of the north field and head for Japan. The last quartet of this particular mission buzzed across the width of the island, and January dropped four more pebbles, aiming for crevices in the pile. One of them stuck nicely.

"There they are!" said Matthews. "They're on the taxiing strip."

January located the 509th's first plane. Today, the first of August, there was something more interesting to watch than the usual Superfortress parade. Word was out that General LeMay wanted to take the 509th's mission away from it. Their commander Colonel Tibbets had gone and bitched to LeMay in person, and the general had agreed the mission was theirs, but on one condition: one of the general's men was to make a test flight with the 509th, to make sure they were fit for combat over Japan. The general's man had arrived, and now he was down there in the strike plane, with Tibbets and the whole first team. January sidled back to his mates to view the takeoff with them.

"Why don't the strike plane have a name, though?" Haddock was saying.

Fitch said, "Lewis won't give it a name because it's not his plane, and he knows it." The others laughed. Lewis and his crew were naturally unpopular, being Tibbets' favorites.

"What do you think he'll do to the general's man?" Matthews asked.

The others laughed at the very idea. "He'll kill an engine at takeoff, I bet you anything," Fitch said. He pointed at the wrecked B-29s that marked the end of every runway, planes whose engines had given out on takeoff. "He'll want to show that he wouldn't go down if it happened to him."

"'Course he wouldn't!" Matthews said.

"You hope," January said under his breath.

"They let those Wright engines out too soon," Haddock said seriously. "They keep busting under the takeoff load."

"Won't matter to the old bull," Matthews said. Then they all started in about Tibbets' flying ability, even Fitch. They all thought Tibbets was the greatest. January, on the other hand, liked Tibbets even less than he liked Fitch. That had started right after he was assigned to the 509th. He had been told he was part of the most important group in the war, and then given a leave. In Vicksburg a couple of fliers just back from England had bought him a lot of whiskies, and since January had spent several months stationed near London they had talked for a good long time and gotten pretty drunk. The two were really curious about what January was up to now, but he had stayed vague on it and kept returning the talk to the blitz. He had been seeing an English nurse, for instance, whose flat had been bombed, family and neighbors killed.... But they had really wanted to know. So he had told them he was onto something special, and they had flipped out their badges and told him they were Army Intelligence, and that if he ever broke security like that again he'd be transferred to Alaska. It was a dirty trick. January had gone back to Wendover and told Tibbets so to his face, and Tibbets had turned red and threatened him some more. January despised him for that. The upshot was that January was effectively out of the war, because Tibbets really played his favorites. January wasn't sure he really minded, but during their year's training he had bombed better than ever, as a way of showing the old bull he was wrong to write January off. Every time their eyes had met it was clear what was going on. But Tibbets never backed off no matter how precise January's bombing got. Just thinking about it was enough to cause January to line up a pebble over an ant and drop it.

"Will you cut that out?" Fitch complained. "I swear you must hang from the ceiling when you take a shit so you can practice aiming for the toilet." The men laughed.

"Don't I bunk over you?" January asked. Then he pointed. "They're going."

Tibbets' plane had taxied to runway Baker. Fitch passed the flask around again. The tropical sun beat on them, and the ocean surrounding the island blazed white. January put up a sweaty hand to aid the bill of his baseball cap.

The four props cut in hard, and the sleek Superfortress quickly trundled up to speed and roared down Baker. Three-quarters of the way down the strip the outside right prop feathered.

"Yow!" Fitch crowed. "I told you he'd do it!"

The plane nosed off the ground and slewed right, then pulled back on course to cheers from the four young men around January. January pointed again. "He's cut number three, too."

The inside right prop feathered, and now the plane was pulled up by the left wing only, while the two right props windmilled uselessly. "Holy smoke!" Haddock cried. "Ain't the old bull something?"

They whooped to see the plane's power, and Tibbets' nervy arrogance.

"By God, LeMay's man will remember this flight," Fitch hooted. "Why, look at that! He's banking!"

Apparently taking off on two engines wasn't enough for Tibbets; he banked the plane right until it was standing on its dead wing, and it curved back toward Tinian.

Then the inside left engine feathered.

War tears at the imagination. For three years Frank January had kept his imagination trapped, refusing to give it any play whatsoever. The dangers threatening him, the effects of the bombs, the fate of the other participants in the war, he had refused to think about any of it. But the war tore at his control. That English nurse's flat. The missions over the Ruhr. The bomber just below him blown apart by flak. And then there had been a year in Utah, and the viselike grip that he had once kept on his imagination had slipped away.

So when he saw the number two prop feather, his heart gave a little jump against his sternum and helplessly he was up there with Ferebee, the first team bombardier. He would be looking over the pilots' shoulders....

"Only one engine?" Fitch said.

"That one's for real," January said harshly. Despite himself he *saw* the panic in the cockpit, the frantic rush to power the two right engines. The plane was dropping fast and Tibbets leveled it off, leaving them on a course back toward the island. The two right props spun, blurred to a shimmer. January held his breath. They needed more lift; Tibbets was trying to pull it over the island. Maybe he was trying for the short runway on the south half of the island.

But Tinian was too tall, the plane too heavy. It roared right into the jungle above the beach, where 42nd Street met their East River. It exploded in a bloom of fire. By the time the sound of the explosion struck them they knew no one in the plane had survived.

Black smoke towered into white sky. In the shocked silence on Mount Lasso insects buzzed and creaked. The air left January's lungs with a gulp. He had been with Ferebee there at the end, had heard the desperate shouts, seen the last green rush, been stunned by the dentist-drill-all-over pain of the impact.

"Oh my God," Fitch was saying. "Oh my God." Matthews was sitting. January picked up the flask, tossed it at Fitch.

"C-come on," he stuttered. He hadn't stuttered since he was sixteen. He led the others in a rush down the hill. When they got to Broadway a jeep careened toward them and skidded to a halt. It was Colonel Scholes, the old bull's exec. "What happened?"

Fitch told him.

"Those damned Wrights," Scholes said as the men piled in. This time one had failed at just the wrong moment; some welder stateside had kept flame to metal a second less than usual—or something equally minor, equally trivial—and that had made all the difference.

They left the jeep at 42nd and Broadway and hiked east over a narrow track to the shore. A fairly large circle of trees was burning. The fire trucks were already there.

Scholes stood beside January, his expression bleak. "That was the whole first team," he said.

"I know," said January. He was still in shock, in imagination crushed, incinerated, destroyed. Once as a kid he had tied sheets to his arms and waist, jumped off the roof and landed right on his chest; this felt like that had. He had no way of knowing what would come of this crash, but he had a suspicion that he had indeed smacked into something hard.

Scholes shook his head. A half hour had passed, the fire was nearly out. January's four mates were over chattering with the Seabees. "He was going to name the plane after his mother," Scholes said to the ground. "He told me that just this morning. He was going to call it *Enola Gay*."

At night the jungle breathed, and its hot wet breath washed over the 509th's compound. January stood in the doorway of his Quonset barracks hoping for a real breeze. No poker tonight. Voices were hushed, faces solemn. Some of the men had helped box up the dead crew's gear. Now most lay on their bunks. January gave up on the breeze, climbed onto his top bunk to stare at the ceiling.

He observed the corrugated arch over him. Cricketsong sawed through his thoughts. Below him a rapid conversation was being carried on in guilty undertones, Fitch at its center.

"January is the best bombardier left," he said. "And I'm as good as Lewis was."

"But so is Sweeney," Matthews said. "And he's in with Scholes."

They were figuring out who would take over the strike. January scowled. Tibbets and the rest were less than twelve hours dead, and they were squabbling over who would replace them.

January grabbed a shirt, rolled off his bunk, put the shirt on.

"Hey, Professor," Fitch said. "Where you going?"

"Out."

Though midnight was near it was still sweltering. Crickets shut up as he walked by, started again behind him. He lit a cigarette. In the dark the MPs patrolling their fenced-in compound were like pairs of walking armbands. The 509th, prisoners in their own army. Fliers from other groups had taken to throwing rocks over the fence. Forcefully January expelled smoke, as if he could expel his disgust with it. They were only kids, he told himself. Their minds had been shaped in the war, by the war, and for the war. They knew you couldn't mourn the dead for long; carry around a load like that and your own engines might fail. That was all right with January. It was an attitude that Tibbets had helped to form, so it was what he deserved. Tibbets would *want* to be forgotten in favor of the mission, all he had lived for was to drop the gimmick on the Japs, he was oblivious to anything else, men, wife, family, anything.

So it wasn't the lack of feeling in his mates that bothered January. And it was natural of them to want to fly the strike they had been training a year for. Natural, that is, if you were a kid with a mind shaped by fanatics like Tibbets, shaped to take orders and never imagine consequences. But January was not a kid, and he wasn't going to let men like Tibbets do a thing to his mind. And the gimmick… the gimmick was not natural. A chemical bomb of some sort, he guessed. Against the Geneva Convention. He stubbed his cigarette against the sole of his sneaker, tossed the butt over the fence. The tropical night breathed over him. He had a headache.

For months now he had been sure he would never fly a strike. The dislike Tibbets and he had exchanged in their looks (January was acutely aware of looks) had been real and strong. Tibbets had understood that January's record of pinpoint accuracy in the runs over the Salton Sea had been a way of showing contempt, a way of saying *you can't get rid of me even though you hate me and I hate you.* The record had forced Tibbets to keep January on one of the four second-string teams, but with the fuss they were making over the gimmick January had figured that would be far enough down the ladder to keep him out of things.

Now he wasn't so sure. Tibbets was dead. He lit another cigarette, found his hand shaking. The Camel tasted bitter. He threw it over the fence at a receding armband, and regretted it instantly. A waste. He went back inside.

Before climbing onto his bunk he got a paperback out of his footlocker. "Hey, Professor, what you reading now?" Fitch said, grinning.

January showed him the blue cover. *Winter's Tales,* by an Isak Dinesen. Fitch examined the little wartime edition. "Pretty racy, eh?"

"You bet," January said heavily. "This guy puts sex on every page." He climbed onto his bunk, opened the book. The stories were strange, hard to follow. The voices below bothered him. He concentrated harder.

As a boy on the farm in Arkansas, January had read everything he could lay his hands on. On Saturday afternoons he would race his father down the muddy lane to the mailbox (his father was a reader too), grab the *Saturday Evening Post* and run off to devour every word of it. That meant he had another week with nothing new to read, but he couldn't help it. His favorites were the Hornblower stories, but anything would do. It was a way off the farm, a way into the world. He had become a man who could slip between the covers of a book whenever he chose.

But not on this night.

The next day the chaplain gave a memorial service, and on the morning after that Colonel Scholes looked in the door of their hut right after mess. "Briefing at eleven," he announced. His face was haggard. "Be there early." He looked at Fitch with bloodshot eyes, crooked a finger. "Fitch, January, Matthews—come with me."

January put on his shoes. The rest of the men sat on their bunks and watched them wordlessly. January followed Fitch and Matthews out of the hut.

"I've spent most of the night on the radio with General LeMay," Scholes said. He looked them each in the eye. "We've decided you're to be the first crew to make a strike."

Fitch was nodding, as if he had expected it.

"Think you can do it?" Scholes said.

"Of course," Fitch replied. Watching him January understood why they had chosen him to replace Tibbets: Fitch was like the old bull, he had that same ruthlessness. The young bull.

"Yes, sir," Matthews said.

Scholes was looking at him. "Sure," January said, not wanting to think about it. "Sure." His heart was pounding directly on his sternum. But Fitch and Matthews looked serious as owls, so he wasn't going to stick out by looking odd. It was big news, after all; anyone would be taken aback by it. Nevertheless, January made an effort to nod.

"Okay," Scholes said. "McDonald will be flying with you as copilot." Fitch frowned. "I've got to go tell those British officers that LeMay doesn't want them on the strike with you. See you at the briefing."

"Yes, sir."

As soon as Scholes was around the corner Fitch swung a fist at the sky. "Yow!" Matthews cried. He and Fitch shook hands. "We did it!" Matthews took January's hand and wrung it, his face plastered with a goofy grin. "We did it!"

"Somebody did it, anyway," January said.

"Ah, Frank," Matthews said. "Show some spunk. You're always so cool."

"Old Professor Stoneface," Fitch said, glancing at January with a trace of amused contempt. "Come on, let's get to the briefing."

The briefing hut, one of the longer Quonsets, was completely surrounded by MPs holding carbines. "Gosh," Matthews said, subdued by the sight. Inside it was already smoky. The walls were covered by the usual maps of Japan. Two blackboards at the front were draped with sheets. Captain

Shepard, the naval officer who worked with the scientists on the gimmick, was in back with his assistant Lieutenant Stone, winding a reel of film onto a projector. Dr. Nelson, the group psychiatrist, was already seated on a front bench near the wall. Tibbets had recently sicced the psychiatrist on the group—another one of his great ideas, like the spies in the bar. The man's questions had struck January as stupid. He hadn't even been able to figure out that Easterly was a flake, something that was clear to anybody who flew with him, or even played him in a single round of poker. January slid onto a bench beside his mates.

The two Brits entered, looking furious in their stiff-upper-lip way. They sat on the bench behind January. Sweeney's and Easterly's crews filed in, followed by the other men, and soon the room was full. Fitch and the rest pulled out Lucky Strikes and lit up; since they had named the plane only January had stuck with Camels.

Scholes came in with several men January didn't recognize, and went to the front. The chatter died, and all the smoke plumes ribboned steadily into the air.

Scholes nodded, and two intelligence officers took the sheets off the blackboards, revealing aerial reconnaissance photos.

"Men," Scholes said, "these are the target cities."

Someone cleared his throat.

"In order of priority they are Hiroshima, Kokura, and Nagasaki. There will be three weather scouts: *Straight Flush* to Hiroshima, *Strange Cargo* to Kokura, and *Full House* to Nagasaki. *The Great Artiste* and *Number 91* will be accompanying the mission to take photos. And *Lucky Strike* will fly the bomb."

There were rustles, coughs. Men turned to look at January and his mates, and they all sat up straight. Sweeney stretched back to shake Fitch's hand, and there were some quick laughs. Fitch grinned.

"Now listen up," Scholes went on. "The weapon we are going to deliver was successfully tested stateside a couple of weeks ago. And now we've got orders to drop it on the enemy." He paused to let that sink in. "I'll let Captain Shepard tell you more."

Shepard walked to the blackboard slowly, savoring his entrance. His forehead was shiny with sweat, and January realized he was excited or nervous. He wondered what the psychiatrist would make of that.

"I'm going to come right to the point," Shepard said. "The bomb you are going to drop is something new in history. We think it will knock out everything within four miles."

Now the room was completely still. January noticed that he could see a great deal of his nose, eyebrows, and cheeks; it was as if he were receding back into his body, like a fox into its hole. He kept his gaze rigidly on Shepard, steadfastly ignoring the feeling. Shepard pulled a sheet back over a blackboard while someone else turned down the lights.

"This is a film of the only test we have made," Shepard said. The film started, caught, started again. A wavery cone of bright cigarette smoke speared the length of the room, and on the sheet sprang a dead gray landscape: a lot of sky, a smooth desert floor, hills in the distance. The projector went *click-click-click-click, click-click-click-click*. "The bomb is on top of the tower," Shepard said, and January focused on the pinlike object sticking out of the desert floor, off against the hills. It was between eight and ten miles from the camera, he judged; he had gotten good at calculating distances. He was still distracted by his face.

Click-click-click-click, click—then the screen went white for a second, filling even their room with light. When the picture returned the desert floor was filled with a white bloom of fire. The fireball coalesced and then quite suddenly it leaped off the earth all the way into the *stratosphere*, by God, like a tracer bullet leaving a machine gun, trailing a whitish pillar of smoke behind it. The pillar gushed up and a growing ball of smoke billowed outward, capping the pillar. January calculated the size of the cloud, but was sure he got it wrong. There it stood. The picture flickered, and then the screen went white again, as if the camera had melted or that part of the world had come apart. But the flapping from the projector told them it was the end of the film.

January felt the air suck in and out of his open mouth. The lights came on in the smoky room and for a second he panicked, he struggled to shove his features into an accepted pattern, the psychiatrist would be looking around at them all—and then he glanced around and realized he needn't have worried, that he wasn't alone. Faces were bloodless, eyes were blinky or bug-eyed with shock, mouths hung open or were clamped whitely shut. For a few moments they all had to acknowledge what they were doing. January, scaring himself, felt an urge to say, "Play it again, will you?" Fitch was pulling his curled black hair off his thug's forehead uneasily. Beyond him January saw that one of the Limeys had already reconsidered how mad he was about missing the flight. Now he looked sick. Someone let out a long *whew*, another whistled. January looked to the front again, where the psychiatrist watched them, undisturbed.

Shepard said, "It's big, all right. And no one knows what will happen when it's dropped from the air. But the mushroom cloud you saw will go to at least thirty thousand feet, probably sixty. And the flash you saw at the beginning was hotter than the sun."

Hotter than the sun. More licked lips, hard swallows, readjusted baseball caps. One of the intelligence officers passed out tinted goggles like welder's glasses. January took his and twiddled the opacity dial.

Scholes said, "You're the hottest thing in the armed forces, now. So no talking, even among yourselves." He took a deep breath. "Let's do it the way Colonel Tibbets would have wanted us to. He picked every one of *you* because you were the best, and now's the time to show he was right. So—so let's make the old man proud."

The briefing was over. Men filed out into the sudden sunlight. Into the heat and glare. Captain Shepard approached Fitch. "Stone and I will be flying with you to take care of the bomb," he said.

Fitch nodded. "Do you know how many strikes we'll fly?"

"As many as it takes to make them quit." Shepard stared hard at all of them. "But it will only take one."

War breeds strange dreams. That night January writhed over his sheets in the hot wet vegetable darkness, in that frightening half sleep when you sometimes know you are dreaming but can do nothing about it, and he dreamed he was walking…

… walking through the streets when suddenly the sun swoops down, the sun touches down and everything is instantly darkness and smoke and silence, a deaf roaring. Walls of fire. His head hurts and in the middle of his vision is a bluewhite blur as if God's camera went off in his face. Ah—the sun fell, he thinks. His arm is burned. Blinking is painful. People stumbling by, mouths open, horribly burned—

He is a priest, he can feel the clerical collar, and the wounded ask him for help. He points to his ears, tries to touch them but can't. Pall of black smoke over everything, the city has fallen into the streets. Ah, it's the end of the world. In a park he finds shade and cleared ground. People crouch under bushes like frightened animals. Where the park meets the river red and black figures crowd into steaming water. A figure gestures from a copse of bamboo. He enters it, finds five or six faceless soldiers huddling. Their eyes have melted, their mouths are holes. Deafness spares him their words. The sighted soldier mimes drinking. The soldiers are thirsty. He nods and goes down to the river in search of a container. Bodies float downstream.

Hours pass as he hunts fruitlessly for a bucket. He pulls people from the rubble. He hears a bird screeching and he realizes that his deafness is the roar of the city burning, a roar like the blood in his ears but he is not deaf, he only thought he was deaf because there are no human cries. The people are suffering in silence. Through the dusky night he stumbles back to the river, pain crashing through his head. In a field men are pulling potatoes out of the ground that have been baked well enough to eat. He shares one with them. At the river everyone is dead—

—and he struggled out of the nightmare drenched in rank sweat, the taste of dirt in his mouth, his stomach knotted with horror. He sat up and the wet rough sheet clung to his skin. His heart felt crushed between lungs desperate for air. The flowery rotting jungle smell filled him and images from the dream flashed before him so vividly that in the dim hut he saw nothing else. He grabbed his cigarettes and jumped off the bunk, hurried out into the compound. Trembling he lit up, started pacing around. For a moment he worried that the idiot psychiatrist might see him, but then he dismissed the idea. Nelson would be asleep. They were all asleep. He shook his head, looked down at his right arm and almost dropped his cigarette—but it was just his stove scar, an old scar, he'd had it most of his life, since the day he'd pulled the frypan off the stove and onto his arm, burning it with oil. He could still remember the round O of fear that his mother's mouth had made as she rushed in to see what was wrong. Just an old burn scar, he thought, let's not go overboard here. He pulled his sleeve down.

For the rest of the night he tried to walk it off, cigarette after cigarette. The dome of the sky lightened until all the compound and the jungle beyond it was visible. He was forced by the light of day to walk back into his hut and lie down as if nothing had happened.

Two days later Scholes ordered them to take one of LeMay's men over Rota for a test run. This new lieutenant colonel ordered Fitch not to play with the engines on takeoff. They flew a perfect run. January put the dummy gimmick right on the aiming point just as he had so often in the Salton Sea, and Fitch powered the plane down into the violent bank that started their 150-degree turn and flight for safety. Back on Tinian the lieutenant colonel congratulated them and shook each of their hands. January smiled with the rest, palms cool, heart steady. It was as if his body were a shell, something he could manipulate from without, like a bombsight. He ate well, he chatted as much as he ever had, and when the psychiatrist ran him to earth for some questions he was friendly and seemed open.

"Hello, Doc."

"How do you feel about all this, Frank?"

"Just like I always have, sir. Fine."

"Eating well?"

"Better than ever."

"Sleeping well?"

"As well as I can in this humidity. I got used to Utah, I'm afraid." Dr. Nelson laughed. Actually January had hardly slept since his dream. He was afraid of sleep. Couldn't the man see that?

"And how do you feel about being part of the crew chosen to make the first strike?"

"Well, it was the right choice, I reckon. We're the b—the best crew left."

"Do you feel sorry about Tibbets' crew's accident?"

"Yes, sir, I do." You better believe it.

After the jokes and firm handshakes that ended the interview January walked out into the blaze of the tropical noon and lit a cigarette. He allowed himself to feel how much he despised the psychiatrist and his blind profession at the same time he was waving good-bye to the man. Ounce brain. Why couldn't he have seen? Whatever happened it would be his fault.... With a rush of smoke out of him January realized how painfully easy it was to fool someone if you wanted to. All action was no more than a mask that could be perfectly manipulated from somewhere else. And all the while in that somewhere else January lived in a *click-click-click* of film, in the silent roaring of a dream, struggling against images he couldn't dispel. The heat of the tropical sun—ninety-three million miles away, wasn't it?—pulsed painfully on the back of his neck.

As he watched the psychiatrist collar their tail-gunner Kochenski, he thought of walking up to the man and saying *I quit.* I don't want to do this. In imagination he saw the look that would form in the man's eye, in Fitch's eye, in Tibbets' eye, and his mind recoiled from the idea. He felt too much contempt for them. He wouldn't for anything give them a means to despise him, a reason to call him coward. Stubbornly he banished the whole complex of thought. Easier to go along with it.

And so a couple of disjointed days later, just after midnight of August 9th, he found himself preparing for the strike. Around him Fitch and Matthews and Haddock were doing the same. How odd were the everyday motions of getting dressed when you were off to demolish a city, to end a hundred thousand lives! January found himself examining his hands, his boots, the cracks in the linoleum. He put on his survival vest, checked the pockets abstractedly for fishhooks, water kit, first aid package, emergency rations. Then the parachute harness, and his coveralls over it all. Tying his bootlaces took minutes; he couldn't do it when watching his fingers so closely.

"Come on, Professor!" Fitch's voice was tight. "The big day is here."

He followed the others into the night. A cool wind was blowing. The chaplain said a prayer for them. They took jeeps down Broadway to runway Able. *Lucky Strike* stood in a circle of spotlights and men, half of them with cameras, the rest with reporter's pads. They surrounded the crew; it reminded January of a Hollywood premiere. Eventually he escaped up the hatch and into the plane. Others followed. Half an hour passed before Fitch joined them, grinning like a movie star. They started the engines, and

January was thankful for their vibrating, thought-smothering roar. They taxied away from the Hollywood scene and January felt relief for a moment until he remembered where they were going. On runway Able the engines pitched up to their twenty-three hundred rpm whine, and looking out the clear windscreen he saw the runway paint-marks move by ever faster. Fitch kept them on the runway till Tinian had run out from under them, then quickly pulled up. They were on their way.

When they got to altitude January climbed past Fitch and McDonald to the bombardier's seat and placed his parachute on it. He leaned back. The roar of the four engines packed around him like cotton batting. He was on the flight, nothing to be done about it now. The heavy vibration was a comfort, he liked the feel of it there in the nose of the plane. A drowsy, sad acceptance hummed through him.

Against his closed eyelids flashed a black eyeless face and he jerked awake, heart racing. He was on the flight, no way out. Now he realized how easy it would have been to get out of it. He could have just said he didn't want to. The simplicity of it appalled him. Who gave a damn what the psychiatrist or Tibbets or anyone else thought, compared to this? Now there was no way out. It was a comfort, in a way. Now he could stop worrying, stop thinking he had any choice.

Sitting there with his knees bracketing the bombsight January dozed, and as he dozed he daydreamed his way out. He could climb the step to Fitch and McDonald and declare he had been secretly promoted to major and ordered to redirect the mission. They were to go to Tokyo and drop the bomb in the bay. The Jap War Cabinet had been told to watch this demonstration of the new weapon, and when they saw that fireball boil the bay and bounce into heaven they'd run and sign surrender papers as fast as they could write, kamikazes or not. They weren't crazy, after all. No need to murder a whole city. It was such a good plan that the generals back home were no doubt changing the mission at this very minute, desperately radioing their instructions to Tinian, only to find out it was too late… so that when they returned to Tinian January would become a hero for guessing what the generals really wanted, and for risking all to do it. It would be like one of the Hornblower stories in the *Saturday Evening Post*.

Once again January jerked awake. The drowsy pleasure of the fantasy was replaced with desperate scorn. There wasn't a chance in hell that he could convince Fitch and the rest that he had secret orders superseding theirs. And he couldn't go up there and wave his pistol around and *order* them to drop the bomb in Tokyo Bay, because he was the one who had to actually drop it, and he couldn't be down in front dropping the bomb and up ordering the others around at the same time. Pipe dreams.

Time swept on, slow as a second hand. January's thoughts, however, matched the spin of the props; desperately they cast about, now this way now that, like an animal caught by the leg in a trap. The crew was silent. The clouds below were a white scree on the black ocean. January's knee vibrated against the squat stand of the bombsight. He was the one who had to drop the bomb. No matter where his thoughts lunged they were brought up short by that. He was the one, not Fitch or the crew, not LeMay, not the generals and scientists back home, not Truman and his advisors. Truman—suddenly January hated him. Roosevelt would have done it differently. If only Roosevelt had lived! The grief that had filled January when he learned of Roosevelt's death reverberated through him again, more strongly than ever. It was unfair to have worked so hard and then not see the war's end. And FDR would have ended it differently. Back at the start of it all he had declared that civilian centers were never to be bombed, and if he had lived, if, if, if. But he hadn't. And now it was smiling bastard Harry Truman, ordering *him*, Frank January, to drop the sun on two hundred thousand women and children. Once his father had taken him to see the Browns play before twenty thousand, a giant crowd—"I never voted for you," January whispered viciously, and jerked to realize he had spoken aloud. Luckily his microphone was off. But Roosevelt would have done it differently, he *would have*.

The bombsight rose before him, spearing the black sky and blocking some of the hundreds of little cruciform stars. *Lucky Strike* ground on toward Iwo Jima, minute by minute flying four miles closer to their target. January leaned forward and put his face in the cool headrest of the bombsight, hoping that its grasp might hold his thoughts as well as his forehead. It worked surprisingly well.

His earphones crackled and he sat up. "Captain January." It was Shepard. "We're going to arm the bomb now, want to watch?"

"Sure thing." He shook his head, surprised at his own duplicity. Stepping up between the pilots, he moved stiffly to the roomy cabin behind the cockpit. Matthews was at his desk taking a navigational fix on the radio signals from Iwo Jima and Okinawa, and Haddock stood beside him. At the back of the compartment was a small circular hatch, below the larger tunnel leading to the rear of the plane. January opened it, sat down and swung himself feet first through the hole.

The bomb bay was unheated, and the cold air felt good. He stood facing the bomb. Stone was sitting on the floor of the bay; Shepard was laid out under the bomb, reaching into it. On a rubber pad next to Stone were tools, plates, several cylindrical blocks. Shepard pulled back, sat up, sucked a scraped knuckle. He shook his head ruefully: "I don't dare wear gloves with this one."

"I'd be just as happy myself if you didn't let something slip," January joked nervously. The two men laughed.

"Nothing can blow till I change those green wires to the red ones," Stone said.

"Give me the wrench," Shepard said. Stone handed it to him, and he stretched under the bomb again. After some awkward wrenching inside it he lifted out a cylindrical plug. "Breech plug," he said, and set it on the mat.

January found his skin goose-pimpling in the cold air. Stone handed Shepard one of the blocks. Shepard extended under the bomb again. "Red ends toward the breech." "I know." Watching them January was reminded of auto mechanics on the oily floor of a garage, working under a car. He had spent a few years doing that himself, after his family moved to Vicksburg. Hiroshima was a river town. One time a flatbed truck carrying bags of cement powder down Fourth Street hill had lost its brakes and careened into the intersection with the River Road, where despite the driver's efforts to turn it smashed into a passing car. Frank had been out in the yard playing, had heard the crash and saw the cement dust rising. He had been one of the first there. The woman and child in the passenger seat of the Model T had been killed. The woman driving was okay. They were from Chicago. A group of folks subdued the driver of the truck, who kept trying to help at the Model T, though he had a bad cut on his head and was covered with white dust.

"Okay, let's tighten the breech plug." Stone gave Shepard the wrench. "Sixteen turns exactly," Shepard said. He was sweating even in the bay's chill, and he paused to wipe his forehead. "Let's hope we don't get hit by lightning." He put the wrench down and shifted onto his knees, picked up a circular plate. Hubcap, January thought. Stone connected wires, then helped Shepard install two more plates. Good old American know-how, January thought, goose pimples rippling across his skin like cat's paws over water. There was Shepard, a scientist, putting together a bomb like he was an auto mechanic changing oil and plugs. January felt a tight rush of rage at the scientists who had designed the bomb. They had worked on it for over a year down there in New Mexico; had none of them in all that time ever stopped to think what they were doing?

But none of them had to drop it. January turned to hide his face from Shepard, stepped down the bay. The bomb looked like a big long trash can, with fins at one end and little antennae at the other. Just a bomb, he thought, damn it, it's just another bomb.

Shepard stood and patted the bomb gently. "We've got a live one now."

Never a thought about what it would do. January hurried by the man, afraid that hatred would crack his shell and give him away. The pistol strapped to his belt caught on the hatchway and he imagined shooting Shepard—shooting Fitch and McDonald and plunging the controls forward so that *Lucky Strike* tilted and spun down into the sea like a spent tracer bullet, like a plane broken by flak, following the arc of all human ambition. Nobody would ever know what had happened to them, and their trash can would be dumped at the bottom of the Pacific where it belonged. He could even shoot everyone and parachute out, and perhaps be rescued by one of the Superdumbos following them....

The thought passed and remembering it January squinted with disgust. But another part of him agreed that it was a possibility. It could be done. It would solve his problem. His fingers explored his holster snap.

"Want some coffee?" Matthews asked.

"Sure," January said, and took his hand from the gun to reach for the cup. He sipped: hot. He watched Matthews and Benton tune the loran equipment. As the beeps came in Matthews took a straightedge and drew lines from Okinawa and Iwo Jima on his map table. He tapped a finger on the intersection. "They've taken the art out of navigation," he said to January. "They might as well stop making the navigator's dome," thumbing up at the little Plexiglas bubble over them.

"Good old American know-how," January said.

Matthews nodded. With two fingers he measured the distance between their position and Iwo Jima. Benton measured with a ruler.

"Rendezvous at five thirty-five, eh?" Matthews said. They were to rendezvous with the two trailing planes over Iwo.

Benton disagreed: "I'd say five-fifty."

"What? Check again, guy, we're not in no tugboat here."

"The wind—"

"Yah, the wind. Frank, you want to add a bet to the pool?"

"Five thirty-six," January said promptly.

They laughed. "See, he's got more confidence in me," Matthews said with a dopey grin.

January recalled his plan to shoot the crew and tip the plane into the sea, and he pursed his lips, repelled. Not for anything would he be able to shoot these men, who, if not friends, were at least companions. They passed for friends. They meant no harm.

Shepard and Stone climbed into the cabin. Matthews offered them coffee. "The gimmick's ready to kick their ass, eh?" Shepard nodded and drank.

January moved forward, past Haddock's console. Another plan that wouldn't work. What to do? All the flight engineer's dials and gauges showed conditions were normal. Maybe he could sabotage something? Cut a line somewhere?

Fitch looked back at him and said, "When are we due over Iwo?"

"Five-forty, Matthews says."

"He better be right."

A thug. In peacetime Fitch would be hanging around a pool table giving the cops trouble. He was perfect for war. Tibbets had chosen his men well—most of them, anyway. Moving back past Haddock, January stopped to stare at the group of men in the navigation cabin. They joked, drank coffee. They were all a bit like Fitch: young toughs, capable and thoughtless. They were having a good time, an adventure. That was January's dominant impression of his companions in the 509th; despite all the bitching and the occasional moments of overmastering fear, they were having a good time. His mind spun forward and he saw what these young men would grow up to be like as clearly as if they stood before him in businessmen's suits, prosperous and balding. They would be tough and capable and thoughtless, and as the years passed and the great war receded in time they would look back on it with ever-increasing nostalgia, for they would be the survivors and not the dead. Every year of this war would feel like ten in their memories, so that the war would always remain the central experience of their lives—a time when history lay palpable in their hands, when each of their daily acts affected it, when moral issues were simple, and others told them what to do—so that as more years passed and the survivors aged, bodies falling apart, lives in one rut or another, they would unconsciously push harder and harder to thrust the world into war again, thinking somewhere inside themselves that if they could only return to world war then they would magically be again as they were in the last one—young, and free, and happy. And by that time they would hold the positions of power, they would be capable of doing it.

So there would be more wars, January saw. He heard it in Matthews' laughter, saw it in their excited eyes. "There's Iwo, and it's five thirty-one. Pay up! I win!" And in future wars they'd have more bombs like the gimmick, hundreds of them no doubt. He saw more planes, more young crews like this one, flying to Moscow no doubt or to wherever, fireballs in every capital, why not? And to what end? To what end? So that the old men could hope to become magically young again. Nothing more sane than that.

They were over Iwo Jima. Three more hours to Japan. Voices from *The Great Artiste* and *Number 91* crackled on the radio. Rendezvous accomplished, the three planes flew northwest, toward Shikoku, the first Japanese island in their path. January went aft to use the toilet. "You okay, Frank?" Matthews asked. "Sure. Terrible coffee, though." "Ain't it always."

January tugged at his baseball cap and hurried away. Kochenski and the other gunners were playing poker. When he was done he returned forward. Matthews sat on the stool before his maps, readying his equipment for the constant monitoring of drift that would now be required. Haddock and Benton were also busy at their stations. January maneuvered between the pilots down into the nose. "Good shooting," Matthews called after him.

Forward it seemed quieter. January got settled, put his headphones on and leaned forward to look out the ribbed Plexiglas.

Dawn had turned the whole vault of the sky pink. Slowly the radiant shade shifted through lavender to blue, pulse by pulse a different color. The ocean below was a glittering blue plane, marbled by a pattern of puffy pink cloud. The sky above was a vast dome, darker above than on the horizon. January had always thought that dawn was the time when you could see most clearly how big the earth was, and how high above it they flew. It seemed they flew at the very upper edge of the atmosphere, and January saw how thin it was, how it was just a skin of air really, so that even if you flew up to its top the earth still extended away infinitely in every direction. The coffee had warmed January, he was sweating. Sunlight blinked off the Plexiglas. His watch said six. Plane and hemisphere of blue were split down the middle by the bombsight. His earphones crackled and he listened in to the reports from the lead planes flying over the target cities. Kokura, Nagasaki, Hiroshima, all of them had six-tenths cloud cover. Maybe they would have to cancel the whole mission because of weather. "We'll look at Hiroshima first," Fitch said. January peered down at the fields of miniature clouds with renewed interest. His parachute slipped under him. Readjusting it he imagined putting it on, sneaking back to the central escape hatch under the navigator's cabin, opening the hatch… he could be out of the plane and gone before anyone noticed. Leave it up to them. They could bomb or not but it wouldn't be January's doing. He could float down onto the world like a puff of dandelion, feel cool air rush around him, watch the silk canopy dome hang over him like a miniature sky, a private world.

An eyeless black face. January shuddered; it was as though the nightmare could return any time. If he jumped nothing would change, the bomb would still fall—would he feel any better, floating on his Inland Sea? Sure, one part of him shouted; maybe, another conceded; the rest of him saw that face….

Earphones crackled. Shepard said, "Lieutenant Stone has now armed the bomb, and I can tell you all what we are carrying. Aboard with us is the world's first atomic bomb."

Not exactly, January thought. Whistles squeaked in his earphones. The first one went off in New Mexico. Splitting atoms: January had heard the term before. Tremendous energy in every atom, Einstein had said. Break one, and—he had seen the result on film. Shepard was talking about radiation, which brought back more to January. Energy released in the form of X rays. Killed by X rays! It would be against the Geneva Convention if they had thought of it.

Fitch cut in. "When the bomb is dropped Lieutenant Benton will record our reaction to what we see. This recording is being made for history, so watch your language." Watch your language! January choked back a laugh. Don't curse or blaspheme God at the sight of the first atomic bomb incinerating a city and all its inhabitants with X rays!

Six-twenty. January found his hands clenched together on the headrest of the bombsight. He felt as if he had a fever. In the harsh wash of morning light the skin on the backs of his hands appeared slightly translucent. The whorls in the skin looked like the delicate patterning of waves on the sea's surface. His hands were made of atoms. Atoms were the smallest building block of matter, it took billions of them to make those tense, trembling hands. Split one atom and you had the fireball. That meant that the energy contained in even one hand… he turned up a palm to look at the lines and the mottled flesh under the transparent skin. A person was a bomb that could blow up the world. January felt that latent power stir in him, pulsing with every hard heart-knock. What beings they were, and in what a blue expanse of a world!—And here they spun on to drop a bomb and kill a hundred thousand of these astonishing beings.

When a fox or raccoon is caught by the leg in a trap, it lunges until the leg is frayed, twisted, perhaps broken, and only then does the animal's pain and exhaustion force it to quit. Now in the same way January wanted to quit. His mind hurt. His plans to escape were so much crap—stupid, useless. Better to quit. He tried to stop thinking, but it was hopeless. How could he stop? As long as he was conscious he would be thinking. The mind struggles longer in its traps than any fox.

Lucky Strike tilted up and began the long climb to bombing altitude. On the horizon the clouds lay over a green island. Japan. Surely it had gotten hotter, the heater must be broken, he thought. Don't think. Every few minutes Matthews gave Fitch small course adjustments. "Two seventy-five, now. That's it." To escape the moment January recalled his childhood. Following a mule and plow. Moving to Vicksburg (rivers). For a while there in Vicksburg, since his stutter made it hard to gain friends, he had played a game with himself. He had passed the time by imagining that everything he did was vitally important and determined the fate of the world. If he crossed a road in front of a certain car, for instance, then the car wouldn't make it through the next intersection before a truck hit it, and so the man driving would be killed and wouldn't be able to invent the flying boat that would save President Wilson from kidnappers—so he had to wait for that car because everything afterward depended on it. Oh damn it, he thought, damn it, think of something *different*. The last Hornblower story he had read—how would *he* get out of this? The round O of his mother's face as she ran in and saw his arm—The Mississippi, mud-brown behind its levees— Abruptly he shook his head, face twisted in frustration and despair, aware at last that no possible avenue of memory would serve as an escape for him now, for now there was no part of his life that did not apply to the situation he was in, and no matter where he cast his mind it was going to shore up against the hour facing him.

Less than an hour. They were at thirty thousand feet, bombing altitude. Fitch gave him altimeter readings to dial into the bombsight. Matthews gave him windspeeds. Sweat got in his eye and he blinked furiously. The sun rose behind them like an atomic bomb, glinting off every corner and edge of the Plexiglas, illuminating his bubble compartment with a fierce glare. Broken plans jumbled together in his mind, his breath was short, his throat dry. Uselessly and repeatedly he damned the scientists, damned Truman. Damned the Japanese for causing the whole mess in the first place, damned yellow killers, they had brought this on themselves. Remember Pearl. American men had died under bombs when no war had been declared; they had started it and now it was coming back to them with a vengeance. And they deserved it. And an invasion of Japan would take years, cost millions of lives—end it now, end it, they deserved it, they deserved it steaming river full of charcoal people silently dying damned stubborn race of maniacs!

"There's Honshu," Fitch said, and January returned to the world of the plane. They were over the Inland Sea. Soon they would pass the secondary target, Kokura, a bit to the south. Seven-thirty. The island was draped more heavily than the sea by clouds, and again January's heart leaped with the idea that weather would cancel the mission. But they did deserve it. It was a mission like any other mission. He had dropped bombs on Africa, Sicily, Italy, all Germany.... He leaned forward to take a look through the sight. Under the X of the crosshairs was the sea, but at the lead edge of the sight was land. Honshu. At two hundred and thirty miles an hour that gave them about a half hour to Hiroshima. Maybe less. He wondered if his heart could beat so hard for that long.

Fitch said, "Matthews, I'm giving over guidance to you. Just tell us what to do."

"Bear south two degrees," was all Matthews said. At last their voices had taken on a touch of awareness, even fear.

"January, are you ready?" Fitch asked.

"I'm just waiting," January said. He sat up, so Fitch could see the back of his head. The bombsight stood between his legs. A switch on its side would start the bombing sequence; the bomb would not leave the plane immediately upon the flick of the switch, but would drop after a fifteen-second radio tone warned the following planes. The sight was adjusted accordingly.

"Adjust to a heading of two sixty-five," Matthews said. "We're coming in directly upwind." This was to make any side-drift adjustments for the bomb unnecessary. "January, dial it down to two hundred and thirty-one miles per hour."

"Two thirty-one."

Fitch said, "Everyone but January and Matthews, get your goggles on."

January took the darkened goggles from the floor. One needed to protect one's eyes or they might melt. He put them on, put his forehead on the headrest. They were in the way. He took them off. When he looked through the sight again there was land under the crosshairs. He checked his watch. Eight o'clock. Up and reading the papers, drinking tea.

"Ten minutes to AP," Matthews said. The aiming point was Aioi Bridge, a T-shaped bridge in the middle of the delta-straddling city. Easy to recognize.

"There's a lot of cloud down there." Fitch nodded. "Are you going to be able to see?"

"I won't be sure until we try it," January said.

"We can make another pass and use radar if we need to," Matthews said.

Fitch said, "Don't drop it unless you're sure, January."

"Yes sir."

Through the sight a grouping of rooftops and gray roads was just visible between broken clouds. Around it green forest. "All right," Matthews exclaimed, "here we go! Keep it right on this heading, Captain! January, we'll stay at two thirty-one."

"And same heading," Fitch said. "January, she's all yours. Everyone make sure your goggles are on. And be ready for the turn."

January's world contracted to the view through the bombsight. A stippled field of cloud and forest. Over a small range of hills and into Hiroshima's watershed. The broad river was mud brown, the land pale hazy green, the growing network of roads flat gray. Now the tiny rectangular shapes of buildings covered almost all the land, and swimming into the sight came the city proper, narrow islands thrusting into a dark blue bay. Under the crosshairs the city moved island by island, cloud by cloud. January had stopped breathing, his fingers were rigid as stone on the switch. And there was Aioi Bridge. It slid right under the crosshairs, a tiny T right in a gap of clouds. January's fingers crushed the switch. Deliberately he took a breath, held it. Clouds swam under the crosshairs, then the next island. "Almost there," he said calmly into his microphone. "Steady." Now that he was committed his heart was humming like the Wrights. He counted to ten. Now flowing under the crosshairs were clouds alternating with green forest, leaden roads. "I've turned the switch, but I'm not getting a tone!" he croaked into the mike. His right hand held the switch firmly in place. Fitch was shouting something—Matthews' voice cracked across it—"Flipping it b-back and forth," January shouted, shielding the bombsight with his body from the eyes of the pilots. "But *still*—wait a second—"

He pushed the switch down. A low hum filled his ears. "That's it! It started!"

"But where will it land?" Matthews cried.

"Hold steady!" January shouted.

Lucky Strike shuddered and lofted up ten or twenty feet. January twisted to look down and there was the bomb, flying just below the plane. Then with a wobble it fell away.

The plane banked right and dove so hard that the centrifugal force threw January against the Plexiglas. Several thousand feet lower Fitch leveled it out and they hurtled north.

"Do you see anything?" Fitch cried.

From the tail-gun Kochenski gasped, "Nothing." January struggled upright. He reached for the welder's goggles, but they were no longer on his head. He couldn't find them. "How long has it been?" he said.

"Thirty seconds," Matthews replied.

January clamped his eyes shut.

The blood in his eyelids lit up red, then white.

On the earphones a clutter of voices: "Oh my God. Oh my God." The plane bounced and tumbled, metallically shrieking. January pressed himself off the Plexiglas. "'Nother shockwave!" Kochenski yelled. The plane rocked again, bounced out of control, this is it, January thought, end of the world, I guess that solves my problem.

He opened his eyes and found he could still see. The engines still roared, the props spun. "Those were the shockwaves from the bomb," Fitch called. "We're okay now. Look at that! Will you look at that sonofabitch go!"

January looked. The cloud layer below had burst apart, and a black column of smoke billowed up from a core of red fire. Already the top of the column was at their height. Exclamations of shock clattered painfully in January's ears. He stared at the fiery base of the cloud, at the scores of fires feeding into it. Suddenly he could see past the cloud, and his fingernails cut into his palms. Through a gap in the clouds he saw it clearly, the delta, the six rivers, there off to the left of the tower of smoke: the city of Hiroshima, untouched.

"We missed!" Kochenski yelled. "We missed it!"

January turned to hide his face from the pilots; on it was a grin like a rictus. He sat back in his seat and let the relief fill him.

Then it was back to it. "God damn it!" Fitch shouted down at him. McDonald was trying to restrain him. "January, get up here!"

"Yes sir." Now there was a new set of problems.

January stood and turned, legs weak. His right fingertips throbbed painfully. The men were crowded forward to look out the Plexiglas. January looked with them.

The mushroom cloud was forming. It roiled out as if it might continue to extend forever, fed by the inferno and the black stalk below it. It looked about two miles wide, and a half-mile tall, and it extended well above the height they flew at, dwarfing their plane entirely. "Do you think we'll all be sterile?" Matthews said.

"I can taste the radiation," McDonald declared. "Can you? It tastes like lead."

Bursts of flame shot up into the cloud from below, giving a purplish tint to the stalk. There it stood: lifelike, malignant, sixty thousand feet tall. One bomb. January shoved past the pilots into the navigation cabin, overwhelmed.

"Should I start recording everyone's reaction, Captain?" asked Benton.

"To hell with that," Fitch said, following January back. But Shepard got there first, descending quickly from the navigation dome. He rushed across the cabin, caught January on the shoulder. "You bastard!" he screamed as January stumbled back. "You lost your nerve, coward!"

January went for Shepard, happy to have a target at last, but Fitch cut in and grabbed him by the collar, pulled him around until they were face to face—

"Is that right?" Fitch cried, as angry as Shepard. "Did you screw up on purpose?"

"No," January grunted, and knocked Fitch's hands away from his neck. He swung and smacked Fitch on the mouth, caught him solid. Fitch staggered back, recovered, and no doubt would have beaten January up, but Matthews and Benton and Stone leaped in and held him back, shouting for order. "Shut up! Shut up!" McDonald screamed from the cockpit, and for a moment it was bedlam, but Fitch let himself be restrained, and soon only McDonald's shouts for quiet were heard. January retreated to between the pilot seats, right hand on his pistol holster.

"The city was in the crosshairs when I flipped the switch," he said. "But the first couple of times I flipped it nothing happened—"

"That's a lie!" Shepard shouted. "There was nothing wrong with the switch, I checked it myself. Besides, the bomb exploded *miles* beyond Hiroshima, look for yourself! That's *minutes*." He wiped spit from his chin and pointed at January. "You did it."

"You don't know that," January said. But he could see the men had been convinced by Shepard, and he took a step back. "You just get me to a board of inquiry, quick. And leave me alone till then. If you touch me again," glaring venomously at Fitch and then Shepard, "I'll shoot you." He turned and hopped down to his seat, feeling exposed and vulnerable, like a treed raccoon.

"They'll shoot *you* for this," Shepard screamed after him. "Disobeying orders—treason—" Matthews and Stone were shutting him up.

"Let's get out of here," he heard McDonald say. "I can taste the lead, can't you?"

January looked out the Plexiglas. The giant cloud still burned and roiled. One atom... Well, they had really done it to that forest. He almost laughed but stopped himself, afraid of hysteria. Through a break in the clouds he got a clear view of Hiroshima for the first time. It lay spread over its islands like a map, unharmed. Well, that was that. The inferno at the base of the mushroom cloud was eight or ten miles around the shore of the bay and a mile or two inland. A certain patch of forest would be gone, destroyed—utterly blasted from the face of the earth. The Japs would be able to go out and investigate the damage. And if they were told it was a demonstration, a warning—and if they acted fast—well, they had their chance. Maybe it would work.

The release of tension made January feel sick. Then he recalled Shepard's words and he knew that whether his plan worked or not he was still in trouble. In trouble! It was worse than that. Bitterly he cursed the Japanese, he even wished for a moment that he *had* dropped it on them. Wearily he let his despair empty him.

A long while later he sat up straight. Once again he was a trapped animal. He began lunging for escape, casting about for plans. One alternative after another. All during the long grim flight home he considered it, mind spinning at the speed of the props and beyond. And when they came down on Tinian he had a plan. It was a long shot, he reckoned, but it was the best he could do.

The briefing hut was surrounded by MPs again. January stumbled from the truck with the rest and walked inside. He was more than ever aware of the looks given him, and they were hard, accusatory. He was too tired to care. He hadn't slept in more than thirty-six hours, and had slept very little since the last time he had been in the hut, a week before. Now the room quivered with the lack of engine vibration to stabilize it, and the silence roared. It was all he could do to hold on to the bare essentials of his plan. The glares of Fitch and Shepard, the hurt incomprehension of Matthews, they had to be thrust out of his focus. Thankfully he lit a cigarette.

In a clamor of question and argument the others described the strike. Then the haggard Scholes and an intelligence officer led them through the bombing run. January's plan made it necessary to hold to his story: "…and when the AP was under the crosshairs I pushed down the switch, but got no signal. I flipped it up and down repeatedly until the tone kicked in. At that point there was still fifteen seconds to the release."

"Was there anything that may have caused the tone to start when it did?"

"Not that I noticed immediately, but—"

"It's impossible," Shepard interrupted, face red. "I checked the switch before we flew and there was nothing wrong with it. Besides, the drop occurred over a minute—"

"Captain Shepard," Scholes said. "We'll hear from you presently."

"But he's obviously lying—"

"Captain Shepard! It's not at all obvious. Don't speak unless questioned."

"Anyway," January said, hoping to shift the questions away from the issue of the long delay, "I noticed something about the bomb when it was falling that could explain why it stuck. I need to discuss it with one of the scientists familiar with the bomb's design."

"What was that?" Scholes asked suspiciously.

January hesitated. "There's going to be an inquiry, right?"

Scholes frowned. "This is the inquiry, Captain January. Tell us what you saw."

"But there will be some proceeding beyond this one?"

"It looks like there's going to be a court-martial, yes, Captain."

"That's what I thought. I don't want to talk to anyone but my counsel, and some scientist familiar with the bomb."

"*I'm* a scientist familiar with the bomb," Shepard burst out. "You could tell me if you really had anything, you—"

"I said I need a scientist!" January exclaimed, rising to face the scarlet Shepard across the table. "Not a G-God damned mechanic." Shepard started to shout, others joined in and the room rang with argument. While Scholes restored order January sat down, and he refused to be drawn out again.

"I'll see you're assigned counsel, and initiate the court-martial," Scholes said, clearly at a loss. "Meanwhile you are under arrest, on suspicion of disobeying orders in combat." January nodded, and Scholes gave him over to the MPs.

"One last thing," January said, fighting exhaustion. "Tell General LeMay that if the Japs are told this drop was a warning, it might have the same effect as—"

"I told you!" Shepard shouted. "I told you he did it on purpose!"

Men around Shepard restrained him. But he had convinced most of them, and even Matthews stared at him with surprised anger.

January shook his head wearily. He had the dull feeling that his plan, while it had succeeded so far, was ultimately not a good one. "Just trying to make the best of it." It took all of his remaining will to force his legs to carry him in a dignified manner out of the hut.

His cell was an empty NCO's office. MPs brought his meals. For the first couple of days he did little but sleep. On the third day he glanced out the office's barred window, and saw a tractor pulling a tarpaulin-draped trolley out of the compound, followed by jeeps filled with MPs. It looked like a military funeral. January rushed to the door and banged on it until one of the young MPs came.

"What's that they're doing out there?" January demanded.

Eyes cold and mouth twisted, the MP said, "They're making another strike. They're going to do it right this time."

"No!" January cried. "No!" He rushed the MP, who knocked him back and locked the door. "*No!*" He beat the door until his hands hurt, cursing wildly. "You don't *need* to do it, it isn't *necessary.*" Shell shattered at last, he collapsed on the bed and wept. Now everything he had done would be rendered meaningless. He had sacrificed himself for nothing.

A day or two after that the MPs led in a colonel, an iron-haired man who stood stiffly and crushed January's hand when he shook it. His eyes were a pale, icy blue.

"I am Colonel Dray," he said. "I have been ordered to defend you in court-martial." January could feel the dislike pouring from the man. "To do that I'm going to need every fact you have, so let's get started."

"I'm not talking to anybody until I've seen an atomic scientist."

"I am your *defense* counsel—"

"I don't care who you are," January said. "Your defense of me depends on you getting one of the scientists *here*. The higher up he is, the better. And I want to speak to him alone."

"I will have to be present."

So he would do it. But now January's lawyer, too, was an enemy.

"Naturally," January said. "You're my lawyer. But no one else. Our atomic secrecy may depend on it."

"You saw evidence of sabotage?"

"Not one word more until that scientist is here."

Angrily the colonel nodded and left.

Late the next day the colonel returned with another man. "This is Dr. Forest."

"I helped develop the bomb," Forest said. He had a crew cut and dressed in fatigues, and to January he looked more Army than the colonel. Suspiciously he stared back and forth at the two men.

"You'll vouch for this man's identity on your word as an officer?" he asked Dray.

"Of course," the colonel said stiffly, offended.

"So," Dr. Forest said. "You had some trouble getting it off when you wanted to. Tell me what you saw."

"I saw nothing," January said harshly. He took a deep breath; it was time to commit himself. "I want you to take a message back to the scientists. You folks have been working on this thing for years, and you must have had time to consider how the bomb should have been used. You know we could have convinced the Japs to surrender by showing them a demonstration—"

"Wait a minute," Forest said. "You're saying you didn't see anything? There wasn't a malfunction?"

"That's right," January said, and cleared his throat. "It wasn't *necessary*, do you understand?"

Forest was looking at Colonel Dray. Dray gave him a disgusted shrug. "He told me he saw evidence of sabotage."

"I want you to go back and ask the scientists to intercede for me," January said, raising his voice to get the man's attention. "I haven't got a chance in that court-martial. But if the scientists defend me then maybe they'll let me live, see? I don't want to get shot for doing something every one of you scientists would have done."

Dr. Forest had backed away. Color rising, he said, "What makes you think that's what we would have done? Don't you think we considered it? Don't you think men better qualified than you made the decision?" He waved a hand— "God damn it—what made you think you were competent to decide something as important as that!"

January was appalled at the man's reaction; in his plan it had gone differently. Angrily he jabbed a finger at Forest. "Because *I* was the man doing it, *Doctor* Forest. You take even one step back from that and suddenly you can pretend it's not your doing. Fine for you, but *I was there.*"

At every word the man's color was rising. It looked like he might pop a vein in his neck. January tried once more. "Have you ever tried to imagine what one of your bombs would do to a city full of people?"

"I've had enough!" the man exploded. He turned to Dray. "I'm under no obligation to keep what I've heard here confidential. You can be sure it will be used as evidence in Captain January's court-martial." He turned and gave January a look of such blazing hatred that January understood it. For these men to admit he was right would mean admitting that they were wrong—that every one of them was responsible for his part in the construction of the weapon January had refused to use. Understanding that, January knew he was doomed.

The bang of Dr. Forest's departure still shook the little office. January sat on his cot, got out a smoke. Under Colonel Dray's cold gaze he lit one shakily, took a drag. He looked up at the colonel, shrugged. "It was my best chance," he explained. That did something—for the first and only time the cold disdain in the colonel's eyes shifted to a little, hard, lawyerly gleam of respect.

The court-martial lasted two days. The verdict was guilty of disobeying orders in combat and of giving aid and comfort to the enemy. The sentence was death by firing squad.

For most of his remaining days January rarely spoke, drawing ever further behind the mask that had hidden him for so long. A clergyman came to see him, but it was the 509th's chaplain, the one who had said the prayer blessing the *Lucky Strike*'s mission before they took off. Angrily January sent him packing.

Later, however, a young Catholic priest dropped by. His name was Patrick Getty. He was a little pudgy man, bespectacled and, it seemed, somewhat afraid of January. January let the man talk to him. When he returned the next day January talked back a bit, and on the day after that he talked some more. It became a habit.

Usually January talked about his childhood. He talked of plowing mucky black bottom land behind a mule. Of running down the lane to the mailbox. Of reading books by the light of the moon after he had been ordered to sleep, and of being beaten by his mother for it with a high-heeled shoe. He told the priest the story of the time his arm had been burnt, and about the car crash at the bottom of Fourth Street. "It's the truck driver's face I remember, do you see, Father?"

"Yes," the young priest said. "Yes."

And he told him about the game he had played in which every action he took tipped the balance of world affairs. "When I remembered that game I thought it was dumb. Step on a sidewalk crack and cause an earthquake—you know, it's stupid. Kids are like that." The priest nodded. "But now I've been thinking that if everybody were to live their whole lives like that, thinking that every move they made really was important, then... it might make a difference." He waved a hand vaguely, expelled cigarette smoke. "You're accountable for what you do."

"Yes," the priest said. "Yes, you are."

"And if you're given orders to do something wrong, you're still accountable, right? The orders don't change it."

"That's right."

"Hmph." January smoked a while. "So they say, anyway. But look what happens." He waved at the office. "I'm like the guy in a story I read—he thought everything in books was true, and after reading a bunch of westerns he tried to rob a train. They tossed him in jail." He laughed shortly. "Books are full of crap."

"Not all of them," the priest said. "Besides, you weren't trying to rob a train."

They laughed at the notion. "Did you read that story?"

"No."

"It was the strangest book—there were two stories in it, and they alternated chapter by chapter, but they didn't have a thing to do with each other! I didn't get it."

"...Maybe the writer was trying to say that everything connects to everything else."

"Maybe. But it's a funny way to say it."

"I like it."

And so they passed the time, talking.

So it was the priest who was the one to come by and tell January that his request for a Presidential pardon had been refused. Getty said awkwardly, "It seems the President approves the sentence."

"That bastard," January said weakly. He sat on his cot.

Time passed. It was another hot, humid day.

"Well," the priest said. "Let me give you some better news. Given your situation I don't think telling you matters, though I've been told not to. The second mission—you know there was a second strike?"

"Yes."

"Well, they missed too."

"What?" January cried, and bounced to his feet. "You're kidding!"

"No. They flew to Kokura, but found it covered by clouds. It was the same over Nagasaki and Hiroshima, so they flew back to Kokura and tried to drop the bomb using radar to guide it, but apparently there was a—a genuine equipment failure this time, and the bomb fell on an island."

January was hopping up and down, mouth hanging open, "So we n-never—"

"We never dropped an atom bomb on a Japanese city. That's right." Getty grinned. "And get this—I heard this from my superior—they sent a message to the Japanese government telling them that the two explosions were warnings, and that if they didn't surrender by September first we would drop bombs on Kyoto and Tokyo, and then wherever else we had to. Word is that the Emperor went to Hiroshima to survey the damage, and when he saw it he ordered the Cabinet to surrender. So…"

"So it worked," January said. He hopped around, "It worked, it worked!"

"Yes."

"Just like I said it would!" he cried, and hopping before the priest he laughed.

Getty was jumping around a little too, and the sight of the priest bouncing was too much for January. He sat on his cot and laughed till the tears ran down his cheeks.

"So—" he sobered quickly. "So Truman's going to shoot me anyway, eh?"

"Yes," the priest said unhappily. "I guess that's right."

This time January's laugh was bitter. "He's a bastard, all right. And proud of being a bastard, which makes it worse." He shook his head. "If Roosevelt had lived…"

"It would have been different," Getty finished. "Yes. Maybe so. But he didn't." He sat beside January. "Cigarette?" He held out a pack, and January noticed the white wartime wrapper. He frowned.

"Oh. Sorry."

"Oh well. That's all right." January took one of the Lucky Strikes, lit up. "That's awfully good news." He breathed out. "I never believed Truman would pardon me anyway, so mostly you've brought good news. Ha. They *missed*. You have no idea how much better that makes me feel."

"I think I do."

January smoked the cigarette.

"… So I'm a good American after all. I *am* a good American," he insisted, "no matter what Truman says."

"Yes," Getty replied, and coughed. "You're better than Truman any day."

"Better watch what you say, Father." He looked into the eyes behind the glasses, and the expression he saw there gave him pause. Since the drop every look directed at him had been filled with contempt. He'd seen it so often during the court-martial that he'd learned to stop looking; and now he had to teach himself to see again. The priest looked at him as if he were... as if he were some kind of hero. That wasn't exactly right. But seeing it...

January would not live to see the years that followed, so he would never know what came of his action. He had given up casting his mind forward and imagining possibilities, because there was no point to it. His planning was ended. In any case he would not have been able to imagine the course of the post-war years. That the world would quickly become an armed camp pitched on the edge of atomic war, he might have predicted. But he never would have guessed that so many people would join a January Society. He would never know of the effect the Society had on Dewey during the Korean crisis, never know of the Society's successful campaign for the test ban treaty, and never learn that thanks in part to the Society and its allies, a treaty would be signed by the great powers that would reduce the number of atomic bombs year by year, until there were none left.

Frank January would never know any of that. But in that moment on his cot looking into the eyes of young Patrick Getty, he guessed an inkling of it—he felt, just for an instant, the impact on history.

And with that he relaxed. In his last week everyone who met him carried away the same impression, that of a calm, quiet man, angry at Truman and others, but in a withdrawn, matter-of-fact way. Patrick Getty, a strong force in the January Society ever after, said January was talkative for some time after he learned of the missed attack on Kokura. Then he became quieter and quieter, as the day approached. On the morning that they woke him at dawn to march him out to a hastily constructed execution shed, his MPs shook his hand. The priest was with him as he smoked a final cigarette, and they prepared to put the hood over his head. January looked at him calmly. "They load one of the guns with a blank cartridge, right?"

"Yes," Getty said.

"So each man in the squad can imagine he may not have shot me?"

"Yes. That's right."

A tight, unhumorous smile was January's last expression. He threw down the cigarette, ground it out, poked the priest in the arm. "But I shot the blank. I *know*." Then the mask slipped back into place for good, making the hood redundant, and with a firm step January went to the wall. One might have said he was at peace.

A SENSITIVE DEPENDENCE
ON INITIAL CONDITIONS

The covering law model of historical explanation states that an event is explained if it can be logically deduced from a set of initial conditions, and a set of general historical laws. These sets are the *explanans,* and the event is the *explanandum.* The general laws are applied to the initial conditions, and the explanandum is shown to be the inevitable result. An explanation, in this model, has the same structure as a prediction.

On the morning of August 6th, 1945, Colonel Paul Tibbets and his crew flew the *Enola Gay* from Tinian Island to Hiroshima, and dropped an atomic bomb on the city. Approximately a hundred thousand people died. Three days later, another crew dropped a bomb on the outskirts of Nagasaki. Approximately seventy thousand people died. The Japanese surrendered.

President Harry Truman, in consultation with his advisors, decided to drop the bombs. Why did he make these decisions? Because the Japanese had fiercely defended many islands in the South Pacific, and the cost of conquering them had been high. Kamikaze attacks had sunk many American ships, and it was said that the Japanese would stage a gigantic kamikaze defense of the home islands. Estimated American casualties resulting from an invasion of the home islands ranged as high as a million men.

These were the conditions. General laws? Leaders want to end wars as quickly as possible, with a minimum of bloodshed. They also like to frighten potential postwar enemies. With the war in Europe ended, the Soviet Army stood ready to go wherever Stalin ordered it. No one could be sure where Stalin might want to go. An end to the Japanese war that frightened him would not be a bad thing.

But there were more conditions. The Japanese were defenseless in the air and at sea. American planes could bomb the home islands at will, and a total naval blockade of Japan was entirely possible. The Japanese civilian population was already starving; a blockade, combined with bombing of military sites, could very well have forced the Japanese leaders to surrender without an invasion.

But Truman and his advisors decided to drop the bombs. A complete explanation of the decision, omitted here due to considerations of length, would have to include an examination of the biographies of Truman, his advisors, the builders of the bomb, and the leaders of Japan and the Soviet Union; as well as a detailed analysis of the situation in Japan in 1945, and of American intelligence concerning that situation.

President Truman was re-elected in 1948, in an upset victory over Thomas Dewey. Two years later the United States went to war in Korea, to keep that country from being overrun by Communists supported by the Soviet Union and China. It was only one of many major wars in the second half of the twentieth century; there were over sixty, and although none of them were nuclear, approximately fifty million people were killed.

Heisenberg's uncertainty principle says that we cannot simultaneously determine both the velocity and the position of a particle. This is not a function of human perception, but a basic property of the universe. Thus it will never be possible to achieve a deterministic prediction of the movement of all particles throughout spacetime. Quantum mechanics, which replaced classical mechanics as the best description of these events, can only predict the probabilities among a number of possible outcomes.

The covering law model of historical explanation asserts that there is no logical difference between historical explanation and scientific explanation. But the model's understanding of scientific explanation is based on classical mechanics. In quantum reality, the covering law model breaks down.

The sufficient conditions model of historical explanation is a modification of the covering law model; it states that if one can describe a set of initial conditions that are sufficient (but not necessary) for the event to occur, then the event can be said to be explained. Deduction from general law is not part of this model, which is descriptive rather than prescriptive, and "seeks only to achieve an acceptable degree of coherent narrative."

In July of 1945, Colonel Tibbets was ordered to demonstrate his crew's ability to deliver an atomic weapon, by flying a test mission in the western Pacific. During the takeoff Tibbets shut down both propellers on the right wing, to show that if this occurred during an armed takeoff, he would still be able to control the plane. The strain of this maneuver, however, caused the inboard left engine to fail, and in the emergency return to Tinian the *Enola Gay* crashed, killing everyone aboard.

A replacement crew was chosen from Tibbets' squadron, and was sent to bomb Hiroshima on August 9th, 1945. During the run over Hiroshima the bombardier, Captain Frank January, deliberately delayed the release of the bomb, so that it missed Hiroshima by some ten miles. Another mission later that week encountered cloud cover, and missed Kokura by accident. January was court-martialed and executed for disobeying orders in battle. The Japanese, having seen the explosions and evaluated the explosion sites, surrendered.

January decided to miss the target because: he had a visionary dream in which he saw the results of the bombing; he had not been in combat for over a year; he was convinced the war was over; he had been in London during the Blitz; he disliked his plane's pilot; he hated Paul Tibbets; he was a loner, older than his fellow squadron members; he had read the Hornblower stories in the *Saturday Evening Post;* he once saw a truck crash into a car, and watched the truck driver in the aftermath; he was burned on the arm by stove oil when a child; he had an imagination.

The inboard left engine on the *Enola Gay* failed because a worker at the Wright manufacturing plant had failed to keep his welding torch flame on a weld for the required twenty seconds. He stopped three seconds too soon. He stopped three seconds too soon because he was tired. He was tired because the previous night he had stayed up late, drinking with friends.

In 1948, President Truman lost to Thomas Dewey in a close election that was slightly influenced by a political group called the January Society. The Korean conflict was settled by negotiation, and in February of 1956 a treaty was signed in Geneva, banning the use and manufacture of nuclear weapons.

Light behaves like either wave or particle, depending on how it is observed. The famous two-slit experiment, in which interference in wave patterns causes light shining through two slits in a partition to hit a screen in a pattern of light and dark bars, is a good example of this. Even when photons are sent at the slits one at a time, the pattern of light and dark bars still appears, implying that the single quantum of light is passing through both slits at the same time, creating an interference pattern with itself.

History is an interference pattern, says the covering law model. The conditions are particles; the laws are waves.

The necessary conditions model states that historical explanation requires merely identifying the kind of historical event being explained, and then locating among its initial conditions some that seem necessary for the event to take place. No general laws of history can help; one can only locate more necessary conditions. As William Dray writes in *Laws and Explanation in History,* an explanandum is explained when we "can trace the course of events by which it came about."

Tibbets and his crew died in a training flight crash, and the *Lucky Strike* was sent in *Enola Gay*'s place. The bombardier, Captain Frank January, after much frantic thought on the flight there, performed just as Tibbets' bombardier would have, and dropped the bomb over the T-shaped Aioi Bridge in Hiroshima. Approximately a hundred thousand people died. Three days later Nagasaki was bombed. The Japanese surrendered. Truman was re-elected. The Korean War led to the Cold War, the assassination of Kennedy on November 22nd, 1963, the Vietnam War, the collapse of the Soviet bloc in the fall of 1989. Replacing one crew with another made no larger difference.

Richard Feynman's notion of a "sum over histories" proposes that a particle does not move from point A to point B by a single path, as in classical mechanics, but rather by every possible path within the wave. Two numbers describe these possible paths, one describing the size of the wave, the other the path's position in the crest-to-trough cycle. When Pauli's exclusion principle, which states that two particles cannot occupy the same position at the same velocity within the mathematical limits of the uncertainty principle, is applied to the sum over histories, it indicates that some possible paths cause interference patterns, and cancel each other out; other paths are phased in a reinforcing way, which makes their occurrence more probable.

Perhaps history has its own sum over histories, so that all possible histories resemble ours. Perhaps every possible bombardier chooses Hiroshima.

The weak covering law model attempts to rescue the notion of general historical laws by relaxing their rigor, to the point where one can no longer deduce the explanandum from the explanans alone; the laws become not laws but tendencies, which help historians by providing "guiding threads" between events and their initial conditions. Thus the uncertainty principle is acknowledged, and the covering law model brought into the twentieth century.

But can any historical model explain the twentieth century? Tibbets crashed, the *Lucky Strike* flew to Hiroshima, and Captain January chose to spare the city. He was executed, the war ended, Dewey won the 1948 election; the Korean conflict was resolved by negotiation; and nuclear weapons were banned by treaty in February of 1956.

But go on. In November of 1956, conflict broke out in the Middle East between Egypt and Israel, and Britain and France quickly entered the conflict to protect their interests in the Suez Canal. President Dewey, soon to be replaced by President-elect Dwight Eisenhower, asked Britain and

France to quit the conflict; his request was ignored. The war spread through the Middle East. In December the Soviet Army invaded West Germany. The United States declared war on the Soviet Union. China launched assaults in Indochina, and the Third World War was under way. Both the United States and the Soviet Union quickly assembled a number of atomic bombs, and in the first week of 1957, Jerusalem, Berlin, Bonn, Paris, London, Warsaw, Leningrad, Prague, Budapest, Beirut, Amman, Cairo, Moscow, Vladivostok, Tokyo, Peking, Los Angeles, Washington, D.C., and Princeton, New Jersey (hit by a bomb targeted for New York) were destroyed. Loss of life in that week and the year following was estimated at a hundred million people.

At normal energies, the strong nuclear force has a property called confinement, which binds quarks tightly together. At the high energies achieved in particle accelerators, however, the strong nuclear force becomes much weaker, allowing quarks and gluons to jet away almost like free particles. This property of dispersion at high energies is called "asymptotic freedom."

History is a particle accelerator. Energies are not always normal. We live in a condition of asymptotic freedom, and every history is possible. Each bombardier has to choose.

In *The Open Society and Its Enemies* Karl Popper writes: "If two armies are equally well-led and well-armed, and one has an enormous numerical superiority, the other will never win." Popper made this proposition to demonstrate that any historical law with broad explanatory power would become so general as to be trivial. For the school of thought that agrees with him, there can be no covering laws.

In June of 1945, seven of the scientists who had worked on the Manhattan Project submitted a document called the Franck Report to the Scientific Panel of the Interim Committee, which was overseeing the progress of the bomb. The Franck Report called for a demonstration of the bomb before observers from many countries, including Japan. The Scientific Panel decided this was a possible option and passed the Report on to the Committee, which passed it on to the White House. "The Buck Stops Here." Truman read the report and decided to invite James Franck, Leo Szilard, Niels Bohr, and Albert Einstein to the White House to discuss the issue. Final consultations included Oppenheimer, Secretary of War Stimson, and the military head of the Manhattan Project, General Leslie Groves. After a week's intense debate Truman instructed Stimson to contact the Japanese leadership and arrange a demonstration drop, to be made on one of the uninhabited islands in the Izu Shichito archipelago, south of Tokyo Bay. An atomic bomb was exploded on Udone Shima on August 24th, 1945; the mushroom cloud was visible from Tokyo. Films of the explosion were shown to Emperor Hirohito. The Emperor instructed his government to surrender, which it did on August 31st, one day before Truman had declared he was going to begin bombing Japanese cities.

Truman won the election of 1948. In 1950 North Korean troops invaded the south, until a series of six so-called Shima blasts, each closer to the north's advance forces, stopped them at the 38th parallel. In 1952 Adlai Stevenson became president, and appointed Leo Szilard the first presidential science advisor. In 1953 Stalin died, and in 1956 Szilard was sent to Moscow for a consultation with Khrushchev. This meeting led to the founding of the International Peace Brigade, which sent internationally integrated teams of young people to work in underdeveloped countries and in countries still recovering from World War Two. In 1960 John Kennedy was elected president, and he was succeeded in 1968 by his brother Robert. In 1976, in the wake of scandals in the administration, Richard Nixon was elected. At this point in time the postwar period is usually considered to have ended. The century itself came to a close without any further large wars. Though there had been a number of local conflicts, the existence of nuclear weapons had ended war as practiced in the first half of the century. In the second half, only about five million people died in war.

The great man theory considers particles; historical materialism considers waves. The wave/particle duality, confirmed many times by experiment, assures us that neither theory can be the complete truth. Neither theory will serve as the covering law.

The defenders of the covering law model reply to its various critiques by stating that it is irrelevant whether historians actually use the model or not; the fact remains that they *should*. If they do not, then an event like "the bottle fell off the table" could be explained by either "the cat's tail brushed it," or "the cat looked at it cross-eyed," and there would be no basis for choosing between the two explanations. Historical explanation is not just a matter of the practice of historians, but of the nature of reality. And in reality, physical events are constrained by general laws—or if they are not laws, they are at least extraordinarily detailed descriptions of the links between an event and those that follow it, allowing predictions that, if not deterministically exact, are still accurate enough to give us enormous power over physical reality. That, for anyone but followers of David Hume, serves as law enough. And humans, as part of the stuff of the universe, are subject to the same physical laws that control all the rest of it. So it makes sense to seek a science of history, and to try to formulate some general historical laws.

What would these general laws look like? Some examples:

· If two armies are equally well-led and well-armed, and one has an enormous numerical superiority, the other will never win.

· A privileged group will never relinquish privilege voluntarily.

· Empires rise, flourish, fall and are replaced, in a cyclical pattern.

· A nation's fortunes depend on its success in war.

· A society's culture is determined by its economic system.

· Belief systems exist to disguise inequality.

· Lastly, unparalleled in both elegance and power, subsuming many of the examples listed above: power corrupts.

So there do seem to be some quite powerful laws of historical explanation. But consider another:

· For want of a nail, the battle was lost.

For instance: on July 29th, 1945, a nomad in Kirgiz walked out of his yurt and stepped on a butterfly. For lack of the butterfly flapping its wings, the wind in the area blew slightly less. A low-pressure front therefore moved over east China more slowly than it would have. And so on August 6th, when the *Enola Gay* flew over Hiroshima, it was covered by ninety percent cloud cover, instead of fifty percent. Colonel Tibbets flew to the secondary target, Nagasaki; it was also covered. The *Enola Gay* had little fuel left, but its crew was able to fly over Kokura on the way back to Tinian, and taking advantage of a break in the clouds, they dropped the bomb there. Ninety thousand people died in Kokura. The *Enola Gay* landed at Tinian with so little fuel left in its tanks that what remained "wouldn't have filled a cigarette lighter." On August 9th a second mission tried Hiroshima again, but the clouds were still there, and the mission eventually dropped the bomb on the less heavily clouded secondary target, Nagasaki, missing the city center and killing only twenty thousand people. The Japanese surrendered a week later.

On August 11th, 1945, a child named Ai Matsui was born in Hiroshima. In 1960 she began to speak in local meetings on many topics, including Hiroshima's special position in the world. Its citizens had escaped annihilation, she said, as if protected by some covering angel (or law); they had a responsibility to the dead of Kokura and Nagasaki, to represent them in the world of the living, to change the world for the good. The Hiroshima Peace Party quickly grew to become the dominant political movement in Hiroshima, and then, in revulsion at the violence of the 1960s in Vietnam and elsewhere, all over Japan. In the 1970s the party became a worldwide movement, gaining the enthusiastic support of ex-President Kennedy, and President Babbitt. Young people from every country joined it as if experiencing a religious conversion. In 1983 Japan began its Asian Assistance League. One of its health care programs saved the life of a young woman in India, sick with malaria. The next year she had a child, a woman destined to become India's greatest leader. In 1987, the nation of Palestine raised its flag over the West Bank and parts of Jordan and Lebanon; a generation of camp children moved into homes. A child was born in Galilee. In 1990 Japan started its African Assistance League. The Hiroshima Peace Party had a billion members.

And so on; so that by July 29th, 2045, no human on Earth was the same as those who would have lived if the nomad in Kirgiz had not stepped on the butterfly a century before.

This phenomenon is known as the butterfly effect, and it is a serious problem for all other models of historical explanation; meaning trouble for you and for me. The scientific term for it is "sensitive dependence on initial conditions." It is an aspect of chaos theory first studied by the meteorologist Edward Lorenz, who, while running computer simulations of weather patterns, discovered that the slightest change in the initial conditions of the simulation would quickly lead to completely different weather.

So the strong covering law model said that historical explanation should equal the rigor of scientific explanation. Then its defenders, bringing the model into the quantum world, conceded that predictions can never be anything but probabilistic at best. The explanandum was no longer deducible from the explanans; one could only suggest probabilities.

Now chaos theory has added new problems. And yet consider: Captain Frank January chose to miss Hiroshima. Ten years later, nuclear weapons were universally banned. Eleven years later, local conflicts in the Middle East erupted into general war, and nuclear weapons were quickly reassembled and used. For it is not easy to forget knowledge, once it is learned; symmetry T, which says that physical laws are the same no matter which way the time arrow is pointed, does not actually exist in nature. There is no going back.

And so by 1990, in this particular world, the bombed cities were rebuilt. The Western industrial nations were rich, the Southern developing nations were poor. Multinational corporations ruled the world's economy. The Soviet bloc was falling apart. Gigantic sums of money were spent on armaments. By the year 2056, there was very little to distinguish this world from the one in which January had dropped the bomb, in which Tibbets had bombed Hiroshima, in which Tibbets had made a demonstration, in which Tibbets bombed Kokura.

Perhaps a sum over histories had bunched the probabilities. Is this likely? We don't know. We are particles, moving in a wave. The wave breaks. No math can predict which bubbles will appear where. But there is a sum over histories. Chaotic systems fall into patterns, following the pull of strange attractors. Linear chaotic figures look completely non-repetitive, but slice them into Poincaré sections and they reveal the simplest kinds of patterns. There is a tide, and we float in it; perhaps it is the flux of the cosmos itself; swim this way or that, the tide still carries us to the same destination. Perhaps.

So the covering law model is amended yet again. Explanations still require laws, but there are not laws for every event. The task of historical explanation becomes the act of making distinctions, between those parts of an event that can be explained by laws, and those that cannot. The component events that combine to create an explanandum are analyzed each in turn, and the historian then concentrates on the explicable components.

Paul Tibbets flies toward Hiroshima. The nomad steps out of his yurt.

Lyapunov exponents are numbers that measure the conflicting effects of stretching, contracting, and folding in the phase space of an attractor. They set the topological parameters of unpredictability. An exponent greater than zero means stretching, so that each alternative history moves farther and farther apart as time passes. An exponent smaller than zero means contraction, so that alternatives tend to come back together. When the exponent equals zero, a periodic orbit results.

What is history's Lyapunov exponent? This is the law that no one can know.

Frank January flies toward Hiroshima. The nomad stops in his yurt.

It is said that the historian's task requires an imaginative reconstruction of the thinking of people who acted in the past, and of the circumstances in which they acted. "An explanation is said to be successful when the historian gets the sense of reliving the past which he is trying to explain."

You are flying toward Hiroshima. You are the bombardier. You have been given the assignment two days before. You know what the bomb will do. You do not know what you will do. You have to decide.

There are a hundred billion neurons in the brain. Some of the neurons have as many as eighty thousand synaptic endings. During thought, neurotransmitter chemicals flow across the synaptic clefts between one neuron's synaptic knobs and another's dendritic spines, reversing a slight electric charge, which passes on a signal. The passage of a signal often leaves changes in the synapses and dendrites along the way, forever altering the structure of the brain. This plasticity makes memory and learning possible. Brains are always growing; intensely in the first five years, then steadily thereafter.

At the moment of choice, then, signals fly through a neural network that has been shaped over a lifetime into a particular and unique structure. Some signals are conscious, other are not. According to Roger Penrose, during the process of decision quantum effects in the brain take over, allowing a great number of parallel and simultaneous computations to take place; the number could be extraordinarily large, 10^{21} or more. Only at the intrusion of the "observation," that is to say a decision, do the parallel computations resolve back into a single conscious thought.

And in the act of deciding, the mind attempts the work of the historian: breaking the potential events down into their component parts, enumerating conditions, seeking covering laws that will allow a prediction of what will follow from the variety of possible choices. Alternative futures branch like dendrites away from the present moment, shifting chaotically, pulled this way and that by attractors dimly perceived. Probable outcomes emerge from those less likely.

And then, in the myriad clefts of the quantum mind, a mystery: the choice is made. We have to choose, that is life in time. Some powerful selection process, perhaps aesthetic, perhaps moral, perhaps practical (survival of the thinker), shoves to consciousness those plans that seem safest, or most right, or most beautiful, we do not know; and the choice is made. And at the moment of this observation the great majority of alternatives disappear without trace, leaving us in our asymptotic freedom to act, uncertainly, in time's asymmetrical flow.

There are few covering laws. Initial conditions are never fully known. The butterfly may be on the wing, it may be crushed underfoot. You are flying toward Hiroshima.

ARTHUR STERNBACH BRINGS THE CURVEBALL TO MARS

He was a tall skinny Martian kid, shy and stooping. Gangly as a puppy. Why they had him playing third base I have no idea. Then again they had me playing shortstop and I'm left-handed. And can't field grounders. But I'm American so there I was. That's what learning a sport by video will do. Some things are so obvious people never think to mention them. Like never put a lefty at shortstop. But on Mars they were making it all new. Some people there had fallen in love with baseball, and ordered the equipment and rolled some fields, and off they went.

So there we were, me and this kid Gregor, butchering the left side of the infield. He looked so young I asked him how old he was, and he said eight and I thought Jeez you're not *that* young, but realized he meant Martian years of course, so he was about sixteen or seventeen, but he seemed younger. He had recently moved to Argyre from somewhere else, and was staying at the local house of his co-op with relatives or friends, I never got that straight, but he seemed pretty lonely to me. He never missed practice even though he was the worst of a terrible team, and clearly he got frustrated at all his errors and strike-outs. I used to wonder why he came out at all. And so shy; and that stoop; and the acne; and the tripping over his own feet, the blushing, the mumbling—he was a classic.

English wasn't his first language, either. It was Armenian, or Moravian, something like that. Something no one else spoke, anyway, except for an elderly couple in his co-op. So he mumbled what passes for English on Mars, and sometimes even used a translation box, but basically tried never to be in a situation where he had to speak. And made error after error. We must have made quite a sight—me about waist-high to him, and both of us letting grounders pass through us like we were a magic show. Or else knocking them down and chasing them around, then winging them past the first baseman. We very seldom made an out. It would have been conspicuous except everyone else was the same way. Baseball on Mars was a high-scoring game.

But beautiful anyway. It was like a dream, really. First of all the horizon, when you're on a flat plain like Argyre, is only three miles away rather than six. It's very noticeable to a Terran eye. Then their diamonds have just over normal-sized infields, but the outfields have to be huge. At my team's ballpark it was nine hundred feet to dead center, seven hundred down the lines. Standing at the plate the outfield fence was like a little green line off in the distance, under a purple sky, pretty near the horizon itself—what I'm telling you is that the baseball diamond about covered *the entire visible world.* It was so great.

They played with four outfielders, like in softball, and still the alleys between fielders were wide. And the air was about as thin as at Everest base camp, and the gravity itself only bats .380, so to speak. So when you hit the ball solid it flies like a golf ball hit by a big driver. Even as big as the fields were, there were still a number of home runs every game. Not many shutouts on Mars. Not till I got there anyway.

I went there after I climbed Olympus Mons, to help them establish a new soil sciences institute. They had the sense not to try that by video. At first I climbed in the Charitums in my time off, but after I got hooked into baseball it took up most of my spare time. Fine, I'll play, I said when they asked me. But I won't coach. I don't like telling people what to do.

So I'd go out and start by doing soccer exercises with the rest of them, warming up all the muscles we would never use. Then Werner would start hitting infield practice, and Gregor and I would start flailing. We were like matadors. Occasionally we'd snag one and whale it over to first, and occasionally the first baseman, who was well over two meters tall and built like a tank, would catch our throws, and we'd slap our gloves together. Doing this day after day Gregor got a little less shy with me, though not much. And I saw that he threw the ball pretty damned hard. His arm was as long as my whole body, and boneless it seemed, like something pulled off a squid, so loose-wristed that he got some real pop on the ball. Of course sometimes it would still be rising when it passed ten meters over the first baseman's head, but it was moving, no doubt about it. I began to see that maybe the reason he came out to play, beyond just being around people he didn't have to talk to, was the chance to throw things really hard. I saw too that he wasn't so much shy as he was surly. Or both.

Anyway our fielding was a joke. Hitting went a bit better. Gregor learned to chop down on the ball and hit grounders up the middle; it was pretty effective. And I began to get my timing together. Coming to it from years of slow-pitch softball, I had started by swinging at everything a week late, and between that and my shortstopping I'm sure my teammates figured they had gotten a defective American. And since they had a rule limiting each team to only two Terrans, no doubt they were disappointed by that. But slowly I adjusted my timing, and after that I hit pretty well. The thing was their pitchers had no breaking stuff. These big guys would rear back and throw as hard as they could, like Gregor, but it took everything in their power just to throw strikes. It was a little scary because they often threw right at you by accident. But if they got it down the pipe then all you had to do was time it. And if you hit one, how the ball flew! Every time I connected it was like a miracle. It felt like you could put one into orbit if you hit it right, in fact that was one of their nicknames for a home run. Oh that's orbital they would say, watching one leave the park headed for the horizon. They had a little bell, like a ship's bell, attached to the backstop, and every time someone hit one out they would ring that bell while you rounded the bases. A very nice local custom.

So I enjoyed it. It's a beautiful game even when you're butchering it. My sorest muscles after practice were in my stomach from laughing so hard. I even began to have some success at short. When I caught balls going to my right I twirled around backwards to throw to first or second. People were impressed though of course it was ridiculous. It was a case of the one-eyed man in the country of the blind. Not that they weren't good athletes, you understand, but none of them had played as kids, and so they had no baseball instincts. They just liked to play. And I could see why—out there on a green field as big as the world, under a purple sky, with the yellow-green balls flying around—it was beautiful. We had a good time.

I started to give a few tips to Gregor, too, though I had sworn to myself not to get into coaching. I don't like trying to tell people what to do. The game's too hard for that. But I'd be hitting flies to the outfielders, and it was hard not to tell them to watch the ball and run under it and then put the glove up and catch it, rather than run all the way with their arms stuck up like the Statue of Liberty's. Or when they took turns hitting flies (it's harder than it looks) giving them batting tips. And Gregor and I played catch all the time during warm-ups, so just watching me—and trying to throw to such a short target—he got better. He definitely threw hard. And I saw there was a whole lot of movement in his throws. They'd come tailing in to me every which way, no surprise given how loose-wristed he was. I had to look sharp or I'd miss. He was out of control, but he had potential.

And the truth was, our pitchers were bad. I loved the guys, but they couldn't throw strikes if you paid them. They'd regularly walk ten or twenty batters every game, and these were five-inning games. Werner would watch

Thomas walk ten, then he'd take over in relief and walk ten more himself. Sometimes they'd go through this twice. Gregor and I would stand there while the other team's runners walked by as in a parade, or a line at the grocery store. When Werner went to the mound I'd stand by Gregor and say, You know Gregor you could pitch better than these guys. You've got a good arm. And he would look at me horrified, muttering, No no no no, not possible.

But then one time warming up he broke off a really mean curve and I caught it on my wrist. While I was rubbing it down I walked over to him.

Did you see the way that ball curved? I said.

Yes, he said, looking away. I'm sorry.

Don't be sorry, that's called a curveball, Gregor. It can be a useful throw. You twisted your hand at the last moment and the ball came over the top of it, like this, see? Here, try it again.

So we slowly got into it. I was all-state in Connecticut my senior year in high school, and it was all from throwing junk—curve, slider, split-finger, change. I could see Gregor throwing most of those just by accident, but to keep from confusing him I just worked on a straight curve. I told him: just throw it to me like you did that first time.

I thought you weren't to coach us, he said.

I'm not coaching you! Just throw it like that. Then in the games throw it straight. As straight as possible.

He mumbled a bit at me in Moravian, and didn't look me in the eye. But he did it. And after a while he worked up a good curve. Of course the thinner air on Mars meant there was little for the balls to bite on. But I noticed that the blue dot balls they played with had higher stitching than the red dot balls. They played with both of them as if there was no difference, but there was. So I filed that away and kept working with Gregor.

We practiced a lot. I showed him how to throw from the stretch, figuring that a wind-up from Gregor was likely to end up in knots. And by mid-season he threw a mean curve from the stretch. We had not mentioned it to anyone else. He was wild with it, but it hooked hard; I had to be really sharp to catch some of them. It made me better at shortstop too. Although finally in one game, behind twenty to nothing as usual, a batter hit a towering pop fly and I took off running back on it, and the wind kept carrying it and I kept following it, until when I got it I was out there sprawled between our startled center fielders.

Maybe you should play outfield, Werner said.

I said, Thank God.

So after that I played left center or right center, and I spent the games chasing line drives to the fence and throwing them back in to the cut-off man. Or more likely, standing there and watching the other team take their walks. I called in my usual chatter, and only then did I notice that no one on Mars ever yelled anything at these games. It was like playing in a league of deaf-mutes. I had to provide the chatter for the whole team from two hundred yards away in center field, including of course criticism of the plate umpire's calls. My view of the plate was miniaturized but I still did a better job than they did, and they knew it too. It was fun. People would walk by and say, Hey there must be an American out there.

One day after one of our home losses, 28 to 12 I think it was, everyone went to get something to eat, and Gregor was just standing there looking off into the distance. You want to come along? I asked him, gesturing after the others, but he shook his head. He had to get back home and work. I was going back to work myself, so I walked with him into town, a place like you'd see in the Texas panhandle. I stopped outside his co-op, which was a big house or little apartment complex, I could never tell which was which on Mars. There he stood like a lamppost, and I was about to leave when an old woman came out and invited me in. Gregor had told her about me, she said in stiff English. So I was introduced to the people in the kitchen there, most of them incredibly tall. Gregor seemed really embarrassed, he didn't want me being there, so I left as soon as I could get away. The old woman had a husband, and they seemed like Gregor's grandparents. There was a young girl there too, about his age, looking at both of us like a hawk. Gregor never met her eye.

Next time at practice I said, Gregor, were those your grandparents?

Like my grandparents.

And that girl, who was she?

No answer.

Like a cousin or something?

Yes.

Gregor, what about your parents? Where are they?

He just shrugged and started throwing me the ball.

I got the impression they lived in another branch of his co-op somewhere else, but I never found out for sure. A lot of what I saw on Mars I liked—the way they run their businesses together in co-ops takes a lot of pressure off them, and they live pretty relaxed lives compared to us on Earth. But some of their parenting systems—kids brought up by groups, or by one parent, or whatever—I wasn't so sure about those. It makes for problems if you ask me. Bunch of teenage boys ready to slug somebody. Maybe that happens no matter what you do.

Anyway we finally got to the end of the season, and I was going to go back to Earth after it. Our team's record was three and fifteen, and we came in last place in the regular season standings. But they held a final weekend tournament for all the teams in the Argyre Basin, a bunch of three-inning games, as there were a lot to get through. Immediately we lost the first game and were in the loser's bracket. Then we were losing the next one too, and all because of walks, mostly. Werner relieved Thomas for a time, then when that didn't work out Thomas went back to the mound to re-relieve Werner. When that happened I ran all the way in from center to join them on the mound. I said, Look you guys, let Gregor pitch.

Gregor! they both said. No way!

He'll be even worse than us, Werner said.

How could he be? I said. You guys just walked eleven batters in a row. Night will fall before Gregor could do that.

So they agreed to it. They were both discouraged at that point, as you might expect. So I went over to Gregor and said, Okay, Gregor, you give it a try now.

Oh no, no no no no no no no. He was pretty set against it. He glanced up into the stands where we had a couple hundred spectators, mostly friends and family and some curious passersby, and I saw then that his like-grandparents and his girl something-or-other were up there watching. Gregor was getting more hangdog and sullen every second.

Come on Gregor, I said, putting the ball in his glove. Tell you what, I'll catch you. It'll be just like warming up. Just keep throwing your curveball. And I dragged him over to the mound.

So Werner warmed him up while I went over and got on the catcher's gear, moving a box of blue dot balls to the front of the ump's supply area while I was at it. I could see Gregor was nervous, and so was I. I had never caught before, and he had never pitched, and bases were loaded and no one was out. It was an unusual baseball moment.

Finally I was geared up and I clanked on out to him. Don't worry about throwing too hard, I said, just put the curveball right in my glove. Ignore the batter. I'll give you the sign before every pitch; two fingers for curve, one for fastball.

Fastball? he says.

That's where you throw the ball fast. Don't worry about that. We're just going to throw curves anyway.

And you said you weren't to coach, he said bitterly.

I'm not coaching, I said, I'm catching.

So I went back and got set behind the plate. Be looking for curveballs, I said to the ump. Curveball? he said.

So we started up. Gregor stood crouched on the mound like a big praying mantis, red-faced and grim. He threw the first pitch right over our heads to the backstop. Two guys scored while I retrieved it, but I threw out the runner going from first to third. I went out to Gregor. Okay, I said, the bases are cleared and we got an out. Let's just throw now. Right into the glove. Just like last time, but lower.

So he did. He threw the ball at the batter, and the batter bailed, and the ball cut right down into my glove. The umpire was speechless. I turned around and showed him the ball in my glove. That was a strike, I told him.

Strike! he hollered. He grinned at me. That was a curveball, wasn't it?

Damn right it was.

Hey, the batter said. What was that?

We'll show you again, I said.

And after that Gregor began to mow them down. I kept putting down two fingers, and he kept throwing curveballs. By no means were they all strikes, but enough were to keep him from walking too many batters. All the balls were blue dot. The ump began to get into it.

And between two batters I looked behind me and saw that the entire crowd of spectators, and all the teams not playing at that moment, had congregated behind the backstop to watch Gregor pitch. No one on Mars had ever seen a curveball before, and now they were crammed back there to get the best view of it, gasping and chattering at every hook. The batter would bail or take a weak swing and then look back at the crowd with a big grin, as if to say, Did you see that? That was a curveball!

So we came back and won that game, and we kept Gregor pitching, and we won the next three games as well. The third game he threw exactly twenty-seven pitches, striking out all nine batters with three pitches each. Walter Feller once struck out all twenty-seven batters in a high school game; it was like that.

The crowd was loving it. Gregor's face was less red. He was standing straighter in the box. He still refused to look anywhere but at my glove, but his look of grim terror had shifted to one of ferocious concentration. He may have been skinny, but he was tall. Out there on the mound he began to look pretty damned formidable.

So we climbed back up into the winner's bracket, then into a semifinal. Crowds of people were coming up to Gregor between games to get him to sign their baseballs. Mostly he looked dazed, but at one point I saw him glance up at his co-op family in the stands and wave at them, with a brief smile.

How's your arm holding out? I asked him.

What do you mean? he said.

Okay, I said. Now look, I want to play outfield again this game. Can you pitch to Werner? Because there were a couple of Americans on the team we played next, Ernie and Caesar, who I suspected could hit a curve. I just had a hunch.

Gregor nodded, and I could see that as long as there was a glove to throw at, nothing else mattered. So I arranged it with Werner, and in the semifinals I was back out in right-center field. We were playing under the lights by this time, the field like green velvet under a purple twilight sky. Looking in from center field it was all tiny, like something in a dream.

And it must have been a good hunch I had, because I made one catch charging in on a liner from Ernie, sliding to snag it, and then another running across the middle for what seemed like thirty seconds, before I got under a towering Texas leaguer from Caesar. Gregor even came up and congratulated me between innings.

And you know that old thing about how a good play in the field leads to a good at bat. Already in the day's games I had hit well, but now in this semifinal I came up and hit a high fastball so solid it felt like I didn't hit it at all, and off it flew. Home run over the center field fence, out into the dusk. I lost sight of it before it came down.

Then in the finals I did it again in the first inning, back-to-back with Thomas—his to left, mine again to center. That was two in a row for me, and we were winning, and Gregor was mowing them down. So when I came up again in the next inning I was feeling good, and people were calling out for another homer, and the other team's pitcher had a real determined look. He was a really big guy, as tall as Gregor but massive-chested as so many Martians are, and he reared back and threw the first one right at my head. Not on purpose, he was out of control. Then I barely fouled several pitches off, swinging very late, and dodging his inside heat, until it was a full count, and I was thinking to myself, Well heck, it doesn't really matter if you strike out here, at least you hit two in a row.

Then I heard Gregor shouting, Come on, coach, you can do it! Hang in there! Keep your focus! All doing a passable imitation of me, I guess, as the rest of the team was laughing its head off. I suppose I had said all those things to them before, though of course it was just the stuff you always say automatically at a ball game, I never meant anything by it, I didn't even know people heard me. But I definitely heard Gregor needling me, and I stepped back into the box thinking, Look I don't even like to coach, I played ten games at shortstop trying not to coach you guys. And I was so irritated I was barely aware of the pitch, but hammered it anyway out over the right field fence, higher and deeper even than my first two. Knee-high fastball, inside. As Ernie said to me afterwards, You *drove* that baby. My teammates rang the little ship's bell all the way around the bases, and I slapped hands with every one of them on the way from third to home, feeling the grin on my face. Afterwards I sat on the bench and felt the hit in my hands. I can still see it flying out.

So we were ahead 4–0 in the final inning, and the other team came up determined to catch us. Gregor was tiring at last, and he walked a couple, then hung a curve and their big pitcher got into it and clocked it far over my head. Now I do okay charging liners, but the minute a ball is hit over me I'm totally lost. So I turned my back on this one and ran for the fence, figuring either it goes out or I collect it against the fence, but that I'd never see it again in the air. But running on Mars is so weird. You get going too fast and then you're pinwheeling along trying to keep from doing a face-plant. That's what I was doing when I saw the warning track, and looked back up and spotted the ball coming down, so I jumped, trying to jump straight up, you know, but I had a lot of momentum, and had completely forgotten about the gravity, so I shot up and caught the ball, amazing, but found myself *flying right over the fence.*

I came down and rolled in the dust and sand, and the ball stayed stuck in my glove. I hopped back over the fence holding the ball up to show everyone I had it. But they gave the other pitcher a home run anyway, because you have to stay inside the park when you catch one, it's a local rule. I didn't care. The whole point of playing games is to make you do things like that anyway. And it was good that that pitcher got one too.

So we started up again and Gregor struck out the side, and we won the tournament. We were mobbed, Gregor especially. He was the hero of the hour. Everyone wanted him to sign something. He didn't say much, but he wasn't stooping either. He looked surprised. Afterwards Werner took two balls and everyone signed them, to make kind-of trophies for Gregor and me. Later I saw half the names on my trophy were jokes, "Mickey Mantle" and other names like that. Gregor had written on it "Hi Coach Arthur, Regards Greg." I have the ball still, on my desk at home.

THE BLIND GEOMETER

When you are born blind, your development is different from that of sighted infants. (I was born blind. I know.) The reasons for this difference are fairly obvious. Much normal early infant development, both physical and mental, is linked to vision, which coordinates all sense and action. Without vision, reality is… (it's hard to describe) a sort of void, in which transitory things come to existence when grasped and mouthed and heard; then, when the things fall silent or are dropped, they melt away, they *cease to exist*. (I wonder if I have not kept a bit of that feeling with me always.) It can be shown that this sense of object permanence must be learned by sighted infants as well—move a toy behind a screen, and very young babies will assume the toy has ceased to exist—but vision (seeing part of a toy [or a person] behind the screen) makes their construction of a sense of object permanence fairly rapid and easy. With the blind child, it is a much harder task; it takes months, sometimes years. And with no sense of an object world, there can be no complementary concept of *self;* without this concept, all phenomena can be experienced as part of an extended "body." (Haptic space [or tactile space, the space of the body] expanding to fill visual space…) Every blind infant is in danger of autism.

> But we also have, and know that we have, the capacity of complete freedom to transform, in thought and phantasy, our human historical existence…
>
> Edmund Husserl, *The Origin of Geometry*

My first memories are of the Christmas morning when I was some three and a half years old, when one of my gifts was a bag of marbles. I was fascinated by the way the handfuls of marbles felt: heavy, glassy spheres, all so smooth and clickety, all so much the same… I was equally impressed by the leather bag that had contained them. It was so pliable, had such a baggy shape, could be drawn up by such a leathery drawstring. (I must tell you, from the viewpoint of tactual aesthetics, there is nothing quite so beautiful as well-oiled leather. My favorite toy was my father's boot.) Anyway, I was rolling on my belly over the marbles spread on the floor (more contact) when I came against the Christmas tree, all prickly and piney. Reaching up to break off some needles to rub between my fingers, I touched an ornament that felt to me, in my excitement, like a lost marble. I yanked on it (and on the branch, no doubt) and—down came the tree.

The alarum afterward is only a blur in my memory, as if it all were on tape, and parts of it forever fast-forwarded to squeaks and trills. Little unspliced snippets of tape: my memory. (My story.)

How often have I searched for snippets before that one, from the long years of my coming to consciousness? How did I first discover the world beyond my body, beyond my searching hands? It was one of my greatest intellectual feats—perhaps the greatest—and yet it is lost to me.

So I read, and learn how other blind infants have accomplished the task. My own life, known to me through words—the world become a text—this happens to me all the time. It is what T. D. Cutsforth called entering the world of "verbal unreality," and it is part of the fate of the curious blind person.

I never did like Jeremy Blasingame. He was a colleague for a few years, and his office was six doors down from mine. It seemed to me that he was one of those people who are fundamentally uncomfortable around the blind; and it's always the blind person's job to put these people at their ease, which gets to be a pain in the ass. (In fact, I usually ignore the problem.) Jeremy always watched me closely (you can tell this by voice), and it was clear that he found it hard to believe that I was one of the co-editors of *Topological Geometry*, a journal he submitted to occasionally. But he was a good mathematician and a fair topologist, and we published most of his submissions, so that he and I remained superficially friendly.

Still, he was always probing, always picking my brains. At this time I was working hard on the geometry of n-dimensional manifolds, and some of the latest results from CERN and SLAC and the big new cyclotron on Oahu were fitting into the work in an interesting way: It appeared that certain subatomic particles were moving as if in a multidimensional manifold, and I had Sullivan and Wu and some of the other physicists from these places asking me questions. With them I was happy to talk, but with Jeremy I couldn't see the point. Certain speculations I once made in conversation with him later showed up in one of his papers, and it just seemed to me that he was looking for help without actually saying so.

And there was the matter of his image. In the sun I perceived him as a shifting, flecked brightness. It's unusual I can see people at all, and as I couldn't really account for this (was it vision, or something else?) it made me uncomfortable.

But no doubt in retrospect I have somewhat exaggerated this uneasiness.

The first event of my life that I recall that has any emotion attached to it (the earlier ones being mere snips of tape that could have come from anyone's life, given how much feeling is associated with them) comes from my eighth year, and has to do, emblematically enough, with math. I was adding columns with my Braille punch, and, excited at my new power, I took the bumpy sheet of figures to show my father. He puzzled over it for a while. "Hmm," he said. "Here, you have to make very sure that the columns are in straight, vertical rows." His long fingers guided mine down a column. "Twenty-two is off to the left, feel that? You have to keep them all straight."

Impatiently I pulled my hand away, and the flood of frustration began its tidal wash through me (most familiar of sensations, felt scores of times a day); my voice tightened to a high whine: "But *why?* It doesn't *matter*—"

"Yeah it does." My father wasn't one for unnecessary neatness, as I already knew well from tripping over his misplaced briefcase, ice skates, shoes... "Let's see." He had my fingers again. "You know how numbers work. Here's twenty-two. Now what that means is two twos and two tens. This two marks the twenty, this two marks the two, even though they're both just two characters, right? Well, when you're adding, the column to the far right is the column of ones. Next over is the column of tens, and next over is the column of hundreds. Here you've got three hundreds, right? Now if you have the twenty-two over to the left too far, you'll add the twenty in the hundreds column, as if the number were two hundred twenty rather than twenty-two. And that'll be wrong. So you have to keep the columns really straight—"

Understanding, ringing me as if I were a big old church bell, and it the clapper. It's the first time I remember feeling that sensation that has remained one of the enduring joys of my life: *to understand.*

And understanding mathematical concepts quickly led to power (and how I craved that!), power not only in the abstract world of math, but in the real world of father and school. I remember jumping up and down, my dad laughing cheerily, me dashing to my room to stamp out columns as straight as the ruler's edge, to add column after column of figures.

Oh, yes: Carlos Oleg Nevsky, here. Mother Mexican, father Russian (military advisor). Born in Mexico City in 2018, three months premature, after my mother suffered a bout of German measles during the pregnancy. Result: almost total blindness (I can tell dark from [bright] light). Lived in Mexico City until father was transferred to Russian embassy in Washington, D.C., when I was five. Lived in Washington almost continuously since then; my parents divorced when I was fifteen. Mathematics professor at George Washington University since 2043.

One cold spring afternoon I encountered Jeremy Blasingame in the faculty lounge as I went to get a coffee refill—in the lounge, where nobody ever hangs out. "Hello, Carlos, how's it going?"

"Fine," I said, reaching about the table for the sugar. "And you?"

"Pretty good. I've got a kind of an interesting problem over at my consulting job, though. It's giving me fits."

Jeremy worked for the Pentagon in military intelligence or something, but he seldom talked about what he did there, and I certainly never asked. "Oh, yes?" I said, as I found the sugar and spooned some in.

"Yes. They've got a coding problem that I bet would interest you."

"I'm not much for cryptography." Spy games—the math involved is really very specific. Sweet smell of sugar, dissolving in the lounge's bad coffee.

"Yes, I know," Jeremy said. "But"—an edge of frustration in his voice; it's hard to tell when I'm paying attention, I know (a form of control)—"but this may be a geometer's code. We have a subject, you see, drawing diagrams."

A *subject*. "Hmph," I said. Some poor spy scribbling away in a cell somewhere…

"So—I've got one of the drawings here. It reminds me of the theorem in your last article. Some projection, perhaps."

"Yes?" Now what spy would draw something like that?

"Yeah, and it seems to have something to do with her speech, too. Her verbal sequencing is all dislocated—words in strange order, sometimes."

"Yes? What happened to her?"

"Well… here, check out the drawing."

I put out a hand. "I'll take a look."

"And next time you want coffee, come ask me. I do a proper job of it in my office."

"All right."

I suppose I have wondered all my life what it would be like to see. And all my work, no doubt, is an effort to envision things in the inward theater. "I see it *feelingly*." In language, in music, most of all in the laws of geometry, I find the best ways I can to see: by analogy to touch, and to sound, and to abstractions. Understand: To know the geometries fully is to comprehend exactly the physical world that light reveals; in a way one is then perceiving something like the Platonic ideal forms underlying the visible phenomena of the world. Sometimes the great ringing of comprehension fills me so entirely that I feel I *must* be seeing; what more could it be? I believe that I see.

Then comes the problem of crossing the street, of finding my misplaced keys. Geometry is little help; it's back to the hands and ears as eyes, at that point. And then I know that I do not see at all.

Let me put it another way. Projective geometry began in the Renaissance, as an aid to painters newly interested in perspective, in the problems of representing the three-dimensional world on a canvas; it quickly became a mathematics of great power and elegance. The basic procedure can be described quickly: When a geometrical figure is *projected* from one plane to another (as light, they tell me, projects the image on a slide onto a wall), certain properties of the figure are changed (lengths of sides, measures of angles), while other properties are not—points are still points, lines lines, and certain proportions still hold, among other things.

Now imagine that the visual world is a geometrical figure, which in a way it is. But then imagine that it has been projected inward onto something different, not onto a plane, but onto a Möbius strip or a Klein bottle, say, or onto a manifold actually much more complex and strange than those (you'd be surprised). Certain features of the figure are gone for good (color, for instance), but other essential features remain. And projective geometry is the art of finding what features or qualities survive the transformations of projection...

Do you understand me?

A geometry for the self—non-Euclidean, of course; in fact, strictly Nevskyan, as it has to be to help me, as I make my projections from visual space to auditive space, to haptic space.

The next time I met Blasingame he was anxious to hear what I thought of his diagram. (There could be an acoustics of emotion—thus a mathematics of emotion; meanwhile, the ears of the blind do these calculations every day.)

"One drawing isn't much to go on, Jeremy. I mean, you're right, it looks like a simple projective drawing, but with some odd lines crossing it. Who knows what they mean? The whole thing might be something scribbled by a kid."

"She's not that young. Want to see more?"

"Well…" This woman he kept mentioning, some sort of Mata Hari prisoner in the Pentagon, drawing geometrical figures and refusing to speak except in riddles… naturally I was intrigued.

"Here, take these anyway. There seems to be a sort of progression."

"It would help if I could talk to this *subject* who's doing all these."

"Actually, I don't think so… but"—seeing my irritation—"I can bring her by, I think, if these interest you."

"I'll check them out."

"Good, good." Peculiar edge of excitement in his voice, tension, anticipation of… Frowning, I took the papers from him.

That afternoon I shuffled them into my special Xerox machine, and the stiff reproductions rolled out of it heavily ridged. I ran my hands over the raised lines and letters slowly.

Here I must confess to you that most geometrical drawings are almost useless to me. If you consider it, you will quickly see why: Most drawings are two-dimensional representations of what a three-dimensional construction *looks* like. This does me no good and in fact is extremely confusing. Say I feel a trapezoid on the page; is that meant to be a trapezoid, or is it rather a representation of a rectangle not coterminous with the page it lies on? Or the conventional representation of a plane? Only a *description* of the drawing will tell me that. Without a description I can only deduce what the figure *appears* to mean. Much easier to have 3-D models to explore with my hands.

But in this case, not possible. So I swept over the mishmash of ridges with both hands, redrew it with my ridging pen several times over, located the two triangles in it, and the lines connecting the two triangles' corners, and the lines made by extending the triangles' sides in one direction. I tried to make from my Taylor collection a 3-D model that accounted for the drawing—try that sometime, and understand how difficult this kind of intellectual feat can be! Projective imagination…

Certainly it seemed to be a rough sketch of Desargues' theorem.

Desargues' theorem was one of the first theorems clearly concerned with projective geometry; it was proposed by Girard Desargues in the mid-seventeenth century, in between his architectural and engineering efforts, his books on music, etc. It is a relatively simple theorem, showing that two triangles that are projections of each other generate a group of points off to one side that lie on a single line. Its chief interest is in showing the kind of elegant connections that projection so often creates.

(It is also true that this theorem is reciprocal; that is, if you postulate two triangles whose extensions of the sides meet at three collinear points, then it is possible to show that the triangles are projections of each other. As they say in the textbooks, I leave the proof of this as an exercise for the reader.)

But so what? I mean, it is a beautiful theorem, with the sort of purity characteristic of Renaissance math—but what was it doing in a drawing made by some poor prisoner of the Pentagon?

I considered this as I walked to my health club, Warren's Spa (considered it secondarily, anyway, and no doubt subconsciously; my primary concerns were the streets and the traffic. Washington's streets bear a certain resemblance to one of those confusing geometrical diagrams I described [the state streets crossing diagonally the regular gridwork, creating a variety of intersections]; happily, one doesn't have to comprehend all the city at once to walk in it. But it is easy to become lost. So as I walked I concentrated on distances, on the sounds of the streets that tended to remain constant, on smells [the dirt of the park at M and New Hampshire, the hot dog vendor on 21st and K]; meanwhile, my cane established the world directly before my feet, my sonar shades whistled rising or falling notes as objects approached or receded... It takes some work just to get from point A to point B without getting disoriented [at which point one has to grind one's teeth and ask for directions] but it can be done, it is one of those small tasks/accomplishments [one chooses which, every time] that the blind cannot escape)—still, I did consider the matter of the drawing as I walked.

On 21st and H, I was pleased to smell the pretzel cart of my friend Ramon, who is also blind. His cart is the only one where the hot plate hasn't roasted several pretzels to that metallic burnt odor that all the other carts put off; Ramon prefers the clean smell of freshly baked dough, and he claims it brings him more customers, which I certainly believe. "Change only, please," he was saying to someone briskly, "there's a change machine on the other side of the cart for your convenience, thanks. Hot pretzels! Hot pretzels, one dollar!"

"Hey there, Superblink!" I called as I approached him.

"Hey yourself, Professor Superblink," he replied. (*Superblink* is a mildly derogatory name used by irritated sighted social service people to describe those of their blind colleagues who are aggressively or ostentatiously competent in getting around, etc., who make a *display* of their competence. Naturally, we have appropriated the term for our own use; sometimes it means the same thing for us—when used in the third person, usually—but in the second person, it's a term of affection.) "Want a pretzel?"

"Sure."

"You off to the gym?"

"Yeah, I'm going to throw. Next time we play you're in trouble."

"That'll be the day, when my main mark starts beating me!"

I put four quarters in his callused hand, and he gave me a pretzel. "Here's a puzzle for you," I said. "Why would someone try to convey a message by geometrical diagram?"

He laughed. "Don't ask me, that's your department!"

"But the message isn't for me."

"Are you sure about that?"

I frowned.

At the health club I greeted Warren and Amanda at the front desk. They were laughing over a headline in the tabloid newspaper Amanda was shaking; they devoured those things and pasted the best headlines all over the gym.

"What's the gem of the day?" I asked.

"How about 'Gay Bigfoot Molests Young Boys'?" Warren suggested.

"Or 'Woman Found Guilty of Turning Husband into Bank President,'" Amanda said, giggling. "She drugged him and did 'bemod' to him until he went from teller to president."

Warren said, "I'll have to do that for you, eh, Amanda?"

"Make me something better than a bank president."

Warren clicked his tongue. "Entirely too many designer drugs, these days. Come on, Carlos, I'll get the range turned on." I went to the locker room and changed, and when I got to the target room Warren was just done setting it up. "Ready to go," he said cheerily as he rolled past me.

I stepped in, closed the door, and walked out to the center of the room, where a waist-high wire column was filled with baseballs. I pulled out a baseball, hefted it, felt the stitching. A baseball is a beautiful object: nicely flared curves of the seams over the surface of a perfect sphere, exactly the right weight for throwing.

I turned on the range with a flick of a switch and stepped away from the feeder, a ball in each hand. Now it was quite silent, only the slightest whirr faintly breathing through the soundproofed walls. I did what I could to reduce the sound of my own breathing, heard my heartbeat in my ears.

Then a *beep* behind me to my left, and low; I whirled and threw. Dull thud. "Right… low," said the machine voice from above, softly. *Beep*—I threw again: "Right… high," it said louder, meaning I had missed by more. "Shit," I said as I got another two balls. "Bad start."

Beep—a hard throw to my left—*clang!* "Yeah!" There is very little in life more satisfying than the bell-like clanging of the target circle when hit square. It rings at about middle C with several overtones, like a small, thick church bell hit with a hammer. The sound of success.

Seven more throws, four more hits. "Five for ten," the machine voice said. "Average strike time, one point three five seconds. Fastest strike time, point eight four seconds."

Ramon sometimes hit the target in half a second or less, but I needed to hear the full beep to keep my average up. I set up for another round, pushed the button, got quiet; *beep* throw, *beep* throw, working to shift my feet faster, to follow through, to use the information from my misses to correct for the next time the target was near the floor, or the ceiling, or behind me (my weakness is the low ones; I can't seem to throw down accurately). And as I warmed up I threw harder and harder... just throwing a baseball as hard as you can is a joy in itself. And then to set that bell ringing! *Clang!* It chimes every cell of you.

But when I quit and took a shower, and stood before my locker and reached in to free my shirt from a snag on the top of the door, my fingers brushed a small metal wire stuck to an upper inside corner, where the door would usually conceal it from both me and my sighted companions; it came away when I pulled on it. Fingering the short length I couldn't be certain what it was, but I had my suspicions, so I took it to my friend James Gold, who works in acoustics in the engineering department, and had him take a confidential look at it.

"It's a little remote microphone, all right," he said, and then joked, "Who's bugging you, Carlos?"

He got serious when I asked him where I could get a system like that for myself.

> John Metcalf—"Blind Jack of Knaresborough"—(1717–1810).
> At six he lost his sight through smallpox, at nine he could get on pretty well unaided, at fourteen he announced his intention of disregarding his affliction thenceforward and of behaving in every respect as a normal human being. It is true that immediately on this brave resolve he fell into a gravel pit and received a serious hurt while escaping, under pursuit, from an orchard he was robbing... fortunately this did not affect his self-reliance. At twenty he had made a reputation as a pugilist. (!)
>
> Ernest Bramah, Introduction,
> *The Eyes of Max Carrados*

When I was young I loved to read Bramah's stories about Max Carrados, the blind detective. Carrados could hear, smell, and feel with incredible sensitivity, and his ingenious deductions were never short of brilliant; he was fearless in a pinch; also, he was rich and had a mansion, and a secretary, manservant, and chauffeur who acted as his eyes. All great stuff for the imaginative young reader, as certainly I was. I read every book I could get my hands on; the voice of my reading machine was more familiar to me than any human voice that I knew. Between that reading and my mathematical work, I could have easily withdrawn from the world of my own experience into Cutsforth's "verbal unreality," and babbled on like Helen Keller about the shapes of clouds and the colors of flowers and the like. The world become nothing but a series of texts; sounds kind of like deconstructionism, doesn't it? And of course at an older age I was enamored of the deconstructionists of the last century. The world as text: Husserl's *The Origin of Geometry* is twenty-two pages long, Derrida's *Introduction to the Origin of Geometry* is 153 pages long; you can see why it would have appealed to me. If, as the deconstructionists seemed to say, the world is nothing but a collection of texts, and I can read, then I am not missing anything by being blind, am I?

The young can be very stubborn, very stupid.

"All right, Jeremy," I said. "Let me meet this mysterious *subject* of yours who draws all this stuff."

"You want to?" he said, trying to conceal his excitement.

"Sure," I replied. "I'm not going to find out any more about all this until I do." My own subtext, yes; but I am better at hiding such things than Jeremy is.

"What have you found out? Do the diagrams mean anything to you?"

"Not much. You know me, Jeremy, drawings are my weakness. I'd rather have her do it in models, or writing, or verbally. You'll have to bring her by if you want me to continue."

"Well, okay. I'll see what I can do. She's not much help, though. You'll find out." But he was pleased.

One time in high school I was walking out of the gym after P.E., and I heard one of my coaches (one of the best teachers I have ever had) in his office, speaking to someone (he must have had his back to me)—he said, "You know, it's not the physical handicaps that will be the problem for most of these kids. It's the emotional problems that tend to come with the handicaps that will be the real burden."

I was in my office listening to my reading machine. Its flat, uninflected mechanical voice (almost unintelligible to some of my colleagues) had over the years become a sort of helpless, stupid friend. I called it George, and was always programming into it another pronunciation rule to try to aid its poor speech, but to no avail; George always found new ways to butcher the language. I put the book facedown on the glass; "Finding first line," croaked George, as the scanner inside the machine thumped around. Then it read from Roberto Torretti, quoting and discussing Ernst Mach. (Hear this spoken in the most stilted, awkward, syllable-by-syllable mispronunciation that you can imagine.)

"'Our notions of space are rooted in our *physiological* constitution'" (George raises his voice in pitch to indicate italics, which also slow him down considerably). "'Geometric concepts are the product of the idealization of *physical* experiences of space.' Physiological space is quite different from the infinite, isotropic, metric space of classical geometry and physics. It can, at most, be structured as a topological space. When viewed in this way, it naturally falls into several components: visual or optic space, tactile or haptic space, auditive space, etc. Optic space is anisotropic, finite, limited. Haptic space or 'the space of our skin corresponds to a two-dimensional, finite, unlimited (closed) Riemannian space.' This is nonsense, for R-spaces are metric, while haptic space is not. I take it that Mach means to say that the latter can naturally be regarded as a two-dimensional compact connected topological space. Mach does not emphasize enough the disconnectedness of haptic from optic space—"

There came four quick knocks at my door. I pressed the button on George that stopped him and said, "Come in!"

The door opened. "Carlos!"

"Jeremy," I said. "How are you?"

"Fine. I've brought Mary Unser with me—you know, the one who drew—"

I stood, feeling/hearing the presence of the other in the room. And there are times (like this one) when you *know* the other is in some odd, undefinable way, *different*, or... (Our language is not made for the experience of the blind.) "I'm glad to meet you."

I have said that I can tell dark from light, and I can, though it is seldom very useful information. In this case, however, I was startled to have my attention drawn to my "sight"—for this woman was darker than other people, she was a sort of bundle of darkness in the room, her face distinctly lighter than the rest of her (or was that her face, exactly?).

A long pause. Then: "On border stand we *n*-dimensional space the," she said. Coming just after George's reading, I was struck by a certain similarity: the mechanical lilt from word to word; the basic incomprehension of a reading machine... Goose bumps rose on my forearms.

Her voice itself, on the other hand, had George beat hands down. Fundamentally vibrant under the odd intonation, it was a voice with a very thick timbre, a bassoon or a hurdy-gurdy of a voice, with the buzz of someone who habitually speaks partly through the sinuses; this combined with over-relaxed vocal cords, what speech pathologists call *glottal fry*. Usually nasal voices are not pleasant, but pitch them low enough…

She spoke again, more slowly (definitely glottal fry): "We stand on the border of *n*-dimensional space."

"Hey," Jeremy said. "Pretty good!" He explained: "Her word order isn't usually as… ordinary as that."

"So I gathered," I said. "Mary, what do you mean by that?"

"I—oh—" A kazoo squeak of distress, pain. I approached her, put out a hand. She took it as if to shake: a hand about the size of mine, narrow, strong fat muscle at base of thumb; trembling distinctly.

"I work on the geometries of topologically complex spaces," I said. "I am more likely than most to understand what you say."

"Are within never see we points us."

"That's true." But there was something wrong here, something I didn't like, though I couldn't tell exactly what it was. Had she spoken toward Jeremy? Speaking to me while she looked at him? Bundle of darkness in the dark… "But why are your sentences so disordered, Mary? Your words don't come out in the order you thought them. You must know that, since you understand us."

"Folded—*oh!*—" Again the double-reed squeak, and suddenly she was weeping, trembling hard; we sat her down on my visitor's couch, and Jeremy got her a glass of water while she quaked in my hands. I stroked her hair (short, loosely curled, wild) and took the opportunity for a quick phrenological check: skull regular and, as far as I could tell, undamaged; temples wide, distinct; same for eye sockets; nose a fairly ordinary pyramidal segment, no bridge to speak of; narrow cheeks, wet with tears. She reached up and took my right hand, squeezed it hard, three times fast, three times slow, all the time sobbing and sort of hiccupping words: "Pain it, station. I, oh, fold end, bright, light, space fold, oh, ohhh…"

Well, the direct question is not always the best way. Jeremy returned with a glass of water, and drinking some seemed to calm her. Jeremy said, "Perhaps we could try again later. Although…" He didn't seem very surprised.

"Sure," I said. "Listen, Mary, I'll talk to you again when you're feeling better."

After Jeremy got her out of the office and disposed of her (how? with whom?) he returned to the seventh floor.

"So what the hell happened to her?" I asked angrily. "Why is she like that?"

"We aren't completely sure," he said slowly. "Here's why. She was one of the scientists staffing Tsiolkovsky Base Five, up in the mountains on the back side of the moon, you know. She's an astronomer and cosmologist. Well—I have to ask you to keep this quiet—one day Base Five stopped all broadcasting, and when they went over to see what was wrong, they found only her, alone in the station in a sort of catatonic state. No sign of the other scientists or station crew—eighteen people gone without a trace. And nothing much different to explain what had happened, either."

I *hmphed*. "What do they think happened?"

"They're still not sure. Apparently, no one else was in the area, or could have been, et cetera. It's been suggested by the Russians, who had ten people there, that this could be first contact—you know, that aliens took the missing ones, and somehow disarranged Mary's thought processes, leaving her behind as a messenger that isn't working. Her brain scans are bizarre. I mean, it doesn't sound very likely…"

"No."

"But it's the only theory that explains everything they found there. Some of which they won't tell me about. So, we're doing what we can to get Mary's testimony, but as you can see, it's hard. She seems most comfortable drawing diagrams."

"Next time we'll start with that."

"Okay. Any other ideas?"

"No," I lied. "When can you bring her back again?"

As if because I was blind I couldn't tell I was being duped! I struck fist into palm angrily. Oh, they were making a mistake, all right. They didn't know how much the voice reveals. The voice's secret expressivity reveals *so much!*—the language really is not adequate to tell it; we need that mathematics of emotion… In the high school for the blind that I briefly attended for some of my classes, it often happened that a new teacher was instantly disliked, for some falseness in his or her voice, some quality of condescension or pity or self-congratulation that the teacher (and his or her superiors) thought completely concealed, if they knew of it at all. But it was entirely obvious to the students, because the voice (if what I have heard is true) is much more revealing than facial expressions; certainly it is less under our control. This is what makes most acting performances so unsatisfactory to me; the vocal qualities are so stylized, so removed from those of real life…

And here, I thought, I was witnessing a performance.

There is a moment in Olivier Messiaen's *Visions de l'Amen* when one piano is playing a progression of major chords, very traditionally harmonic, while on another piano high pairs of notes plonk down across the other's chords, ruining their harmony, crying out, Something's wrong! Something's wrong!

I sat at my desk and swayed side to side, living just such a moment. Something was wrong.

When I collected myself I called the department secretary, who had a view of the hall to the elevator. "Delphina, did Jeremy just leave?"

"Yes, Carlos. Do you want me to try and catch him?"

"No, I only need a book he left in his office. Can I borrow the master key and get it?"

"Okay."

I got the key, entered Jeremy's office, closed the door. One of the tiny pickups that James Gold had gotten for me fit right under the snap-in plug of the telephone cord. Then a microphone under the desk, behind a drawer. And out. (I have to be bold every day, you see, just to get by. But they didn't know that.)

Back in my office I closed and locked the door, and began to search. My office is big: two couches, several tall bookcases, my desk, a file cabinet, a coffee table…. When the partitions on the seventh floor of the Gelman Library were moved around to make more room, Delphina and George Hampton, who was chairman that year, had approached me nervously: "Carlos, you wouldn't mind an office with no windows, would you?"

I laughed. All of the full professors had offices on the outer perimeter of the floor, with windows.

"You see," George said, "since none of the windows in the building opens anyway, you won't be missing out on any breezes. And if you take this room in the inner core of the building, then we'll have enough space for a good faculty lounge."

"Fine," I said, not mentioning that I could see sunlight, distinguish light and dark. It made me angry that they hadn't remembered that, hadn't thought to ask. So I nicknamed my office "The Vault," and I had a lot of room, but no windows. The halls had no windows either, so I was really without sun, but I didn't complain.

Now I got down on hands and knees and continued searching, feeling like it was hopeless. But I found one, on the bottom of the couch. And there was another in the phone. Bugged. I left them in position and went home.

Home was a small top-floor apartment up near 21st and N streets, and I supposed it was bugged too. I turned up Stockhausen's *Telemusik* as loud as I could stand it, hoping to drive my listeners into a suicidal fugal state, or at least give them a headache. Then I slapped together a sandwich, downed it angrily.

I imagined I was captain of a naval sailing ship (like Horatio Hornblower), and that because of my sharp awareness of the wind I was the best captain afloat. They had had to evacuate the city and all the people I knew were aboard depending on me. But we were caught against a lee shore by two large ships of the line, and in the ensuing broadsides (roar of cannon, smell of gunpowder and blood, screams of wounded like shrieking seagulls), everyone I knew fell—chopped in half, speared by giant splinters, heads removed by cannonball, you name it. Then when they were all corpses on the sand-strewn splintered decking, I felt a final broadside discharge, every ball converging on me as if I were point 0 at the tip of a cone. Instant dissolution and death.

I came out of it feeling faintly disgusted with myself. But because it actively defends the ego by eradicating those who attack its self-esteem, Cutsforth calls this type of fantasy in the blind subject healthy. (At least in fourteen-year-olds.) So be it. Here's to health. Fuck all of you.

Geometry is a language, with a vocabulary and syntax as clear and precise as humans can make them. In many cases definitions of terms and operations are explicitly spelled out, to help achieve this clarity. For instance, one could say:

Let (parentheses) designate corollaries.
Let [brackets] designate causes.
Let {braces} designate…
But would it be true, in this other language of the heart?

Next afternoon I played beepball with my team. Sun hot on my face and arms, spring smell of pollen and wet grass. Ramon got six runs in the at-bat before mine (beepball is a sort of cricket/softball mix, played with softball equipment ["It proves you can play cricket blind" one Anglophobe {she was Irish} said to me once]), and when I got up I scratched out two and then struck out. Swinging *too* hard. I decided I liked outfield better. The beepball off in the distance, lofted up in a short arc, smack of bat, follow the ball up and up—out toward me!—drift in its direction, the rush of fear, glove before face as it approaches, stab for it, off after it as it rolls by—pick it up—Ramon's voice calling clearly, "Right here! Right here!"—and letting loose with a throw—really putting everything into it—and then, sometimes, hearing that beepball lance off into the distance and smack into Ramon's glove. It was great. Nothing like outfield.

And next inning I hit one *hard*, and that's great too. That feeling goes right up your arms and all through you.

Walking home I brooded over Max Carrados, blind detective, and over Horatio Hornblower, sighted naval captain. Over Thomas Gore, the blind senator from Oklahoma. As a boy his fantasy was to become a senator. He read the *Congressional Record*, joined the debate team, organized his whole life around the project. And he became senator. I knew that sort of fantasy as well as I knew the vengeful adolescent daydreams: All through my youth I dreamed of being a mathematician. And here I was. So one could do it. One could imagine doing something, and then do it.

But that meant that one had, by definition, imagined something *possible*. And one couldn't always say ahead of the attempt whether one had imagined the possible or the impossible. And even if one had imagined something possible, that didn't guarantee a successful execution of the plan.

The team we had played was called *Helen Keller Jokes* (there are some good ones, too [they come {of course} from Australia] but I won't go into that). It's sad that such an intelligent woman was so miseducated—not so much by Sullivan as by her whole era: all that treacly Victorian sentimentality poured into her: "The fishing villages of Cornwall are very picturesque, seen either from the beaches or the hilltops, with all their boats riding to their moorings or sailing about in the harbor. When the moon, large and serene, floats up the sky, leaving in the water a long track of brightness like a plow breaking up a soil of silver, I can only sigh my ecstasy"—come on, Helen. Now *that* is living in a world of texts.

But didn't I live most (all?) of my life in texts as least as unreal to me as moonlight on water was to Helen Keller? These n-dimensional manifolds… I suppose the basis for my abilities in them was the lived reality of haptic space, but still, it was many removes from my actual experience. And so was the situation I found myself confronted with now, Jeremy and Mary acting out some drama I did not comprehend… and so was my plan to deal with it. Verbalism… words versus reality.

I caressed my glove, refelt the knock of bat against beepball. Brooded over my plan.

The next time Jeremy brought Mary Unser by my office, I said very little. I got out my "visitor's supply" of paper and pencils and set her down at the coffee table. I brought over my models: subatomic particles breaking up in a spray of wire lines, like water out of a showerhead; strawlike Taylor sticks for model making; polyhedric blocks of every kind. And I sat down with the ridged sheets made from her earlier drawings, as well as the models I had attempted to make of them, and I started asking very limited questions. "What does this line mean? Does it go before or behind? Is this R or R *prime*? Have I got this right?"

And she would honk a sort of laugh, or say, "No, no, no, no" (no problem with sequencing there), and draw furiously. I took the pages as she finished them and put them in my Xerox, took out the ridged, bumpy sheets and had her guide my fingers over them. Even so they were difficult, and with a squeak of frustration she went to the straw models, clicking together triangles, parallels, etc. This was easier, but eventually she reached a limit here too. "Need drawing beyond," she said.

"Fine. Write down whatever you want."

She wrote and then read aloud to me, or I put it through the Xerox machine marked *translation to Braille*. And we forged on, with Jeremy looking over our shoulders the whole time.

And eventually we came very close to the edge of my work, following subatomic particles down into the microdimensions where they appeared to make their "jumps." I had proposed an n-dimensional topological manifold, where $1 < n <$ infinity, so that the continuum being mapped fluctuated between one and some finite number of dimensions, going from a curving line to a sort of n-dimensional Swiss cheese, if you like, depending on the amounts of energy displayed in the area, in any of the four "forms" of electromagnetism, gravity, or the strong and weak interactions. The geometry for this manifold-pattern (so close to the experience of haptic space) had, as I have said, attracted the attention of physicists at CERN and SLAC—but there were still unexplained data, as far as I could tell, and the truth was, *I had not published this work.*

So here I was "conversing" with a young woman who in ordinary conversations could not order her words correctly—who in this realm spoke with perfect coherence—who was in fact speaking about (inquiring about?) the edges of my own private work.

The kind of work that Jeremy Blasingame used to ask me about so curiously.

I sighed. We had been going on for two or three hours, and I sat back on the couch. My hand was taken up in Mary's, given a reassuring squeeze. I didn't know what to make of it. "I'm tired."

"I feel better," she said. "Easier to talk way—this way."

"Ah," I said. I took up the model of a positron hitting a "stationary" muon: a wire tree, trunk suddenly bursting into a mass of curling branches. So it was here: one set of events, a whole scattering of explanations. Still, the bulk of the particles shot out in a single general direction (the truths of haptic space).

She let go of my hand to make one last diagram. Then she Xeroxed it for me, and guided my hands over the ridged copy.

Once again it was Desargues' theorem.

At this point Mary said, "Mr. Blasingame, I need a drink of water." He went out to the hall water dispenser, and she quickly took my forefinger between her finger and thumb (pads flattening with an inappropriate pressure, until my finger ached)—squeezed twice, and jabbed my finger first onto her leg, then onto the diagram, tracing out one of the triangles. She repeated the movements, then poked my leg and traced out the other triangle. Then she traced down the line off to the side, the one generated by the projection of the two triangles, over and over. What did she mean?

Jeremy returned, and she let my hand go. Then in a while, after the amenities (hard handshake, quivering hand), Jeremy whisked her off.

When he returned, I said, "Jeremy, is there any chance I can talk to her alone? I think she's made nervous by your presence—the associations, you know. She really does have an interesting perspective on the n-dimensional manifold, but she gets confused when she stops and interacts with you. I'd just like to take her for a walk, you know—down by the canal, or the Tidal Basin, perhaps, and talk things over with her. It might get the results you want."

"I'll see what they say," Jeremy said in an expressionless voice.

That night I put on a pair of earplugs and played the tape of Jeremy's phone conversations. In one when the phone was picked up he said, "He wants to talk with her alone now."

"Fine," said a tenor voice. "She's prepared for that."

"This weekend?"

"If he agrees." Click.

I listen to music. I listen to twentieth-century composers the most, because many of them made their music out of the sounds of the world we live in now, the world of jets and sirens and industrial machinery, as well as bird song and woodblock and the human voice. Messiaen, Partch, Reich, Glass, Shapiro, Subotnik, Ligeti, Penderecki—these first explorers away from the orchestra and the classical tradition remain for me the voices of our age; they speak to me. In fact, they speak for me; in their dissonance and confusion and anger I hear myself being expressed. And so I listen to their difficult, complex music because I understand it, which gives me pleasure, and because while doing so I am participating fully, I am excelling, no one can bring more to the act than I. I am *in control*.

I listened to music.

You see, these n-dimensional manifolds… if we understand them well enough to manipulate them, to tap their energy… well, there is a tremendous amount of energy contained in those particles. That kind of energy means power, and power… draws the powerful. Or those seeking power, fighting for it. I began to feel the extent of the danger.

She was quiet as we walked across the Mall toward the Lincoln Memorial. I think she would have stopped me if I had spoken about anything important. But I knew enough to say nothing, and I think she guessed I knew she was bugged. I held the back of her upper arm loosely in my left hand and let her guide us. A sunny, windy day, with occasional clouds obscuring the sun for a minute or two. Down by the Mall's lake the slightly stagnant smell of wet algae tinged all the other scents: grass, dust, the double strand of charcoal and cooking meat… The sink of darkness swirling around the Vietnam Memorial. Pigeons cooed their weird, larger-than-life coos and flapped away noisily as we walked through their affairs. We sat on grass that had been recently cut, and I brushed a hand over the stiff blades.

A curious procedure, this conversation. No visuals, for me; and perhaps we were being watched, as well. (Such a common anxiety of the blind, the fear of being watched—and here it was true.) And we couldn't talk freely, even though at the same time we had to say something, to keep Blasingame and friends from thinking I was aware of anything wrong. "Nice day." "Yeah, I'd love to be out on the water on a day like this." "Really?" "Yeah."

And all the while, two fingers held one finger. My hands are my eyes, and always have been. Now they were as expressive as voice, as receptive as ever touch can be, and into haptic space we projected a conversation of rare urgency. Are you okay? I'm okay. Do you know what's going on? Not entirely, can't explain.

"Let's walk down to the paddle boats and go out on the basin, then."

I said, "Your speech is much better today."

She squeezed my hand thrice, hard. False information? "I… had… electroshock." Her voice slid, slurred; it wasn't entirely under control.

"It seems to have helped."

"Yes. Sometimes."

"And the ordering of your mathematical thought?"

Buzzing laugh, hurdy-gurdy voice. "I don't know—more disarranged, perhaps—complementary procedure? You'll have to tell me."

"As a cosmologist did you work in this area?"

"The topology of the microdimensions apparently determines both gravity and the weak interaction, wouldn't you agree?"

"I couldn't say. I'm not much of a physicist."

Three squeezes again. "But you must have an idea or two about it?"

"Not really. You?"

"Perhaps… once. But it seems to me your work is directly concerned with it."

"Not that I know of."

Stalemate. Was that right? I was becoming more and more curious about this woman, whose signals to me were so mixed… Once again she seemed a bundling of darkness in the day, a whirlpool where all lightness disappeared, except for around her head. (I suppose I imagine all that I "see," I suppose they are always haptic visions.)

"Are you wearing dark clothes?"

"Not really. Red, beige…"

As we walked I held her arm more tightly. She was about my height. Her arm muscles were distinct, and her lats pushed out from her ribs. "You must swim."

"Weight lifting, I'm afraid. They made us on Luna."

"On Luna," I repeated.

"Yes," and she fell silent.

This was really impossible. I didn't think she was completely an ally—in fact I thought she was lying—but I felt an underlying sympathy from her, and a sense of conspiracy with her, that grew more powerful the longer we were together. The problem was, what did that feeling mean? Without the ability to converse freely, I was stymied in my attempts to learn more; pushed this way and that in the cross-currents of her behavior, I could only wonder what she was thinking. And what our listeners made of this mostly silent day in the sun.

So we paddled out onto the Tidal Basin and talked from time to time about the scene around us. I loved the feel of being on water—the gentle rocking over other boats' wakes, the wet stale smell. "Are the cherry trees blossoming still?"

"Oh, yes. Not quite at the peak, but just past. It's beautiful. Here"—she leaned out—"here's one about to drown." She put it in my hand. I sniffed at it. "Do they smell?"

"No, not much," I said. "The prettier people say flowers are, the less scent they seem to have. Did you ever notice that?"

"I guess. I like the scent of roses."

"It's faint, though. These blossoms must be very beautiful—they smell hardly at all."

"En masse they are lovely. I wish you could see them."

I shrugged. "And I wish you could touch their petals, or feel us bouncing about as I do. I have enough sense data to keep entertained."

"Yes… I suppose you do." She left her hand covering mine. "I suppose we're out quite a ways," I said. So that we couldn't be seen well from the shore, I meant.

"From the dock, anyway. We're actually almost across the basin."

I moved my hand from under hers and held her shoulder. Deep hollow behind her collarbone. This contact, this conversation of touch… it was most expressive hand to hand, and so I took her hand again, and our fingers made random entanglements, explorations. Children shouting, then laughing in boats to our left, voices charged with excitement. How to speak in this language of touch?

Well, we all know that. Fingertips, brushing lines of the palm; ruffling the fine hair at the back of the wrist; fingers pressing each other back: these are sentences, certainly. And it is a difficult language to lie in. That catlike, sensuous stretch, under my stroking fingertips…

"We've got a clear run ahead of us," she said after a time, voice charged with humming overtones.

"Stoke the furnaces," I cried. "Damn the torpedoes!" And with a gurgling *clug-clug-clug-clug* we paddle-wheeled over the basin into the fresh wet wind, sun on our faces, laughing at the release from tension (bassoon and baritone), crying out, "Mark Twain!" or "Snag dead ahead!" in jocular tones, entwined hands crushing the other as we pedaled harder and harder… "Down the Potomac!" "Across the sea!" "Through the gates of Hercules!" "On to the Golden Fleece!" Spray cold on the breeze—

She stopped pedaling, and we swerved left.

"We're almost back," she said quietly.

We let the boat drift in, without a word.

My bugs told me that my office had been broken into, by two, possibly three, people, only one of whom spoke—a man, in an undertone: "Try the file cabinet." The cabinet drawers were rolled out (familiar clicking of the runners over the ball bearings), and the desk drawers too, and then there was the sound of paper shuffling, of things being knocked about.

I also got an interesting phone conversation over Jeremy's phone. The call was incoming; Jeremy said, "Yes?" and a male voice—the same one Jeremy had called earlier—said, "She says he's unwilling to go into any detail."

"That doesn't surprise me," Jeremy said. "But I'm sure he's got—"

"Yes, I know. Go ahead and try what we discussed."

The break-in, I supposed.

"Okay." Click.

No doubt it never even occurred to them that I might turn the tables on them, or act against them in any way, or even figure out that something was strange. It made me furious.

At the same time I was frightened. You feel the lines of force, living in Washington, D.C.; feel the struggle for power among the shadowy groups surrounding the official government; read of the unsolved murders, of shadowy people whose jobs are not made clear… As a blind person, one feels apart from the nebulous world of intrigue and hidden force, on the edge by reason of disability. ("No one harms a blind man.") Now I knew I was part of it, pulled in and on my own. It was frightening.

One night I was immersed in Harry Partch's *Cloud Chamber Music*, floating in those big glassy notes, when my doorbell rang. I picked up the phone. "Hello?"

"It's Mary Unser. May I come up?"

"Sure." I pushed the button and walked onto the landing.

She came up the stairs alone. "Sorry to bother you at home," she buzzed, out of breath. Such a voice. "I looked up your address in the phone book. I'm not supposed…"

She stood before me, touched my right arm. I lifted my hand and held her elbow. "Yes?"

Nervous, resonant laugh. "I'm not supposed to be here."

Then you'll soon be in trouble, I wanted to say. But surely she knew my apartment would be bugged? Surely she *was* supposed to be here? She was trembling violently, enough so that I put up my other hand and held her by the shoulders. "Are you all right?"

"Yes. No." Falling oboe tones, laugh that was not a laugh… She seemed frightened, very frightened. I thought, if she is acting she is *very* good.

"Come on in," I said, and led her inside. I went to the stereo and turned down the Partch—then reconsidered, and turned it back up. "Have a seat—the couch is nice." I was nervous myself. "Would you like something to drink?" Quite suddenly it all seemed unreal, a dream, one of my fantasies. Phantasmagoric cloud chamber ringing to things, how did I know what was real?

"No. Or yes." She laughed again, that laugh that was not a laugh.

"I've got some beer." I went to the refrigerator, got a couple of bottles, opened them.

"So what's going on?" I said as I sat down beside her. As she spoke I drank from my beer, and she stopped from time to time to take long swallows.

"Well, I feel that the more I understand what you're saying about the transfer of energies between n-dimensional manifolds, the better I understand what… happened to me." But now there was a different sound to her voice—an overtone was gone, it was less resonant, less nasal.

I said, "I don't know what I can tell you. It's not something I can talk about, or even write down. What I can express, I have, you know. In papers." This a bit louder, for the benefit of our audience. (If there was one.)

"Well..." and her hand, under mine, began to tremble again.

We sat there for a very long time, and all during that time we conversed through those two hands, saying things I can scarcely recall now, because we have no language for that sort of thing. But they were important things nevertheless, and after a while I said, "Here. Come with me. I'm on the top floor, so I have a sort of porch on the roof. Finish your beer. It's a pleasant night out, you'll feel better outside." I led her through the kitchen to the pantry, where the door to the backstairs was. "Go on up." I went back to the stereo and put on Jarrett's *Köln Concert*, loud enough so we'd be able to hear it. Then I went up the stairs onto the roof, and crunched over the tarred gravel.

This was one of my favorite places. The sides of the building came up to the chest around the edge of the roof, and on two sides large willows draped their branches over it, making it a sort of haven. I had set a big old wreck of a couch out there, and on certain nights when the wind was up and the air was cool, I would lie back on it with a bumpy Braille planisphere in my hands, listening to Scholz's *Starcharts* and feeling that with those projections I knew what it was to see the night sky.

"This is nice," she said.

"Isn't it?" I pulled the plastic sheet from the couch, and we sat.

"Carlos?"

"Yes?"

"I—I—" that double-reed squeak.

I put an arm around her. "Please," I said, suddenly upset myself. "Not now. Not now. Just relax. Please." And she turned into me, her head rested on my shoulder; she trembled. I dug my fingers into her hair and slowly pulled them through the tangles. Shoulder length, no more. I cupped her ears, stroked her neck. She calmed.

Time passed, and I only caressed. No other thought, no other perception. How long this went on I couldn't say—perhaps a half-hour? Perhaps longer. She made a sort of purring kazoo sound, and I leaned forward and kissed her. Jarrett's voice, crying out briefly over a fluid run of piano notes. She pulled me to her; her breath caught, rushed out of her. The kiss became intense, tongues dancing together in a whole intercourse of their own, which I felt all through me in that *chakra* way, neck, spine, belly, groin, nothing but kiss. And without the slightest bit of either intention or resistance, I fell into it.

I remember a college friend once asked me, hesitantly, if I didn't have trouble with my love life. "Isn't it hard to tell when they... want to?" I had laughed. The whole process, I had wanted to say, was amazingly easy. The blinds' dependence on touch puts them in an advance position, so to speak: Using hands to see faces, being led by the hand (being dependent), one has already crossed what Russ calls the border between the world of not-sex and the world of sex; once over that border (with an other feeling protective)...

My hands explored her body, discovering it then and there for the first time—as intensely exciting a moment as there is, in the whole process. I suppose I expect narrow-cheeked people to be narrow hipped (it's mostly true, you'll find), but it wasn't so, in this case—her hips flared in those feminine curves that one can only hold, without ever getting used to (without ever [the otherness of the other] quite believing). On their own my fingers slipped under clothes, between buttons, as adroit as little mice, clever, lusty little creatures, unbuttoning blouse, reaching behind to undo bra with a twist. She shrugged out of them both and I felt the softness of her breasts while she tugged at my belt. I shifted, rolled, put my ear to her hard sternum, kissing the inside of one breast as it pressed against my face, feeling that quick heartbeat speak to me... She moved me back, got me unzipped, we paused for a speedy moment and got the rest of our clothes off, fumbling at our own and each other's until they were clear. Then it was flesh to flesh, skin to skin, in a single haptic space jumping with energy, with the insistent *yes* of caresses, mouth to mouth, four hands full, body to body, with breasts and erect penis crushed, as it were, between two pulsing walls of muscle.

The skin is the ultimate voice.

So we made love. As we did (my feet jabbing the end of the couch, which was quite broad enough, but a little too short) I arched up and let in the breeze between us (cool on our sweat), leaned down and sucked on first one nipple and then the other—

(thus becoming helpless in a sense, a needy infant, utterly dependent [because for the blind from birth, mother love is even more crucial than for the rest of us; the blind depend on their mothers for almost *everything*, for the sense of object permanence, for the education that makes the distinction between self and world, for the beginning of language, and also for the establishment of a private language that compensates for the lack of sight {if your mother doesn't know that a sweeping hand means "*I want*"} and bridges the way to the common tongue—without all that, which only a mother can give, the blind infant is lost; without mother love beyond mother love, the blind child will very likely go mad] so that to suck on a lover's nipple brings back that primal world of trust and need, I am sure of it)

—I was sure of it even then, as I made love to this strange other Mary Unser, a woman as unknown to me as any I had ever spoken with. At least until now. Now with each plunge into her (cylinder capped by cone, sliding through cylinder into rough sphere, neuron to neuron, millions of them fusing across, so that I could not tell where I stopped and she began) I learned more about her, the shape of her, her rhythms, her whole nerve-reality, spoken to me in movement and touch (spread hands holding my back, flanks, bottom) and in those broken bassoon tones that were like someone humming, briefly, involuntarily. "Ah," I said happily at all this sensation, all this new knowledge, feeling all my skin and all my nerves swirl up like a gust of wind into my spine, the back of my balls, to pitch into her all my self—

When we were done (oboe squeaks) I slid down, bending my knees so my feet stuck up in the air. I wiggled my toes in the breeze. Faint traffic noises played a sort of city music to accompany the piano in the apartment. From the airshaft came the sound of a chorus of pigeons, sounding like monkeys with their jaws wired shut, trying to chatter. Mary's skin was damp and I licked it, loving the salt. Patch of darkness in my blur of vision, darkness bundling in it… She rolled onto her side and my hands played over her. Her biceps made a smooth, hard bulge. There were several moles on her back, like little raisins half buried in her skin. I pushed them down, fingered the knobs of her spine. The muscles of her back put her spine in a deep trough of flesh.

I remembered a day my blind science class was taken to a museum, where we were allowed to feel a skeleton. All those hard bones, in just the right places; it made perfect sense, it was exactly as if felt under skin, really—there were no big surprises. But I remember being so upset by the experience of feeling the skeleton that I had to go outside and sit down on the museum steps. I don't know to this day exactly why I was so shaken, but I suppose (all those hard things left behind) it was something like this: it was frightening to know how *real* we were!

Now I tugged at her, gently. "Who are you, then?"

"Not now." And as I started to speak again she put a finger to my mouth (scent of us): "A friend." Buzzing nasal whisper, like a tuning fork, like a voice I was beginning (and this scared me, for I knew I did not know her) to love: "A friend…."

At a certain point in geometrical thinking, vision becomes only an obstruction. Those used to visualizing theorems (as in Euclidean geometry) reach a point, in the n-dimensional manifolds or elsewhere, where the concepts simply *can't* be visualized; and the attempt to do so only leads to confusion and misunderstanding. Beyond that point an interior geometry, a haptic geometry, guided by a kinetic esthetics, is probably the best sensory analogy we have; and so I have my advantage.

But in the real world, in the geometrics of the heart, do I ever have any comparable advantage? Are there things we feel that can never be seen?

The central problem for everyone concerned with the relationship between geometry and the real world is the question of how one moves from the incommunicable impressions of the sensory world (vague fields of force, of danger), to the generally agreed-upon abstractions of the math (the explanation). Or, as Edmund Husserl puts it in *The Origin of Geometry* (and on this particular morning George was enunciating this passage for me with the utmost awkwardness): "How does geometrical ideality (just like that of all the sciences) proceed from its primary intrapersonal origin, where it is a structure within the conscious space of the first inventor's soul, to its ideal objectivity?"

At this point Jeremy knocked at my door: four quick raps. "Come in, Jeremy," I said, my pulse quickening.

He opened the door and looked in. "I have a pot of coffee just ready to go," he said. "Come on down and have some."

So I joined him in his office, which smelled wonderfully of strong French roast. I sat in one of the plush armchairs that circled Jeremy's desk, accepted a small glazed cup, sipped from it. Jeremy moved about the room restlessly as he chattered about one minor matter after another, obviously avoiding the topic of Mary and all that she represented. The coffee sent a warm flush through me—even the flesh of my feet buzzed with heat, though in the blast of air-conditioned air from the ceiling vent I didn't start to sweat. At first it was a comfortable, even pleasant sensation. The bitter, murky taste of the coffee washed over my palate, through the roof of my mouth into my sinuses, from there up behind my eyes, through my brain, all the way down my throat, into my lungs: I breathed coffee, my blood singing with warmth.

... I had been talking about something. Jeremy's voice came from directly above and before me, and it had a crackly, tinny quality to it, as if made by an old carbon microphone: "And what would happen if the Q energy from this manifold were directed through these vectored dimensions into the macrodimensional manifold?"

Happily I babbled, "Well, provide each point P of an n-dimensional differentiable manifold M with the analogue of a tangent plane, an n-dimensional vector space $Tp(M)$, called the tangent space at P. Now we can define a *path* in manifold M as a differentiable mapping of an open interval of R into M. And along this path we can fit the *whole* of the forces defining K the submanifold of M, a lot of energy to be sure," and I was writing it down, when the somatic effect of the drug caught up with the mental effect, and I recognized what was happening. ("Entirely too many new designer drugs these days…") Jeremy's breathing snagged as he looked up to see what had stopped me; meanwhile, I struggled with a slight wave of nausea, caused more by the realization that I had been drugged than by the chemicals themselves, which had very little "noise." What had I told him? And why, for God's sake, did it matter so much?

"Sorry," I muttered through the roar of the ventilator. "Bit of a headache."

"Sorry to hear that," Jeremy said, in a voice exactly like George's. "You look a little pale."

"Yes," I said, trying to conceal my anger. (Later, listening to the tape of the conversation, I thought I only sounded confused.) (And I hadn't said much about my work, either—mostly definitions.) "Sorry to run out on you, but it really is bothering me."

I stood, and for a moment I panicked; the location of the room's door—the most fundamental point of orientation, remembered without effort in every circumstance—wouldn't come to me. I was damned if I would ask Jeremy Blasingame about such a thing, or stumble about in front of him. I consciously fought to remember: desk faces door, chair faces desk, door therefore behind you…

"Let me walk you to your office," Jeremy said, taking me by the arm. "Listen, maybe I can give you a lift home?"

"That's all right," I said, shrugging him off. I found the door by accident, it seemed, and left him. Down to my office, wondering if I would get the right door. My blood was hot Turkish coffee. My head spun. The key worked, so I had found the right door. Locked in, I went to my couch and lay down. I was as dizzy there as standing, but found I couldn't move again. I spun in place helplessly. I had read that the designer drugs used for such purposes had almost no somatic effect, but perhaps this was true only for subjects less sensitive to their kinetic reality —otherwise, why was I reacting so? Fear. Or Jeremy had put something beyond the truth drug in me. A warning? Against? Suddenly I was aware of the tight boundaries of my comprehension, beyond it the wide manifold of action I did not understand—and the latter threatened to completely flood the former, so that there would be left nothing at all that I understood about this matter. Such a prospect terrified me.

Some time later—perhaps as much as an hour—I felt I had to get home. Physically I felt much better, and it was only when I got outside in the wind that I realized that the psychological effects of the drug were still having their way with me. Rare, heavy waft of diesel exhaust, a person wearing clothes rank with old sweat: these smells overwhelmed any chance I had of locating Ramon's cart by nose. My cane felt unusually long, and the rising and falling whistles of my sonar glasses made a musical composition like something out of Messiaen's *Catalogue d'Oiseaux*. I stood entranced by the effect. Cars zoomed past with their electric whirrs, the wind made more sound than I could process. I couldn't find Ramon and decided to give up trying; it would be bad to get him mixed up in any of this anyway. Ramon was my best friend. All those hours at Warren's throwing together, and when we played beeper ping-pong at his apartment we sometimes got to laughing so hard we couldn't stand—what else is friendship than that, after all?

Distracted by thoughts such as these, and by the bizarre music of wind and traffic, I lost track of which street I was crossing. The *whoosh* of a car nearly brushing me as I stepped up from a curb. Lost! "Excuse me, is this Pennsylvania or K?" Fuckyouverymuch. Threading my way fearfully between broken bottles, punji-stick nails poking up out of boards on the sidewalk, low-hanging wires holding up tree branch or street sign, dog shit on the curb waiting like banana peel to skid me into the street under a bus, speeding cars with completely silent electric motors careening around the corner, muggers who didn't care if I was blind or paraplegic or whatever, manholes left open in the crosswalks, rabid dogs with their toothy jaws stuck out between the rails of a fence, ready to bite… Oh, yes, I fought off all these dangers and more, and I must have looked mad tiptoeing down the sidewalk, whapping my cane about like a man beating off devils.

By the time I got into my apartment I was shaking with fury. I turned on Steve Reich's *Come Out* (in which the phrase "Come out to show them" is looped countless times) as loud as I could stand it, and barged around my place alternately cursing and crying (that stinging of the eyes), all under the sound of the music. I formulated a hundred impossible plans of revenge against Jeremy Blasingame and his shadowy employers. I brushed my teeth for fifteen minutes to get the taste of coffee out of my mouth.

By the next morning I had a workable plan: it was time for some confrontation. It was a Saturday, and I was able to work in my office without interruption. I entered the office and unlocked a briefcase, opened my file cabinet and made sounds of moving papers from briefcase to cabinet. Much more silently, I got out a big mousetrap that I had bought that morning. On the back of it I wrote, *You're caught. The next trap kills.* I set the trap and placed it carefully behind the new file I had added to the cabinet. This was straight out of one of my adolescent rage fantasies, of course, but I didn't care; it was the best way I could think of to both punish them and warn them from a distance. When the file was pulled from the cabinet, the trap would release onto the hand pulling the file out, and it would also break tape set in a pattern only I would be able to feel. So if the trap went off, I would know.

The first step was ready.

In Penderecki's *Threnody for the Victims of Hiroshima*, a moment of deadly stillness, strings humming dissonant strokes as the whole world waits.

Cut shaving; the smell of blood.

Across the road, a carpenter hammering nails on a roof, each set of seven strokes a crescendo: tap-tap-tap-tap-tap-tap-*tap!* Tap-tap-tap-tap-tap-tap-*tap!*

In that mathematics of emotion, stress calculations to measure one's tension: already there for us to use. Perhaps all of math already charts states of consciousness, moments of being.

She came to me again late at night, with the wind swirling by her through the doorway. It was late, the wind was chill and blustery, the barometer was falling. Storm coming.

"I wanted to see you," she said.

I felt a great thrill of fear, and another of pleasure, and I could not tell which was stronger, or, after a time, which was which.

"Good." We entered the kitchen, I served her water, circled her unsteadily, my voice calm as we discussed trivia in fits and starts. After many minutes of this I very firmly took her by the hand. "Come along." I led her into the pantry, up the narrow musty stairs, out the roof door into the wind. A spattering of big raindrops hit us. "Carlos—" "Never mind that!" The whoosh of the wind was accompanied by the rain smell of wet dust and hot asphalt and a certain electricity in the air. Off in the distance, to the south, a low rumble of thunder shook the air.

"It's going to rain," she ventured, shouting a bit over the wind.

"Quiet," I told her, and kept her hand crushed in mine. The wind gusted through our clothes, and mixed with my anger and my fear I felt rising the electric elation that storms evoke in me. Face to the wind, hair pulled back from my scalp, I held her hand and waited: "Listen," I said, "watch, feel the storm." And after a time I felt —no, I saw, I *saw*—the sudden jerk of lightness that marked lightning. "Ah," I said aloud, counting to myself. The thunder pushed us about ten seconds later. Just a couple of miles away.

"Tell me what you see," I commanded, and heard in my own voice a vibrancy that could not be denied.

"It's—it's a thunderstorm," she replied, uncertain of me in this new mood. "The clouds are very dark, and fairly low at their bottoms, but broken up in places by some largish gaps. Kind of like immense boulders rolling overhead. The lightning—there! You noticed that?"

I had jumped. "I can see lightning," I said, grinning. "I have a basic perception of light and darkness, and everything flashes to lightness for a moment. As if the sun had turned on and then off."

"Yes. It's sort of like that, only the light is shaped in jagged white lines, extending from cloud to ground. Like that model you have of subatomic particles breaking up—a sort of broken wire sculpture, white as the sun, forking the earth for just an instant, as bright as the thunder is loud." Her voice rasped with an excitement that had sparked across our hands—also with apprehension, curiosity, I didn't know what. *Light...* BLAM, the thunder struck us like a fist and she jumped. I laughed. "That was off to the side!" she said fearfully. "We're in the middle of it!"

I couldn't control a laugh. "More!" I shouted. "Pick up the pace!" And as if I were a weathermonger, the lightning snapped away the darkness around us, *flash*-BLAM... *flash*-BLAM... *flash*-**BLAM!!**

"We should get down!" Mary shouted over the wind's ripping, over the reverberating crashes of thunder. I shook my head back and forth and back and forth, gripped her by the arm so hard it must have hurt.

"*No!* This is *my* visual world, do you understand? This is as beautiful as it ever—" *flash-crack*-BLAM.

"*Carlos*—"

"No! Shut up!" *Flash-flash-flash*-**BOOM!** Rolling thunder, now, hollow casks the size of mountains, rolling across a concrete floor.

"I'm afraid," she said miserably, tugging away from me.

"You feel the exposure, eh?" I shouted at her, as lightning flashed and the wind tore at us, and raindrops pummeled the roof, throwing up a tarry smell to mix with the lightning's ozone. "You feel what it's like to stand helpless before a power that can kill you, is that right?"

Between thunderclaps she said, desperately, "Yes!"

"Now you know how I've felt around you people!" I shouted. BLAM! BLAM!! "Goddammit," I said, pain searing my voice as the lightning seared the air, "I can go sit in the corner park with the drug dealers and the bums and the crazies and I *know* I'll be safe, because even those people still have the idea that it isn't right to hurt a blind man. But you people!" I couldn't go on. I shoved her away from me and staggered back, remembering it all. *Flash*-BLAM! *Flash*-BLAM!

"Carlos—" Hands pulling me around.

"What?"

"I didn't—"

"The hell you didn't! You came in and gave me that story about the moon, and talked backwards, and drew stuff, and all to steal my work—how could you do it? How could you do it?"

"I *didn't*, Carlos, I didn't!" I batted her hands away, but it was as if a dam had burst, as if only now, charged to it in the storm, was she able to speak: "*Listen to me!*" Flash-BLAM. "*I'm just like you*. They made me do it. They took me because I have some math background, I guess, and they ran me through more memory implants than I can even count!" Now the charged, buzzing timbre of her desperate voice scraped directly across my nervous system: "You know what they can do with those drugs and implants. They can program you just like a machine. You walk through your paces and watch yourself and can't do a thing about it." BLAM. "And they programmed me and I went in there and spouted it all off to you on cue. But you *know*"—BLAM—"was trying, you know there's the parts of the mind they can't touch—I fought them as hard as I could, don't you see?"

Flash-BLAM. Sizzle of scorched air, ozone, ringing eardrums. That one was close.

"I took TNPP-50," she said, calmer now. "That and MDMA. I just *made* myself duck into a pharmacy on my way to meet you alone, and I used a blank prescription pad I keep and got them. I was so drugged up when we went to the Tidal Basin that I could barely walk. But it helped me to speak, helped me to fight the programming."

"You were drugged?" I said, amazed. (I know, Max Carrados would have figured it out. But me...)

"Yes!" BOOM. "Every time I saw you after that time. And it's worked better every time. But I've had to pretend I was still working on you, to protect us both. The last time we were up here"—BOOM—"you *know* I'm with you, Carlos, do you think I would have faked that?"

Bassoon voice, hoarse with pain. Low rumble of thunder in the distance. Flickers in the darkness, no longer as distinct as before: my moments of vision were coming to an end. "But what do they *want?*" I cried.

"Blasingame thinks your work will solve the problems they're having getting sufficient power into a very small particle-beam weapon. They think they can channel energy out of the microdimensions you've been studying." BLAM. "Or so I guess, from what I've overheard."

"Those fools." Although to an extent there might be something to the idea. I had almost guessed it, in fact. So much energy... "Blasingame is such a *fool*. He and his stupid Pentagon bosses—"

"*Pentagon!*" Mary exclaimed. "Carlos, these people are *not* with the Pentagon! I don't know who they are—a private group, from Germany, I think. But they kidnapped me right out of my apartment, and I'm a statistician for the defense department! The Pentagon has nothing to do with it!"

Blam. "But Jeremy..." My stomach was falling.

"I don't know how he got into it. But whoever they are, they're dangerous. I've been afraid they'll kill us both. I know they've discussed killing you, I've heard them. They think you're onto them. Ever since the Tidal Basin I've been injecting myself with Fifty and MDMA, a lot of it, and telling them you don't know a thing, that you just haven't *got* the formula yet. But if they were to find out you know about them…"

"God I hate this spy shit," I exclaimed bitterly. And the oh-so-clever trap in my office, warning Jeremy off…

It started to rain hard. I let Mary lead me down into my apartment. No time to lose, I thought. I had to get to my office and remove the trap. But I didn't want her at risk; I was suddenly frightened more for this newly revealed ally than for myself.

"Listen, Mary," I said when we were inside. Then I remembered, and whispered in her ear, "Is this room bugged?"

"No."

"For God's sake." All those silences—she must have thought me deranged! "All right. I want to make some calls, and I'm sure my phones are bugged. I'm going to go out for a bit, but I want you to stay right here. All right?" She started to protest and I stopped her. "Please! *Stay right here.* I'll be right back. Just stay here and wait for me, *please.*"

"Okay, okay. I'll stay."

"You promise?"

"I promise."

Down on the street I turned left and took off for my offices. Rain struck my face and I automatically thought to return for an umbrella, then angrily shook the thought away. Thunder still rumbled overhead from time to time, but the brilliant ("brilliant!" I say—meaning I saw a certain lightness in the midst of a certain darkness) the brilliant flashes that had given me a momentary taste of vision were gone.

Repeatedly I cursed myself, my stupidity, my presumption. I had made axioms out of theorems (humanity's most common logical-syntactic flaw?), never pausing to consider that my whole edifice of subsequent reasoning rested on them. And now, having presumed to challenge a force I didn't understand, I was in real danger, no doubt about it; and no doubt (as corollary) Mary was as well. The more I thought of it the more frightened I became, until finally I was as scared as I should have been all along.

The rain shifted to an irregular drizzle. The air was cooled, the wind had dropped to an occasional gust. Cars hissed by over wet 21st Street, humming like Mary's voice, and everywhere water sounded, squishing and splashing and dripping. I passed 21st and K, where Ramon sometimes set up his cart; I was glad that he wouldn't be there, that I wouldn't have to walk by him in silence, perhaps ignoring his cheerful invitation to buy, or even his specific hello. I would have hated to fool him so. Yet if I had wanted to, how easy it would have been! Just walk on by—he would have had no way of knowing.

A sickening sensation of my disability swept over me, all the small frustrations and occasional hard-learned limits of my entire life balling up and washing through me in a great wave of fear and apprehension, like the flash-*boom* of the lightning and thunder, the drenching of the downpour: Where was I, where was I going, how could I take even one step more?

This fear paralyzed me. I felt as though I had never come down from the drugs Jeremy had given me, as though I struggled under their hallucinatory influence still. I literally had to stop walking, had to lean on my cane.

And so I heard their footsteps. Henry Cowell's *The Banshee* begins with fingernails scraping repeatedly up the high wires of an open piano; the same music played my nervous system. Behind me three or four sets of footsteps had come to a halt, just a moment after I myself had stopped.

For a while my heart hammered so hard within me that I could hear nothing else. I forced it to slow, took a deep breath. Of course I was being followed. It made perfect sense. And ahead, at my office…

I started walking again. The rain picked up on a gust of wind, and silently I cursed it; it is difficult to hear well when rain is pattering down everywhere, so that one stands at the center of a universal *puh-puh-puh-puh*. But attuned now to their presence, I could hear them behind me, three or four (likely three) people walking, walking at just my pace.

Detour time. Instead of continuing down 21st Street I decided to go west on Pennsylvania, and see what they did. No sound of nearby cars so I stood still; I crossed swiftly, nearly losing my cane as it struck the curb. As casually, as "accidentally" as I could, I turned and faced the street; the sonar glasses whistled up at me, and I knew people were approaching though I could not hear their footsteps in the rain. More fervently than ever before I blessed the glasses, turned and struck off again, hurrying as much as seemed natural.

Wind and rain, the electric hum and tire hiss of a passing car. Washington late on a stormy spring night, unusually quiet and empty. Behind me the wet footsteps were audible again. I forced myself to keep a steady pace, to avoid giving away the fact that I was aware of their presence. Just a late-night stroll to the office…

At 22nd I turned south again. Ordinarily, no one would have backtracked on Pennsylvania like that, but these people followed me. Now we approached the university hospital, and there was a bit more activity, people passing to left and right, voices across the street discussing a movie, an umbrella being shaken out and folded, cars passing… Still the footsteps were back there, farther away now, almost out of earshot.

As I approached Gelman Library my pulse picked up again, my mind raced through a network of plans, all unsatisfactory in different ways. Outdoors, I couldn't evade pursuit. Given. In the building…

My sonar whistled up as Gelman loomed over me, and I hurried down the steps from the sidewalk to the foyer containing the elevator to the sixth and seventh floors. I missed the door and adrenaline flooded me, then there it was just to my left. The footsteps behind me hurried down the sidewalk steps as I slipped inside and stepped left into the single elevator, punched the button for the seventh floor. The doors stood open, waiting… then mercifully they slid together, and I was off alone.

A curious feature of Gelman Library is that there are no stairways to the sixth and seventh floors (the offices above the library proper) that are not fire escapes, locked on the outside. To get to the offices, you are forced to take the single elevator, a fact I had complained about many times before—I liked to walk. Now I was thankful, as the arrangement would give me some time. When the elevator opened at the seventh floor I stepped out, reached back in and punched the buttons for all seven floors, then ran for my office, jangling through my keys for the right one.

I couldn't find the key.

I slowed down. Went through them one by one. Found the key, opened my door, propped it wide with the stopper at its base. Over to the file cabinet, where I opened the middle drawer and very carefully slid one hand down the side of the correct file.

The mousetrap was gone. They knew that I knew.

I don't know how long I stood there thinking; it couldn't have been long, though my thoughts spun madly through scores of plans. Then I went to my desk and got the scissors from the top drawer. I followed the power cord of the desk computer to its wall socket beside the file cabinet. I pulled out the plugs there, opened the scissors wide, fitted one point into a socket, jammed it in, and twisted it hard.

Crack. The current held me cramped down for a moment—intense pain pulsed through me—I was knocked away, found myself on my knees slumping against the file cabinets.

(For a while, when I was young, I fancied I was allergic to novocaine, and my dentist drilled my teeth without anesthetic. It was horribly uncomfortable, but tangent to normal pain: pain beyond pain. So it was with the shock that coursed through me. Later I asked my brother, who is an electrician, about it, and he said that the nervous system was indeed capable of feeling the sixty cycles per second of the alternating current: "When you get hit you always feel it pumping like that, very fast but distinct." He also said that with my wet shoes I could have been killed. "The current cramps the muscles down so that you're latched onto the source, and that can kill you. You were lucky. Did you find blisters on the bottoms of your feet?" I had.)

Now I struggled up, with my left arm aching fiercely and a loud hum in my ear. I went to my desk. As they beeped fairly loudly, I took my glasses off and put them on a bookshelf facing the door. I tested the radio—it had no power. Wondering if the whole floor was dead, I went into the hall briefly to look into a ceiling light. Nothing. Back at the desk I took stapler and water tumbler, put them beside the file cabinet. Went to the bookshelves and gathered all the plastic polyhedral shapes (the sphere was just like a big cue ball) and took them to the file cabinet as well. Then I found the scissors on the floor.

Out in the hall the elevator doors opened. "It's dark—" "Shh." Hesitant steps, into the hall. I tiptoed to the doorway. Here it was possible to tell for sure that there were only three of them. There would be light from the elevator, I recalled: it wouldn't do to be illuminated. I stepped back.

(Once Max Carrados was caught in a situation similar to mine, and he simply announced to his assailants that he had a gun on them and would shoot the first person to move. In his case it had worked; but now I saw that the plan was insanely risky.)

"Down here," one whispered. "Spread out, and be quiet." Rustling, quiet footsteps, three small clicks (gun safeties?). I retreated into the office, behind the side of the file cabinet. Stilled my breathing and was silent in a way they'd never be able to achieve. If they heard anything it would be my glasses...

"It's here," the first voice whispered. "Door's open, watch it." Their breathing was quick. They were bunched up outside the door, and one said, "Hey, I've got a lighter," so I threw the pulled-open scissors overhand.

"*Ah!* Ah—" Clatter, hard bump against the hall wall, voices clashing. "What—" "Threw a knife—" "Ah—"

I threw the stapler as hard as I could, *wham*—the wall above, I guessed— and threw the dodecahedron as they leaped back. I don't know what I hit. I jumped almost to the doorway and heard a voice whisper, "Hey." I threw the cue-ball sphere right at the voice. *Ponk.* It sounded like—like nothing else I have ever heard. (Although every once in a while some outfielder takes a beepball in the head, and it sounded something like that, wooden and hollow.) The victim fell right to the hall floor, making a heavy sound like a car door closing; a metallic clatter marked his gun skidding across the floor. Then CRACK! CRACK! CRACK! another of them shot into the office. I cowered on the floor and crawled swiftly back to the file cabinet, ears ringing painfully, hearing wiped out, fear filling me like the smell of cordite leaking into the room. No way of telling what they were doing. The floor was carpet on concrete, with no vibrations to speak of. I hung my mouth open, trying to focus my hearing on the sound of my glasses. They would whistle up if people entered the room quickly, perhaps (again) more loudly than the people would be on their own. The glasses were still emitting their little beep, now heard through the pulsing wash of noise the gunshots had set off in my ears.

I hefted the water tumbler—it was a fat glass cylinder, with a heavy bottom. A rising whistle, and then, in the hall, the rasp of a lighter flint being sparked.

I threw the tumbler. *Crash*, tinkle of glass falling. A man entered the office. I picked up the pentahedron and threw it—thump of it against far wall. I couldn't find any of the other polyhedrons—somehow they weren't there beside the cabinet. I crouched and pulled off a shoe.

He swept my glasses aside and I threw the shoe. I think it hit him, but nothing happened. There I was, without a weapon, utterly vulnerable, revealed in the glow of a God-damned cigarette lighter…

When the shots came I thought they had missed, or that I was hit and couldn't feel it; then I realized some shots had come from the doorway, others from the bookcase. Sounds of bodies hit, staggering, falling, writhing—and all the while I cowered in my corner, trembling.

Then I heard a nasal groan from the hall, a groan like a viola bowed by a rasp. "Mary," I cried, and ran into the hallway to her, tripped on her. She was sitting against the wall—"Mary!" Blood on her. "Carlos," she squeaked painfully, sounding surprised.

Fortunately, it turned out that she had only been wounded; the bullet had entered just under the shoulder, wrecking it but doing no fatal damage.

I learned all this later, at the hospital. An hour or more after our arrival a doctor came out and told me, and the sickening knot of tension in my diaphragm untied all at once, making me feel sick in another way, dizzy and nauseated with relief, unbelievably intense relief.

After that I went through a session with the police, and Mary talked a lot with her employers, and after that we both answered a lot of questions from the FBI. (In fact, that process took days.) Two of our assailants were dead (one shot, another hit in the temple with a sphere), and the third had been stabbed: What had happened? I stayed up all through that first night explaining, retrieving and playing my tapes, and so on, and still they didn't go for Jeremy until dawn; by that time he was nowhere to be found.

Eventually I got a moment alone with Mary, about ten the following morning.

"You didn't stay at my place," I said.

"No. I thought you were headed for Blasingame's apartment, and I drove there, but it was empty. So I drove to your office and came upstairs. The elevator opened just as shots were being fired, so I hit the deck and crawled right over a gun. But then I had a hell of a time figuring out who was where. I don't know how you do it."

"Ah."

"So I broke my promise."

"I'm glad."

"Me too."

Our hands found each other and embraced, and I leaned forward until my forehead touched her shoulder (the good one), and rested.

A couple of days later I said to her, "But what were all those diagrams of Desargues' theorem about?"

She laughed, and the rich timbre of it cut through me like a miniature of the current from my wall socket. "Well, they programmed me with all those geometrical questions for you, and I was roboting through all that, you know, and struggling underneath it all to understand what was going on, what they wanted. And later, how I could alert you. And to tell you the truth, Desargues' theorem was the only geometry of my own that I could remember from school. I'm a statistician, you know, most of my training is in that and analysis… So I kept drawing it to try to get your attention to *me*. I had a message in it, you see. You were the triangle in the first plane, and I was the triangle in the second plane, but we were both controlled by the point of projection—"

"But I knew that already!" I exclaimed.

"Did you? But also I marked a little *J* with my thumbnail by the point of projection, so you would know Jeremy was doing it. Did you feel that?"

"No. I Xeroxed your drawings, and an impression like that wouldn't show up." So my indented copy, ironically enough, had missed the crucial indentation.

"I know, but I was hoping you would brush it or something. Stupid. Well, anyway, between us all we were making the three collinear points off to the side, which is what they were after, you see, determined in this case by point *J* and his projection…"

I laughed. "It never occurred to me," I said, and laughed again, "but I sure do like your way of thinking!"

I saw, however, that the diagram had a clearer symbolism than that.

When I told Ramon about it, he laughed too. "Here you're the mathematician, and you never got it! It was too simple for you!"

"I don't know if I'd call it *too simple*—"

"And wait—wait—you say you told this here girlfriend of yours to stay behind at your house, when you knew you were going to run into those thugs at your office?"

"Well, I didn't *know* they'd be there right then. But…"

"Now *that* was superblink."

"Yeah." I had to admit it; I had been stupid, I had gone too far. And it occurred to me then that in the realm of thought, of analysis and planning, I had consistently and spectacularly failed. Whereas in the physical continuum of action, I had (up to a point—a point that I didn't like to remember [*ponk* of sphere breaking skull, cowering revealed in a lighter's glare]) done pretty well. And though it was disturbing, in the end this reflection pleased me. For a while there, anyway, I had been almost free of the world of texts.

Naturally it took a while for Mary to regain her health; the kidnapping, the behavior programming, the shooting, and most of all the repeated druggings her captors and she had subjected herself to had left her quite sick, and she was in the hospital for some weeks. I visited every day; we talked for hours.

And, naturally, it took quite a while for us to sort things out. Not only with the authorities, but with each other. What was real and permanent between us, and what was a product of the strange circumstances of our meeting—no one could say for sure which was which, there.

And maybe we never did disentangle those strands. The start of a relationship remains a part of it forever; and in our case, we had seen things in each other that we might never have otherwise, to our own great good. I know that years later, sometimes, when her hand touched mine, I would feel that primal thrill of fear and exhilaration that her first touches had caused in me, and I would shiver again under the mysterious impact of the unknown other… And sometimes, arm in arm, the feeling floods me that we are teamed together, in an immense storm of trouble and threat that cracks and thunders all around us. So that it seems clear to me, now, that loves forged in the smithy of intense and dangerous circumstances are surely the strongest loves of all.

I leave the proof of this as an exercise for the reader.

OUR TOWN

I found my friend Desmond Kean at the northeast corner of the penthouse viewing terrace, assembling a telescope with which to look at the world below. He took a metal cylinder holding a lens and screwed it into the side of the telescope, then put his eye to the lens, the picture of concentrated absorption. How often I had found him like this in recent months! It made me shiver a little; this new obsession of his, so much more intense than the handmade clocks, or the stuffed birds, or the geometric proofs, seemed to me a serious malady.

Clearing my throat did nothing to get his attention, so I ventured to say, "Desmond, you're wanted inside."

"Look at this," he replied. "Just look at it!" He stepped back, and I put my eye to his device.

I have never understood how looking through two pieces of curved glass can bring close distant sights; doesn't the same amount of light hit the first lens as would hit a plain circle of glass? And if so, what then could possibly be done to that amount of light within two lenses, to make it reveal so much more? Mystified, I looked down at the lush greenery of Tunisia. There in the shimmery circle of glass was a jumble of wood and thatch in a rice paddy, pale browns on light green. "Amazing," I said.

I directed the telescope to the north. On certain days, as Desmond once explained to me, when the temperature gradients layer the atmosphere in the right way, light is curved through the air (and tell me how that works!) so that one can see farther over the horizon than usual. This was one of those strange days, and in the lens wavered a black dot, resting on top of a silver pin that stuck up over the horizon. The black dot was Rome, the silver pin was the top of the graceful spire that holds the Eternal City aloft. My heart leaped to know that I gazed from Carthage to Rome.

"It's beautiful," I said.

"No, no," Desmond exclaimed angrily. "Look down! Look what's below!"

I did as he directed, even leaning a tiny bit over the railing to do so. Our new Carthage has a spire of its own, one every bit the equal of Rome's, or that of any other of the great cities of the world. The spire seemed to the naked eye a silver rope, a thread, a strand of gossamer. But through the telescope I saw the massy base of the spire, a concrete block like an immense blind fortress.

"Stunning," I said.

"No!" He seized the spyglass from me. "Look at the people camped there on the base! Look what they're doing!"

I looked through the glass where he had aimed it. Smoky fires, huts of cardboard, ribs perfectly delineated under taut brown skin... "See," Desmond hissed. "There where the bonfires are set. They keep the fires going for days, then pour water on the concrete. To crack it, do you see?"

I saw, there in the curved glass surface; it was just as he had said. "At that pace it will take them ten thousand years," Desmond said bitterly.

I stood back from the railing. "Please, Desmond. The world has gotten itself into a sorry state, and it's very distressing, but what can any one person do?"

He took the telescope, looked through it again. For a while I thought he wouldn't answer. But then he said, "I... I'm not so sure, friend Roarick. It's a good question, isn't it. But I feel that someone with knowledge, with expertise, could make a bit of a difference. Heal the sick, or... give advice about agricultural practices. I've been studying upon that pretty hard. They're wrecking their soil. Or... or just put one more shoulder to the wheel! Add one more hand to tend that fire!... I don't know. I don't know! Do we ever know, until we act?"

"But Desmond," I said. "Do you mean down there?"

He looked up at me. "Of course."

I shivered again. Up at our altitude the air stays pretty chill all the time, even in the sun. "Come back inside, Desmond," I said, feeling sorry for him. These obsessions...."The exhibition is about to open, and if you're not there for it Cleo will press for the full set of sanctions."

"Now there's something to fear," he said nastily.

"Come on inside. Don't give Cleo the chance. You can return here another day."

With a grimace he put the telescope in the big duffel bag, picked it up and followed me in.

Inside the glass wall, jacaranda trees showered the giant curved greenhouse-gallery with purple flowers. All the tableaux of the exhibit were still covered by saffron sheets, but soon after we entered the sheets were raised, all at once. The human form was revealed in all its variety and beauty, frozen in place yet still pulsing with life. I noted a man loping, a pair of women fighting, a diver launched in air, four drunks playing cards, a couple stopped forever at orgasm. I felt the familiar opening-night quiver of excitement, caused partly by the force fields of the tableaux as they kept the living ectogenes stopped in place, but mostly by rapture, by a physical response to art and natural beauty. "At first glance it seems a good year," I said. "I already see three or four pieces of merit."

"Obscene travesties," said Desmond.

"Now, now, it isn't as bad as all that. Some imitation of last year, yes, but no more than usual."

We walked down the hall to see how my entry had been placed. Like Desmond, before he quit sculpting, I was chiefly interested in finding and isolating moments of dance that revealed, by themselves, all the grace of the whole act. This year I had stopped a pair of ballet dancers at the end of a pas de deux, the ballerina just off the base of the display as her partner firmly but delicately returned her to the boards. How long I had worked with the breeders, to get ectogenes with these lean dancers' bodies! How many hours I had spent, programming their unconscious education, and training and choreographing them in their brief waking hours! And then at the end, how very often I had had them dance on the tableau base, and stopped them in the force field, before I caught them in the exact moment that I had envisioned! Yes, I had spent a great deal of time in my sculpting chamber, this year; and now my statue stood before us like the epitome of all that is graceful in the human spirit. At a proper angle to the viewers, too, I was pleased to see, and under tolerable lighting. On the two faces were expressions that said that for these two, nothing existed but dance; and in this case it was almost literally true. Yes, it was satisfactory.

Desmond only shook his head. "No, Roarick. You don't understand. We can't keep doing this—"

"Desmond!" cried Cleo, flowing through the crowd of sculptors and their guests. Her smile was wide, her eyes bright with malice. "Come see my latest, dear absent one!"

Wordlessly Desmond followed her, his face so blank of expression that all his thoughts showed clear. A whole crew followed us discreetly, for Desmond and Cleo's antipathy was legendary. How it had started none remembered, although some said they had once been lovers. If so, it was before I knew them. Others said Desmond hated Cleo for her success in the sculpture competitions, and some of the more sharp-tongued gossips said that this envy explained Desmond's new, morbid interest in the world below—sour grapes, you know. But Desmond had always been interested in things no one else cared about—rediscovering little scientific truths and the like—and to me it was clear that his fascination was simply the result of his temperament, and of what his telescope had newly revealed to him. No, his and Cleo's was a more fundamental hatred, a clash of contrary natures.

Now Desmond stared at Cleo's new statue. It is undeniable that Cleo is a superb artist, especially in facial expressions, those utterly complex projections of unique emotional states; and this work displayed her usual brilliance in that most difficult medium. It was a solo piece: a red-haired young woman looked back over one shoulder with an expression of intense vulnerability and confusion, pierced by a sharp melancholy. It was exquisite.

The sight of this sculpture snapped some final restraint in Desmond Kean; I saw it happen. His eyes filled with pity and disgust; his lip curled, and he said loudly, "How did you do it, Cleo? What did you do to her in your little bubble world to get that expression out of her?"

Now, this was a question one simply didn't ask. Each artist's arcology was his or her own sovereign ground, a physical projection of the artist's creative unconscious, an entirely private cosmos. What one did to one's material there was one's own business.

But the truth was no one had forgotten the unfortunate Arthur Magister, who had exhibited increasingly peculiar and morbid statues over a period of years, ending with one of a maiden who had had on her face such an expression that no one could bear to look at it. Though the rule of privacy was maintained, there were of course questions muttered; but no one would ever have found out the answers, if Arthur had not blown up himself and his arcology, revealing in the wreckage, among other things, a number of unpleasantly dismembered ectogenes.

So it was a sensitive issue; and when Desmond asked Cleo his brazen question, with its dark implication, she blanched, then reddened with anger. Disdainfully (though I sensed she was afraid, too) she refused to reply. Desmond stared fiercely at us all; were he an ectogene, I would have stopped him at just that instant.

"Little gods," he snarled, and left the room.

That would cost him, in reputation if not in actual sanctions. But the rest of us forgot his distemper, relieved that we could now begin the exhibit's opening reception in earnest. Down at the drink tables champagne corks were already bringing down a fresh shower of jacaranda blooms.

It was just a few hours later, when the reception was a riotous party, that I heard the news, passed from group to group instantly, that someone had broken the locks on the tableaux (this was supposed to be impossible) and turned their force fields off, letting most of the statues free. And it was while we rushed to the far end of the greenhouse-gallery, around the great curve of the perimeter of the penthouse, that I heard that Desmond Kean had been seen, leaving the gallery with Cleo's red-headed ectogene.

Utter scandal. This would cost Desmond more than money; they would exile him to some tedious sector of the city, to scrub walls with robots or teach children or the like: they would make him pay in time. And Cleo! I groaned; he would never live to see the end of her wrath.

Well, a friend can only do so much, but while the rest were rounding up and pacifying the disoriented ectogenes (which included, alas, my two dancers, who were huddled in each other's arms) I went in search of Desmond, to warn him that he had been seen. I knew his haunts well, having shared most of them, and I hurried to them through the uncrowded, vaguely Parisian boulevards of the penthouse's northern quarter.

My first try was the broken planetaria near the baths; I opened the door with the key we had quietly reproduced years before. An indiscretion!—for Desmond and the young ectogene were making love on the dais in the middle of the chamber, Desmond on his back, the woman straddling him, arced as if all the energy of the great spire were flowing up into her... he was breaking all the taboos this night. Immediately I shut the door, but given the situation saw fit to pound loudly on it. "Desmond! It's Roarick! They saw you with the girl, you've got to leave!"

Silence. What to do in such a situation? I had no precedent. After a good thirty seconds had passed I opened the door again. No Desmond, no girl.

I, however, was one of those who with Desmond had first discovered the other exit from the planetaria, and I hurried to the central ball of optical fibers which even he could not fix, and pulled up the trap door beside it. Down the stairs and along the passageway, into one of the penthouse's other infrastructures I ran.

I will not detail my long search, nor my desperate and ludicrous attempts to evade rival search parties. Despite my knowledge of Desmond's ways and my anxious thoroughness, I did not find him until I thought of the place that should have occurred to me first. I returned to the northeast corner of the viewing terrace, right there outside the glass wall of the greenhouse-gallery, where (as it was now dusk) if the artists inside could have seen through their own reflections, they would have looked right at him.

He and the redhead were standing next to Desmond's telescope, their elbows on the railing as they looked over the edge side by side. Desmond had his duffel bag at his feet. Something in their stance kept me from emerging from the shadows. They looked as though they had just finished the most casual and intimate of conversations—a talk about trivial, inessential things, the kind of talk lovers have together after years of companionship. Such calmness, such resignation... I could only look, at what seemed to me then an unbreakable, eternal tableau.

Desmond sighed and turned to look at her. He took a red curl of her hair between his fingers, watched the gold in it gleam in a band across the middle of the curl. "There are three kinds of red hair," he said sadly. "Red black, red brown, and red gold. And the greatest of these is...."

"Black," said the girl.

"Gold," said Desmond. He fingered the curl....

The woman pointed. "What's all that down there?"

Dusky world below, long since in night: vast dark Africa, the foliage like black fur, sparking with the sooty flares of a thousand bonfires, little pricks of light like yellow stars. "That's the world," Desmond said, voice tightened to a burr. "I suppose you don't know a thing about it. Around those fires down there are people. They are slaves, they live lives even worse than yours, almost."

But his words didn't appear to touch the woman. She turned away, and lifted an empty glass left on the railing. On her face was an expression so... lost—a sudden echo of her expression as statue—that I shivered in the cold wind. She didn't have the slightest idea what was going on.

"Damn," she said. "I wish I'd remembered to bring another drink."

A conversation from another world, resumed here. I saw Desmond Kean's face then, and I know that I did right to interrupt at that moment. "Desmond!" I rushed forward and grasped his arm. "There's no time, you really must get to one of our private rooms and hide! You don't want to find out what sort of sentence they might hand down for this sort of thing!"

A long moment: I shudder to think of the tableau we three made. The world is a cruel sculptor.

"All right," Desmond said at last. "Here, Roarick, take her and get her out of here." He bent over to fumble in his bag. "They'll put her down after all this if they catch her."

"But—but where should I go?" I stammered.

"You know this city as well as I! Try the gallery's service elevator, and get on the underfloor—you know," he insisted, and yet he was about to give me further directions when the far greenhouse door burst open and a whole mob poured out. We were forced to run for it; I took the woman by the hand and sprinted for the closer greenhouse door. The last I saw of Desmond Kean, he was climbing over the railing. *My God,* I thought, *he's going to kill himself*—but then I saw the purposefully rectangular package strapped to his back.

ESCAPE FROM
KATHMANDU

I

Usually I'm not much interested in other people's mail. I mean when you get right down to it, even my own mail doesn't do that much for me. Most of it's junk mail or bills, and even the real stuff is, like, official news from my sister-in-law, xeroxed for the whole clan, or at best an occasional letter from a climbing buddy that reads like a submission to the *Alpine Journal for the Illiterate*. Taking the trouble to read some stranger's version of this kind of stuff? You must be kidding.

But there was something about the dead mail at the Hotel Star in Kathmandu that drew me. Several times each day I would escape the dust and noise of Alice's Second City, cross the sunny paved courtyard of the Star, enter the lobby and get my key from one of the zoned-out Hindu clerks—nice guys all—and turn up the uneven stairs to go to my room. And there at the bottom of the stairs was a big wooden letter rack nailed to the wall, absolutely *stuffed* with mail. There must have been two hundred letters and postcards stuck up there—thick packets, blue airmail pages, dog-eared postcards from Thailand or Peru, ordinary envelopes covered with complex addresses and purple postal marks—all of them bent over the wooden retainer bars of the rack, all of them gray with dust. Above the rack a cloth print of Ganesh stared down with his sad elephant gaze, as if he represented all the correspondents who had mailed these letters, whose messages were never going to reach their destinations. It was dead mail at its deadest.

And after a while it got to me. I became curious. Ten times a day I passed this sad sight, which never changed—no letters taken away, no new ones added. Such a lot of wasted effort! Once upon a time these names had taken off for Nepal, a long way away no matter where they were from. And back home some relative or friend or lover had taken the time to sit down and

163

write a letter, which to me is like dropping a brick on your foot as far as entertainment is concerned. Heroic, really. "Dear George Fredericks!" they cried. "Where are you, how are you? Your sister-in-law had her baby, and I'm going back to school. When will you be home?" Signed, Faithful Friend, Thinking of You. But George had left for the Himal, or had checked into another hotel and never been to the Star, or was already off to Thailand, Peru, you name it; and the heartfelt effort to reach him was wasted.

One day I came into the hotel a little wasted myself, and noticed this letter to George Fredericks. Just glancing through them all, you know, out of curiosity. My name is George, also—George Fergusson. And this letter to George was the thickest letter-sized envelope there, all dusty and bent permanently across the middle. "George Fredericks—Hotel Star—Thamel Neighborhood—Kathmandu—NEPAL." It had a trio of Nepali stamps on it—the King, Cho Oyo, the King again—and the postmark date was illegible, as always.

Slowly, reluctantly, I shoved the letter back into the rack. I tried to satisfy my curiosity by reading a postcard from Koh Samui: "Hello! Do you remember me? I had to leave in December when I ran out of money. I'll be back next year. Hello to Franz and Badim Badur—Michel."

No, no. I put the card back and hoisted myself upstairs. Postcards are all alike. *Do you remember me?* Exactly. But that letter to George, now. About half-an-inch thick! Maybe six or eight ounces—some sort of epic, for sure. And apparently written in Nepal, which naturally made it more interesting to me. I'd spent most of the previous several years in Nepal, you see, climbing and guiding treks and hanging out; and the rest of the world was beginning to seem pretty unreal. These days I felt the same sort of admiration for the ingenuity of the writers of *The International Herald Tribune* that I used to feel for the writers of *The National Enquirer*. "Jeez," I'd think as I scanned a *Tribbie* in front of a Thamel bookstore, and read of strange wars, unlikely summits, bizarre hijackings. "How do they think these things up?"

But an epic from Nepal, now. That was reality. And addressed to a "George F." Maybe they had misspelled the last name, eh? And anyway, it was clear by the way the letter was doubled over, and the envelope falling apart, that it had been stuck there for years. A dead loss to the world, if someone didn't save it and read it. All that agony of emotions, of brain cells, of finger muscles, all *wasted*. It was a damn shame.

So I took it.

II

My room, one of the nicest in all Thamel, was on the fourth floor of the

Star. The view was eastward, toward the tall bat-filled trees of the King's palace, overlooking the jumble of Thamel shops. A lot of big evergreens dotted the confusion of buildings; in fact, from my height it looked like a city of trees. In the distance I could see the green hills that contained the Kathmandu Valley, and before the clouds formed in the mornings I could even see some white spikes of the Himal to the north.

The room itself was simple: a bed and a chair, under the light of a single bare bulb hanging from the ceiling. But what else do you really need? It's true that the bed was lumpy; but with my foam pad from my climbing gear laid over it to level it out, it was fine. And I had my own bathroom. It's true the seatless toilet leaked pretty badly, but since the shower poured directly onto the floor and leaked also, it didn't matter. It was also true that the shower came in two parts, a waist-high faucet and a showerhead near the ceiling, and the showerhead didn't work, so that to take a shower I had to sit on the floor under the faucet. But that was okay—it was all okay—because that shower was *hot*. The water heater was right there in the room hanging over the toilet, and the water that came from it was so hot that when I took a shower I actually had to turn on the cold water too. That in itself made it one of the finest bathrooms in Thamel.

Anyway, this room and bath had been my castle for about a month, while I waited for my next trekkers' group from Want To Take You Higher Ltd. to arrive. When I entered it with the lifted letter in hand I had to kick my way through clothes, climbing gear, sleeping bag, food, books, maps, *Tribbies*—sweep a pile of such stuff off the chair—and clear a space for the chair by the windowsill. Then I sat down, and tried to open the bent old envelope without actually ripping it.

No way. It wasn't a Nepali envelope, and there was some real glue on the flap. I did what I could, but the CIA wouldn't have been proud of me.

Out it came. Eight sheets of lined paper, folded twice like most letters, and then bent double by the rack. Writing on both sides. The handwriting was miniaturized and neurotically regular, as easy to read as a paperback. The first page was dated June 2, 1985. So much for my guess concerning its age, but I would have sworn the envelope looked four or five years old. That's Kathmandu dust for you. A sentence near the beginning was underlined heavily: "*You must not tell ANYBODY about this!!!*" Whoah, heavy! I glanced out the window, even. A letter with some secrets in it! How great! I tilted the chair back, flattened the pages, and began to read.

June 2nd, 1985

Dear Freds—

I know, it's a miracle to get even a postcard from me, much less a letter like this one's going to be. But an amazing thing has happened to me and you're the only friend I can trust to keep it to himself. *You must not tell ANYBODY about this!!!* Okay? I know you won't—ever since we were roommates in the dorm you've been the one I can talk to about anything, in confidence. And I'm glad I've got a friend like you, because I've found I really have to tell this to somebody, or go crazy.

As you may or may not remember, I got my Master's in Zoology at U.C. Davis soon after you left, and I put in more years than I care to recall on a Ph.D. there before I got disgusted and quit. I wasn't going to have anything more to do with any of that, but last fall I got a letter from a friend I had shared an office with, a Sarah Hornsby. She was going to be part of a zoological/botanical expedition to the Himalayas, a camp modeled on the Cronin expedition, where a broad range of specialists set up near treeline, in as pure a wilderness as they can conveniently get to. They wanted me along because of my "extensive experience in Nepal," meaning they wanted me to be sirdar, and my degree didn't have a thing to do with it. That was fine by me. I took the job and went hacking away at the bureaucratic underbrush in Kathmandu. You would have done it better, but I did okay. Central Immigration, Ministry of Tourism, Forests and Parks, RNAC, the whole horrible routine, which clearly was designed by someone who had read too much Kafka. But eventually it got done and I took off in the early spring with four animal behaviorists, three botanists, and a ton of supplies, and flew north. We were joined at the airstrip by 22 local porters and a real sirdar, and we started trekking.

I'm not going to tell you exactly where we went. Not because of you; it's just too dangerous to commit it to print. But we were up near the top of one of the watersheds, near the crest of the Himalayas and the border with Tibet. You know how those valleys end: tributaries keep getting higher and higher, and finally there's a last set of box canyon-type valleys fingering up into the highest peaks. We set our base camp where three of these dead-end valleys met, and members of the group could head upstream or down depending on their project. There was a trail to the camp, and a bridge over the river near it, but the three upper valleys were wilderness, and it was tough to get through the forest up into them. It was what these folks wanted, however—untouched wilderness, almost.

When the camp was set the porters left, and there the eight of us were. My old friend Sarah Hornsby was the ornithologist—she's quite good at it, and I spent some time working with her. But she had a boyfriend along, the mammalogist (no, not that, Freds), Phil Adrakian. I didn't like him much, from the start. He was the expedition leader, and absolutely Mr. Animal Behavior—but he sure had a tough time finding any mammals up there.

Then Valerie Budge was the entomologist—no problem finding subjects for her, eh? (Yes, she did bug me. Another expert.) And Armaat Ray was the herpetologist, though he ended up helping Phil a lot with the night blinds. The botanists were named Kitty, Dominique, and John; they spent a lot of time to themselves, in a large tent full of plant samplings.

So—camp life with a zoological expedition. I don't suppose you've ever experienced it. Compared to a climbing expedition it isn't that exciting, I'll tell you. On this one I spent the first week or two crossing the bridge and establishing the best routes through the forest into the three high valleys; after that I helped Sarah with her project, mostly. But the whole time I entertained myself watching this crew—being an animal behaviorist for the animal behaviorists, so to speak.

What interests me, having once given it a try and decided it wasn't worth it, is why others carry on. Following animals around, then explaining every little thing you see, and then arguing intensely with everyone else about the explanations—for a *career*? Why on earth would anyone do it?

I talked about it with Sarah, one day when we were up the middle valley looking for beehives. I told her I had formed a classification system.

She laughed. "Taxonomy! You can't escape your training." And she asked me to tell her about it.

First, I said, there were the people who had a genuine and powerful fascination with animals. She was that way herself, I said; when she saw a bird flying, there was a look on her face... it was like she was seeing a miracle.

She wasn't so sure she approved of that; you have to be scientifically detached, you know. But she admitted the type certainly existed.

Then, I said, there were the stalkers. These people liked to crawl around in the bush tailing other creatures, like kids playing a game. I went on to explain why I thought this was such a powerful urge; it seemed to me that the life it led to was very similar to the lives led by our primitive ancestors, for a million long years. Living in camps, stalking animals in the woods: to get back to that style of life is a powerfully satisfying feeling.

Sarah agreed, and pointed out that it was also true that nowadays when you got sick of camp life you could go out and sit in a hot bath drinking brandy and listening to Beethoven, as she put it.

"That's right!" I said. "And even in camp there's quite a night life, you've all got your Dostoevski and your arguments over E. O. Wilson... it's the best of both worlds. Yeah, I think most of you are stalkers on some level."

"But you always say, 'you people,'" Sarah pointed out to me. "Why are you outside it, Nathan? Why did you quit?"

And here it got serious; for a few years we had been on the same path, and now we weren't, because I had left it. I thought carefully about how to explain myself. "Maybe it's because of type three, the theorists. Because we must remember that animal behavior is a Very Respectable Academic Field! It has to have its intellectual justification, you can't just go into the academic senate and say, 'Distinguished colleagues, we do it because we like the way birds fly, and it's fun to crawl in the bushes!'"

Sarah laughed at that. "It's true."

And I mentioned ecology and the balance of nature, population biology and the preservation of species, evolution theory and how life became what it is, sociobiology and the underlying animal causes for social behavior... But she objected, pointing out that those were real concerns.

"Sociobiology?" I asked. She winced. I admitted, then, that there were indeed some excellent angles for justifying the study of animals, but I claimed that for some people these became the most important part of the field. As I said, "For most of the people in our department, the theories became more important than the animals. What they observed in the field was just more data for their theory! What interested them was on the page or at the conference, and a lot of them only do field work because you have to prove you can."

"Oh, Nathan," she said. "You sound cynical, but cynics are just idealists who have been disappointed. I remember that about you—you're such an idealist!"

I know, Freds—you will be agreeing with her: Nathan Howe, idealist. And maybe I am. That's what I told her: "Maybe I am. But jeez, the atmosphere in the department made me sick. Theorists backstabbing each other over their pet ideas, and sounding just as scientific as they could, when it isn't really scientific at all! You can't test these theories by designing an experiment and looking for reproducibility, and you can't isolate your factors or vary them, or use controls—it's just observation and untestable hypothesis, over and over! And yet they acted like such solid scientists, math models and all, like chemists or something. It's just scientism."

Sarah just shook her head at me. "You're too idealistic, Nathan. You want things perfect. But it isn't so simple. If you want to study animals, you have to make compromises. As for your classification system, you should write it up for the *Sociobiological Review*! But it's just a theory, remember. If you forget that, you fall into the trap yourself."

She had a point, and besides we caught sight of some bees and had to hurry to follow them upstream. So the conversation ended. But during the following evenings in the tent, when Valerie Budge was explaining to us how human society behaved pretty much like ants—or when Sarah's boyfriend Adrakian, frustrated by his lack of sightings, went off on long analytical jags like he was the hottest theorist since Robert Trivers—she would give me a look and a smile, and I knew I had made my point. Actually, though he talked a big line, I don't think Adrakian was all that good; his publications wouldn't exactly give a porter backstrain, if you know what I mean. I couldn't figure out what Sarah saw in him.

One day soon after that, Sarah and I returned to the middle high valley to hunt again for beehives. It was a cloudless morning, a classic Himalayan forest climb: cross the bridge, hike among the boulders in the streambed, ascending from pool to pool; then up through damp trees and underbrush, over lumpy lawns of moss. Then atop the wall of the lower valley, and onto the floor of the upper valley, much clearer and sunnier up there in a big rhododendron forest. The rhododendron blooms still flared on every branch, and with the flowers' pink intensity, and the long cones of sunlight shafting down through the leaves to illuminate rough black bark, orange fungi, bright green ferns—it was like hiking through a dream. And three thousand feet above us soared a snowy horseshoe ring of peaks. The Himalayas—you know.

So we were in good spirits as we hiked up this high valley, following the streambed. And we were in luck, too. Above one small turn and lift the stream widened into a long narrow pool; on the south face above it was a cliff of striated yellowish granite, streaked with big horizontal cracks. And spilling down from these cracks were beehives. Parts of the cliff seemed to pulsate blackly, clouds of bees drifted in front of it, and above the quiet sound of the stream I could hear the mellow buzz of the bees going about their work. Excited, Sarah and I sat on a rock in the sun, got out our binoculars, and started watching for bird life. Goraks upvalley on the snow, a lammergeier sailing over the peaks, finches beeping around as always—and then I saw it—a flick of yellow, just bigger than the biggest hummingbird. A warbler, bobbing on a twig that hung before the hive cliff. Down it flew, to a fallen piece of hive wax; peck peck peck; wax into bird. A honey warbler. I nudged Sarah and pointed it out, but she had already seen it. We were still for a long time, watching.

Edward Cronin, leader of a previous expedition of this kind to the Himalayas, did one of the first extensive studies of the honey warbler, and I knew that Sarah wanted to check his observations and continue the work. Honey warblers are unusual birds, in that they manage to live off the excess wax of the honeycombs, with the help of some bacteria in their gastro-intestinal systems. It's a digestive feat hardly any other creature on earth has managed, and it's obviously a good move for the bird, as it means they have a very large food source that nothing else is interested in. This makes them very worthy of study, though they hadn't gotten a whole lot of it up to that point—something Sarah hoped to change.

When the warbler, quick and yellow, flew out of sight, Sarah stirred at last—took a deep breath, leaned over and hugged me. Kissed me on the cheek. "Thanks for getting me here, Nathan."

I was uncomfortable. The boyfriend, you know—and Sarah was so much finer a person than he was… And besides, I was remembering, back when we shared that office, she had come in one night all upset because the boyfriend of the time had declared for someone else, and what with one thing and another—well, I don't want to talk about it. But we had been *good friends*. And I still felt a lot of that. So to me it wasn't just a peck on the cheek, if you know what I mean. Anyway, I'm sure I got all awkward and formal in my usual way.

In any case, we were pretty pleased at our discovery, and we returned to the honey cliff every day after that for a week. It was a really nice time. Then Sarah wanted to continue some studies she had started of the goraks, and so I hiked on up to Honey Cliff on my own a few times.

It was on one of those days by myself that it happened. The warbler didn't show up, and I continued upstream to see if I could find the source. Clouds were rolling up from the valley below and it looked like it would rain later, but it was still sunny up where I was. I reached the source of the stream—a spring-fed pool at the bottom of a talus slope—and stood watching it pour down into the world. One of those quiet Himalayan moments, where the world seems like an immense chapel.

Then a movement across the pool caught my eye, there in the shadow of two gnarled oak trees. I froze, but I was right out in the open for anyone to see. There under one of the oaks, in shadow darker for the sunlight, a pair of eyes watched me. They were about my height off the ground. I thought it might be a bear, and was mentally reviewing the trees behind me for climbability, when it moved again—it blinked. And then I saw that the eyes had whites visible around the iris. A villager, out hunting? I didn't think so. My heart began to hammer away inside me, and I couldn't help swallowing. Surely that was some sort of *face* there in the shadows? A bearded face?

Of course I had an idea what I might be trading glances with. The yeti, the mountain man, the elusive creature of the snows. The *Abominable Snowman*, for God's sake! My heart's never pounded faster. What to do? The whites of its eyes… baboons have white eyelids that they use to make threats, and if you look at them directly they see the white of your eyes, and believe you are threatening them; on the off-chance that this creature had a similar code, I tilted my head down and looked at him indirectly. I swear it appeared to nod back at me.

Then another blink, only the eyes didn't return. The bearded face and the shape below it were gone. I started breathing again, listened as hard as I could, but never heard anything except for the chuckle of the stream.

After a minute or two I crossed the stream and took a look at the ground under the oak. It was mossy, and there were areas of moss that had been stepped on by something at least as heavy as me; but no clear tracks, of course. And nothing more than that, in any direction.

I hiked back down to camp in a daze; I hardly saw a thing, and jumped at every little sound. You can imagine how I felt—a sighting like that…!

And that very night, while I was trying to quietly eat my stew and not reveal that anything had happened, the group's conversation veered onto the topic of the yeti. I almost dropped my fork. It was Adrakian again—he was frustrated at the fact that despite all of the spoor visible in the area, he had only actually seen some squirrels and a distant monkey or two. Of course it would have helped if he'd spent the night in the night blinds more often. Anyway, he wanted to bring up something, to be the center of attention and take the stage as The Expert. "You know these high valleys are exactly the zone the yeti live in," he announced matter-of-factly.

That's when the fork almost left me. "It's almost certain they exist, of course," Adrakian went on, with a funny smile.

"Oh, Philip," Sarah said. She said that a lot to him these days, which didn't bother me at all.

"It's true." Then he went into the whole bit, which of course all of us knew: the tracks in the snow that Eric Shipton photographed, George Schaller's support for the idea, the prints Cronin's party found, the many other sightings… "There are thousands of square miles of impenetrable mountain wilderness here, as we now know firsthand."

Of course I didn't need any convincing. And the others were perfectly willing to concede the notion. "Wouldn't that be something if we found one!" Valerie said. "Got some good photos—"

"Or found a body," John said. Botanists think in terms of stationary subjects.

Phil nodded slowly. "Or if we captured a live one…"

"We'd be famous," Valerie said.

Theorists. They might even get their names latinized and made part of the new species' name. *Gorilla montani adrakianias-budgeon*.

I couldn't help myself; I had to speak up. "If we found good evidence of a yeti it would be our duty to get rid of it and forget about it," I said, perhaps a bit too loudly.

They all stared at me. "Whatever for?" Valerie said.

"For the sake of the yeti, obviously," I said. "As animal behaviorists you're presumably concerned about the welfare of the animals you study, right? And the ecospheres they live in? But if the existence of the yeti were confirmed, it would be disastrous for both. There would be an invasion of expeditions, tourists, poachers—yetis in zoos, in primate center cages, in laboratories under the knife, stuffed in museums—" I was getting upset. "I mean what's the real value of the yeti for us, anyway?" They only stared at me: value? "Their *value* is the fact that they're unknown, they're beyond science. They're the part of the wilderness we can't touch."

"I can see Nathan's point," Sarah remarked in the ensuing silence, with a look at me that made me lose my train of thought. Her agreement meant an awful lot more than I would have expected…

The others were shaking their heads. "A nice sentiment," Valerie said. "But really, hardly any of them would be affected by study. Think what they'd add to our knowledge of primate evolution!"

"Finding one would be a contribution to science," Phil said, glaring at Sarah. And he really believed that, too, I have to give him that.

Armaat said slyly, "It wouldn't do any harm to our chances for tenure, either."

"There is that," Phil admitted. "But the real point is, you have to abide by what's true. If we found a yeti we'd be obliged to say so, because it was so—no matter how we felt about it. Otherwise you get into suppressing data, altering data, all that kind of thing."

I shook my head. "There are values that are more important than scientific integrity."

And the argument went on from there, mostly repeating points. "You're an idealist," Phil said to me at one point. "You can't *do* zoology without disturbing some subject animals to a certain extent."

"Maybe that's why I got out," I said. And I had to stop myself from going further. How could I say that he was corrupted by the tremendous job pressures in the field to the point where he'd do anything to make a reputation, without the argument getting ugly? Impossible. And Sarah would be upset with me. I only sighed. "What about the subject animal?"

Valerie said indignantly, "They'd trank it, study it, put it back in its environment. Maybe keep one in captivity, where it would live a lot more comfortably than in the wild."

Total corruption. Even the botanists looked uncomfortable with that one.

"I don't think we have to worry," Armaat said with his sly smile. "The beast is supposed to be nocturnal." —Because Phil had shown no enthusiasm for night blinds, you see.

"Exactly why I'm starting a high-valley night blind," Phil snapped, tired of Armaat's needling. "Nathan, I'll need you to come along and help set it up."

"And find the way," I said. The others continued to argue, Sarah taking my position, or at least something sympathetic to it; I retired, worried about the figure in the shadows I had seen that day. Phil watched me suspiciously as I left.

So, Phil had his way, and we set up a tiny blind in the upper valley to the west of the one I had made the sighting in. We spent several nights up in an oak tree, and saw a lot of Himalayan spotted deer, and some monkeys at dawn. Phil should have been pleased, but he only got sullen. It occurred to me from some of his mutterings that he had hoped all along to find the yeti; he had come craving that big discovery.

And one night it happened. The moon was gibbous, and thin clouds let most of its light through. About two hours before dawn I was in a doze, and Adrakian elbowed me. Wordlessly he pointed at the far side of a small pool in the stream.

Shadows in shadows, shifting. A streak of moonlight on the water—then, silhouetted above it, an upright figure. For a moment I saw its head clearly, a tall, oddly shaped, furry skull. It looked almost human.

I wanted to shout a warning; instead I shifted my weight on the platform. It creaked very slightly, and instantly the figure was gone.

"Idiot!" Phil whispered. In the moonlight he looked murderous. "I'm going after him!" He jumped out of the tree and pulled what I assumed was a tranquilizer pistol from his down jacket.

"You can't find anything out there at night!" I whispered, but he was gone. I climbed down and took off after him—with what purpose I wasn't sure.

Well, you know the forest at night. Not a chance of seeing animals, or of getting around very easily, either. I have to give it to Adrakian —he was fast, and quiet. I lost him immediately, and after that only heard an occasional snapped branch in the distance. More than an hour passed, and I was only wandering through the trees. The moon had set and the sky was about halfway to dawn light when I returned to the stream.

I rounded a big boulder that stood on the bank and almost ran straight into a yeti coming the other way, as if we were on a busy sidewalk and had veered the same direction to avoid each other. He was a little shorter than me; dark fur covered his body and head, but left his face clear—a patch of pinkish skin that in the dim light looked quite human. His nose was as much human as primate—broad, but protruding from his face—like an extension of the occipital crest that ridged his skull fore-to-aft. His mouth was broad and his jaw, under its ruff of fur, very broad—but nothing that took him outside the parameters of human possibility. He had thick eyebrow crests bent high over his eyes, so that he had a look of permanent surprise, like a cat I once owned.

At this moment I'm sure he really was surprised. We both were as still as trees, swaying gently in the wind of our confrontation—but no other movement. I wasn't even breathing. What to do? I noticed he was carrying a small smoothed stick, and there in the fur on his neck were some objects on a cord. His face—tools—ornamentation: a part of me, the part outside the shock of it all, was thinking (I suppose I am still a zoologist at heart), *They aren't just primates, they're hominid.*

As if to confirm this idea, he spoke to me. He hummed briefly; squeaked; sniffed the air hard a few times; lifted his lip (quite a canine was revealed) and whistled, very softly. In his eyes there was a question, so calmly, gently, and intelligently put forth that I could hardly believe I couldn't understand and answer it.

I raised my hand, very slowly, and tried to say "Hello." I know, stupid, but what do you say when you meet a yeti? Anyway, nothing came out but a strangled "Huhn."

He tilted his head to the side inquisitively, and repeated the sound. "Huhn. Huhn. Huhn."

Suddenly he jacked his head forward and stared past me, upstream. He opened his mouth wide and stood there listening. He stared at me, trying to judge me. (I swear I could tell these things!)

Upstream there was a crash of branches, and he took me by the arm and wham, we were atop the stream bank and in the forest. Hoppety-hop through the trees and we were down on our bellies behind a big fallen log, lying side-by-side in squishy wet moss. My arm hurt.

Phil Adrakian appeared down in the streambed, looking considerably the worse for wear. He'd scraped through some brush and torn the nylon of his down jacket in several places, so that fluffy white down wafted away from him as he walked. And he'd fallen in mud somewhere. The yeti squinted hard as he looked at him, clearly mystified by the escaping down.

"Nathan!" Phil cried. "Naaaa—thannnn!" He was still filled with energy, it seemed. "I saw one! Nathan, where are you, dammit!" He continued downstream, yelling, and the yeti and I lay there and watched him pass by.

I don't know if I've ever experienced a more satisfying moment.

When he had disappeared around a bend in the stream, the yeti sat up and sprawled back against the log like a tired backpacker. The sun rose, and he only squeaked, whistled, breathed slowly, watched me. What was he thinking? At this point I didn't have a clue. It was even frightening me;

I couldn't imagine what might happen next.

His hands, longer and skinnier than human hands, plucked at my clothes. He plucked at his own necklace, pulled it up over his head. What looked like fat seashells were strung on a cord of braided hemp. They were fossils, of shells very like scallop shells—evidence of the Himalayas' days underwater. What did the yeti make of them? No way of knowing. But clearly they were valued, they were part of a culture.

For a long time he just looked at this necklace of his. Then, very carefully, he placed this necklace over my head, around my neck. My skin burned in an instant flush, everything blurred through tears, my throat hurt—I felt just like God had stepped from behind a tree and blessed me, and for no reason, you know? I didn't deserve it.

Without further ado he hopped up and walked off bowleggedly, without a glance back. I was left alone in the morning light with nothing except for the necklace, which hung solidly on my chest. And a sore arm. So it *had* happened, I hadn't dreamed it. I had been blessed.

When I had collected my wits I hiked downstream and back to camp. By the time I got there the necklace was deep in one of my down jacket's padded pockets, and I had a story all worked out.

Phil was already there, chattering to the entire group. "There you are!" he shouted. "Where the hell were you? I was beginning to think they had gotten you!"

"I was looking for you," I said, finding it very easy to feign irritation. "Who's this *they*?"

"The yeti, you fool! You saw him too, don't deny it! And I followed him and saw him again, up the river there."

I shrugged and looked at him dubiously. "I didn't see anything."

"You weren't in the right place! You should have been with me." He turned to the others. "We'll shift the camp up there for a few days, very quietly. It's an unprecedented opportunity!"

Valerie was nodding, Armaat was nodding, even Sarah looked convinced. The botanists looked happy to have some excitement.

I objected that moving that many people upvalley would be difficult, and disruptive to whatever life was up there. And I suggested that what Phil had seen was a bear. But Phil wasn't having it. "What I saw had a big occipital crest, and walked upright. It was a yeti."

So despite my protests, plans were made to move the camp to the high valley and commence an intensive search for the yeti. I didn't know what to do. More protests from me would only make it look suspiciously like I had seen what Phil had seen. I have never been very clever at thinking up subterfuges to balk the plans of others; that's why I left the university in the first place.

I was at my wit's end when the weather came through for me with an early monsoon rainstorm. It gave me an idea. The watershed for our valley was big and steep, and one day's hard rain, which we got, would quickly elevate the level of water in our river. We had to cross the bridge before we could start up the three high valleys, and we had to cross two more to get back out to the airstrip.

So I had my chance. In the middle of the night I snuck out and went down to the bridge. It was the usual village job: piles of big stones on each bank, supporting the three half logs of the span. The river was already washing the bottom of the stone piles, and some levering with a long branch collapsed the one on our shore. It was a strange feeling to ruin a bridge, one of the most valuable human works in the Himalayas, but I went at it with a will. Quickly the logs slumped and fell away from each other, and the end of the downstream one floated away. It was easy enough to get the other two under way as well. Then I snuck back into camp and into bed.

And that was that. Next day I shook my head regretfully at the discovery, and mentioned that the flooding would be worse downstream. I wondered if we had enough food to last through the monsoon, which of course we didn't; and another hour's hard rain was enough to convince Armaat and Valerie and the botanists that the season was up. Phil's shrill protests lost out, and we broke camp and left the following morning, in a light mist that turned to brilliant wet sunshine by noon. But by then we were well downtrail, and committed.

There you have it, Freds. Are you still reading? I lied to, concealed data from, and eventually scared off the expedition of old colleagues that hired me. But you can see I had to do it. There is a creature up there, intelligent and full of peace. Civilization would destroy it. And that yeti who hid with me—somehow he *knew* I was on their side. Now it's a trust I'd give my life to uphold, really. You can't betray something like that.

On the hike back out, Phil continued to insist he had seen a yeti, and I continued to disparage the idea, until Sarah began to look at me funny. And I regret to report that she and Phil became friendly once again as we neared J—, and the end of our hike out. Maybe she felt sorry for him, maybe she somehow knew that I was acting in bad faith. I wouldn't doubt it; she knew me pretty well. But it was depressing, whatever the reason. And nothing to be done about it. I had to conceal what I knew, and lie, no matter how much it screwed up that friendship, and no matter how much it hurt. So when we arrived at J—, I said good-bye to them all. I was pretty sure that the funding difficulties endemic in zoology would keep them away for a good long time to come, so that was okay. As for Sarah—well—damn it...

a bit reproachfully I said farewell to her. And I hiked back to Kathmandu rather than fly, to get away from her, and work things off a bit.

The nights on this hike back have been so long that I finally decided to write this, to occupy my mind. I hoped writing it all down would help, too; but the truth is, I've never felt lonelier. It's been a comfort to imagine you going nuts over my story—I can just see you jumping around the room and shouting "YOU'RE KIDDING!" at the top of your lungs, like you used to. I hope to fill you in on any missing details when I see you in person this fall in Kathmandu. Till then—

your friend, Nathan

III

Well, blow my mind. When I finished reading that letter all I could say was "Wow." I went back to the beginning and started to reread the whole thing, but quickly skipped ahead to the good parts. A meeting with the famed Abominable Snowman! What an event! Of course all this Nathan guy had managed to get out was "Huhn." But the circumstances were unusual, and I suppose he did his best.

I've always wanted to meet a yeti myself. Countless mornings in the Himal I've gotten up in the light before dawn and wandered out to take a leak and see what the day was going to be like, and almost every time, especially in the high forests, I've looked around and wondered if that twitch at the corner of my sleep-crusted eye wasn't something abominable, moving.

It never had been, so far as I know. And I found myself a bit envious of this Nathan and his tremendous luck. Why had this yeti, member of the shyest race in Central Asia, been so relaxed with him? It was a mystery to consider as I went about in the next few days, doing my business. And I wished I could do more than that, somehow. I checked the Star's register to look for both Nathan and George Fredericks, and found Nathan's perfect little signature back in mid-June, but no sign of George, or Freds, as Nathan called him. The letter implied they would both be around this fall, but where?

Then I had to ship some Tibetan carpets to the States, and my company wanted me to clear three "videotreks" with the Ministry of Tourism, at the same time that Central Immigration decided I had been in the country long enough; and dealing with these matters, in the city where mailing a letter can take you all day, made me busy indeed. I almost forgot about it.

But when I came into the Star late one sunny blue afternoon and saw that some guy had gone berserk at the mail rack, had taken it down and scattered the poor paper corpses all over the first flight of stairs, I had a feeling I might know what the problem was. I was startled, maybe even a little guilty-feeling, but not at all displeased. I squashed the little pang of guilt and stepped past the two clerks, who were protesting in rapid Nepali. "Can I help you find something?" I said to the distraught person who had wreaked the havoc.

He straightened up and looked me straight in the eye. Straight-shooter, all the way. "I'm looking for a friend of mine who usually stays here." He wasn't panicked yet, but he was close. "The clerks say he hasn't been here in a year, but I sent him a letter this summer, and it's gone."

Contact! Without batting an eye I said, "Maybe he dropped by and picked it up without checking in."

He winced like I'd stuck a knife in him. He looked about like what I had expected from his epic: tall, upright, dark-haired. He had a beard as thick and fine as fur, neatly trimmed away from the neck and below the eyes—just about a perfect beard, in fact. That beard and a jacket with leather elbows would have got him tenure at any university in America.

But now he was seriously distraught, though he was trying not to show it. "I don't know how I'm going to find him, then…"

"Are you sure he's in Kathmandu?"

"He's supposed to be. He's joining a big climb in two weeks. But he always stays here!"

"Sometimes it's full. Maybe he had to go somewhere else."

"Yeah, that's true." Suddenly he came out of his distraction enough to notice he was talking to me, and his clear, gray-green eyes narrowed as he examined me.

"George Fergusson," I said, and stuck out my hand. He tried to crush it, but I resisted just in time.

"My name's Nathan Howe. Funny about yours," he said without a smile. "I'm looking for a George Fredericks."

"Is that right! What a coincidence." I started picking up all the Star's bent mail. "Well, maybe I can help you. I've had to find friends in Kathmandu before—it's not easy, but it can be done."

"Yeah?" It was like I'd thrown him a lifebuoy; what was his problem?

"Sure. If he's going on a climb he's had to go to Central Immigration to buy the permits for it. And on the permits you have to write down your local address. I've spent too many hours at C. I., and have some friends there. If we slip them a couple hundred rupees baksheesh they'll look it up for us."

"Fantastic!" Now he was Hope Personified, actually quivering with it. "Can we go now?" I saw that his heartthrob, the girlfriend of The Unscrupulous One, had had him pegged; he was an idealist, and his ideas shined through him like the mantle of a Coleman lantern gleaming through the glass. Only a blind woman wouldn't have been able to tell how he felt about her; I wondered how this Sarah had felt about him.

I shook my head. "It's past two—closed for the day." We got the rack back on the wall, and the clerks returned to the front desk. "But there's a couple other things we can try, if you want." Nathan nodded, stuffing mail as he watched me. "Whenever I try to check in here and it's full, I just go next door. We could look there."

"Okay," said Nathan, completely fired up. "Let's go."

So we walked out of the Star and turned right to investigate at the Lodge Pheasant—or Lodge Pleasant—the sign is ambiguous on that point.

Sure enough, George Fredericks had been staying there. Checked out that very morning, in fact. "Oh my God no," Nathan cried, as if the guy had just died. Panic time was really getting close.

"Yes," the clerk said brightly, pleased to have found the name in his thick book. "He is go on trek."

"But he's not due to leave here for two weeks!" Nathan protested.

"He's probably off on his own first," I said. "Or with friends."

That was it for Nathan. Panic, despair; he had to go sit down. I thought about it. "If he was flying out, I heard all of RNAC's flights to the mountains were canceled today. So maybe he came back in and went to dinner. Does he know Kathmandu well?"

Nathan nodded glumly. "As well as anybody."

"Let's try the Old Vienna Inn, then."

IV

In the blue of early evening Thamel was jumping as usual. Lights snapped on in the storefronts that opened on the street, and people were milling about. Big Land Rovers and little Toyota taxis forged through the crowd abusing their horns; cows in the street chewed their cud and stared at it all with expressions of faint surprise, as if they'd been magically zipped out of a pasture just seconds before.

Nathan and I walked single file against the storefronts, dodging bikes and jumping over the frequent puddles. We passed carpet shops, climbing outfitters, restaurants, used bookstores, trekking agents, hotels, and souvenir stands, and as we made our way we turned down a hundred offers from the young men of the street: "Change money?" "No." "Smoke dope?" "No." "Buy a nice carpet?" "No." "Good hash!" "No." "Change money?" "No." Long ago I had simplified walking in the neighborhood, and just said "No" to everyone I passed. "No, no, no, no, no, no, no." Nathan had a different method that seemed to work just as well or better, because the hustlers didn't think I was negative enough; he would nod politely with that straight-shooter look, and say "No, thank you," and leave them open-mouthed in the street.

We passed K.C.'s, threaded our way through "Times Square," a crooked intersection with a perpetual traffic jam, and started down the street that led out of Thamel into the rest of Kathmandu. Two merchants stood in the doorway of their shop, singing along with a cassette of Pink Floyd's *The Wall*. "We don't need no education, we don't need no thought control." I almost got run over by a bike. Where the street widened and the paving began, I pushed a black goat to one side, and we leaped over a giant puddle into a tunnellike hall that penetrated one of the ramshackle street-side buildings. In the hall, turn left up scuzzy concrete stairs. "Have you been here before?" I asked Nathan.

"No, I always go to K.C.'s or Red Square." He looked as though he wasn't sorry, either.

At the top of the stairs we opened the door, and stepped into the Austro-Hungarian Empire. White tablecloths, paneled partitions between deep booths, red wallpaper in a fleur-de-lis pattern, plush upholstery, tasteful kitschy lamps over every table; and, suffusing the air, the steamy pungent smell of sauerkraut and goulash. Strauss waltzes on the box. Except for the faint honking from the street below, it was absolutely the real item.

"My Lord," Nathan said, "how did they get *this* here?"

"It's mostly her doing." The owner and resident culinary genius, a big plump friendly woman, came over and greeted me in stiff Germanic English.

"Hello, Eva. We're looking for a friend—" But then Nathan was already past us, and rushing down toward a small booth at the back.

"I think he finds him," Eva said with a smile.

By the time I got to the table Nathan was pumping the arm of a short, long-haired blond guy in his late thirties, slapping his back, babbling with relief—overwhelmed with relief, by the look of it. "Freds, thank God I found you!"

"Good to see you too, bud! Pretty lucky, actually—I was gonna split with some Brits for the hills this morning, but old Reliability Negative Airline bombed out again." Freds had a faint southern or country accent, and talked as fast as anyone I'd ever heard, sometimes faster.

"I know," Nathan said. He looked up and saw me. "Actually, my new friend here figured it out. George Fergusson, this is George Fredericks."

We shook hands. "Nice name!" George said. "Call me Freds, everyone does." We slid in around his table while Freds explained that the friends he was going to go climbing with were finding them rooms. "So what are you up to, Nathan? I didn't even know you were in Nepal. I thought you were back in the States working, saving wildlife refuges or something."

"I was," Nathan said, and his grim do-or-die expression returned. "But I had to come back. Listen—you didn't get my letter?"

"No, did you write me?" said Freds.

Nathan stared right at me, and I looked as innocent as I could. "I'm going to have to take you into my confidence," he said to me. "I don't know you very well, but you've been a big help today, and the way things are I can't really be…"

"Fastidious?"

"No no no—I can't be over-cautious, you see. I tend to be over-cautious, as Freds will tell you. But I need help, now." And he was dead serious.

"Just giving you a hard time," I reassured him, trying to look trustworthy, loyal, and all that; difficult, given the big grin on Freds's face.

"Well, here goes," Nathan said, speaking to both of us. "I've got to tell you what happened to me on the expedition I helped in the spring. It still isn't easy to talk about, but…"

And ducking his head, leaning forward, lowering his voice, he told us the tale I had read about in his lost letter. Freds and I leaned forward as well, so that our heads practically knocked over the table. I did all I could to indicate my shocked surprise at the high points of the story, but I didn't have to worry about that too much, because Freds supplied all the amazement necessary. "You're kidding," he'd say. "No. Incredible. I can't believe it. Yetis are usually so skittish! And this one just *stood there*? You're *kidding*! In-fucking-credible, man! I can't *believe* it! How great! What?—oh, no! You didn't!" And when Nathan told about the yeti giving him the necklace, sure enough, just as Nathan had predicted, Freds jumped up out of the booth and leaned back in and shouted, "YOU'RE KIDDING!!"

"Shh!" Nathan hissed, putting his face down on the tablecloth. "No! Get back down here, Freds! Please!"

So he sat down and Nathan went on, to the same sort of response ("You tore the fucking BRIDGE DOWN!?!" "Shhhh!!"); and when he was done we all leaned back in the booth, exhausted. Slowly the other customers stopped staring at us. I cleared my throat: "But then today, you um, you indicated that there was still a problem, or some new problem…?"

Nathan nodded, lips pursed. "Adrakian went back and got money from a rich old guy in the States whose hobby used to be *big game hunting*. J. Reeves Fitzgerald. Now he keeps a kind of a photo zoo on a big estate. He came over here with Adrakian, and Valerie, and Sarah too even, and they went right back up to the camp we had in the spring. I found out about it from Armaat and came here quick as I could. Right after I arrived, they checked into a suite at the Sheraton. A bellboy told me they came in a Land Rover with its windows draped, and he saw someone funny hustled upstairs, and now they're locked into that suite like it's a fort. And I'm afraid—I think—I think they've *got one up there*."

Freds and I looked at each other. "How long ago was this?" I asked.

"Just two days ago! I've been hunting for Freds ever since, I didn't know what else to do!"

Freds said, "What about that Sarah? Is she still with them?"

"Yes," Nathan said, looking at the table. "I can't believe it, but she is." He shook his head. "If they're hiding a yeti up there—if they've got one—then, well, it's all over for the yetis. It'll just be a disaster for them."

I supposed that was true enough. Freds was nodding automatically, agreeing just because Nathan had said it. "It would be a zoo up there, ha ha."

"So you'll help?" Nathan asked.

"Of course, man! Naturally!" Freds looked surprised Nathan would even ask.

"I'd like to," I said. And that was the truth, too. The guy brought it out in you, somehow.

"Thanks," said Nathan. He looked very relieved. "But what about this climb you were going on, Freds?"

"No prob. I was a late add-on anyway, just for fun. They'll be fine. I was beginning to wonder about going with them this time anyway. They got themselves a Trivial Pursuit game for this climb, to keep them from going bonkers in their tents. We tried it out yesterday and you know I'm real good at Trivial Pursuit, except for the history, literature and entertainment categories, but this here game was the *British* version. So we get a buzz on and start to playing and suddenly I'm part of a Monty Python routine, I mean they just don't play it the same! You know how when we play it and you don't know the answer everyone says 'Ha, too bad'—but here I take my turn and go for sports and leisure which is my natural forte, and they pull the card and ask me, 'Who was it bowled three hundred and sixty-five consecutive sticky wickets at the West Indian cricket match of 1956,' or whatever, and they like to *died* they were laughing so hard. They jumped up and danced around me and *howled*. 'Yew don't know, dew yew! Yew don't have the slightest fookin' *idear* who bowled those sticky wickets, dew yew!' It was really hard to concentrate on my answer. So. Going with them this time might have been a mistake anyway. Better to stay here and help you."

Nathan and I could only agree.

Then Eva came by with our food, which we had ordered after Nathan's epic. The amazing thing about the Old Vienna Inn is that the food is even better than the decor. It would be good anywhere, and in Kathmandu, where almost everything tastes a little like cardboard, it's simply unbelievable. "Look at this steak!" Freds said. "Where the hell do they get the meat?"

"Didn't you ever wonder how they keep the street cow population under control?" I asked.

Freds liked that. "I can just imagine them sneaking one of them big honkers into the back here. Wham!"

Nathan began to prod dubiously at his schnitzel. And then, over a perfect meal, we discussed the problem facing us. As usual in situations like this, I had a plan.

V

I have never known baksheesh to fail in Kathmandu, but that week at the Everest Sheraton International the employees were bottled up tight. They didn't even want to *hear* about anything out of the ordinary, much less be part of it, no matter the gain. Something was up, and I began to suspect that J. Reeves Fitzgerald had a very big bankroll indeed. So Plan A for getting into Adrakian's room was foiled, and I retired to the hotel bar, where Nathan was hidden in a corner booth, suitably disguised in sunglasses and an Australian outback hat. He didn't like my news.

The Everest Sheraton International is not exactly like Sheratons elsewhere, but it is about the quality of your average Holiday Inn, which makes it five-star in Kathmandu, and just about as incongruous as the Old Vienna. The bar looked like an airport bar, and there was a casino in the room next to us, which clearly, to judge by the gales of laughter coming from it, no one could take seriously. Nathan and I sat and nursed our drinks and waited for Freds, who was casing the outside of the hotel.

Suddenly Nathan clutched my forearm. "Don't look!"

"Okay."

"Oh my God, they must have hired a whole bunch of private security cops. Jeez, look at those guys. No, don't look!"

Unobtrusively I glanced at the group entering the bar. Identical boots, identical jackets, with little bulges under the arm; clean-cut looks, upright, almost military carriage… They looked a little bit like Nathan, to tell the truth, but without the beard. "Hmm," I said. Definitely not your ordinary tourists. Fitzgerald's bankroll must have been *very* big.

Then Freds came winging into the bar and slid into our booth. "Problems, man."

"Shh!" Nathan said. "See those guys over there?"

"I know," said Freds. "They're Secret Service agents."

"They're *what?*" Nathan and I said in unison.

"Secret Service agents."

"Now *don't* tell me this Fitzgerald is a close friend of Reagan's," I began, but Freds was shaking his head and grinning.

"No. They're here with Jimmy and Rosalynn Carter. Haven't you heard?"

Nathan shook his head, but I had a sudden sinking feeling as I remembered a rumor of a few weeks back. "He wanted to see Everest…?"

"That's right. I met them all up in Namche a week ago, actually. But now they're back, and staying here."

"Oh my God," Nathan said. "Secret Service men, *here.*"

"They're nice guys, actually," Freds said. "We talked to them a lot in Namche. Real straight, of course—real straight—but nice. They could tell us what was happening in the World Series, because they had a satellite dish, and they told us what their jobs were like, and everything. Of course sometimes we asked them questions about the Carters and they just looked around like no one had said anything, which was weird, but mostly they were real normal."

"And *what* are they doing here?" I said, still not quite able to believe it.

"Well, Jimmy wanted to go see Everest. So they all helicoptered into Namche just as if there was no such thing as altitude sickness, and took off for Everest! I was talking just now with one of the agents I met up there, and he told me how it came out. Rosalynn got to fifteen thousand feet and turned back, but Jimmy kept on trudging. Here he's got all these young tough Secret Service guys to protect him, you know, but they started to get sick, and every day they were helicoptering out a number of them because of altitude sickness, pneumonia, whatever, until there were hardly any left! He hiked his whole crew right into the ground! What is he, in his sixties? And here all these young agents were dropping like flies while he motored right on up to Kala Pattar, and Everest Base Camp too. I love it!"

"That's great," I said. "I'm happy for him. But now they're back."

"Yeah, they're doing the Kathmandu culture scene for a bit."

"That's too bad."

"Ah! No luck getting a key to the yeti's room, is that it?"

"*Shhhhh,*" Nathan hissed.

"Sorry, I forgot. Well, we'll just have to think of something else, eh? The Carters are going to be here another week."

"The windows?" I asked.

Freds shook his head. "I could climb up to them no problem, but the ones to their room overlook the garden and it wouldn't be all that private."

"God, this is bad," Nathan said, and downed his Scotch. "Phil could decide to reveal the—what he's got, at a press conference while the Carters are here. Perfect way to get enhanced publicity fast—that would be just like him."

We sat and thought about it for a couple of drinks.

"You know, Nathan," I said slowly, "there's an angle we haven't discussed yet, that you'd have to take the lead in."

"What's that?"

"Sarah."

"What? Oh, no. No. I couldn't. I can't talk to her, really. It just—well, I just don't want to."

"But why?"

"She wouldn't care what I said." He looked down at his glass and swirled the contents nervously. His voice turned bitter: "She'd probably just tell Phil we were here, and then we'd *really* be in trouble."

"Oh, I don't know. I don't think she's the kind of person to do that, do you, Freds?"

"I don't know," Freds said, surprised. "I never met her."

"She couldn't be, surely." And I kept after him for the rest of our stay, figuring it was our best chance at that point. But Nathan was stubborn about it, and still hadn't budged when he insisted we leave.

So we paid the bill and took off. But we were crossing the foyer, and near the broad set of front doors, when Nathan suddenly stopped in his tracks. A tall, good-looking woman with large owl-eye glasses had just walked in. Nathan was stuck in place. I guessed who the woman must be, and nudged him. "Remember what's at stake."

A good point to make. He took a deep breath. And as the woman was about to pass us, he whipped off his hat and shades. "Sarah!"

The woman jumped back. "Nathan! My God! What—what are you doing here!"

Darkly: "You know why I'm here, Sarah." He drew himself up even straighter than usual, and glared at her. If she'd been convicted of murdering his mother I don't think he could have looked more accusing.

"What—?" Her voice quit on her.

Nathan's lip curled disdainfully. I thought he was kind of overdoing the laying-on-of-guilt trip, and I was even thinking of stepping in and trying a less confrontational approach, but then right in the middle of the next sentence his voice twisted with real pain: "I didn't think you'd be capable of this, Sarah."

With her light brown hair, bangs, and big glasses, she had a schoolgirlish look. Now that schoolgirl was hurting; her lip quivered, she blinked rapidly; "I—I—" And then her face crumpled, and with a little cry she tottered toward Nathan and collapsed against his broad shoulder. He patted her head, looking flabbergasted.

"Oh, Nathan," she said miserably, sniffing. "It's so *awful…*"

"It's all right," he said, stiff as a board. "I know."

The two of them communed for a while. I cleared my throat. "Why don't we go somewhere else and have a drink," I suggested, feeling that things were looking up a trifle.

VI

We went to the hotel Annapurna coffee shop, and there Sarah confirmed all of Nathan's worst fears. "They've got him in there locked in the *bathroom.*" Apparently the yeti was eating less and less, and Valerie Budge was urging Mr. Fitzgerald to take him out to the city's funky little zoo immediately, but Fitzgerald was flying in a group of science and nature writers so he could hold a press conference, the next day or the day after that, and he and Phil wanted to wait. They were hoping for the Carters' presence at the unveiling, as Freds called it, but they couldn't be sure about that yet.

Freds and I asked Sarah questions about the setup at the hotel. Apparently Phil, Valerie Budge and Fitzgerald were taking turns in a continuous watch on the bathroom. How did they feed him? How docile was he? Question, answer, question, answer. After her initial breakdown, Sarah proved to be a tough and sensible character. Nathan, on the other hand, spent the time repeating, "We've got to get him out of there, we've got to do it soon, it'll be the *end* of him." Sarah's hand on his just fueled the flame. "We'll just have to *rescue* him."

"I know, Nathan," I said, trying to think. "We know that already." A plan was beginning to fall into place in my mind. "Sarah, you've got a key to the room?" She nodded. "Okay, let's go."

"What, now?" Nathan cried.

"Sure! We're in a hurry, right? These reporters are going to arrive, and they're going to notice Sarah is gone… And we've got to get some stuff together, first."

VII

When we returned to the Sheraton it was late afternoon. Freds and I were on rented bikes, and Nathan and Sarah followed in a taxi. We made sure our cabbie understood that we wanted him to wait for us out front; then Freds and I went inside, gave the all-clear to Nathan and Sarah, and headed straight for the lobby phones. Nathan and Sarah went to the front desk and checked into a room; we needed them out of sight for a while.

I called all the rooms on the top floor of the hotel (the fourth), and sure enough half of them were occupied by Americans. I explained that I was J. Reeves Fitzgerald, assistant to the Carters, who were fellow guests in the hotel. They all knew about the Carters. I explained that the Carters were hosting a small reception for the Americans at the hotel, and we hoped that they would join us in the casino bar when it was convenient—the Carters would be down in an hour or so. They were all delighted at the invitation (except for one surly Republican that I had to cut off), and they promised to be down shortly.

The last call got Phil Adrakian, in room 355; I identified myself as Lionel Hodding. It went as well as the others; if anything Adrakian was even more enthusiastic. "We'll be right down, thanks—we have a reciprocal invitation to make, actually." I was prejudiced, but he did sound like a pain. Nathan's epithet, *theorist*, didn't really make it for me; I preferred something along the lines of, say, *asshole*.

"Fine. Look forward to seeing all your party, of course."

Freds and I waited in the bar and watched the elevators. Americans in their safari best began to pile out and head for the casino; you wouldn't have thought there was that much polyester in all Kathmandu, but I guess it travels well.

Two men and a plump woman came down the broad stairs beside the elevator. "Them?" Freds asked. I nodded; they fitted Sarah's descriptions exactly. Phil Adrakian was shortish, slim, and good-looking in a California Golden Boy kind of way. Valerie Budge wore glasses and had a lot of curly hair pulled up; somehow she looked intellectual where Sarah only looked studious. The money man, J. Reeves Fitzgerald, was sixtyish and very fit-looking, though he did smoke a cigar. He wore a safari jacket with eight pockets on it. Adrakian was arguing a point with him as they crossed the foyer to the casino bar, and I heard him say, "*better* than a press conference."

I had a final inspiration and returned to the phones. I asked the hotel operator for Jimmy Carter, and got connected; but the phone was answered by a flat Midwestern voice, very businesslike indeed. "Hello?"

"Hello, is this the Carters' suite?"

"May I ask who's speaking?"

"This is J. Reeves Fitzgerald. I'd like you to inform the Carters that the Americans in the Sheraton have organized a reception for them in the hotel's casino bar, for this afternoon."

"… I'm not sure their scheduling will allow them to attend."

"I understand. But if you'd just let them know."

"Of course."

Back to Freds, where I downed a Star beer in two gulps. "Well," I said, "*something* should happen. Let's get up there."

VIII

I gave Nathan and Sarah a buzz and they joined us at the door of Room 355. Sarah let us in. Inside was a big suite—style, generic Holiday Inn—it could have been in any city on earth. Except that there was a slight smell of wet fur.

Sarah went to the bathroom door, unlocked it. There was a noise inside. Nathan, Freds and I shifted around behind her uncomfortably. She opened the door. There was a movement, and there he was, standing before us. I found myself staring into the eyes of the yeti.

In the Kathmandu tourist scene, there are calendars, postcards, and embroidered T-shirts with a drawing of a yeti on them. It's always the same drawing, which I could never understand; why should everyone agree to use the same guess? It annoyed me: a little furball thing with his back to you, looking over his shoulder with a standard monkey face, and displaying the bottom of one big bare foot.

I'm happy to report that the real yeti didn't look anything like that. Oh he was furry, all right; but he was about Fred's height, and had a distinctly humanoid face, surrounded by a beardlike ruff of matted reddish fur. He looked a little like Lincoln—a short and very ugly Lincoln, sure, with a squashed nose and rather prominent eyebrow ridges—but the resemblance was there. I was relieved to see how human his face looked; my plan depended on it, and I was glad Nathan hadn't exaggerated in his description. The only feature that really looked unusual was his occipital crest, a ridge of bone and muscle that ran fore-and-aft over the top of his head, like his skull itself had a Mohawk haircut.

Well, we were all standing there like a statue called "People Meet Yeti," when Freds decided to break the ice; he stepped forward and offered the guy a hand. "Namaste!" he said.

"No, no—" Nathan brushed by him and held out the necklace of fossil shells that he had been given in the spring.

"Is this the same one?" I croaked, momentarily at a loss. Because up until that bathroom door opened, part of me hadn't really believed in it all.

"I think so."

The yeti reached out and touched the necklace and Nathan's hand. Statue time again. Then the yeti stepped forward and touched Nathan's face with his long, furry hand. He whistled something quiet. Nathan was quivering; there were tears in Sarah's eyes. I was impressed myself. Freds said, "He looks kind of like Buddha, don't you think? He doesn't have the belly, but those eyes, man. Buddha to the max."

We got to work. I opened my pack and got out baggy overalls, a yellow "Free Tibet" T-shirt, and a large anorak. Nathan was taking his shirt off and putting it back on to show the yeti what we had in mind.

Slowly, carefully, gently, with many a soft-spoken sound and slow gesture, we got the yeti into the clothes. The T-shirt was the hardest part; he squeaked a little when we pulled it over his head. The anorak was zippered, luckily. With every move I made I said, "Namaste, blessed sir, namaste."

The hands and feet were a problem. His hands were strange, fingers skinny and almost twice as long as mine, and pretty hairy as well; but wearing mittens in the daytime in Kathmandu was almost worse. I suspended judgement on them and turned to his feet. This was the only area of the tourist drawing that was close to correct; his feet were huge, furry, and just about square. He had a big toe like a very fat thumb. The boots I had brought, biggest I could find in a hurry, weren't wide enough. Eventually I put him in Tibetan wool socks and Birkenstock sandals, modified by a penknife to let the big toe hang over the side.

Lastly I put my blue Dodgers cap on his head. The cap concealed the occipital crest perfectly, and the bill did a lot to obscure his rather low forehead and prominent eyebrows. I topped everything off with a pair of mirrored wraparound sunglasses. "Hey, neat," Freds remarked. Also a Sherpa necklace, made of five pieces of coral and three giant chunks of rough turquoise, strung on black cord. Principle of distraction, you know.

All this time Sarah and Nathan were ransacking the drawers and luggage, stealing all the camera film and notebooks and whatever else might have contained evidence of the yeti. And throughout it all the yeti stood there, calm and attentive: watching Nathan, sticking his hand down a sleeve like a millionaire with his valet, stepping carefully into the Birkenstocks, adjusting the bill of the baseball cap, everything. I was really impressed, and so was Freds. "He really is like Buddha, isn't he?" I thought the physical resemblance was a bit muted at this point, but his attitude couldn't have been more mellow if he'd been the Gautama himself.

When Nathan and Sarah were done searching they looked up at our handiwork. "*God* he looks weird," Sarah said.

Nathan just sat on the bed and put his head in his hands. "It'll never work," he said. "Never."

"Sure it will!" Freds exclaimed, zipping the anorak up a little farther. "You see people on Freak Street looking like this all the time! Man, when I went to school I played football with a whole team of guys that looked just like him! Fact is, in my state he could run for Senator—"

"Whoah, whoah," I said. "No time to waste, here. Give me the scissors and brush, I still have to do his hair." I tried brushing it over his ears with little success, then gave him a trim in back. One trip, I was thinking, just one short walk down to a taxi. And in pretty dark halls. "Is it even on both sides?"

"For God's sake, George, let's go!" Nathan was getting antsy, and we had been a while. We gathered our belongings, filled the packs, and tugged old Buddha out into the hall.

IX

I have always prided myself on my sense of timing. Many's the time I've surprised myself by how perfectly I've managed to be in the right place at the right time; it goes beyond all conscious calculation, into deep mystic communion with the cycles of the cosmos, etc. etc. But apparently in this matter I was teamed up with people whose sense of timing was so cosmically awful that mine was completely swamped. That's the only way I can explain it.

Because there we were, escorting a yeti down the hallway of the Everest Sheraton International and we were walking casually along, the yeti kind of bowlegged—very bowlegged—and long-armed, too—so that I kept worrying he might drop to all fours—but otherwise, passably normal. Just an ordinary group of tourists in Nepal. We decided on the stairs, to avoid any awkward elevator crowds, and stepped through the swinging doors into the stairwell. And there coming down the stairs toward us were Jimmy Carter, Rosalynn Carter, and five Secret Service men.

"Well!" Freds exclaimed. "Damned if it isn't Jimmy Carter! And Rosalynn too!"

I suppose that was the best way to play it, not that Freds was doing anything but being natural. I don't know if the Carters were on their way to something else, or if they were actually coming down to attend my reception; if the latter, then my last-minute inspiration to invite them had been really a bad one. In any case, there they were, and they stopped on the landing. We stopped on the landing. The Secret Service men, observing us closely, stopped on the landing.

What to do? Jimmy gave us his famous smile, and it might as well have been the cover of *Time* magazine, it was such a familiar sight; just the same. Only not quite. Not exactly. His face was older, naturally, but also it had the look of someone who had survived a serious illness, or a great natural disaster. It looked like he had been through the fire, and come back into the world knowing more than most people about what the fire was. It was a good face, it showed what a man could endure. And he was relaxed; this kind of interruption was part of daily life, part of the job he had volunteered for nine years before.

I was anything but relaxed. In fact, as the Secret Service men did their hawk routine on Buddha, their gazes locked, I could feel my heart stop, and I had to give my torso a little twist to get it started up again. Nathan had stopped breathing from the moment he saw Carter, and he was turning white above the sharp line of his beard. It was getting worse by the second when Freds stepped forward and extended a hand. "Hey, Mr. Carter, namaste! We're happy to meet you."

"Hi, how are y'all." More of the famous smile. "Where are y'all from?"

And we answered "Arkansas," "California," "M-Massa-chusetts," "Oregon," and at each one he smiled and nodded with recognition and pleasure, and Rosalynn smiled and said "Hello, hello," with that faint look I had seen before during the Presidential years, that seemed to say she would have been just as happy somewhere else, and we all shuffled around so that we could all shake hands with Jimmy—until it was Buddha's turn.

"This is our guide, B-Badim Badur," I said. "He doesn't speak any English."

"I understand," Jimmy said. And he took Buddha's hand and pumped it up and down.

Now, I had opted to leave Buddha barehanded, a decision I began to seriously regret. Here we had a man who had shaken at least a million hands in his life, maybe ten million; nobody in the whole world could have been more of an expert at it. And as soon as he grasped Buddha's long skinny hand, he knew that something was different. This wasn't like any of the millions of other hands he had shaken before. A couple of furrows joined the network of fine wrinkles around his eyes, and he looked closer at Buddha's peculiar get-up. I could feel the sweat popping out and beading on my forehead. "Um, Badim's a bit shy," I was saying, when suddenly the yeti squeaked.

"Naa-maas-tayy," it said, in a hoarse, whispery voice.

"Namaste!" Jimmy replied, grinning the famous grin.

And that, folks, was the first recorded conversation between yeti and human.

Of course Buddha had only been trying to help—I'm sure of that, given what happened later—but despite all we did to conceal it, his speech had obviously surprised us pretty severely. As a result the Secret Service guys were about to go cross-eyed checking us out, Buddha in particular.

"Let's let these folks get on with things," I said shakily, and took Buddha by the arm. "Nice to meet you," I said to the Carters. We all hung there for a moment. It didn't seem polite to precede the ex-President of the United States down a flight of stairs, but the Secret Service men damn well didn't want us *following* them down either; so finally I took the lead, with Buddha by the arm, and I held onto him tight as we descended.

We reached the foyer without incident. Sarah conversed brightly with the Secret Service men who were right behind us, and she distracted their attention very successfully, I thought. It appeared we would escape the situation without further difficulties, when the doors to the casino bar swung back, and Phil Adrakian, J. Reeves Fitzgerald, and Valerie Budge walked out. (Timing, anyone?)

Adrakian took in the situation at a glance. "They're kidnapping him!" he yelled. "Hey! *Kidnapping!*"

Well, you might just as well have put jumper cables on those Secret Service agents. After all, it's kind of a question why anyone would want to assassinate an ex-President, but as a hostage for ransom or whatnot, you've got a prime target. They moved like mongooses to get between us and the Carters. Freds and I were trying to back Buddha out the front doors without actually moving our legs; we weren't making much progress, and I don't doubt we could've gotten shot for our efforts, if it weren't for Sarah. She jumped right out in front of the charging Adrakian and blocked him off.

"*You're* the kidnapper, you liar," she cried, and slapped him in the face so hard he staggered. "*Help!*" she demanded of the Secret Service guys, blushing bright red and shoving Valerie Budge back into Fitzgerald. She looked so tousled and embattled and beautiful that the agents were confused; the situation wasn't at all clear. Freds, Buddha and I bumped out the front door and ran for it.

Our taxi was gone. "Shit," I said. No time to think. "The bikes?" Freds asked.

"Yep." No other choice—we ran around the side of the building and unlocked our two bikes. I got on mine and Freds helped Buddha onto the little square rack over the back wheel. People around front were shouting, and I thought I heard Adrakian among them. Freds gave me a push from behind and we were off; I stood to pump up some speed, and we wavered side to side precariously.

I headed up the road to the north. It was just wider than one lane, half-paved and half-dirt. Bike and car traffic on it was heavy, as usual, and between dodging vehicles and potholes, looking back for pursuers, and keeping the bike from tipping under Buddha's shifting weight, I was kept pretty busy.

The bike was a standard Kathmandu rental, Hero Jet by brand name: heavy frame, thick tires, low handlebars, one speed. It braked when you pedaled backwards, and had one handbrake, and it had a big loud bell, which is a crucial piece of equipment. This bike wasn't a bad specimen either, in that the handbrake worked and the handlebars weren't loose and the seat wasn't putting a spring through my ass. But the truth is, the Hero Jet is a solo vehicle. And Buddha was no lightweight. He was built like a cat, dense and compact, and I bet he weighed over two hundred pounds. With him in back, the rear tire was squashed flat—there was about an eighth of an inch clearance between rim and ground, and every time I misnavigated a pothole there was an ugly *thump* as we bottomed out.

So we weren't breaking any speed records, and when we turned left on Dilli Bazar Freds shouted from behind, "They're after us! See, there's that Adrakian and some others in a taxi!"

Sure enough, back a couple hundred yards was Phil Adrakian, hanging out the side window of a little white Toyota taxi, screaming at us. We pedaled over the Dhobi Khola bridge and shot by the Central Immigration building before I could think of anything to yell that might have brought the crowd there into the street. "Freds!" I said, panting. "Make a diversion! Tie up traffic!"

"Right on." Without a pause he braked to a halt in the middle of the road, jumped off and threw his Hero Jet to the pavement. The three-wheeled motorcab behind him ran over it before the driver could stop. Freds screamed abuse, he pulled the bike out and slung it under a Datsun going the other way, which crunched it and screeched to a halt. More abuse from Freds, who ran around

pulling the drivers from their vehicles, shouting at them with all the Nepalese he knew: "Chiso howa!" (Cold wind.) "Tato pani!" (Hot water.) "Rhamrao dihn!" (Nice day.)

I only caught glimpses of this as I biked away, but I saw he had bought a little time and I concentrated on negotiating the traffic. Dilli Bazar is one of the most congested streets in Kathmandu, which is really saying a lot. The two narrow lanes are fronted by three-story buildings containing grocery markets and fabric wholesalers, which open directly onto the street and use it for cash register lines and so on, despite the fact that it's a major truck route. Add to that the usual number of dogs, goats, chickens, taxis, young schoolgirls walking three abreast with their arms linked, pedicabs with five-foot-tall operators pedaling whole families along at three miles an hour, and the occasional wandering sacred cow, and you can see the extent of the problem. Not only that, but the potholes are fierce—some could be mistaken for open manholes.

And the hills! I was doing all right until that point, weaving through the crowd and ringing my bell to the point of thumb cramp. But then Buddha shook my arm and I looked back and saw that Adrakian had somehow gotten past Freds and hired another taxi, and he was trailing us again, stuck behind a colorfully painted bus some distance behind. And then we started up the first of three fairly steep up-and-downs that Dilli Bazar makes before it reaches the city center.

Hero Jets are not made for hills. The city residents get off theirs and walk them up inclines like that one, and only Westerners, still in a hurry even in Nepal, stay on and grind up the slopes. I was certainly a Westerner in a hurry that day, and I stood up and started pumping away. But it was heavy going, especially after I had to brake to a dead stop to avoid an old man blowing his nose with his finger. Adrakian's taxi had rounded the bus, in an explosion of honks, and he was gaining on us fast. I sat back on the seat, huffing and puffing, legs like big blocks of wood, and it was looking like I'd have to find a diplomatic solution to the problem, when suddenly both my feet were kicked forward off the pedals; we surged forward, just missing a pedicab.

Buddha had taken over. He was holding onto the seat with both hands, and pedaling from behind. I had seen tall Westerners ride their rental bikes like that before, to keep from smashing their knees into the handlebars on every upswing. But you can't get much downthrust from back there, and you didn't ever see them doing that while biking uphill. For Buddha, this was not a problem. I mean this guy was *strong*. He pumped away so hard that the poor Hero Jet squeaked under the strain, and we surged up the hill and flew down the other side like we had jumped onto a motorcycle.

A motorcycle without brakes, I should add. Buddha did not seem up on the theory of the footbrake, and I tried the handbrake once or twice and found that it only squealed like a pig and reduced our stability a bit. So as we fired down Dilli Bazar I could only put my feet up on the frame and dodge obstacles, as in one of those race-car video games. I rang the bell for all it was worth, and spent a lot of time in the right lane heading at oncoming traffic (they drive on the left). Out the corner of my eye I saw pedestrians goggling at us as we flew by; then the lanes ahead cleared as we rounded a semi, and I saw we were approaching the "Traffic Engineers' Intersection," usually one of my favorites. Here Dilli Bazar crosses another major street, and the occasion is marked by four traffic lights, all four of them *permanently green twenty-four hours a day.*

This time there was a cow for a traffic cop. "Bistarre!" (Slowly) I yelled, but Buddha's vocabulary apparently remained restricted to "Namaste," and he pedaled right on. I charted a course, clamped down the handbrake, crouched over the handlebars, rang the bell.

We shot the gap between a speeding cab and the traffic cow, with three inches to spare on each side, and were through the intersection before I even had time to blink. No problem. Now *that's* timing.

After that, it was just a matter of navigation. I took us the wrong way up the one-way section of Durbar Marg, to shorten our trip and throw off pursuit for good, and having survived that it was simple to make it the rest of the way to Thamel.

As we approached Thamel, we passed the grounds of the Royal Palace; as I mentioned, the tall trees there are occupied day and night by giant brown bats, hanging head down from the bare upper branches. As we passed the palace, those bats must have caught the scent of the yeti, or something, because all of a sudden the whole flock of them burst off the branches, squeaking like my handbrake and flapping their big skin wings like a hundred little Draculas. Buddha slowed to stare up at the sight, and everyone else on the block, even the cow on the corner, stopped and looked up as well, to watch that cloud of bats fill the sky.

It's moments like that that make me love Kathmandu.

In Thamel, we fit right in. A remarkable number of people on the street looked a lot like Buddha—so much so that the notion hit me that the city was being secretly infiltrated by yeti in disguise. I chalked the notion up to hysteria caused by the Traffic Engineers' Intersection, and directed our Hero Jet into the Hotel Star courtyard. At that point walls surrounded us and Buddha consented to stop pedaling. We got off the bike, and shakily I led him upstairs to my room.

X

So. We had liberated the imprisoned yeti. Although I had to admit, as I locked us both into my room, that he was only partway free. Getting him completely free, back on his home ground, might turn out to be a problem. I still didn't know exactly where his home was, but they don't rent cars in Kathmandu, and the bus rides, no matter the destination, are long and crowded. Would Buddha be able to hold it together for ten hours in a crowded bus? Well, knowing him, he probably would. But would his disguise hold up? That was doubtful.

Meanwhile, there was the matter of Adrakian and the Secret Service being on to us. I had no idea what had happened to Nathan and Sarah and Freds, and I worried about them, especially Nathan and Sarah. I wished they would arrive. Now that we were here and settled, I felt a little uncomfortable with my guest; with him in there, my room felt awfully small.

I went in the bathroom and peed. Buddha came in and watched me, and when I was done he found the right buttons on the overalls, and did the same thing! The guy was amazingly smart. Another point—I don't know whether to mention this—but in the hominid-versus-primate debate,

I've heard it said that most primate male genitals are quite small, and that human males are by far the size champs in that category. Hurray for us. But Buddha, I couldn't help noticing, was more on the human side of the scale. Really, the evidence was adding up. The yeti was a hominid, and a highly intelligent hominid at that. Buddha's quick understanding, his rapid adaptation to changing situations, his recognition of friends and enemies, his *cool*, all indicated smarts of the first order.

Of course, it made sense. How else could they have stayed concealed so well for so long? They must have taught their young all the tricks, generation to generation; keeping close track of all tools or artifacts, hiding their homes in the most hard-to-find caves, avoiding all human settlements, practicing burial of the dead...

Then it occurred to me to wonder: If the yetis were so smart, and so good at concealment, why was Buddha here with me in my room? What had gone wrong? Why had he revealed himself to Nathan, and how had Adrakian managed to capture him?

I found myself speculating on the incidence of mental illness among yetis, a train of thought that made me even more anxious for Nathan's arrival. Nathan was not a whole lot of help in some situations, but the man had a rapport with the yeti that I sadly lacked.

Buddha was crouched on the bed, hunched over his knees, staring at me brightly. We had taken his sunglasses off on arrival, but the Dodgers cap was still on. He looked observant, curious, puzzled. What next? he seemed to say. Something in his expression, something about the way he was coping with it all, was both brave and pathetic—it made me feel for him. "Hey, guy. We'll get you back up there. Namaste."

He formed the words with his lips.

Perhaps he was hungry. What do you feed a hungry yeti? Was he vegetarian, carnivorous? I didn't have much there in the room: some packages of curried chicken soup, some candy (would sugar be bad for him?), beef jerky, yeah, a possibility; Nebico malt biscuits, which were little cookielike wafers made in India that figured large in my diet... I opened a package of these and one of jerky, and offered some to him.

He sat back on the bed and crossed his legs in front of him. He tapped the bed as if to indicate my spot. I sat down on the bed across from him. He took a stick of jerky in his long fingers, sniffed it, stuck it between his toes. I ate mine for example. He looked at me as if I'd just used the wrong fork for the salad. He began with a Nebico wafer, chewing it slowly. I found I was hungry, and from the roundness of his eyes I think he felt the same. But he was cool; there was a procedure here, he had me know; he handled all the wafers carefully first, sniffed them, ate them very slowly; took the jerky from between his toes, tried half of it; looked around the room, or at me, chewing very slowly. So calm, so peaceful he was! I decided the candy would be okay, and offered him the bag of jelly beans. He tried one and his eyebrows lifted; he picked one of the same color (green) from the bag, and gave it to me.

Pretty soon we had all the food I owned scattered out there on the bed between us, and we tried first one thing and then another, in silence, as slowly and solemnly as if it were all some sacred ritual. And you know, after a while I felt just like it was.

XI

About an hour after our meal Nathan, Sarah, and Freds all arrived at once. "You're here!" they cried. "All right, George! Way to go!"

"Thank Buddha," I said. "He got us here."

Nathan and Buddha went through a little hand ritual with the fossil shell necklace. Freds and Sarah told me the story of their adventures. Sarah had fought with Adrakian, who escaped her and ran after us, and then with Valerie Budge, who stayed behind with Fitzgerald, to trade blows and accusations. "It was a joy to pound on her, she's been coming on to Phil for months now—not that I care anymore, of course," Sarah added quickly as Nathan eyed her. Anyway, she had pushed and shoved and denounced Budge and Fitzgerald and Adrakian, and by the time she was done no one at the Sheraton had the slightest idea what was going on. A couple of Secret Service men had gone after Adrakian; the rest contented themselves with shielding the Carters, who were being called on by both sides to judge the merits of the case. Naturally the Carters were reluctant to do this, uncertain as they were of what the case was. Fitzgerald and Budge didn't want to come right out and say they had had a yeti stolen from them, so they were hamstrung; and when Freds returned to see what was up, Nathan and Sarah had already ordered a cab. "I think the Carters ended up on our side," Sarah said with satisfaction.

"All well and good," added Freds, "but there I had old Jimmy right at hand, no yeti to keep me polite, and man I had a bone to pick with that guy! I was in San Diego in 1980 and along about six o'clock on election day me and a bunch of friends were going down to vote and I argued *heavily* with them that we should vote for Carter rather than Anderson, because Anderson would just be a gesture whereas I thought Carter might still have a chance to win, since I don't believe in polls. I really went at it and I convinced every one of them, probably the peak of my political career, and then when we got home and turned on the TV we found out that Carter had already conceded the election a couple of hours before!

My friends were so mad at me! John Drummond threw his beer at me and hit me right here. In fact they soaked me. So I had a bone to pick with old Jimmy, you bet, and I was going to go up to him and ask him why he had done such a thing. But he was looking kind of confused by all the ruckus, so I decided not to."

"The truth is I dragged him away before he could," said Sarah.

Nathan got us back to the problem at hand. "We've still got to get the yeti out of Kathmandu, and Adrakian knows we've got him—he'll be searching for us. How are we going to do it?"

"I've got a plan," I said. Because after my meal with Buddha I had been thinking. "Now where is Buddha's home? I need to know."

Nathan told me.

I consulted my maps. Buddha's valley was pretty near the little airstrip at J—. I nodded. "Okay, here's how we'll do it…"

XII

I spent most of the next day through the looking glass, inside the big headquarters of the Royal Nepal Airline Corporation, getting four tickets for the following day's flight to J—. Tough work, even though as far as I could tell the plane wasn't even close to sold out. J—wasn't near any trekking routes, and it wasn't a popular destination. But that doesn't mean anything at RNAC. Their purpose as a company, as far as I can tell, is not so much to fly people places as it is to *make lists*. Waiting lists. I would call it their secret agenda, only it's no secret.

Patience, a very low-keyed pigheadedness, and lots of baksheesh are the keys to getting from the lists to the status of ticket-holder; I managed it, and in one day too. So I was pleased, but I called my friend Bill, who works in one of the city's travel agencies, to establish a little backup plan. He's good at those, having a lot of experience with RNAC. Then I completed the rest of my purchases, at my favorite climbing outfitters in Thamel. The owner, a Tibetan woman, put down her copy of *The Far Pavilions* and stopped doing her arm aerobics, and got me all the clothes I asked for, in all the right colors. The only thing she couldn't find me was another Dodgers cap, but I got a dark blue "ATOM" baseball cap instead.

I pointed at it. "What is this 'ATOM,' anyway?" Because there were caps and jackets all over Nepal with that one word on them. Was it a company, and if so, what kind?

She shrugged. "Nobody knows."

Extensive advertising for an unknown product: yet another Great Mystery of Nepal. I stuffed my new belongings into my backpack and left. I was on my way home when I noticed someone dodging around in the crowd behind me. Just a glance and I spotted him, nipping into a newsstand: Phil Adrakian.

Now I couldn't go home, not straight home. So I went to the Kathmandu Guest House, next door, and told one of the snooty clerks there that Jimmy Carter would be visiting in ten minutes and his secretary would be arriving very shortly. I walked through into the pretty garden that gives the Guest House so many of its pretensions, and hopped over a low spot in the back wall. Down an empty garbage alley, around the corner, over another wall, and past the Lodge Pleasant or Pheasant into the Star's courtyard. I was feeling pretty covert and all when I saw one of the Carters' Secret Service men, standing in front of the Tantric Used Book Store. Since I was already in the courtyard, I went ahead and hurried on up to my room.

XIII

"I think they must have followed you here," I told our little group. "I suppose they might think we really were trying a kidnapping yesterday."

Nathan groaned. "Adrakian probably convinced them we're part of that group that bombed the Hotel Annapurna this summer."

"That should reassure them," I said. "When that happened the opposition group immediately wrote to the King and told him they were suspending all operations against the government until the criminal element among them was captured by the authorities."

"Hindu guerrillas are heavy, aren't they?" said Freds.

"Anyway," I concluded, "all this means is that we have a damn good reason to put our plan into effect. Freds, are you sure you're up for it?"

"Sure I'm sure! It sounds like fun."

"All right. We'd better all stay here tonight, just in case. I'll cook up some chicken soup."

So we had a spartan meal of curried chicken soup, Nebico wafers, Toblerone white chocolate, jelly beans, and iodinated Tang. When Nathan saw the way Buddha went for the jelly beans, he shook his head. "We've got to get him out of here *fast.*"

When we settled down, Sarah took the bed, and Buddha immediately joined her, with a completely innocent look in his eye, as if to say: Who, me? This is just where I sleep, right? I could see Nathan was a bit suspicious of this, worried about the old Fay Wray complex maybe, and in fact he curled up on the foot of the bed. I assume there weren't any problems. Freds and I threw down the mildewed foam pads I owned and lay down on the floor.

"Don't you think Buddha is sure to get freaked by the flight tomorrow?" Sarah asked when the lights were off.

"Nothing's seemed to bother him much so far," I said. But I wondered; I don't like flying myself.

"Yeah, but this isn't remotely like anything he's ever done before."

"Standing on a high ridge is kind of like flying. Compared to our bike ride it should be easy."

"I'm not so sure," Nathan said, worried again. "Sarah may be right—flying can be upsetting even for people who know what it is."

"That's usually the heart of the problem," I said, with feeling.

Freds cut through the debate: "I say we should get him stoned before the flight. Get a hash pipe going good and just get him *wasted*."

"You're crazy!" Nathan said. "That'd just freak him out more!"

"Nah."

"He wouldn't know what to make of it," Sarah said.

"Oh yeah?" Freds propped himself up on one arm. "You really think those yetis have lived all this time up there among all those pot plants, and haven't figured them out? No way! In fact that's probably why no one ever sees them! Man, the pot plants up there are as big as *pine trees*. They probably use the buds for food."

Nathan and Sarah doubted that, and they further doubted that we should do any experimenting about it at such a crucial time.

"You got any hash?" I asked Freds with interest.

"Nope. Before this Ama Dablam climb came through I was going to fly to Malaysia to join a jungle mountain expedition that Doug Scott put together, you know? So I got rid of it all. I mean, do you fly drugs into Malaysia is not one of the harder questions on the IQ test, you know? In fact I had too much to smoke in the time I had left, and when I was hiking down from Namche to Lukla I was loading my pipe and dropped this chunk on the ground, a really monster chunk, about ten grams. *And I just left it there!* Just left it lying on the ground! I've always wanted to do that.

"Anyway, I'm out. I could fix that in about fifteen minutes down on the street if you want me to, though—"

"No, no. That's okay." I could already hear the steady breathing of Buddha, fast asleep above me. "He'll be more relaxed than any of us tomorrow." And that was true.

XIV

We got up before dawn, and Freds dressed in the clothes that Buddha had worn the day before. We pasted some swatches of Buddha's back fur onto Freds's face to serve as a beard. We even had some of the russet fur taped to the inside of the Dodgers cap, so it hung down behind. With mittens on, and a big pair of snow boots, he was covered; slip the shades onto his nose and he looked at least as weird as Buddha had in the Sheraton. Freds walked around the room a bit, trying it out. Buddha watched him with that surprised look, and it cracked Freds up. "I look like your long-lost brother, hey Buddha?"

Nathan collapsed on the bed despondently. "This just isn't going to work."

"That's what you said last time," I objected.

"Exactly! And look what happened! You call that *working*? Are you telling me that things *worked* yesterday?"

"Well, it depends on what you mean when you say *worked*. I mean here we are, right?" I began packing my gear. "Relax, Nathan." I put a hand on his shoulder, and Sarah put both her hands on his other shoulder. He bucked up a bit, and I smiled at Sarah. That woman was tough; she had saved our ass at the Sheraton, and she kept her nerve well during the waiting, too. I wouldn't have minded asking her on a long trek into the Himal myself, really, and she saw that and gave me a brief smile of appreciation that also said, no chance. Besides, double-crossing old Nathan would have been like the Dodgers giving away Vin Scully. People like that you can't double-cross, not if you want to look yourself in the mirror.

Freds finished getting pointers in carriage from Buddha, and he and I walked out of the room. Freds stopped and looked back inside mournfully, and I tugged him along, irritated at the Method acting; we wouldn't be visible to anyone outside the Star until we got downstairs.

But I must say that overall Freds did an amazing job. He hadn't seen all that much of Buddha, and yet when he walked across that courtyard and into the street, he caught the yeti's gait exactly: a bit stiff-hipped and bowlegged, a rolling sailor's walk from which he could drop to all fours instantly, or so it seemed. I could hardly believe it.

The streets were nearly empty: a bread truck, scavenging dogs (they passed Freds without even a glance—would that give us away?), the old beggar and his young daughter, a few coffee freaks outside the German Pumpernickel Bakery, shopkeepers opening up… Near the Star we passed a parked taxi with three men in it, carefully looking the other way. Westerners. I hurried on. "Contact," I muttered to Freds. He just whistled a little.

There was one taxi in Times Square, the driver asleep. We hopped in and woke him, and asked him to take us to the Central Bus Stop. The taxi we had passed followed us. "Hooked," I said to Freds, who was sniffing the ashtrays, tasting the upholstery, leaning out the window to eat the wind like a dog. "Try not to overdo it," I said, worried about my Dodgers cap with all that hair taped in it flying away.

We passed the big clock tower and stopped, got out and paid the cabbie.

Our tail stopped farther up the block, I was pleased to see. Freds and I walked down the broad, mashed-mud driveway into the Central Bus Stop.

The bus stop was a big yard of mud, about five or eight feet lower than the level of the street. Scores of buses were parked at all angles in the yard, and their tires had torn the mud up until the yard looked like a vehicular Verdun. All of the buses were owned by private companies—one bus per company, usually, with a single route to run—and all of their agents at the wood-and-cloth booths at the entrance clamored for our attention, as if we might have come in without a particular destination in mind, and would pick the agent that made the loudest offer.

Actually, this time it was almost true. But I spotted the agent for the Jiri bus, which is where I had thought to send Freds, and I bought two tickets, in a crowd of all the other agents, who criticized my choice. Freds hunkered down a little, looking suitably distressed. A big hubbub arose; one of the companies had established its right to leave the yard next, and now its bus was trying to make it up the driveway, which was the one and only exit from the yard.

Each departure was a complete test of the driver, the bus's clutch and tires, and the advisory abilities of the agents standing around. After a lot of clutching and coaching this brightly painted bus squirted up the incline, and the scheduling debate began anew. Only three buses had unblocked access to the driveway, and the argument among their agents was fierce.

I took Freds in hand and we wandered around the track-torn mud, looking for the Jiri bus. Eventually we found it: gaily painted in yellow, blue, green and red, like all the rest, ours also had about forty decals of Ganesh stuck all over the windshield, to help the driver see. As usual, the company's "other bus" was absent, and this one was double-booked. We shoved our way on board and through the tightly packed crowd in the aisle, then found empty seats at the back. The Nepalis like to ride near the front. After more boardings, the crowd engulfed us even in the back. But we had Freds at a window, which is what I wanted.

Through the mud-flecked glass I could just see our tail: Phil Adrakian, and two men who might have been Secret Service agents, though I wasn't sure about that. They were fending off the bus agents and trying to get into the yard at the same time, a tough combination. As they sidestepped the bus agents they got in the driveway and almost got run over by the bus currently sliding up and down the slope; one slipped in the mud scrambling away, and fell on his ass. The bus agents thought this was great. Adrakian and the other two hurried off, and squished from bus to bus trying to look like they weren't looking for anything. They were pursued by the most persistent agents, and got mired in the mud from time to time, and I worried after a while that they wouldn't be able to find us. In fact it took them about twenty minutes. But then one saw Freds at the window, and they ducked behind a bus hulk that had sunk axle-deep, waving off the agents in desperate sign language. "Hooked for good," I said.

"Yeah," Freds replied without moving his lips.

The bus was now completely packed; an old woman had even been insinuated between Freds and me, which suited me fine. But it was going to be another miserable trip. "You're really doing your part for the cause," I said to Freds as I prepared to depart, thinking of the cramped day ahead of him.

"No hroblem!" he said liplessly. "I like these 'us trits!'"

Somehow I believed him. I weaseled my way upright in the aisle and said good-bye. Our tails were watching the bus's only door, but that wasn't really much of a problem. I just squirmed between the Nepalis, whose concept of personal "body space" is pretty much exactly confined to the space their bodies are actually occupying—none of this eighteen-inch bullshit for them—and got to a window on the other side of the bus. There was no way our watchers could have seen across the interior of that bus, so I was free to act. I apologized to the Sherpa I was sitting on, worked the window open, and started to climb out. The Sherpa very politely helped me, without the slightest suggestion I was going anything out of the ordinary, and I jumped down into the mud. Hardly anyone on the bus even noticed my departure. I snuck through the no-man's-land of the back buses. Quickly enough I was back on Durbar Marg and in a cab on my way to the Star.

XV

I got the cabbie to park almost inside the Star's lobby, and Buddha barreled into the backseat like a fullback hitting the line. While we drove he kept his head down, just in case, and the taxi took us out to the airport.

Things were proceeding exactly according to my plan, and you might imagine I was feeling pretty pleased, but the truth is that I was more nervous than I'd been all morning. Because we were walking up to the RNAC desk, you see...

When I got there and inquired, the clerk told us our flight had been canceled for the day.

"What?" I cried. "Canceled! What for?"

Now, our counter agent was the most beautiful woman in the world. This happens all the time in Nepal—in the country you pass a peasant bent over pulling up rice, and she looks up and it's a face from the cover of *Cosmopolitan*, only twice as pretty and without the vampire makeup.

This ticket clerk could have made a million modeling in New York, but she didn't speak much English, and when I asked her "What for?" she said, "It's raining," and looked past me for another customer.

I took a deep breath. Remember, I thought: RNAC. What would the Red Queen say? I pointed out the window. "It's not raining. Take a look."

Too much for her. "It's raining," she repeated. She looked around for her supervisor, and he came on over; a thin Hindu man with a red dot on his forehead. He nodded curtly. "It's raining up at J—."

I shook my head. "I'm sorry, I got a report on the shortwave from J—, and besides you can look north and see for yourself. It's not raining."

"The airstrip at J— is too wet to land on," he said.

"I'm sorry," I said, "but you landed there twice yesterday, and it hasn't rained since."

"We're having mechanical trouble with the plane."

"I'm sorry, but you've got a whole fleet of small planes out there, and when one has a problem you just substitute for it. I know, I switched planes three times here once." Nathan and Sarah didn't look too happy to hear that one.

The supervisor's supervisor was drawn by the conversation: another serious, slender Hindu. "The flight is canceled," he said. "It's political."

I shook my head. "RNAC pilots only strike the flights to Lukla and Pokhara—they're the only ones that have enough passengers for the strike to matter." My fears concerning the real reason for the cancellation were being slowly confirmed. "How many passengers on this flight?"

All three of them shrugged. "The flight is canceled," the first supervisor said. "Try tomorrow."

And I knew I was right. They had less than half capacity, and were waiting until tomorrow so the flight would be full. (Maybe more than full, but did they care?) I explained the situation to Nathan and Sarah and Buddha, and Nathan stormed up to the desk demanding that the flight fly as scheduled, and the supervisors had their eyebrows raised like they might actually get some fun out of this after all, but I hauled him away. While I was dialing my friend in the travel agency, I explained to him how maddening irate customers had been made into a sport (or maybe an art form) by Asian bureaucrats. After three tries I got my friend's office. The receptionist answered and said, "Yeti Travels?" which gave me a start; I'd forgotten the company's name. Then Bill got on and I outlined the situation. "Filling planes again, are they?" He laughed. "I'll call in that group of six we 'sold' yesterday, and you should be off."

"Thanks, Bill." I gave it fifteen minutes, during which time Sarah and I calmed Nathan, and Buddha stood at the window staring at the planes taking off and landing. "We've got to get out today!" Nathan kept repeating. "They'll never go for another ruse after today!"

"We know that already, Nathan."

I returned to the desk. "I'd like to get boarding passes for flight 2 to J—, please?"

She made out the boarding passes. The two supervisors stood off behind a console, studiously avoiding my gaze. Normally it wouldn't have gotten to me, but with the pressure to get Buddha out I was a little edgy. When I had the passes in hand I said to the clerk, loud enough for the supervisors to hear, "No more cancellation, eh?"

"Cancellation?"

I gave up on it.

XVI

Of course a boarding pass is only a piece of paper, and when only eight passengers got on the little two-engine plane, I got nervous again; but we took off right on schedule. When the plane left the ground I sat back in my chair, and the relief blew through me like wash from the props. I hadn't known how nervous I was until that moment. Nathan and Sarah were squeezing hands and grinning in the seats ahead, and Buddha was in the window seat beside me, staring out at Kathmandu Valley, or the shimmy gray circle of the prop, I couldn't tell. Amazing guy, that Buddha: *so* cool.

We rose out of the green, terraced, faintly Middle-Earth perfection of Kathmandu Valley, and flew over the mountains to the north, up into the land of snows. The other passengers, four Brits, were looking out their windows and exclaiming over the godlike views, and they didn't give a damn if one of their fellow passengers was an odd-looking chap. There was no problem there. After the plane had leveled out at cruising altitude one of the two stewards came down the aisle and offered us all little wrapped pieces of candy, just as on other airlines they offer drinks or meals. It was incredibly cute, almost like kids playing at running an airline, which is the sort of thought that seems cute itself until you remember you are at seventeen thousand feet with these characters, and they are now going to fly you over the biggest mountains on earth in order to land you on the smallest airstrips. At that point the cuteness goes away and you find yourself swallowing deeply and trying not to think of downdrafts, life insurance, metal fatigue, the afterlife…

I shifted forward in my seat, hoping that the other passengers were too preoccupied to notice that Buddha had swallowed his candy without removing the wrapper. I wasn't too sure about the two across from us, but they were Brits so even if they did think Buddha was strange, it only meant they would look at him less. No problem.

It wasn't long before the steward said, "No smoking, if it please you," and the plane dipped over and started down toward a particularly spiky group of snowy peaks. Not a sign of a landing strip; in fact the idea of one being down there was absurd on the face of it. I took a deep breath. I hate flying, to tell you the truth.

I suppose some of you are familiar with the Lukla airstrip below the Everest region. It's set on a bench high on the side of the Dudh Khosi gorge, and the grass strip, tilted about fifteen degrees from horizontal and only two hundred yards long, aims straight into the side of the valley wall. When you land there all you can really see is the valley wall, and it looks like you're headed right into it. At the last minute the pilot pulls up and hits the strip, and after the inevitable bounces you roll to a stop quickly because you're going uphill so steeply. It's a heavy experience, some people get religion from it, or at least quit flying.

But the truth is that there are at least a dozen RNAC strips in Nepal that are *much worse* than the one at Lukla, and unfortunately for us, the strip at J— was at about the top of that list. First of all, it hadn't begun life as an airstrip at all—it began as a barley terrace, one terrace among many on a mountainside above a village. They widened it and put a wind sock at one end, and tore out all the barley of course, and that was it. Instant airstrip. Not only that, but the valley it was in was a deep one—say five thousand feet—and very steep-sided, with a nearly vertical headwall just a mile upstream from the airstrip, and a sharp dogleg just a mile or so downstream, and really, nobody in their right *minds* would think to put an airstrip there. I became more and more convinced of this as we made a ten-thousand-foot dive into the dogleg, and pulled up against one wall of the valley, so close to it that I could have made a good estimate of the barley count per hectare if I'd been inclined to. I tried to reassure Buddha, but he was working my candy wrapper out of the ashtray and didn't want to be disturbed. Nice to be a yeti sometimes. I caught sight of our landing strip, and watched it grow bigger—say to the size of a ruler—and then we landed on it. Our pilot was good; we only bounced twice, and rolled to a stop with yards to spare.

XVII

And so we came to the end of our brief association with Buddha the yeti, having successfully liberated him from men who would no doubt become major lecturers on the crank circuit forever after.

I have to say that Buddha was one of the nicest guys I've ever had the pleasure of knowing, and certainly among the coolest. Unflappable, really.

But to finish: we collected our packs, and hiked all that afternoon, up the headwall of that valley and along a forested high valley to the west of it. We camped that night on a broad ledge above a short falls, between two monster boulders. Nathan and Sarah shared one tent, Buddha and I another. Twice I woke and saw Buddha sitting in the tent door, looking out at the immense valley wall facing us.

The next day we hiked long and hard, up continuously, and finally came to the site of the expedition's spring camp. We dropped our packs and crossed the river on a new bridge made of bamboo, and Nathan and Buddha led us up the cross-country route, through the forest to the high box canyon where they had first met. By the time we got up there it was late afternoon, and the sun was behind the mountains to the west.

Buddha seemed to understand the plan, as always. He took off my Dodgers cap and gave it back to me, having shed all the rest of his clothes back at camp. I had always treasured that cap, but now it only seemed right to give it back to Buddha; he nodded when I did, and put it back on his head. Nathan put the fossil necklace around Buddha's neck; but the yeti took it off and bit the cord apart, and gave a fossil seashell to each of us. It was quite a moment. Who knows but what yetis didn't eat these shellfish, in a previous age? I know, I know, I've got the timescales wrong, or so they say, but believe me, there was a look in that guy's eye when he gave us those shells that was ancient. I mean *old*. Sarah hugged him, Nathan hugged him, I'm not into that stuff, I shook his skinny strong right hand. "Good-bye for Freds, too," I told him.

"Na-mas-te," he whispered.

"Oh, Buddha," Sarah said, sniffling, and Nathan had his jaw clamped like a vise. Quite the sentimental moment. I turned to go, and sort of pulled the other two along with me; there wasn't that much light left, after all. Buddha took off upstream, and last I saw him he was on top of a riverside boulder, looking back down at us curiously, his wild russet fur suddenly groomed and perfect-looking in its proper context; my Dodgers cap looked odd indeed. That yeti was a hard man to read, sometimes, but it seemed to me then that his eyes were sad. His big adventure was over.

On the way back down it occurred to me to wonder if he wasn't in fact a little crazy, as I had thought once before. I wondered if he might not walk right into the next camp he found, and sit down and croak "Namaste," blowing all the good work we'd done to save him from civilization. Maybe civilization had corrupted him already, and the natural man was gone for good. I hoped not. If so, you've probably already heard about it.

Well, things were pretty subdued in the old expedition camp that night. We got up the tents by lantern light, and had some soup and sat there looking at the blue flames of the stove. I almost made a real fire to cheer myself up, but I didn't feel like it.

Then Sarah said, with feeling, "I'm proud of you, Nathan," and he began to do his Coleman lantern glow, he was so happy. I would be, too. In fact, when she said, "I'm proud of you too, George," and gave me a peck on the cheek, it made me grin, and I felt a pang of… well, a lot of things. Pretty soon they were off to their tent. Fine for them, and I was happy for them, really, but I was also feeling a little like old Snideley Whiplash at the end of the Dudley Do-Right episode: left out in the cold, with Dudley getting the girl. Of course I had my fossil seashell, but it wasn't quite the same.

I pulled the Coleman over, and looked at that stone shell for a while. Strange object. What had the yeti who drilled the little hole through it been thinking? What was it *for*?

I remembered the meal on my bed, Buddha and me solemnly chomping on wafers and picking over the supply of jelly beans. And then I was all right; that was enough for me, and more than enough.

XVIII

Back in Kathmandu we met Freds and found out what had happened to him, over schnitzel Parisienne and apple strudel at the Old Vienna. "By noon I figured you all were long gone, so when the bus stopped for a break at Lamosangu I hopped off and walked right up to these guys' taxi. I did my Buddha thing and they almost died when they saw me coming. It was Adrakian and two of those Secret Service guys who chased us out of the Sheraton. When I took off the cap and shades they were fried, naturally. I said, 'Man, I made a mistake! I wanted to go to Pokhara! This isn't Pokhara!' They were so mad they started yelling at each other. 'What's that?' says I. 'You all made some sort of mistake too? What a shame!' And while they were screaming at each other and all I made a deal with the taxi driver to take me back to Kathmandu too. The others weren't too happy about that, and they didn't want to let me in, but the cabbie was already pissed at them for hiring him to take his car over that terrible road, no matter what the fare. So when I offered him a lot of rupes he was pleased to stick those guys somehow, and he put me in the front seat with him, and we turned around and drove back to Kathmandu."

I said, "You drove back to Kathmandu with the *Secret Service?* How did you explain the fur taped to the baseball cap?"

"I didn't! So anyway, on the way back it was silent city behind me, and it got pretty dull, so I asked them if they'd seen the latest musical disaster movie from Bombay."

"What?" Nathan said. "What's that?"

"Don't you go see them? They're showing all over town. We do it all the time, it's great. You just smoke a few bowls of hash and go see one of these musicals they make, they last about three hours, no subtitles or anything, and they're killers! Incredible! I told these guys that's what they should do—"

"You told the Secret Service guys they should smoke bowls of *hash*?"

"Sure! They're Americans, aren't they? Anyway, they didn't seem too convinced, and we still had a hell of a long way to go to Kathmandu, so I told them the story of the last one I saw. It's still in town, you sure you're not going to see it? I don't want to spoil it for you."

We convinced him he wouldn't.

"Well, it's about this guy who falls in love with a gal he works with. But she's engaged to their boss, a real crook who is contracted to build the town's dam. The crook is building the dam with some kinda birdshit, it looked like, instead of cement, but while he was scamming that he fell into a mixer and was made part of the dam. So the guy and the gal get engaged, but she burns her face lighting a stove. She heals pretty good, but after that when he looks at her he sees through her to her skull and he can't handle it, so he breaks the engagement and she sings a lot, and she disguises herself by pulling her hair over that side of her face and pretending to be someone else. He meets her and doesn't recognize her and falls in love with her, and she reveals who she is and sings that he should fuck off. Heavy singing on all sides at that point, and he tries to win her back and she says no way, and all the time it's raining cats and dogs, and finally she forgives him and they're all happy again, but the dam breaks right where the crook was weakening it and the whole town is swept away singing like crazy. But these two both manage to grab hold of a stupa sticking up out of the water, and then the floods recede and there they are hanging there together, and they live happily ever after. Great, man. A classic."

"How'd the Secret Service like it?" I asked.

"They didn't say. I guess they didn't like the ending."

But I could tell, watching Nathan and Sarah grinning hand-in-hand across the table, that they liked the ending just fine.

XIX

Oh, one more thing: *you must not tell ANYONE about this!!!*

Okay?

REMAKING HISTORY

"The point is *not* to make an exact replica of the Teheran embassy compound." Exasperated, Ivan Venutshenko grabbed his hair in one hand and pulled up, which gave him a faintly Oriental look. "It's the *spirit* of the place that we want to invoke here."

"This has the spirit of our storage warehouse, if you ask me."

"This *is* our storage warehouse, John. We make all our movies here."

"But I thought you said we were going to correct all the lies of the first movie," John Rand said to their director. "I thought you said *Escape from Teheran* was a dumb TV docudrama, only worth remembering because of De Niro's performance as Colonel Jackson. We're going to get the true story on film at last, you said."

Ivan sighed. "That's right, John. Admirable memory. But what you must understand is that when making a film, *true* doesn't mean an absolute fidelity to the real."

"I'll bet that's just what the director of the docudrama said."

Ivan hissed, which he did often while directing their films, to show that he was letting off steam and avoiding an explosion. "Don't be obstructionist, John. We're not doing anything like that hackwork, and you know it. Lunar gravity alone makes it impossible for us to make a completely realist film. We are working in a world of dream, in a surrealist intensification of what really happened. Besides, we're doing these movies for our own entertainment up here! Remake bad historical films! Have a good time!"

"Sure, Ivan. Sure. Except the ones *you've* directed have been getting some great reviews downside. They're saying you're the new Eisenstein and these little remakes are the best thing to hit the screen since *Kane*. So now the pressure is on and it's not just a game anymore, right?"

"Wrong!" Ivan karate-chopped the air. "I refuse to believe that. When we stop having fun doing this"—nearly shouting—"I quit!"

"Sure, Sergei."

"Don't call me that!"

"Okay, Orson."

"JOHN!"

"But that's *my* name. If I call you that we'll all get confused."

Melina Gourtsianis, their female lead, came to Ivan's rescue. "Come on, John, you'll give him a heart attack, and besides it's late. Let's get on with it."

Ivan calmed down, ran his hands through his hair. He loved doing his maddened director routine, and John loved maddening him. As they disagreed about nearly everything, they made a perfect team. "Fine," Ivan said. "Okay. We've got the set ready, and it may not be an *exact* replica of the compound—" fierce glare at John—"but it's good enough.

"Now, let's go through it one more time. It's night in Teheran. This whole quarter of the city has been gassed with a paralyzing nerve gas, but there's no way of telling when the Revolutionary Guards might come barreling in from somewhere else with gas masks or whatever, and you can't be sure some of them haven't been protected from the gas in sealed rooms. Any moment they might jump out firing. Your helicopters are hovering just overhead, so it's tremendously noisy. There's a blackout in the compound, but searchlights from other parts of the city are beginning to pin the choppers. They've been breaking like cheap toys all the way in, so now there are only five left, and you have no assurances that they will continue to work, especially since twice that number have already broken. You're all wearing gas masks and moving through the rooms of the compound, trying to find and move all fifty-three of the hostages—it's dark and most of the hostages are knocked out like the guards, but some of the rooms were well sealed, and naturally these hostages are shouting for help. For a while—and this is the effect I want to emphasize more than any other—for a while, things inside are absolutely chaotic. No one can find Colonel Jackson, no one knows how many of the hostages are recovered and how many are still in the embassy, it's dark, it's noisy, there are shots in the distance. I want an effect like the scene at the end of *The Lady from Shanghai,* when they're in the carnival's house of mirrors shooting at each other. Multiplied by ten. Total chaos."

"Now hold on just a second here," John said, exaggerating his Texas accent, which came and went according to his convenience. "I like the chaos bit, and the allusion to Welles, but let's get back to this issue of the facts. Colonel Jackson was the hero of this whole thing! He was the one that decided to go on with all them helicopters busting out in the desert, and he was the one that found Annette Bellows in the embassy to lead them around, and all in all he was on top of every minute of it. That's why they gave him all them medals!"

Ivan glared. "What part are you playing, John?"

"Why, Colonel Jackson." John drew himself up. "Natch."

"However." Ivan tapped the side of his head, to indicate thought. "You don't just want to do a bad imitation of the De Niro performance, do you? You want to do a new interpretation, don't you? It seems to me a foolish idea to try an imitation of De Niro."

"I like the idea, myself," John said. "Show him how."

Ivan waved him away. "You got all you know about this affair from that stupid TV movie, just like everyone else. I, however, have been reading the accounts of the hostages and the Marines on those helicopters, and the truth is that Colonel Jackson's best moment was out there in the desert, when he decided to go on with the mission even though only five helicopters were still functioning. That was his peak of glory, his moment of heroism. And you did a perfectly adequate job of conveying that when we filmed the scene. We could see every little gear in there, grinding away." He tapped his skull.

"De Niro would have been proud," Melina said.

John pursed his lips and nodded. "We need great men like that. Without them history would be dead. It'd be nothing but a bunch of broken-down helicopters out in a desert somewhere."

"A trenchant image of history," Ivan said. "Too bad Shelley got to it first. Meanwhile, the truth is that after making the decision to go on with the raid, Colonel Jackson appeared, in the words of his subordinates, somewhat stunned. When they landed on the embassy roof he led the first unit in, and when they got lost inside, the whole force was effectively without leadership for most of the crucial first half-hour. All the accounts of this period describe it as the utmost chaos, saved only when Sergeant Payton—*not* Colonel Jackson; the TV movie lied about that—when Payton found Ms. Bellows, and she led them to all the hostage rooms they hadn't found."

"All right, all right." John frowned. "So I'm supposed to be kind of spaced out in this scene."

"Don't go for too deep an analysis, John, you might strain something. But essentially you have it. Having committed the force to the raid, even though you're vastly undermanned because of the damned helicopters breaking down, you're a bit frozen by the risk of it. Got that?"

"Yeah. But I don't believe it. Jackson was a hero."

"Fine, a hero, lots of medals. Roomfuls of medals. If he pinned them on he'd look like the bride after the dollar dance. He'd collapse under their weight. But now let's try showing what really happened."

"All right." John drew himself up. "I'm ready."

The shooting of the scene was the part they all enjoyed the most; this was the heart of the activity, the reason they kept making movies to occupy their free hours at Luna Three. Ivan and John and Melina and Pierre-Paul, the theoreticians who traded directing chores from project to project, always blocked the scenes very loosely, allowing a lot of room for improvisation. Thus scenes like this one, which were supposed to be chaotic, were played out with a manic gusto. They were good at chaos.

And so for nearly a half-hour they rushed about the interior of their Teheran embassy compound—the base storage warehouse, with its immense rows of boxes arranged behind white panels of plywood to resemble the compound's buildings and their interiors. Their shouts were nearly drowned by the clatter of recorded helicopters, while intermittent lights flashed in the darkness. Cutouts representing the helicopters were pasted to the clear dome overhead, silhouetted against the unearthly brilliance of the stars—these last had become a trademark of Luna Three Productions, as their frequent night scenes always had these unbelievably bright stars overhead, part of the films' dreamlike effect.

The actors playing Marines bounded about the compound in their gas masks, looking like aliens descended to ravage a planet; the actors playing hostages and Revolutionary Guards lay scattered on the floor, except for a few in protected rooms, who fought or cried for help. John and Pierre-Paul and the rest hunted the compound for Melina, playing Annette Bellows. For a while it looked as if John would get to her first, thus repeating the falsehood of the De Niro film. But eventually Pierre-Paul, playing Sergeant Payton, located her room, and he and his small unit rushed about after the clear-headed Bellows, who, as she wrote later, had spent most of her months in captivity planning what she should do if this moment ever came. They located the remaining comatose hostages and lugged them quickly to the plywood helicopter on the compound roof. The sound of shots punctuated the helicopters' roar. They leaped through the helicopter's door, shafts of white light stabbing the air like Islamic swords.

That was it; the flight away would be filmed in their little helicopter interior. Ivan turned off the helicopter noise, shouted "Cut!" into a megaphone. Then he shut down all the strategically placed minicams, which had been recording every minute of it.

"What bothers me about your movies, Ivan," John said, "is that you always take away the hero. Always!"

They were standing in the shallow end of the base pool, cooling off while they watched the day's rushes on a screen filling one wall of the natatorium. Many of the screens showed much the same result: darkness, flickering light, alien shapes moving in the elongated dance-like way that audiences on Earth found so surreal, so mesmerizing. There was little indication of the pulsing rhythms and wrenching suspense that Ivan's editing would create from this material. But the actors were happy, seeing arresting images of desperation, of risk, of heroism in the face of a numbingly loud confusion.

Ivan was not as pleased. "Shit!" he said. "We're going to have to do it again."

"Looks okay to me," John remarked. "Son of Film Noir Returns from the Grave. But really, Ivan, you've got to do something about this prejudice against heroes. I saw *Escape from Teheran* when I was a kid, and it was an inspiration to me. It was one of the big reasons I got into engineering."

Pierre-Paul objected. "John, just how did seeing a commando film get you interested in engineering?"

"Well," John replied, frowning, "I thought I'd design a better helicopter, I guess." He ignored his friends' laughter. "I was pretty shocked at how unreliable they were. But the way old De Niro continued on to Teheran! The way he extricated all the hostages and got them back safely, even with the choppers dropping like flies. It was great! We need heroes, and history tells the story of the few people who had what it takes to be one. But you're always downplaying them."

"The Great Man Theory of History," Pierre-Paul said scornfully.

"Sure!" John admitted. "Great Woman too, of course," nodding quickly at the frowning Melina. "It's the great leaders who make the difference. They're special people, and there aren't many of them. But if you believe Ivan's films, there aren't any at all."

With a snort of disgust, Ivan took his attention from the rushes. "Hell, we are going to have to do that scene again. As for my theory of history, John, you both have it and you don't. As far as I understand you." He cocked his head and looked at his friend attentively. On the set they both played their parts to the teeth: Ivan the tormented, temperamental director, gnashing his teeth and ordering people about; John the stubborn, temperamental star, questioning everything and insisting on his preeminence. Mostly this was role-playing, part of the game, part of what made their hobby entertaining to them. Off the set the roles largely disappeared, except to make a point, or have some fun. Ivan was the base's head of computer operations, while John was an engineer involved in the Mars voyage; they were good friends, and their arguments had done much to shape Ivan's ideas for his revisionist historical films, which were certainly the ones from their little troupe making the biggest splash downside—though John claimed this was because of the suspenseful plots and the weird low-gee imagery, not because of what they were saying about history. "*Do* I understand you?" Ivan asked curiously.

"Well," John said, "take the one you did last time, about the woman who saved John Lennon's life. Now that was a perfect example of heroic action, as the 1982 docudrama made clear. There she was, standing right next to a man who had pulled out a damn big gun, and quicker than he could pull the trigger she put a foot in his crotch and a fist in his ear. But in your remake, all we concentrated on was how she had just started the karate class that taught her the moves, and how her husband encouraged her to take the class, and how that cabbie stopped for her even though she was going the other direction, and how that other cabbie told her that Lennon had just walked into his apartment lobby, and all that. You made it seem like it was just a coincidence!"

Ivan took a mouthful of pool water and spurted it at the spangled dome, looking like a fountain statue. "It took a lot of coincidences to get Margaret Arvis into the Dakota lobby at the right time," he told John. "But some of them weren't coincidences—they were little acts of generosity or kindness or consideration that put her where she could do what she did. I didn't take the heroism away. I just spread it around to all the places it belonged."

John grimaced, drew himself up into his star persona. "I suppose this is some damn Commie notion of mass social movements, sweeping history along in a consensus direction."

"No, no," Ivan said. "I always concentrate on individuals. What I'm saying is that all our individual actions add up to history, to the big visible acts of our so-called 'leaders.' You know what I mean; you hear people saying all the time that things are better now because John Lennon was such a moral force, traveling everywhere, Nobel Peace Prize, secular pope, the conscience of the world or whatnot."

"Well, he *was* the conscience of the world!"

"Sure, sure, he wrote great songs. And he got a lot of antagonists to talk. But without Margaret Arvis he would have been killed at age forty. And without Margaret Arvis's husband, and her karate instructor, and a couple cabbies in New York, and so on, she wouldn't have been there to save his life. So we all become part of it, see? The people who say it was all because of Lennon, or Carter, or Gorbachev—they're putting on a few people what we *all* did."

John shook his head, scattering water everywhere. "Very sophisticated, I'm sure! But in fact it was precisely Lennon and Carter and Gorbachev who made huge differences, all by themselves. Carter started the big swing toward human rights. Palestine, the new Latin America, the American Indian nations—none of those would have existed without him."

"In fact," Melina added, glancing mischievously at Pierre-Paul, "if I understand the Margaret Arvis movie correctly, if she hadn't been going to see Carter thank his New York campaign workers for the 1980 victory, she wouldn't have been in the neighborhood of the Dakota, and so she wouldn't have had the chance to save Lennon's life."

John rose up like a whale breaching. "So it's Carter we have to thank for that, too! As for Gorbachev, well, I don't have to tell you what all he did. That was a hundred-eighty-degree turnaround for you Russkies, and no one can say it would have happened without him."

"Well—he was an important leader, I agree."

"Sure was! And Carter was just as crucial. Their years were the turning point, when the world started to crawl out from under the shadow of World War Two. And that was their doing. There just aren't many people who could've done it. Most of us don't have it in us."

Ivan shook his head. "Carter wouldn't have been able to do what he did unless Colonel Ernest Jackson had saved the rescue mission to Teheran, by deciding to go on."

"So Jackson is a hero too!"

"But then Jackson wouldn't have been a hero if the officer back in the Pentagon hadn't decided at the last minute to send sixteen helicopters instead of eight."

"And," Melina pointed out quickly, "if Annette Bellows hadn't spent most of a year daydreaming about what she would do in a rescue attempt, so that she knew blindfolded where every other hostage was being kept. They would have left about half the hostages behind without her, and Carter wouldn't have looked so good."

"Plus they needed Sergeant Payton to find Bellows," Ivan added

"Well shit!" John yelled defensively, which was his retort in any tight spot. He changed tack. "I ain't so sure that Carter's reelection hinged on those hostages anyway. He was running against a flake, I can't remember the guy's name, but he was some kind of idiot."

"So?" Melina said. "Since when has that made any difference?"

With a roar John dove at her, making a big splash. She was much faster than he was, however, and she evaded him easily as he chased her around the pool; it looked like a whale chasing a dolphin. He was reduced to splashing at her from a distance, and the debate quickly degenerated into a big splash fight, as it often did.

"Oh well," John declared, giving up the attack and floating in the shallow end. "I love watching Melina swim the butterfly. In this gravity it becomes a godlike act. Those muscular arms, that sinuous dolphin motion…"

Pierre-Paul snorted. "You just like the way the butterfly puts her bottom above water so often."

"No way! Women are just more hydrodynamic than men, don't you think?"

"Not the way you like them."

"Godlike. Gods and goddesses."

"You look a bit godlike yourself," Melina told him. "Bacchus, for instance."

"Hey." John waved her off, jabbed a finger at the screens. "I note that all this mucho sophisticated European theorizing has been sunk. Took a bit of Texas logic, is all."

"Only Texas logic could do it," Pierre-Paul said.

"Right. You admit my point. In the end it's the great leaders who have to act, the rare ones, no matter if we ordinary folks help them into power."

"When you revise your proposition like that," Ivan said, "you turn it into mine. Leaders are important, but they are leaders because we made them leaders. They are a collective phenomenon. They are expressions of us."

"Now wait just a minute! You're going over the line again! You're talking like heroic leaders are a dime a dozen, but if that were true it wouldn't matter if Carter had lost in 1980, or if Lennon had been killed by that guy. But look at history, man! Look what happened when we did lose great leaders! Lincoln was shot; did they come up with another leader comparable to him? No way! Same with Gandhi, and the Kennedys, and King, and Sadat, and Olof Palme. When those folks were killed their countries suffered the lack of them, because they were special."

"They *were* special," Ivan agreed, "and obviously it was a bad thing they were killed. And no doubt there was a short-term change for the worse. But they're not irreplaceable, because they're human beings just like us. None of them, except maybe Lincoln or Gandhi, was any kind of genius or saint. It's only afterward we think of them that way, because we want heroes so much. But we're the heroes. All of us put them in place. And there are a lot of capable, brilliant people out there to replace the loss of them, so that in the long run we recover."

"The *real* long run," John said darkly. "A hundred years or more, for the South without Lincoln. They just aren't that common. The long run proves it."

"Speaking of the long run," Pierre-Paul said, "is anyone getting hungry?"

They all were. The rushes were over, and Ivan had dismissed them as unusable. They climbed out of the pool and walked toward the changing room, discussing restaurants. There were a considerable number of them in the station, and new ones were opening every week. "I just tried the new Hungarian restaurant," Melina said. "The food was good, but we had trouble, when the meal was over, finding someone to give us the check!"

"I thought you said it was a Hungarian restaurant," John said. They threw him back in the pool.

The second time they ran through the rescue scene in the compound, Ivan had repositioned most of the minicams, and many of the lights; his instructions to the actors remained the same. But once inside the hallways of the set, John Rand couldn't help hurrying in the general direction of Annette Bellows's room.

All right, he thought. Maybe Colonel Jackson had been a bit hasty to rush into the compound in search of hostages, leaving the group without a commander. But his heart had been in the right place, and the truth was, he had found a lot of the hostages without any help from Bellows at all. It was easy; they were scattered in ones and twos on the floor of almost every room he and his commandos entered, and stretched out along with the guards in the rooms and in the halls, paralyzed by the nerve gas. Damn good idea, that nerve gas. Guards and hostages, tough parts to play, no doubt, as they were getting kicked pretty frequently by commandos running by. He hustled his crew into room after room, then sent them off with hostages draped over their shoulders, pretending to stagger down the halls, banging into walls—*really* tough part to play, hostage—and clutching at gas masks and such; great images for the minicams, no doubt about it.

When all his commandos had been sent back, he ran around a corner in what he believed to be the direction of Annette Bellows's room. Over the racket of the helicopters, and the occasional round of automatic fire, he thought he could make out Melina's voice, shouting hoarsely. So Pierre-Paul hadn't gotten to her yet. Good. Now he could find her and be the one to follow her around rescuing the more obscurely housed hostages, just as De Niro had in the docudrama. It would give Ivan fits, but they could argue it out afterward. No way of telling what had really happened in that compound twenty years before, after all; and it made a better *story* his way.

Their set was only one story tall, which was one of the things that John had objected to; the compound in Teheran had been four stories high, and getting up stairs had been part of the hassle. But Ivan was going to play with the images and shoot a few stair scenes later on, to achieve the effect of multiple floors. Fine, it meant he had only to struggle around a couple of narrow corners, jumping comatose Revolutionary Guards, looking fierce for the minicams wherever they were. It was really loud this time around; *really* loud.

Then one of the walls fell over on him, the plywood pinning him to the ground, the boxes behind it tumbling down and filling the hallway. "Hey!" he cried out, shocked. This wasn't the way it had happened. What was going on? The noise of the helicopters cut off abruptly, replaced by a series of crashes, a whooshing sound. That sound put a fine electric thrill down his spine; he had heard it before, in training routines. Air leaving the chamber. The dome must have been breached.

He heaved up against the plywood. Stuck. Flattening himself as much as possible he slithered forward, under the plywood and out into a small space among fallen boxes. Hard to tell where the hallway had been, and it was pitch-dark. There wouldn't be too much time left. He thought of his little gas mask, then cursed; it wasn't connected to a real oxygen supply. That's what comes from using fake props! he thought angrily. A gas mask with nothing attached to it. Open to the air, which was departing rapidly. Not much time.

He found room among the boxes to stand, and he was about to run over them to the door leading out of the warehouse—assuming the whole station hadn't been breached—when he remembered Melina. Stuck in her embassy room down the hall, wouldn't she still be there? Hell. He groped along in the dark, hearing shouts in the distance. He saw lights, too. Good. He was holding his breath, for what felt like minutes at a time, thought it was probably less than thirty seconds. Every time he sucked in a new breath he expected it to be the freezing vacuum, but the supply of rushing, cold—very cold—air continued to fill him. Emergency supply pouring out into the breach, actually a technique he had helped develop himself. Seemed to be working, at least for the moment.

He heard a muffled cry to one side, began to pull at the boxes before him. Squeak in the gloom, ah-ha, there she was. Not fully conscious. Legs wet, probably blood, uh-oh. He pulled hard at boxes, lifted her up. Adrenaline and lunar gravity made him feel like Superman with that part of things, but there didn't seem to be anywhere near as much air as before, and what was left was damned cold. Hurt to breathe. And harder than hell to balance as he hopped over objects with Melina in his arms. Feeling faint, he climbed over a row of boxes and staggered toward a distant light. A sheet of plywood smacked his shin and he cried out, then fell over. "Hey," he said. The air was gone.

When he came to he was lying in a bed in the station hospital. "Great," he muttered. "Whole station wasn't blown up."

His friends laughed, relieved to hear him speak. The whole film crew was in there, it seemed. Ivan, standing next to the bed, said, "It's okay."

"What the hell happened?"

"A small meteor, apparently. Hit out in our sector, in the shuttle landing chambers, ironically. But it wrecked our storage space as well, as you no doubt noticed."

John nodded painfully. "So it finally happened."

"Yes." This was one of the great uncontrollable dangers of the lunar stations; meteors small and large were still crashing down onto the moon's airless surface, by the thousands every year. Odds were poor that any one would hit something as small as the surface parts of their station, but coming down in such numbers.... In the long run they were reduced to a safety status somewhat equivalent to that of mountain climbers. Rockfall could always get you.

"Melina?" John said, jerking up in his bed.

"Over here," Melina called. She was a few beds down, and had one leg in a cast. "I'm fine, John." She got out of bed to prove it, and came over to kiss his cheek. "Thanks for the rescue!"

John snorted. "What rescue?"

They laughed again at him. Pierre-Paul pointed a forefinger at him. "There are heroes everywhere, even among the lowest of us. Now you have to admit Ivan's argument."

"The hell I do."

"You're a hero," Ivan said to him, grinning. "Just an ordinary man, so to speak. Not one of the great leaders at all. But by saving Melina, you've changed history."

"Not unless she becomes president," John said, and laughed. "Hey Melina! Go out and run for office! Or save some promising songwriter or something."

Ivan just shook his head. "Why are you so stubborn? It's not so bad if I'm right, John. Think about it. If I am right, then we aren't just sitting around waiting for leaders to guide us." A big grin lit his face. "We become the masters of our fate, we make our own decisions and act on them—we choose our leaders, and instruct them by consensus, so that we can take history any direction we please! Just as you did in the warehouse."

John lay back in his bed and was silent. Around him his friends grinned; one of them was bringing up a big papier-mâché medal, which vaguely resembled the one the Wizard of Oz pins to the Cowardly Lion. "Ah hell," John said.

"When the expedition reaches Mars, they'll have to name something after you," Melina said.

John thought about it for a while. He took the big medal, held it limply. His friends watched him, waiting for him to speak.

"Well, I still say it's bullshit," he told Ivan. "But if there is any truth to what you say, it's just the good old spirit of the Alamo you're talking about, anyway. We've been doing it like that in Texas for years."

They laughed at him.

He rose up from the bed again, swung the medal at them furiously.

"I swear it's true! Besides, it's all Robert De Niro's fault anyway! I was *imitating* the real heroes, don't you see? I was crawling around in there all dazed, and then I saw De Niro's face when he was playing Colonel Jackson in the Teheran embassy, and I said to myself, well hell, what would he have done in this here situation? And that's just what I did."

THE TRANSLATOR

Owen Rumford had a breakfast of postage stamp glue and mineral water. Combination of a rather strict diet and the fact that it was time again to send the bills to all the citizens of Rannoch Station. Rumford himself had had the stamps printed, and now he carefully counted out payment for them and shifted the money from the tavern's register to the postmaster strongbox, kept under the bar. A bit silly using stamps at all, since Rumford was the mailman as well as the postmaster—also the town's banker, tavern and hotel keeper, judge, and mayor. So he would be delivering the bills himself. But he liked stamps. These had a nice picture of Rannoch seen from space, all gray ocean with a chunk of onyx in it. Besides, in a town as small and isolated as Rannoch Station it was important to keep up the proprieties. Good for morale. Must, however, consider upgrading the quality of the stamp glue.

A quiet morning in the empty tavern. Hotel above empty as well; nothing had come in to the spaceport in the last few days. Unusual. Rumford decided to take advantage of the rare lull and go for a walk. On with his heavy orange overcoat. Tentlike. Rumford was a big man, tall and stout. Big fleshy face, cropped black hair, big walrus moustache that he tugged at frequently, as he did now while bidding a brief farewell to his daughters. Out into the stiff cold onshore wind. Felt good.

Down the black cobblestones of Rannoch Station's steep main street. Hellos to Simon the butcher, chopping away at a flank of mutton; then to the McEvoys, who helped administer the mines. Pleasant sound of construction behind the general store, tinsmiths and stonemasons banging and clacking away. Then left at the bottom of the street where it crossed the stream, up the track of hard black mud until he was out of the town and on the low hills overlooking the sea.

All views on the planet Rannoch were a bit dark. Its sun, G104938, known locally as the Candle, cast a pale and watery light. And the hills of Rannoch Island—the planet's only continent, located in subarctic latitudes—were composed mostly of black rock, mottled with black lichen and a bit of black bracken, all overlooking a dark sea. The dirt between stones had a high component of carbon ash, and even the perpetual frost on the bracken had gray algae growing in it. In short, only the white wrack thrown onto the black sand by the black waves gave any relief to the general gloom. It was a landscape you had to learn to be fond of.

Rumford had. Sniffing at the cold wind he observed with satisfaction the waves mushing onto the beach below the town. All the dories out fishing except the spavined ones, drawn up above the high tide mark. Town sitting above them nice and cozy, tucked into the crease made by the stream's last approach to the sea, to get out of the perpetual wind. Houses and public buildings all made of round black stones, some cracked open to reveal white quartz marbling. Materials at hand. Roofs were tin, glinting nicely in the low rays of the late morning sun. Tin mined here for local use, not for export. They had found deposits of the ore next to the big manganese mines. Easy to work it. Slag heaps inland of the town just looked like more hills, fit in very nicely in fact. Helped block the wind. Bracken already growing on them.

Altogether satisfactory. "A wild and unearthly place," as the song said. Rumford remembered trees from his childhood on a faraway planet, name forgotten. Only thing he missed. Trees, wonderful things. Would be nice for the girls. He'd told them tales till they'd cried for trees, for picnics in a grove, even though they hadn't the slightest. Flowering ones, perhaps. Grow in the ravines the streams cut, perhaps. Out of the wind. Worth thinking about. Damned difficult to get hold of, though; none native to this star cluster, and they were something traders out here didn't usually deal in. A shame.

Rumford was still thinking of trees when the steep black waves sweeping onto the town beach burst apart, revealing a submarine craft apparently made to roll over the sea floor. Big, dull green metal, lot of wheels, a few small windows. Some of the Ba'arni again, making a visit. Rumford frowned. Bizarre creatures, the Ba'arni. Inscrutable. It was obvious to Rumford that they were as alien to Rannoch as humans were, though he'd never gotten a Ba'ar to admit it. Good traders, though. Fishing rights for plastics, metal nodules gathered off seafloor for refined product, deep sea oddities for machine parts and miscellaneous utensils. Still, what they got from Rannoch Station wasn't enough to sustain an undersea colony. And how start it?

Aliens were strange.

The sea tank rolled above the high water mark and stopped. Door on one side clanked open, becoming a ramp. Three Ba'arni trotted out, one spotted him and they veered, trundled toward him. He walked down to meet them.

Strange looking, of course. The fishermen called them sea hippos, talked about them as if they were intelligent ocean-going hippopotami, nothing more. Ludicrous. The usual fallacy when dealing with aliens: think of them as the terran species they most resemble. Let it go at that. Rumford snorted at the idea. Really only the heads looked like hippos. Bodies too of course, to a limited extent. Massive, foursquare, rounded, etc. But the analogy held up poorly when you examined the fine bluish fur, the squat dexterous fingers on all four feet, and of course the row of walnut-sized excrescences that protruded from their spines. Purpose unknown. Like mushrooms growing out of their backs. Not a pleasant sight.

Then again the pictures of hippos Rumford had seen were none too beautiful. Still, in hippos' eyes, even in pictures, you could see something you could understand. Expression maybe hostile, but perfectly comprehensible. Not so with a Ba'ar. Faces quite hippo-like, sure. Giant faces, butt ugly as the fishermen said. The eyes did it—round and big as plates, and almost as flat. And with a look in them you just couldn't read. Curious, that. The fishermen claimed to see them swimming free in the depths, above seafloor mansions of great size. That was after they'd had a few, but still. Obviously alien to Rannoch, nothing more advanced than bracken here. At least on the land. Different in the planet-wide ocean, perhaps; evolutionary advances all submarine, perhaps down in tropics? Impossible to say. But probably visitors, like the humans. Urge to travel fairly widespread among intelligent species. Spaceships filled with seawater. Funny thought.

The three Ba'arni stopped before Rumford. The one on the left opened his voluminous mouth and made a short sequence of whistles and clicks. From experience Rumford knew this was the usual greeting given him, meaning something like "Hello, trading coordinator." Unfortunately, he usually relied on his translation box to make the actual sound of his response, and though he knew what it sounded like he didn't find it easy making the sounds himself. And the box was back at the tavern.

He gave it a try and made the first few clicks that the box emitted when he typed in his usual hello. Then he added another click-combination, meaning, he thought, "Trade, interrogative?"

The Ba'ar on the left replied swiftly. Trade negative, he appeared to say. Something else, well, Rumford had relied too often on the box to do the exact listening, but it seemed to him they were referring to the box itself.

Rumford shrugged. Only one course. He tried the whistle for translation, added the English words "Rannoch Station," and pointed to the town.

Agreement clicks from the spokesBa'ar.

Sonic booms rolled over the hills. They all looked up; Rannoch's gray sky was split by white contrails. Landing craft, coming down in a very steep descent from orbit, toward the town's spaceport a couple miles inland. Rumford identified the craft by their extreme trajectory. Iggglas.

Then an extraordinary thing happened; all three of the Ba'arni rose up on their hind legs and took swipes at the sky, roaring louder than the sonic booms.

A bad sign. One time it had taken a shotgun blast to get a pack of Iggglas off a lone Ba'ar outside the tavern. Never understood the motive; only time he had ever seen the two species together. Not a good omen. And if the Ba'arni needed translation help—

The three of them returned to all fours with a distinct thump, then more or less herded Rumford down the track to the town. Not much chance of disagreement with them; they were remarkably fast on their feet, and must have weighed a couple of tons each. Drafted.

Rumford entered his tavern and got the translation box from the shelf behind the bar. It was an old bulky thing, in many ways obsolete; you had to type in the English half of things, and it would only translate between English and the alien languages in its program—no chance of any alien-to-alien direct contact. Made for some trouble in the tavern.

Without explanation to his daughters he was out the door. Again the Ba'arni herded him up the street. Quickly they were out of town in the other direction, onto the stony windswept road leading to the spaceport and the mines beyond.

They were still hurrying up this road, the Ba'arni moving at a brisk trot and Rumford loping, when they came round a hill and ran into a party of Iggglas. A dozen or so of them, flapping about the road and squawking loudly. The Ba'arni froze in their tracks and Rumford stumbled to a halt out in front of them.

He shuddered as he always did on first sight of an Igggla. They were beyond ugly; they were... well, beyond words. Languages, human languages at any rate, depend a great deal on analogies. Most abstract ideas are expressed by sometimes hidden analogies to physical things and processes, and most new things are described by analogies to older things. Naturally all these analogies are to things within human ken. But analogies to the human realm largely broke down when dealing with the Iggglas, for there was simply nothing to compare them to.

Still, Rumford thought. Analogies all we have, after all. Especially for things alien. So the Iggglas were inevitably compared to vultures, because of body configuration. Fine except that their skins were covered by a white mucous substance instead of feathers. And then wings were not so much for flying as for hitting things. And then heads were distinctly fishlike, with long underslung jaws that made them resemble gars. Vultures with gars' heads, covered in whitish mucus: fair enough, only the analogy didn't really do justice to their sickening quality. Because above all they were *alien,* weird and hideous beyond appearance alone. Not even sure they occupied the same reality as other creatures; they seemed to *flicker* a little, as if disturbing the membrane between their physical realm and ordinary spacetime. Yes; disgusting. Next to them the Ba'arni seemed handsome beasts. Almost family one might say.

Rumford stepped forward to offer some kind of greeting to the Iggglas, make sure the Ba'arni didn't have to. Touchy situation. He had dealt with Iggglas before; they came from the next planet in, and used Rannoch Station as a trade center. Trade again. Remarkable what kind of thing it put you in contact with, out in this stellar group. Certainly had to get used to these creatures. Language of theirs very loud and squawky. Every once in a while they'd spit in each other's mouths for emphasis. Some kind of chemical transfer of information. Box wasn't equipped to deal with that, luckily. Their speech was enough, although it appeared to be an odd grammar. Lacked tenses, or even verbs for that matter. Another indication of different reality.

The Iggglas liked to stick out a claw and shake humans by the hand, maybe to see if they would vomit. But Rumford could do it with hardly a quiver. No worse than a cockroach in the hand, certainly. So he shook hands with the wet claw of the biggest Igggla. Hot bodies, high metabolism. It turned its head to the side to inspect him with its left eye. Foul smell, like asafoetida.

Two of the other Iggglas led a long string of little furball creatures, a bit like rabbits without legs, up to the one Rumford had shaken hands with. Rumford sighed. Probably the high metabolisms, but still. Note the others weren't doing it—

Abruptly the biggest one snapped that gar's head down and devoured the first rabbit-thing in line, swallowing it whole so that it disappeared instantly, as in a conjuring trick. The Igggla would interrupt itself to do the same throughout the rest of the interview. It made Rumford nervous.

The Igggla squawked loudly and at length. "Croownekkkseetrun-p!" it sounded like. Rumford turned on the translator, switched it to *Iggglas* and typed in the message, *"Again, please."*

After a short interval the box made a short screech. With a loud honk and a quick drumming of its talon-like feet, the big Igggla squawked its initial message again.

A moment later a message appeared in print on the small screen of the translator box. *"Hunger interrogative."*

The Igggla batted one of the worried-looking rabbit-things forward.

"No thank you," Rumford typed steadily, and waited for the box to speak. Then: *"Why do you come to Rannoch interrogative."*

The head Igggla listened to the box's hooting, did a quick hopping dance, struck one of the other Iggglas in the head, and replied.

The box's screen eventually produced a sentence. *"Warlike viciously now descendant death fat food flame death."*

A typical grammatical artifact produced by the box when dealing with the Iggglas. Rumford pondered it, switched the box to *Ba'arni,* and typed in *"The Iggglas express a certain hostility toward the Ba'arni."*

The box whistled and clicked in the oddly high-pitched Ba'arni language. The Ba'ar on the left, which was not the same one that had spoken to Rumford at first, whistled and clicked in reply. The box's screen printed out, *"Tell them we are ready to (x-click B-flat to C-sharp click sequence; see dictionary) and the hateful poison birds will die in traditional manner."*

Hmm. Problems everywhere. With the Iggglas you got grammatic hash. With Ba'arni, too many trips to the dictionary. Which was a problem in itself. The box was not entirely satisfactory, and that was the truth.

Needed to be seated to type on the keyboard properly, too. So, despite the fact that it might seem undignified, Rumford sat on the ground between the two parties of aliens, called up the Ba'arni dictionary function of the box, and typed in an inquiry. The definition appeared quickly:

"X-click B-flat to C-sharp click sequence: 1. Fish market. 2. Fish harvest. 3. Sunspots visible from a depth of 10 meters below the surface of the ocean on a calm day. 4. Traditional festival 5. Astrological configuration in galactic core."

Rumford sighed. The Ba'arni dictionary could be nearly useless. Never sure if it was really serious. No idea who actually wrote the thing. Basic programming provided by linguists working for the company that made the box, of course, but in the years since then (and it was a very old box), its various owners had entered new information of their own. In fact this one was jammed with languages that factory-new boxes didn't have. No other box Rumford had seen had a Ba'arni program; that was why Rumford had bought this one when it was offered by a passing spacecraft pilot. But who in fact had added the Ba'arni program? Rather puckish individual, from the look of it. Or perhaps the Ba'arni relied more than most on context. Some languages like that. Impossible to be sure. The box had worked to this point, and that was all Rumford could say about it. Trade a different matter, however. Not quite as delicate as this.

After thinking it over, Rumford typed in another question to the Ba'arni. *"Clarification please. What do you mean by x-click B-flat to C-sharp click sequence, in context of previous sentence interrogative."*

The Ba'arni listened, and the one on the left replied.

"Ba'arni and poison birds fight war in (z-click double sequence; see dictionary) cycle that now returns. Time for this ritual war."

Very good. Clear as a bell. Unfortunate message, of course, but at least he understood it. Must have meant definition four, perhaps tied to the timing of three, or five. Add new definition later.

Before he could convey the Ba'arni sentiments to the Iggglas, the chief Igggla ate another rabbit-thing, danced in a circle and screeched for quite some time. The box hummed a bit, and the screen flickered.

"Fine fiery wonderful this land always again war's heat slag battlefield dead fat food flame death yes now."

Rumford squinted at the screen.

Finally he typed in, *"Clarification please: where is location of ritual war interrogative,"* and sent it to the Iggglas.

The chief Igggla replied at length, howling shrilly.

On the screen: *"Fine fiery wonderful this land always again war's heat slag battlefield dead fat food flame death yes now yes."*

The Iggglas were not much on clarification.

Rumford decided to ask the same of the Ba'arni, and switched the box over. *"Clarification please: where is location of ritual war interrogative."*

The box whistled, the Ba'ar on the left clicked. The screen flickered and printed out: *"Clarification unnecessary as poison birds know every twelve squared years for twelve cubed years ritual dodecimation has taken place on same ritual ground. Tell them to stop wasting time. We are ready for conflict."*

A small vertical line appeared between Rumford's eyebrows.

He switched back and forth from Iggglas to Ba'arni, asking questions concerning this ritual war, explaining that the questions were essential for proper translation. Every Iggglas answer a long string of violent nouns, adjectives, and so forth, with never a verb. Every Ba'arni answer a hunt through the dictionary. Slowly Rumford put together a picture of Ba'arni and Iggglas contingents battling each other. Ritual phrases from the Ba'arni concerned *Air people opposition water people destruction land,* and so on. The Iggglas concentrated on *fat food,* although obviously it was a ritual for them as well—a sort of game, from the sounds of it. The origins of such a curious conflict remained completely obscure to Rumford; some things the Ba'arni said seemed to indicate that they may have had a religious ceremony of coming out onto land in great numbers during maximum sunspot activity, and that for many cycles now the Iggglas had been there to transform this ceremony into a bloody battle. Possibly indicating that the Ba'arni were in fact not native to Rannoch, as Rumford has speculated earlier. But he couldn't be sure. No way of knowing, really. Accident, misunderstanding; no doubt they themselves didn't have the faintest anymore.

In any case ritual war well established, this was clear. And either during or after the battle—sequentiality was difficult to determine, given the lack of tenses in the Iggglas—the two belligerent forces apparently torched, in a kind of sacrifice, the profane land they fought on.

Hmm. Rumford sat cross-legged on the ground between the two groups, thinking. Rannoch Station had only been there for the past thirty years or so. All that carbon in their dirt, sign of great fires in the past. But mining geologists said no vulcanism. Tremendous heat, one said. Solar flares? Or weapons. Tremendous heat. Tin would melt. It was possible. And after all, here they were.

Rumford cleared his throat. Sticky. He hesitated for a bit, and would have hesitated more, but some thirty sets of alien eyes (counting the rabbit-things) stared fixedly at him, and impelled him to action. He tugged his moustache. Sunspots underwater, astrology... really a shame he didn't know more about these creatures. Now where was he? Ah yes— Ba'arni had indicated readiness for conflict. We are ready for conflict. The line between his eyebrows deepened, and finally he shrugged. He clicked the box over to *Iggglas* and typed away.

"*Ba'arni explain that their priest-caste have performed submarine astrology which contra-indicates ritual war this time. Request war be postponed until next scheduled time twelve squared Rannoch years from now in order to achieve proper equilibrium with the stars.*"

The box honked that out in a series of Iggglasian words. All the Iggglas listeners snapped their big gar jaws as they heard it, then leaped in circles thrashing the dust. Several of the rabbit-things disappeared. The chief Igggla hopped toward Rumford and shrieked for a long while.

On the screen: "*War heat slag death fat food exclamation. Delay impossible war as scheduled astrology stupid exclamation.*"

Rumford tugged his moustache. Not gone over so well. The three Ba'arni were staring at him curiously, waiting for him to translate what the Iggglas had just so vehemently squawked. The line between his eyebrows deepened even more. Ba'arni had visited him more frequently in last year. Now what had they been trading for?

He switched the box to Ba'arni, typed: "*Iggglas state that they do not want ritual war to take place this time. They note the Ba'arni are suffering famine and therefore population difficulties. Thus ritual dodecimation could lead to extinction of Ba'arni and end of beloved war for Iggglas. They suggest skipping this time and returning to war next twelve squared years."*

A lot of clicks and whistles to convey that. The Ba'arni retreated and conferred among themselves, while the Iggglas squawked derisively at them. Rumford watched anxiously. Ba'arni had been trading rather actively for foodstuffs. Brow needed wiping. He tugged on his moustache. The Ba'arni returned in a new line-up and the one on the left clicked.

On screen: *"Ba'arni completely capable of sustaining their part in (x-click B-flat to C-sharp click sequence; see dictionary). Ba'arni (z-click z-click; see dictionary) insist ritual be carried out as always. Poison birds will die."*

Rumford let out a deep breath, switched the box to dictionary function and inquired about z-click z-click.

"Z-click z-click: 1. (double n-1 click sequence, B-flat; see dictionary). 2. Magnetic sense located in supra-spinal nerve nodules. 3. Eggs. 4. Large bearings. 5. Sense of place or of location. 6. Money."

Nothing there seemed completely appropriate, so he tried looking up double n-1 click sequence, B-flat.

"Double n-1 click sequence, B-flat: 1. (q-click A-flat; see dictionary). 2. Honor. 3. Pride. 4. Shame. 5. Face. 6. Molar teeth."

Bit of an infinite regress there, could have you jumping around the dictionary forever. Definitely a prankster, whoever had entered this language in the box. But assume the Ba'arni meant some kind of pride, saving face, that kind of thing. Made sense. Every species must have a version of the concept. Fine. Assume clarification on that front. Now, where was he with the Iggglas? Looking fairly ready for an answer, they were. Rumford pursed his lips so hard that his moustache tips almost met under his chin. Astrologer bit not gone over very far. Iggglas pretty aggressive types. He clicked over to Iggglas and typed away.

"Ba'arni live by submarine astrologer's divine words and intend to decline ritual war. Iggglas insistence will make no difference. Ba'arni have assured this by placement of heat bombs on floor of all seas on Iggglas. Twelve squared heat of weapons used in ritual war. If Iggglas insist on ritual war Ba'arni have no choice but to escalate to total war and annihilate Iggglas seas. Apologies but astrologers insist."

While the box spoke this message in Iggglas (and how was it doing it without verbs?), Rumford pulled a handkerchief from his coat pocket and wiped his brow. Uncommonly warm. Hunger made him feel a bit weak. Have to start eating breakfasts.

The Iggglas began to squawk among themselves very vigorously, and Rumford took a quick glance down at the screen to see if the box was translating their squabble. It was, although apparently it was having problems with the fact that two or three of the Iggglas were always speaking at the same time: *"Lying fat food no meteor shower maybe total war then purpose ambiguous no exclamation one miss translator liar idiot meteor shower no explanation maybe box direct Iggglas fat food why not meteor shower maybe,"* and so on. Rumford tried to direct one eye to the screen and the other to the hopping Iggglas. Looked like the second-largest one might be making the comments about the translator and the box. Yes, even pointing at him as he spat in leader's mouth. Problem.

The Ba'arni were whistling among themselves, so Rumford quickly typed in another message to the Iggglas:

"Ba'arni wish to deal with senior Igggla, suggest that perhaps second-biggest Igggla is one qualified to speak for Iggglas in this matter."

The box squawked this out and Rumford helpfully pointed to the Igggla he had in mind. The chief Iggglas took in the import of the message and shrieked, leaped in the air, jumped at his lieutenant and beat him with a flurry of quick wing blows. Knocked the squealing creature flat and faster than Rumford could see had the lieutenant's skinny vulture-neck between his long toothy jaws. The lieutenant squeaked something dismal and was allowed to live; it crawled to the back of the group of Iggglas. The leader then strode forward and spoke to Rumford and the Ba'arni.

On the screen: *"Astrology stupid war heat fat food death always compact between Iggglas and fat food change never good annihilation of home planet outside compact realm of total war insistence on ritual war heat fat food death."*

Rumford's brow wrinkled as he read this. Getting nowhere with the garheads. After a moment's thought he switched the box to Ba'arni, and typed in, very carefully, the following:

"Iggglas understand Ba'arni capable of sustaining ritual war and intend no slur on Ba'arni (double n-1 sequence, B-flat)." Possibly it was a mistake to try directly for Ba'arni terms to add power to the message. Box could mess it up entirely, in context of sentence. He typed on: *"Iggglas too have sense of honor and save face by suggestion that Ba'arni weakness is only source of problem in ritual war, but Iggglas also have famine trouble, and demand ritual war be postponed twelve squared years to keep both Iggglas and Ba'arni in sufficient numbers to sustain ritual war in perpetuity. Suggest mutual expression of honor (exclamation) by recognition of ritual promise for next time."*

Clicks and whistles, the Ba'arni listening with their big hippo ears tilted down toward the box. Rumford felt the sweat trickling down the inside of his shirt. Extraordinarily hot for Rannoch. The Ba'arni were discussing the matter among themselves, and again Rumford put one eye to the box to see what it could tell him.

"We must not give (z-click z-click; see dictionary) exclamation. Necessary to (middle C to high C; see dictionary)."

Surreptitiously he switched over to the dictionary function and looked up middle C to high C.

"Middle C to high C: 1. Stand still 2. Run. 3. Show interest. 4. Lose. 5. Alternate. 6. Repair. 7. Replace. 8. Subtend. 9. (high C to middle C; see dictionary). 10. Glance through turbid water."

Useful word. Rumford gave up on it.

Finally the Ba'ar on the left, the third one to speak from that position, raised its head and spoke. *"Ba'arni (z-click z-click; see dictionary) satisfied by expression of (n-1 click sequence, B-flat; see dictionary) by poison birds toward Ba'arni and sacred dodecimation ground, if agreed that ritual war should be resumed in twelve squared years at prescribed time."*

Rumford could not prevent his eyebrows from lifting a bit. One down, apparently. Now where was he with the others? Ah yes. Tricky still, the stubborn buzzards. Entirely possible they might take up his threat of total war and act on it, which would leave the Ba'arni considerably confused. And Rannoch torched. Hmm. A problem.

He thought hard and fast. Each side a different understanding of war. Ba'arni thought of it as religious event and perhaps population control, but couldn't sustain it when population already low from famine. Thus agreeable to postponement, if face saved, and quick to arrange talk when Iggglas seen approaching. Fine, clear. And Iggglas? Food source, population control, game, who could tell? Certainly didn't care what Ba'arni astrologers thought of things. Not big on religion, the Iggglas.

Need to give reasons convincing to receiver of message, not sender. Rumford blinked at this sudden realization. Senders not hearing message, after all—not even sending it in fact. Receiver all that mattered.

He switched the box to Iggglas. *"Ba'arni suffer from famine and fear war would reduce them to extinction, in which case no more ritual wars, no more fat food. Want postponement only."* The Iggglas shrieked at this in derision, but the box's screen included among the printed hash the word *understanding.* Perhaps they now had a reason they could comprehend. Best to press the point. He typed another message to the Iggglas:

"Dodecimation and fat food rely on population existence, as you say. If there is no population there is no dodecimation or fat food and ritual war is ended forever. Ba'arni therefore insist on postponement of ritual war and if Iggglas attempt to wage it regardless of traditional cooperation of the Ba'arni then Ba'arni have no choice but total war and mass suicide for all parties. Suggest therefore postponement. Astrologer's decision necessary given population of Ba'arni."

The box hooted and squawked, the Iggglas leader cocked his head to one side and listened, watching Rumford carefully. When the message was completed the leader did a little dance of its own, all on one spot. Then suddenly it approached the Ba'arni directly. Rumford held his breath. The Iggglas leader shrieked at the Ba'arni, sweeping one wing at them in a ferocious gesture.

All three Ba'arni opened their immense mouths, which appeared to split their immense heads in half, and whistled loud and high. Rumford had to hold his hands over his ears, and the Iggglas leader stepped back. Impressive sight, those three open mouths. The Igggla opened his long mouth as if to mock them; lot of teeth in there. Impressive as well. Battle of mouths. All right if it didn't lead to anything. Tense. Need to get a response in squawks from old gar face. Couldn't seem to intrude too much, however.

A long minute's wait as the two parties stared each other down. The Iggglas leader suddenly turned and squawked.

On screen: *"Heat death fat food postponement replacement cannibalism for Iggglas assurance renewal of slag heat war fat food in twelve squared years."* Rumford let out a long breath.

He switched to Ba'arni, typed.

"Iggglas agree to acknowledge Ba'arni honor, promise renewal of honorable battle next time in twelve squared years."

Whistle, click, whistle. The Ba'ar on the left spoke quickly.

"The Ba'arni accept postponement and acknowledgement of their honor."

When Rumford conveyed the news to the Iggglas leader, it too was agreeable. Appeared to like the promise that the conflict would be renewed. But then it squawked on at length:

"Iggglas negative continuance until next ritual war with heat death bombs in Iggglas seas, insistence removal immediate."

Hmm. Bit of a problem, to tell the Ba'arni to remove bombs they didn't know existed. Meanwhile they were looking at Rumford to see what had been said, and to gain time Rumford switched to Ba'arni and typed, *"Iggglas agree to honor Ba'arni and agree to return to ritual war next time."*

A repeat of the previous message to them, but Rumford was too busy to think of anything else, and happily the Ba'arni didn't seem to notice. They agreed again, and Rumford returned to Iggglas.

"Ba'arni state weapons on Iggglas seafloor will be de-activated. All they can do as weapons cannot be relocated."

The Iggglas leader shrieked, pummelled the dust. *"War war war total annihilation war fat food heat death unless sea bombs removal exclamation."*

Hmm. Wouldn't do to stop a small ritual war by starting a total war even more likely to destroy Rannoch Island. Rumford quickly got the Ba'arni's assurances that they would return in twelve squared years, then returned to Iggglas:

"Ba'arni state detonator will be given to Iggglas. Detonation wavelength determined by detonator and Iggglas can change this and render bombs inoperative. Demonstration of this on small scale can be arranged in Rannoch ocean. Translator agrees to convey detonator and run demonstration as ritual forbids Ba'arni speaking to Iggglas in between ritual wars."

Could get a good long-distance detonator from the manganese mines, set up an offshore explosion. Hopefully convince them.

After a long and apparently thoughtful dance, the Iggglas leader ate two of the rabbit-things, and indicated his acceptance of this plan. The Iggglas abruptly turned and hopped back down the road to the spaceport. The meeting was over.

Owen Rumford stood up unsteadily, and feeling drained he accompanied the three Ba'arni back to the beach. As they got into their seacraft, the one on the left said something; but Rumford had his box in his coat pocket. After the Ba'arni craft rolled under the black waves, he took the box out, turned it on and tried to imitate the last set of whistles. The box printed it as, *"(y-click x-click; see dictionary.)"* He switched to the dictionary function and looked it up.

"Y-click x-click: 1. Ebb tide. 2. Twisted, knotted, complex. 3. The ten forefingers. 4. Elegance. 5. The part of the moon visible in a partial eclipse. 6. Tree."

"Hmm," Rumford said.

He walked slowly up toward the town. Y-click x-click. Those big plate eyes, staring at him. Their half of the conversation had gone pretty smoothly. Very smoothly. And all his assumptions, about the famine, the rituals. Could they be... just a little.... But no language barrier as troublesome in telepathy as in speech, after all. Maybe.

Y-click x-click. If he had gotten the whistle right. But he thought he had. Why have word for something they'd never seen? But Ba'arni had traded with earlier passersby, witness box. Curious.

Tin roofs glinting in the light. Black stone walls, veined with white quartz. Black cobblestones. Very neat. Fine little town. In a hundred and forty-four years, they would have to figure something out. Well, that was their problem. More warning next time. Nothing to be done about it now.

He walked into the tavern and sat down heavily. His daughters had just finished preparing the tables for lunch. "Papa, you look exhausted," Isabel said. "Have you been trying to exercise again?"

"No, no." He looked around with a satisfied expression, heaved out a long breath. "Just a spot of translation." He got up and went behind the bar, started drawing a beer from the tap. Suddenly the corners of his moustache lifted a little. "Might get a bit of payment for it," he told her. "If so—still care for a picnic?"

GLACIER

"This is Stella," Mrs. Goldberg said. She opened the cardboard box and a gray cat leaped out and streaked under the corner table.

"That's where we'll put her blanket," Alex's mother said.

Alex got down on hands and knees to look. Stella was a skinny old cat; her fur was an odd mix of silver, black, and pinkish tan. Yellow eyes. Part tortoise-shell, Mom had said. The color of the fur over her eyes made it appear her brow was permanently furrowed. Her ears were laid flat.

"Remember she's kind of scared of boys," Mrs. Goldberg said.

"I know." Alex sat back on his heels. Stella hissed. "I was just looking." He knew the cat's whole story. She had been a stray that began visiting the Goldbergs' balcony to eat their dog's food, then—as far as anyone could tell—to hang out with the dog. Remus, a stiff-legged ancient thing, seemed happy to have the company, and after a while the two animals were inseparable. The cat had learned how to behave by watching Remus, and so it would go for a walk, come when you called it, shake hands and so on. Then Remus died, and now the Goldbergs had to move. Mom had offered to take Stella in, and though Father sighed heavily when she told him about it, he hadn't refused.

Mrs. Goldberg sat on the worn carpet beside Alex, and leaned forward so she could see under the table. Her face was puffy. "It's okay, Stell-bell," she said. "It's okay."

The cat stared at Mrs. Goldberg with an expression that said *You've got to be kidding.* Alex grinned to see such skepticism.

Mrs. Goldberg reached under the table; the cat squeaked in protest as it was pulled out, then lay in Mrs. Goldberg's lap quivering like a rabbit. The two women talked about other things. Then Mrs. Goldberg put Stella in Alex's mother's lap. There were scars on its ears and head. It breathed

237

fast. Finally it calmed under Mom's hands. "Maybe we should feed her something," Mom said. She knew how distressed animals could get in this situation: they themselves had left behind their dog Pongo, when they moved from Toronto to Boston. Alex and she had been the ones to take Pongo to the Wallaces; the dog had howled as they left, and walking away Mom had cried. Now she told Alex to get some chicken out of the fridge and put it in a bowl for Stella. He put the bowl on the couch next to the cat, who sniffed at it disdainfully and refused to look at it. Only after much calming would it nibble at the meat, nose drawn high over one sharp eyetooth. Mom talked to Mrs. Goldberg, who watched Stella eat. When the cat was done it hopped off Mom's lap and walked up and down the couch. But it wouldn't let Alex near; it crouched as he approached, and with a desperate look dashed back under the table. "Oh Stella!" Mrs. Goldberg laughed. "It'll take her a while to get used to you," she said to Alex, and sniffed. Alex shrugged.

Outside the wind ripped at the treetops sticking above the buildings. Alex walked up Chester Street to Brighton Avenue and turned left, hurrying to counteract the cold. Soon he reached the river and could walk the path on top of the embankment. Down in its trough the river's edges were crusted with ice, but midstream was still free, the silty gray water riffled by white. He passed the construction site for the dam and came to the moraine, a long mound of dirt, rocks, lumber, and junk. He climbed it with big steps, and stood looking at the glacier.

The glacier was immense, like a range of white hills rolling in from the west and north. The Charles poured from the bottom of it and roiled through a cut in the terminal moraine; the glacier's snout loomed so large that the river looked small, like a gutter after a storm. Bright white iceberg chunks had toppled off the face of the snout, leaving fresh blue scars and clogging the river below.

Alex walked the edge of the moraine until he was above the glacier's side. To his left was the razed zone, torn streets and fresh dirt and cellars open to the sky; beyond it Allston and Brighton, still bustling with city life. Under him, the sharp-edged mound of dirt and debris. To his right, the wilderness of ice and rock. Looking straight ahead it was hard to believe that the two halves of the view came from the same world. Neat. He descended the moraine's steep loose inside slope carefully, following a path of his own.

The meeting of glacier and moraine was a curious juncture. In some places the moraine had been undercut and had spilled across the ice in wide fans; you couldn't be sure if the dirt was solid or if it concealed crevasses. In other places melting had created a gap, so that a thick cake of ice stood over empty air, and dripped into gray pools below. Once Alex had seen a car in one of these low wet caves, stripped of its paint and squashed flat.

In still other places, however, the ice sloped down and overlay the moraine's gravel in a perfect ramp, as if fitted by carpenters. Alex walked the trough between dirt and ice until he reached one of these areas, then took a big step onto the curved white surface. He felt the usual quiver of excitement: he was on the glacier.

It was steep on the rounded side slope, but the ice was embedded with thousands of chunks of gravel. Each pebble, heated by the sun, had sunk into a little pocket of its own, and was then frozen into position in the night; this process had been repeated until most chunks were about three-quarters buried. Thus the glacier had a peculiarly pocked, rocky surface, which gripped the torn soles of Alex's shoes. A non-slip surface. No slope on the glacier was too steep for him. Crunch, crunch, crunch: tiny arabesques of ice collapsed under his feet with every step. He could change the glacier, he was part of its action. Part of it.

Where the side slope leveled out the first big crevasses appeared. These deep blue fissures were dangerous, and Alex stepped between two of them and up a narrow ramp very carefully. He picked up a fist-sized rock, tossed it in the bigger crack. *Clunk clunk...splash.* He shivered and walked on, ritual satisfied. He knew from these throws that at the bottom of the glacier there were pockets of air, pools of water, streams running down to form the Charles... a deadly subglacial world. No one who fell into it would ever escape. It made the surface ice glow with a magical danger, an internal light.

Up on the glacier proper he could walk more easily. Crunch crunch crunch, over an undulating broken debris-covered plain. Ice for miles on miles. Looking back toward the city he saw the Hancock and Prudential towers to the right, the lower MIT towers to the left, poking up at low scudding clouds. The wind was strong here and he pulled his jacket hood's drawstring tighter. Muffled hoot of wind, a million tricklings. There were little creeks running in channels cut into the ice: it was almost like an ordinary landscape, streams running in ravines over a broad rocky meadow. And yet everything was different. The streams ran into crevasses or potholes and instantly disappeared, for instance. It was wonderfully strange to look down such a rounded hole: the ice was very blue and you could see the air bubbles in it, air from some year long ago.

Broken seracs exposed fresh ice to the sun. Scores of big erratic boulders dotted the glacier, some the size of houses. He made his way from one to the next, using them as cover. There were gangs of boys from Cambridge who occasionally came up here, and they were dangerous. It was important to see them before he was seen.

A mile or more onto the glacier, ice had flowed around one big boulder, leaving a curving wall some ten feet high—another example of the glacier's whimsy, one of hundreds of odd surface formations. Alex had wedged some stray boards into the gap between rock and ice, making a seat that was tucked out of the west wind. Flat rocks made a fine floor, and in the corner he had even made a little fireplace. Every fire he lit sank the hearth of flat stones a bit deeper into the otherwise impervious ice.

This time he didn't have enough kindling, though, so he sat on his bench, hands deep in pockets, and looked back at the city. He could see for miles. Wind whistled over the boulder. Scattered shafts of sunlight broke against ice. Mostly shadowed, the jumbled expanse was faintly pink. This was because of an algae that lived on nothing but ice and dust. Pink; the blue of the seracs; gray ice; patches of white, marking snow or sunlight. In the distance dark clouds scraped the top of the blue Hancock building, making it look like a distant serac. Alex leaned back against his plank wall, whistling one of the songs of the Pirate King.

Everyone agreed the cat was crazy. Her veneer of civilization was thin, and at any loud noise—the phone's ring, the door slamming—she would jump as if shot, then stop in mid-flight as she recalled that this particular noise entailed no danger; then lick down her fur, pretending she had never jumped in the first place. A flayed sensibility.

She was also very wary about proximity to people; this despite the fact that she had learned to love being petted. So she would often get in moods where she would approach one of them and give an exploratory, half-purring mew; then, if you responded to the invitation and crouched to pet her, she would sidle just out of arm's reach, repeating the invitation but retreating with each shift you made, until she either let you get within petting distance—just—or decided it wasn't worth the risk, and scampered away. Father laughed at this intense ambivalence. "Stella, you're too stupid to live, aren't you," he said in a teasing voice.

"Charles," Mom said.

"It's the best example of approach avoidance behavior I've ever seen," Father said. Intrigued by the challenge, he would sit on the floor, back against the couch and legs stretched ahead of him, and put Stella on his thighs. She would either endure his stroking until it ended, when she could jump away without impediment—or relax, and purr. She had a rasping loud purr, it reminded Alex of a chainsaw heard across the glacier. "Bug brain," Father would say to her. "Button head."

After a few weeks, as August turned to September and the leaves began to wither and fall, Stella started to lap sit voluntarily—but always in Mom's lap. "She likes the warmth," Mom said.

"It's cold on the floor," Father agreed, and played with the cat's scarred ears. "But why do you always sit on Helen's lap, huhn, Stell? I'm the one who started you on that." Eventually the cat would step onto his lap as well, and stretch out as if it was something she had always done. Father laughed at her.

Stella never rested on Alex's lap voluntarily, but would sometimes stay if he put her there and stroked her slowly for a long time. On the other hand she was just as likely to look back at him, go cross-eyed with horror and leap desperately away, leaving claw marks in his thighs. "She's so weird," he complained to Mom after one of these abrupt departures.

"It's true," Mom said with her low laugh. "But you have to remember that Stella was probably an abused kitty."

"How can you abuse a stray?"

"I'm sure there are ways. And maybe she was abused at home, and ran away."

"Who would do that?"

"Some people would."

Alex recalled the gangs on the glacier, and knew it was true. He tried to imagine what it would be like to be at their mercy, all the time. After that he thought he understood her permanent frown of deep concentration and distrust, as she sat staring at him. "It's just me, Stell-bells."

Thus when the cat followed him up onto the roof, and seemed to enjoy hanging out there with him, he was pleased. Their apartment was on the top floor, and they could take the pantry stairs and use the roof as a porch. It was a flat expanse of graveled tarpaper, a terrible imitation of the glacier's non-slip surface, but it was nice on dry days to go up there and look around, toss pebbles onto other roofs, see if the glacier was visible, and so on. Once Stella pounced at a piece of string trailing from his pants, and next time he brought up a length of Father's yarn. He was astonished and delighted when Stella responded by attacking the windblown yarn enthusiastically, biting it, clawing it, wrestling it from her back when Alex twirled it around her, and generally behaving in a very kittenish way. Perhaps she had never played as a kitten, Alex thought, so that it was all coming out now that she felt safe. But the play always ended abruptly; she would come to herself in mid-bite or bat, straighten up, and look around with a forbidding expression, as if to say *What is this yarn doing draped over* me?—then lick her fur and pretend the preceding minutes hadn't happened. It made Alex laugh.

Although the glacier had overrun many towns to the west and north, Watertown and Newton most recently, there was surprisingly little evidence of that in the moraines, or in the ice. It was almost all natural: rock and dirt and wood. Perhaps the wood had come from houses, perhaps some of the gravel had once been concrete, but you couldn't tell that now. Just dirt and rock and splinters, with an occasional chunk of plastic or metal thrown in. Apparently the overrun towns had been plowed under on the spot, or moved. Mostly it looked like the glacier had just left the White Mountains.

Father and Gary Jung had once talked about the latest plan from MIT. The enormous dam they were building downstream, between Allston and Cambridge, was to hold the glacier back. They were going to heat the concrete of the inner surface of the dam, and melt the ice as it advanced. It would become a kind of frozen reservoir. The meltwater would pour through a set of turbines before becoming the Charles, and the electricity generated by these turbines would help to heat the dam. Very neat.

The ice of the glacier, when you got right down to look at it, was clear for an inch or less, cracked and bubble-filled; then it turned a milky white. You could see the transition. Where the ice had been sheared vertically, however—on the side of a serac, or down in a crevasse—the clear part extended in many inches. You could see air bubbles deep inside, as if it were badly made glass. And this ice was distinctly blue. Alex didn't understand why there should be that difference, between the white ice lying flat and the blue ice cut vertically. But there it was.

Up in New Hampshire they had tried slowing the glacier—or at least stopping the abrupt "Alaskan slides"—by setting steel rods vertically in concrete, and laying the concrete in the glacier's path. Later they had hacked out one of these installations, and found the rods bent in perfect ninety degree angles, pressed into the scored concrete.

The ice would flow right over the dam.

One day Alex was walking by Father's study when Father called out. "Alexander! Take a look at this."

Alex entered the dark book-lined room. Its window overlooked the weed-filled space between buildings, and green light slanted onto Father's desk. "Here, stand beside me and look in my coffee cup. You can see the reflection of the Morgelis' window flowers on the coffee."

"Oh yeah! Neat."

"It gave me a shock! I looked down and there were these white and pink flowers in my cup, bobbing against a wall in a breeze, all of it tinted sepia as if it were an old-fashioned photo. It took me a while to see where it was coming from, what was being reflected." He laughed. "Through a looking glass."

Alex's father had light brown eyes, and fair wispy hair brushed back from a receding hairline. Mom called him handsome, and Alex agreed: tall, thin, graceful, delicate, distinguished. His father was a great man. Now he smiled in a way Alex didn't understand, looking into his coffee cup.

Mom had friends at the street market on Memorial Drive, and she had arranged work for Alex there. Three afternoons a week he walked over the Charles to the riverside street and helped the fishmongers gut fish, the vegetable sellers strip and clean the vegetables. He also helped set up stalls and take them down, and he swept and hosed the street afterwards. He was popular because of his energy and his willingness to get his hands wet in raw weather. The sleeves of his down jacket were permanently discolored from the frequent soakings—the dark blue almost a brown—a fact that distressed his mom. But he could handle the cold better than the adults; his hands would get a splotchy bluish white and he would put them to the red cheeks of the women and they would jump and say My *God*, Alex, how can you stand it?

This afternoon was blustery and dark but without rain, and it was enlivened by an attempted theft in the pasta stands, and by the appearance of a very mangy, very fast stray dog. This dog pounced on the pile of fishheads and entrails and disappeared with his mouth stuffed, trailing slick white-and-red guts. Everyone who saw it laughed. There weren't many stray dogs left these days, it was a pleasure to see one.

An hour past sunset he was done cleaning up and on his way home, hands in his pockets, stomach full, a five-dollar bill clutched in one hand. He showed his pass to the National Guardsman and walked out onto Weeks Bridge. In the middle he stopped and leaned over the railing, into the wind. Below the water churned, milky with glacial silt. The sky still held a lot of light. Low curving bands of black cloud swept in from the northwest, like great ribs of slate. Above these bands the white sky was leached away by dusk. Raw wind whistled over his hood. Light water rushing below, dark clouds rushing above... he breathed the wind deep into him, felt himself expand until he filled everything he could see.

That night his parents' friends were gathering at their apartment for their bi-weekly party. Some of them would read stories and poems and essays and broadsides they had written, and then they would argue about them; and after that they would drink and eat whatever they had brought, and argue some more. Alex enjoyed it. But tonight when he got home Mom was rushing between computer and kitchen and muttering curses as she hit command keys or the hot water faucet, and the moment she saw him she said, "Oh Alex I'm glad you're here, could you please run down to the laundry and do just one load for me? The Talbots are staying over tonight and there aren't any clean sheets and I don't have anything to wear tomorrow either—thanks, you're a dear." And he was back out the door with a full laundry bag hung over his shoulder and the box of soap in the other hand, stomping grumpily past a little man in a black coat, reading a newspaper on the stoop of 19 Chester.

Down to Brighton, take a right, downstairs into the brightly lit basement laundromat. He threw laundry and soap and quarters into their places, turned the machine on and sat on top of it. Glumly he watched the other people in there, sitting on the washers and dryers. The vibrations put a lot of them to sleep. Others stared dully at the wall. Back in his apartment the guests would be arriving, taking off their overcoats, slapping arms over chests and talking as fast as they could. David and Sara and John from next door, Ira and Gary and Ilene from across the street, the Talbots, Kathryn Grimm, and Michael Wu from Father's university, Ron from the hospital. They would settle down in the living room, on couches and chairs and floor, and talk and talk. Alex liked Kathryn especially, she could talk twice as fast as anyone else, and she called everyone darling and laughed and chattered so fast that everyone was caught up in the rhythm of it. Or David with his jokes, or Jay Talbot and his friendly questions. Or Gary Jung, the way he would sit in his corner like a bear, drinking beer and challenging everything that everyone read. "Why abstraction, why this distortion from the real? How does it help us, how does it speak to us? We should forget the abstract!" Father and Ira called him a vulgar Marxist, but he didn't mind. "You might as well be Plekhanov, Gary!" "Thank you very much!" he would say with a sharp grin, rubbing his unshaven jowls. And someone else would read. Mary Talbot once read a fairy tale about the Thing under the glacier; Alex had *loved* it. Once they even got Michael Wu to bring his violin along, and he hmm'd and hawed and pulled at the skin of his neck and refused and said he wasn't good enough, and then shaking like a leaf he played a melody that stilled them all. And Stella! She hated these parties, she spent them crouched deep in her refuge, ready for any kind of atrocity.

And here he was sitting on a washer in the laundromat.

When the laundry was dry he bundled it into the bag, then hurried around the corner and down Chester Street. Inside the glass door of Number 21 he glanced back out, and noticed that the man who had been reading the paper on the stoop next door was still sitting there. Odd. It was cold to be sitting outdoors.

Upstairs the readings had ended and the group was scattered through the apartment, most of them in the kitchen, as Mom had lit the stovetop burners and turned the gas up high. The blue flames roared airily under their chatter, making the kitchen bright and warm. "Wonderful the way white gas burns so clean." "And then they found the poor thing's head and intestines in the alley—it had been butchered right on the spot."

"Alex, you're back! Thanks for doing that. Here, get something to eat."

Everyone greeted him and went back to their conversations. "Gary, you are so *conservative*," Kathryn cried, hands held out over the stove. "It's not conservative at all," Gary replied. "It's a radical goal and I guess it's so radical that I have to keep reminding you it exists. Art should be used to *change* things."

"Isn't that a distortion from the real?"

Alex wandered down the narrow hall to his parents' room, which overlooked Chester Street. Father was there, saying to Ilene, "It's one of the only streets left with trees. It really seems residential, and here we are three blocks from Comm Ave. Hi, Alex."

"Hi, Alex. It's like a little bit of Brookline made it over to Allston."

"Exactly."

Alex stood in the bay window and looked down, licking the last of the carrot cake off his fingers. The man was still down there.

"Let's close off these rooms and save the heat. Alex, you coming?"

He sat on the floor in the living room. Father and Gary and David were starting a game of hearts, and they invited him to be the fourth. He nodded happily. Looking under the corner table he saw yellow eyes, blinking back at him; Stella, a frown of the deepest disapproval on her flat face. Alex laughed. "I knew you'd be there! It's okay, Stella. It's okay."

They left in a group, as usual, stamping their boots and diving deep into coats and scarves and gloves and exclaiming at the cold of the stairwell. Gary gave Mom a brief hug. "Only warm spot left in Boston," he said, and opened the glass door. The rest followed him out, and Alex joined them. The man in the black coat was just turning right onto Brighton Avenue, toward the university and downtown.

Sometimes clouds took on just the mottled gray of the glacier, low dark points stippling a lighter gray surface as cold showers draped down. At these times he felt he stood between two planes of some larger structure, two halves: icy tongue, icy roof of mouth....

He stood under such a sky, throwing stones. His target was an erratic some forty yards away. He hit the boulder with most of his throws. A rock that big was an easy target. A bottle was better. He had brought one with him, and he set it up behind the erratic, on a waist-high rock. He walked back to a point where the bottle was hidden by the erratic. Using flat rocks he sent spinners out in a trajectory that brought them curving in from the side, so that it was possible to hit the concealed target. This was very important for the rock fights that he occasionally got involved in; usually he was outnumbered, and to hold his own he relied on his curves and his accuracy in general, and on a large number of ammunition caches hidden here and there. In one area crowded with boulders and crevasses he could sometimes create the impression of two throwers.

Absorbed in the exercise of bringing curves around the right side of the boulder—the hard side for him—he relaxed his vigilance, and when he heard a shout he jumped around to look. A rock whizzed by his left ear.

He dropped to the ice and crawled behind a boulder. Ambushed! He ran back into his knot of boulders and dashed a layer of snow away from one of his big caches, then with hands and pockets full looked carefully over a knobby chunk of cement, in the direction the stone had come from.

No movement. He recalled the stone whizzing by, the brief sight of it and the *zip* it made in passing. That had been close! If that had hit him! He shivered to think of it, it made his stomach shrink.

A bit of almost frozen rain pattered down. Not a shadow anywhere. On overcast days like this one it seemed things were lit from below, by the white bulk of the glacier. Like plastic over a weak neon light. Brittle huge blob of plastic, shifting and groaning and once in a while cracking like a gunshot, or grumbling like distant thunder. Alive. And Alex was its ally, its representative among men. He shifted from rock to rock, saw movement and froze. Two boys in green down jackets, laughing as they ran off the ice and over the lateral moraine, into what was left of Watertown. Just a potshot, then. Alex cursed them, relaxed.

He went back to throwing at the hidden bottle. Occasionally he recalled the stone flying by his head, and threw a little harder. Elegant curves of flight as the flat rocks bit the air and cut down and in. Finally one rock spun out into space and turned down sharply. Perfect slider. Its disappearance behind the erratic was followed by a tinkling crash. "Yeah!" Alex exclaimed, and ran to look. Icy glass on glassy ice.

Then, as he was leaving the glacier, boys jumped over the moraine shouting "Canadian!" and "There he is!" and "Get him!" This was more a chase than a serious ambush, but there were a lot of them and after emptying hands and pockets Alex was off running. He flew over the crunchy irregular surface, splashing meltwater, jumping narrow crevasses and surface rills. Then a wide crevasse blocked his way, and to start his jump he leaped onto a big flat rock; the rock gave under his foot and lurched down the ice into the crevasse.

Alex turned in and fell, bringing shoe-tips, knees, elbows and hands onto the rough surface. This arrested his fall, though it hurt. The crevasse was just under his feet. He scrambled up, ran panting along the crevasse until it narrowed, leaped over it. Then up the moraine and down into the narrow abandoned streets of west Allston.

Striding home, still breathing hard, he looked at his hands and saw that the last two fingernails on his right hand had been ripped away from the flesh; both were still there, but blood seeped from under them. He hissed and sucked on them, which hurt. The blood tasted like blood.

If he had fallen into the crevasse, following the loose rock down… if that stone had hit him in the face… he could feel his heart, thumping against his sternum. Alive.

Turning onto Chester Street he saw the man in the black coat, leaning against the florid maple across the street from their building. Watching them still! Though the man didn't appear to notice Alex, he did heft a bag and start walking in the other direction. Quickly Alex picked a rock out of the gutter and threw it at the man as hard as he could, spraying drops of blood onto the sidewalk. The rock flew over the man's head like a bullet, just missing him. The man ducked and scurried around the corner onto Comm Ave.

Father was upset about something. "They did the same thing to Gary and Michael and Kathryn, and their classes are even smaller than mine! I don't know what they're going to do. I don't know what *we're* going to do."

"We might be able to attract larger classes next semester," Mom said. She was upset too. Alex stood in the hall, slowly hanging up his jacket.

"But what about now? And what about later?" Father's voice was strained, almost cracking.

"We're making enough for now, that's the important thing. As for later—well, at least we know now rather than five years down the road."

Father was silent at the implications of this. "First Vancouver, then Toronto, now here—"

"Don't worry about all of it at once, Charles."

"How can I help it!" Father strode into his study and closed the door, not noticing Alex around the corner. Alex sucked his fingers. Stella poked her head cautiously out of his bedroom.

"Hi Stell-bell," he said quietly. From the living room came the plastic clatter of Mom's typing. He walked down the long hallway, past the silent study to the living room. She was hitting the keys hard, staring at the screen, mouth tight.

"What happened?" Alex said.

She looked up. "Hi, Alex. Well—your father got bad news from the university."

"Did he not get tenure again?"

"No, no, it's not a question of that."

"But now he doesn't even have the chance?"

She glanced at him sharply, then back at the screen, where her work was blinking. "I suppose that's right. The department has shifted all the new faculty over to extension, so they're hired by the semester, and paid by the class. It means you need a lot of students…."

"Will we move again?"

"I don't know," she said curtly, exasperated with him for bringing it up. She punched the command key. "But we'll really have to save money, now. Everything you make at the market is important."

Alex nodded. He didn't mention the little man in the black coat, feeling obscurely afraid. Mentioning the man would somehow make him significant—Mom and Father would get angry, or frightened—something like that. By not telling them he could protect them from it, handle it on his own, so they could concentrate on other problems.

Besides, the two matters couldn't be connected, could they? Being watched; losing jobs. Perhaps they could. In which case there was nothing his parents could do about it anyway. Better to save them that anger, that fear.

He would make sure his throws hit the man next time.

Storms rolled in and the red and yellow leaves were ripped off the trees. Alex kicked through piles of them stacked on the sidewalks. He never saw the little man. He put up flyers for his father, who became even more distracted and remote. He brought home vegetables from work, tucked under his down jacket, and Mom cooked them without asking if he had bought them. She did the wash in the kitchen sink and dried it on lines in the back space between buildings, standing knee deep in leaves and weeds. Sometimes it took three days for clothes to dry back there; often they froze on the line.

While hanging clothes or taking them down she would let Stella join her. The cat regarded each shifting leaf with dire suspicion, then after a few exploratory leaps and bats would do battle with all of them, rolling about in a frenzy.

One time Mom was carrying a basket of dry laundry up the pantry stairs when a stray dog rounded the corner and made a dash for Stella, who was still outside. Mom ran back down shouting, and the dog fled; but Stella had disappeared. Mom called Alex down from his studies in a distraught voice, and they searched the back of the building and all the adjacent backyards for nearly an hour, but the cat was nowhere to be found. Mom was really upset. It was only after they had quit and returned upstairs that they heard her, miaowing far above them. She had climbed the big oak tree. "Oh *smart* Stella," Mom cried, a wild note in her voice. They called her name out the kitchen window, and the desperate miaows redoubled.

Up on the roof they could just see her, perched high in the almost bare branches of the big tree. "I'll get her," Alex said. "Cats can't climb down." He started climbing. It was difficult: the branches were close-knit, and they swayed in the wind. And as he got closer the cat climbed higher. "No, Stella, don't do that! Come here!" Stella stared at him, clamped to her branch of the moment, cross-eyed with fear.

Below them Mom said over and over, "Stella, it's okay—it's okay, Stella." Stella didn't believe her.

Finally Alex reached her, near the tree's top. Now here was a problem: he needed his hands to climb down, but it seemed likely he would also need them to hold the terrified cat. "Come here, Stella." He put a hand on her flank; she flinched. Her side pulsed with her rapid breathing. She hissed faintly. He had to maneuver up a step, onto a very questionable branch; his face was inches from her. She stared at him without a trace of recognition. He pried her off her branch, lifted her. If she cared to claw him now she could really tear him up. Instead she clung to his shoulder and chest, all her claws dug through his clothes, quivering under his left arm and hand.

Laboriously he descended, using only the one hand. Stella began miaowing fiercely, and struggling a bit. Finally he met Mom, who had climbed the tree quite a ways. Stella was getting more upset. "Hand her to me." Alex detached her from his chest paw by paw, balanced, held the cat down with both hands. Again it was a tricky moment; if Stella went berserk they would all be in trouble. But she fell onto Mom's chest and collapsed, a catatonic ball of fur.

Back in the apartment she dashed for her blanket under the table. Mom enticed her out with food, but she was very jumpy and she wouldn't allow Alex anywhere near her; she ran away if he even entered the room. "Back to square one, I see," Mom commented.

"It's not fair! I'm the one that saved her!"

"She'll get over it." Mom laughed, clearly relieved. "Maybe it'll take some time, but she will. Ha! This is clear proof that cats are smart enough to be crazy. Irrational, neurotic—just like a person." They laughed, and Stella glared at them balefully. "Yes you are, aren't you! You'll come around again."

Often when Alex got home in the early evenings his father was striding back and forth in the kitchen talking loudly, angrily, fearfully, while Mom tried to reassure him. "They're doing the same thing to us they did to Rick Stone! But why!" When Alex closed the front door the conversation would stop. Once when he walked tentatively down the quiet hallway to the kitchen he found them standing there, arms around each other, Father's head in Mom's short hair.

Father raised his head, disengaged, went to his study. On his way he said, "Alex, I need your help."

"Sure."

Alex stood in the study and watched without understanding as his father took books from his shelves and put them in the big laundry bag. He threw the first few in like dirty clothes, then sighed and thumped in the rest in a businesslike fashion, not looking at them.

"There's a used book store in Cambridge, on Mass Ave. Antonio's."

"Sure, I know the one." They had been there together a few times.

"I want you to take these over there and sell them to Tony for me," Father said, looking at the empty shelves. "Will you do that for me?"

"Sure." Alex picked up the bag, shocked that it had come to this. Father's books! He couldn't meet his father's eye. "I'll do that right now," he said uncertainly, and hefted the bag over one shoulder. In the hallway Mom approached and put a hand on his shoulder—her silent thanks—then went into the study.

Alex hiked east toward the university, crossed the Charles River on the great iron bridge. The wind howled in the superstructure. On the Cambridge side, after showing his pass, he put the heavy bag on the ground and inspected its contents. Ever since the infamous incident of the spilled hot chocolate, Father's books had been off-limits to him; now a good twenty of them were there in the bag to be touched, opened, riffled through. Many in this bunch were in foreign languages, especially Greek and Russian, with their alien alphabets. Could people really read such marks? Well, Father did. It must be possible.

When he had inspected all the books he chose two in English—*The Odyssey* and *The Colossus of Maroussi*—and put those in his down jacket pockets. He could take them to the glacier and read them, then sell them later to Antonio's—perhaps in the next bag of books. There were many more bagfuls in Father's study.

A little snow stuck to the glacier now, filling the pocks and making bright patches on the north side of every boulder, every serac. Some of the narrower crevasses were filled with it—bright white lines on the jumbled gray. When the whole surface was white the crevasses would be invisible, and the glacier too dangerous to walk on. Now the only danger was leaving obvious footprints for trackers. Walking up the rubble lines would solve that. These lines of rubble fascinated Alex. It looked just as if bulldozers had clanked up here and shoved the majority of the stones and junk into straight lines down the big central tongue of the glacier. But in fact they were natural features. Father had attempted to explain on one of the walks they had taken up here. "The ice is moving, and it moves faster in the middle than on the outer edges, just like a stream. So rocks on the surface tend to slide over time, down into lines in the middle."

"Why are there two lines, then?"

Father shrugged, looking into the blue-green depths of a crevasse. "We really shouldn't be up here, you know that?"

Now Alex stopped to inspect a tire caught in the rubble line. Truck tire, tread worn right to the steel belting. It would burn, but with too much smoke. There were several interesting objects in this neat row of rock and sand: plastic jugs, a doll, a lampbase, a telephone.

His shelter was undisturbed. He pulled the two books from his pockets and set them on the bench, propping them with rock bookends.

He circled the boulder, had a look around. The sky today was a low smooth pearl gray sheet, ruffled by a set of delicate waves pasted to it. The indirect light brought out all the colors: the pink of the remarkable snow algae, the blue of the seracs, the various shades of rock, the occasional bright spot of junk, the many white patches of snow. A million dots of color under the pewter sheet of cloud.

Three creaks, a crack, a long shuddering rumble. Sleepy, muscular, the great beast had moved. Alex walked across its back to his bench, sat. On the far lateral moraine some gravel slid down. Puffs of brown dust in the air.

He read his books. *The Odyssey* was strange but interesting. Father had told him some of the story before. *The Colossus of Maroussi* was long-winded but funny—it reminded Alex of his uncle, who could turn the smallest incident into an hour's comic monologue. What he could have made of Stella's flight up the tree! Alex laughed to think of it. But his uncle was in jail.

He sat on his bench and read, stopped occasionally to look around. When the hand holding the book got cold, he changed hands and put the cold one in a pocket of his down jacket. When both hands were blue he hid the books in rocks under his bench and went home.

There were more bags of books to be sold at Antonio's and other shops in Cambridge. Each time Alex rotated out a few that looked interesting, and replaced them with the ones on the glacier. He daydreamed of saving all the books and earning the money some other way—then presenting his father with the lost library, at some future undefined but appropriate moment.

Eventually Stella forgave him for rescuing her. She came to enjoy chasing a piece of yarn up and down their long narrow hallway, skidding around the corner by the study. It reminded them of a game they had played with Pongo, who would chase anything, and they laughed at her, especially when she jerked to a halt and licked her fur fastidiously, as if she had never been carousing. "You can't fool us, Stell! We *remember!*"

Mom sold most of her music collection, except for her favorites. Once Alex went out to the glacier with the *Concierto de Aranjuez* coursing through him—Mom had had it on in the apartment while she worked. He hummed the big theme of the second movement as he crunched over the ice: clearly it was the theme of the glacier, the glacier's song. How had a blind composer managed to capture the windy sweep of it, the spaciousness? Perhaps such things could be heard as well as seen. The wind said it, whistling over the ice. It was a terrifically dark day, windy, snowing in gusts. He could walk right up the middle of the great tongue, between the rubble lines; no one else would be up there today. Da-da-da… da da da da da da, da-da-da…. Hands in pockets, chin on chest, he trudged into the wind humming, feeling like the whole world was right there around him. It was too cold to stay in his shelter for more than a minute.

Father went off on trips, exploring possibilities. One morning Alex woke to the sound of *The Pirates of Penzance*. This was one of their favorites, Mom played it all the time while working and on Saturday mornings, so that they knew all the lyrics by heart and often sang along. Alex especially loved the Pirate King, and could mimic all his intonations.

He dressed and walked down to the kitchen. Mom stood by the stove with her back to him, singing along. It was a sunny morning and their big kitchen windows faced east; the light poured in on the sink and the dishes and the white stove and the linoleum and the plants in the window and Stella, sitting contentedly on the window sill listening.

His mom was tall and broad-shouldered. Every year she cut her hair shorter; now it was just a cap of tight brown curls, with a somewhat longer patch down the nape of her neck. That would go soon, Alex thought, and then her hair would be as short as it could be. She was lost in the song, one slim hand on the white stove top, looking out the window. She had a low, rich, thrilling voice, like a real singer's only prettier. She was singing along with the song that Mabel sings after she finds out that Frederic won't be able to leave the pirates until 1940.

When it was over Alex entered the kitchen, went to the pantry. "That's a short one," he said.

"Yes, they had to make it short," Mom said. "There's nothing funny about that one."

One night while Father was gone on one of his trips, Mom had to go over to Ilene and Ira and Gary's apartment: Gary had been arrested, and Ilene and Ira needed help. Alex and Stella were left alone.

Stella wandered the silent apartment miaowing. "I *know*, Stella," Alex said in exasperation. "They're *gone*. They'll be back tomorrow." The cat paid no attention to him.

He went into Father's study. Tonight he'd be able to read something in relative warmth. It would only be necessary to be *very careful*.

The bookshelves were empty. Alex stood before them, mouth open. He had no idea they had sold that many of them. There were a couple left on Father's desk, but he didn't want to move them. They appeared to be dictionaries anyway. "It's all Greek to me."

He went back to the living room and got out the yarn bag, tried to interest Stella in a game. She wouldn't play. She wouldn't sit on his lap. She wouldn't stop miaowing. "Stella, shut up!" She scampered away and kept crying. Vexed, he got out the jar of catnip and spread some on the linoleum in the kitchen. Stella came running to sniff at it, then roll in it. Afterwards she played with the yarn wildly, until it caught around her tail and she froze, staring at him in a drugged paranoia. Then she dashed to her refuge and refused to come out. Finally Alex put on *The Pirates of Penzance* and listened to it for a while. After that he was sleepy.

They got a good lawyer for Gary, Mom said. Everyone was hopeful. Then a couple of weeks later Father got a new job; he called them from work to tell them about it.

"Where is it?" Alex asked Mom when she was off the phone.

"In Kansas."

"So we will be moving."

"Yes," Mom said. "Another move."

"Will there be glaciers there too?"

"I think so. In the hills. Not as big as ours here, maybe. But there are glaciers everywhere."

He walked onto the ice one last time. There was a thin crust of snow on the tops of everything. A fantastically jumbled field of snow. It was a clear day, the sky a very pale blue, the white expanse of the glacier painfully bright. A few cirrus clouds made sickles high in the west. The snow was melting a bit and there were water droplets all over, with little sparks of colored light in each drip. The sounds of water melting were everywhere, drips, gurgles, splashes. The intensity of light was stunning, like a blow to the brain, right through the eyes.

It pulsed.

The crevasse in front of his shelter had widened, and the boards of his bench had fallen. The wall of ice turning around the boulder was splintered, and shards of bright ice lay over the planks.

The glacier was moving. The glacier was alive. No heated dam would stop it. He felt its presence, huge and supple under him, seeping into him like the cold through his wet shoes, filling him up. He blinked, nearly blinded by the light breaking everywhere on it, a surgical glare that made every snow-capped rock stand out like the color red on a slide transparency. The white light. In the distance the ice cracked hollowly, moving somewhere. Everything moved: the ice, the wind, the clouds, the sun, the planet. All of it rolling around.

As they packed up their possessions Alex could hear them in the next room. "We can't," Father said. "You know we can't. They won't let us."

When they were done the apartment looked odd. Bare walls, bare wood floors. It looked smaller. Alex walked the length of it: his parents' room overlooking Chester Street; his room; his father's study; the living room; the kitchen with its fine morning light. The pantry. Stella wandered the place miaowing. Her blanket was still in its corner, but without the table it looked moth-eaten, fur-coated, ineffectual. Alex picked her up and went through the pantry, up the back stairs to the roof.

Snow had drifted into the corners. Alex walked in circles, looking at the city. Stella sat on her paws by the stairwell shed, watching him, her fur ruffled by the wind.

Around the shed snow had melted, then froze again. Little puddles of ice ran in flat curves across the pebbled tar paper. Alex crouched to inspect them, tapping one speculatively with a fingernail. He stood up and looked west, but buildings and bare treetops obscured the view.

Stella fought to stay out of the box, and once in it she cried miserably.

Father was already in Kansas, starting the new job. Alex and Mom and Stella had been staying in the living room of Michael Wu's place while Mom finished her work; now she was done, it was moving day, they were off to the train. But first they had to take Stella to the Talbots'.

Alex carried the box and followed Mom as they walked across the Commons and down Comm Ave. He could feel the cat shifting over her blanket, scrabbling at the cardboard against his chest. Mom walked fast, a bit ahead of him. At Kenmore they turned south.

When they got to the Talbots', Mom took the box. She looked at him. "Why don't you stay down here," she said.

"Okay."

She rang the bell and went in with the buzzer, holding the box under one arm.

Alex sat on the steps of the walk-up. There were little ones in the corner: flat fingers of ice, spilling away from the cracks.

Mom came out the door. Her face was pale, she was biting her lip. They took off walking at a fast pace. Suddenly Mom said, "Oh, Alex, she was *so scared*," and sat down on another stoop and put her head on her knees.

Alex sat beside her, his shoulder touching hers. Don't say anything, don't put arm around shoulders or anything. He had learned this from Father. Just sit there, be there. Alex sat there like the glacier, shifting a little. Alive. The white light.

After a while she stood. "Let's go," she said.

They walked up Comm Ave. toward the train station. "She'll be all right with the Talbots," Alex said. "She already likes Jay."

"I know." Mom sniffed, tossed her head in the wind. "She's getting to be a pretty adaptable cat." They walked on in silence. She put an arm over his shoulders. "I wonder how Pongo is doing." She took a deep breath. Overhead clouds tumbled like chunks of broken ice.

THE LUNATICS

They were very near the center of the moon, Jakob told them. He was the newest member of the bullpen, but already their leader.

"How do you know?" Solly challenged him. It was stifling, the hot air thick with the reek of their sweat, and a pungent stink from the waste bucket in the corner. In the pure black, under the blanket of the rock's basalt silence, their shifting and snuffling loomed large, defined the size of the pen. "I suppose you see it with your third eye."

Jakob had a laugh as big as his hands. He was a big man, never a doubt of that. "Of course not, Solly. The third eye is for seeing in the black. It's a natural sense just like the others. It takes all the data from the rest of the senses, and processes them into a visual image transmitted by the third optic nerve, which runs from the forehead to the sight centers at the back of the brain. But you can only focus it by an act of the will—same as with all the other senses. It's not magic. We just never needed it till now."

"So how do you know?"

"It's a problem in spherical geometry, and I solved it. Oliver and I solved it. This big vein of blue runs right down into the core, I believe, down into the moon's molten heart where we can never go. But we'll follow it as far as we can. Note how light we're getting. There's less gravity near the center of things."

"I feel heavier than ever."

"You are heavy, Solly. Heavy with disbelief."

"Where's Freeman?" Hester said in her crow's rasp.

No one replied.

Oliver stirred uneasily over the rough basalt of the pen's floor. First Naomi, then mute Elijah, now Freeman. Somewhere out in the shafts and caverns, tunnels and corridors—somewhere in the dark maze of mines, people were disappearing. Their pen was emptying, it seemed. And the other pens?

"Free at last," Jakob murmured.

"There's something out there," Hester said, fear edging her harsh voice, so that it scraped Oliver's nerves like the screech of an ore car's wheels over a too-sharp bend in the tracks. "Something out there!"

The rumor had spread through the bullpens already, whispered mouth to ear or in huddled groups of bodies. There were thousands of shafts bored through the rock, hundreds of chambers and caverns. Lots of these were closed off, but many more were left open, and there was room to hide—miles and miles of it. First some of their cows had disappeared. Now it was people too. And Oliver had heard a miner jabbering at the low edge of hysteria, about a giant foreman gone mad after an accident took both his arms at the shoulder—the arms had been replaced by prostheses, and the foreman had escaped into the black, where he preyed on miners off by themselves, ripping them up, feeding on them—

They all heard the steely squeak of a car's wheel. Up the mother shaft, past cross tunnel Forty; had to be foremen at this time of shift. Would the car turn at the fork to their concourse? Their hypersensitive ears focused on the distant sound; no one breathed. The wheels squeaked, turned their way. Oliver, who was already shivering, began to shake hard.

The car stopped before their pen. The door opened, all in darkness. Not a sound from the quaking miners.

Fierce white light blasted them and they cried out, leaped back against the cage bars vainly. Blinded, Oliver cringed at the clawing of a foreman's hands, searching under his shirt and pants. Through pupils like pinholes he glimpsed brief black-and-white snapshots of gaunt bodies undergoing similar searches, then blows. Shouts, cries of pain, smack of flesh on flesh, an electric buzzing. Shaving their heads, could it be that time again already? He was struck in the stomach, choked around the neck. Hester's long wiry brown arms, wrapped around her head. Scalp burned, *buzzz* all chopped up. Thrown to the rock.

"Where's the twelfth?" In the foremen's staccato language. No one answered.

The foremen left, light receding with them until it was black again, the pure dense black that was their own. Except now it was swimming with bright red bars, washing around in painful tears. Oliver's third eye opened a little, which calmed him, because it was still a new experience; he could make out his companions, dim redblack shapes in the black, huddled over themselves, gasping.

Jakob moved among them, checking for hurts, comforting. He cupped Oliver's forehead and Oliver said, "It's seeing already."

"Good work." On his knees Jakob clumped to their shit bucket, took off the lid, reached in. He pulled something out. Oliver marveled at how clearly he was able to see all this. Before, floating blobs of color had drifted in the black; but he had always assumed they were afterimages, or hallucinations. Only with Jakob's instruction had he been able to perceive the patterns they made, the vision that they constituted. It was an act of will. That was the key.

Now, as Jakob cleaned the object with his urine and spit, Oliver found that the eye in his forehead saw even more, in sharp blood etchings. Jakob held the lump overhead, and it seemed it was a little lamp, pouring light over them in a wavelength they had always been able to see, but had never needed before. By its faint ghostly radiance the whole pen was made clear, a structure etched in blood, redblack on black. "Promethium," Jakob breathed. The miners crowded around him, faces lifted to it. Solly had a little pug nose, and squinched his face terribly in the effort to focus. Hester had a face to go with her voice, stark bones under skin scored with lines. "The most precious element. On Earth our masters rule by it. All their civilization is based on it, on the movement inside it, electrons escaping their shells and crashing into neutrons, giving off heat and more blue as well. So they condemn us to a life of pulling it out of the moon for them."

He chipped at the chunk with a thumbnail. They all knew precisely its clayey texture, its heaviness, the dull silvery gray of it, which pulsed green under some lasers, blue under others. Jakob gave each of them a sliver of it. "Take it between two molars and crush hard. Then swallow."

"It's poison, isn't it?" said Solly.

"After years and years." The big laugh, filling the black. "We don't have years and years, you know that. And in the short run it helps your vision in the black. It strengthens the will."

Oliver put the soft heavy sliver between his teeth, chomped down, felt the metallic jolt, swallowed. It throbbed in him. He could see the others' faces, the mesh of the pen walls, the pens farther down the concourse, the robot tracks—all in the lightless black.

"Promethium is the moon's living substance," Jakob said quietly. "We walk in the nerves of the moon, tearing them out under the lash of the foremen. The shafts are a map of where the neurons used to be. As they drag the moon's mind out by its roots, to take it back to Earth and use it for their own enrichment, the lunar consciousness fills us and we become its mind ourselves, to save it from extinction."

They joined hands: Solly, Hester, Jakob and Oliver. The surge of energy passed through them, leaving a sweet afterglow.

Then they lay down on their rock bed, and Jakob told them tales of his home, of the Pacific dockyards, of the cliffs and wind and waves, and the way the sun's light lay on it all. Of the jazz in the bars, and how trumpet and clarinet could cross each other. "How do you remember?" Solly asked plaintively. "They turned me blank."

Jakob laughed hard. "I fell on my mother's knitting needles when I was a boy, and one went right up my nose. Chopped the hippocampus in two. So all my life my brain has been storing what memories it can somewhere else. They burned a dead part of me, and left the living memory intact."

"Did it hurt?" Hester croaked.

"The needles? You bet. A flash like the foremen's prods, right there in the center of me. I suppose the moon feels the same pain, when we mine her. But I'm grateful now, because it opened my third eye right at that moment. Ever since then I've seen with it. And down here, without our third eye it's nothing but the black."

Oliver nodded, remembering.

"And something out there," croaked Hester.

Next shift start Oliver was keyed by a foreman, then made his way through the dark to the end of the long, slender vein of blue he was working. Oliver was a tall youth, and some of the shaft was low; no time had been wasted smoothing out the vein's irregular shape. He had to crawl between the narrow tracks bolted to the rocky uneven floor, scraping through some gaps as if working through a great twisted intestine.

At the shaft head he turned on the robot, a long low-slung metal box on wheels. He activated the laser drill, which faintly lit the exposed surface of the blue, blinding him for some time. When he regained a certain visual equilibrium—mostly by ignoring the weird illumination of the drill beam—he typed instructions into the robot, and went to work drilling into the face, then guiding the robot's scoop and hoist to the broken pieces of blue. When the big chunks were in the ore cars behind the robot, he jackhammered loose any fragments of the ore that adhered to the basalt walls, and added them to the cars before sending them off.

This vein was tapering down, becoming a mere tendril in the lunar body, and there was less and less room to work in. Soon the robot would be too big for the shaft, and they would have to bore through basalt; they would follow the tendril to its very end, hoping for a bole or a fan.

At first Oliver didn't much mind the shift's work. But IR-directed cameras on the robot surveyed him as well as the shaft face, and occasional shocks from its prod reminded him to keep hustling. And in the heat and bad air, as he grew ever more famished, it soon enough became the usual desperate, painful struggle to keep to the required pace.

Time disappeared into that zone of endless agony that was the latter part of a shift. Then he heard the distant klaxon of shift's end, echoing down the shaft like a cry in a dream. He turned the key in the robot and was plunged into noiseless black, the pure absolute of Nonbeing. Too tired to try opening his third eye, Oliver started back up the shaft by feel, following the last ore car of the shift. It rolled quickly ahead of him and was gone.

In the new silence distant mechanical noises were like creaks in the rock. He measured out the shift's work, having marked its beginning on the shaft floor: eighty-nine lengths of his body. Average.

It took a long time to get back to the junction with the shaft above his. Here there was a confluence of veins and the room opened out, into an odd chamber some seven feet high, but wider than Oliver could determine in every direction. When he snapped his fingers there was no rebound at all. The usual light at the far end of the low chamber was absent. Feeling sandwiched between two endless rough planes of rock, Oliver experienced a sudden claustrophobia; there was a whole world overhead, he was buried alive.... He crouched and every few steps tapped one rail with his ankle, navigating blindly, a hand held forward to discover any dips in the ceiling.

He was somewhere in the middle of this space when he heard a noise behind him. He froze. Air pushed at his face. It was completely dark, completely silent. The noise squeaked behind him again: a sound like a fingernail, brushed along the banded metal of piano wire. It ran right up his spine, and he felt the hair on his forearms pull away from the dried sweat and stick straight out. He was holding his breath. Very slow footsteps were placed softly behind him, perhaps forty feet away... an airy snuffle, like a big nostril sniffing. For the footsteps to be so spaced out it would have to be....

Oliver loosened his joints, held one arm out and the other forward, tiptoed away from the rail, at right angles to it, for twelve feathery steps. In the lunar gravity he felt he might even float. Then he sank to his knees, breathed through his nose as slowly as he could stand to. His heart knocked at the back of his throat, he was sure it was louder than his breath by far. Over that noise and the roar of blood in his ears he concentrated his hearing to the utmost pitch. Now he could hear the faint sounds of ore cars and perhaps miners and foremen, far down the tunnel that led from the far side of this chamber back to the pens. Even as faint as they were, they obscured further his chances of hearing whatever it was in the cavern with him.

The footsteps had stopped. Then came another metallic *scrick* over the rail, heard against a light sniff. Oliver cowered, held his arms hard against his sides, knowing he smelled of sweat and fear. Far down the distant shaft a foreman spoke sharply. If he could reach that voice.... He resisted the urge to run for it, feeling sure somehow that whatever was in there with him was fast.

Another *scrick*. Oliver cringed, trying to reduce his echo profile. There was a chip of rock under his hand. He fingered it, hand shaking. His forehead throbbed and he understood it was his third eye, straining to pierce the black silence and *see*....

A shape with pillar-thick legs, all in blocks of redblack. It was some sort of....

Scrick. Sniff. It was turning his way. A flick of the wrist, the chip of rock skittered, hitting ceiling and then floor, back in the direction he had come from.

Very slow soft footsteps, as if the legs were somehow... they were coming in his direction.

He straightened and reached above him, hands scrabbling over the rough basalt. He felt a deep groove in the rock, and next to it a vertical hole. He jammed a hand in the hole, made a fist; put the fingers of the other hand along the side of the groove, and pulled himself up. The toes of his boot fit the groove, and he flattened up against the ceiling. In the lunar gravity he could stay there forever. Holding his breath.

Step... step... snuffle, fairly near the floor, which had given him the idea for this move. He couldn't turn to look. He felt something scrape the hip pocket of his pants and thought he was dead, but fear kept him frozen; and the sounds moved off into the distance of the vast chamber, without a pause.

He dropped to the ground and bolted doubled over for the far tunnel, which loomed before him redblack in the black, exuding air and faint noise. He plunged right in it, feeling one wall nick a knuckle. He took the sharp right he knew was there and threw himself down to the intersection of floor and wall. Footsteps padded by him, apparently running on the rails.

When he couldn't hold his breath any longer he breathed. Three or four minutes passed and he couldn't bear to stay still. He hurried to the intersection, turned left and slunk to the bullpen. At the checkpoint the monitor's horn squawked and a foreman blasted him with a searchlight, pawed him roughly. "Hey!" The foreman held a big chunk of blue, taken from Oliver's hip pocket. What was this?

"Sorry boss," Oliver said jerkily, trying to see it properly, remembering the thing brushing him as it passed under. "Must've fallen in." He ignored the foreman's curse and blow, and fell into the pen tearful with the pain of the light, with relief at being back among the others. Every muscle in him was shaking.

But Hester never came back from that shift.

Sometime later the foremen came back into their bullpen, wielding the lights and the prods to line them up against one mesh wall. Through pinprick pupils Oliver saw just the grossest slabs of shapes, all grainy black-and-gray: Jakob was a big stout man, with a short black beard under the shaved head, and eyes that popped out, glittering even in Oliver's silhouette world.

"Miners are disappearing from your pen," the foreman said, in the miners' language. His voice was like the quartz they tunneled through occasionally: hard, and sparkly with cracks and stresses, as if it might break at any moment into a laugh or a scream.

No one answered.

Finally Jakob said, "We know."

The foreman stood before him. "They started disappearing when you arrived."

Jakob shrugged. "Not what I hear."

The foreman's searchlight was right on Jakob's face, which stood out brilliantly, as if two of the searchlights were pointed at each other. Oliver's third eye suddenly opened and gave the face substance: brown skin, heavy brows, scarred scalp. Not at all the white cutout blazing from the black shadows. "You'd better be careful, miner."

Loudly enough to be heard from neighboring pens, Jakob said, "Not my fault if something out there is eating us, boss."

The foreman struck him. Lights bounced and they all dropped to the floor for protection, presenting their backs to the boots. Rain of blows, pain of blows. Still, several pens had to have heard him.

Foremen gone. White blindness returned to black blindness, to the death velvet of their pure darkness. For a long time they lay in their own private worlds, hugging the warm rock of the floor, feeling the bruises blush. Then Jakob crawled around and squatted by each of them, placing his hands on their foreheads. "Oh yeah," he would say. "You're okay. Wake up now. Look around you." And in the after-black they stretched and stretched, quivering like dogs on a scent. The bulks in the black, the shapes they made as they moved and groaned... yes, it came to Oliver again, and he rubbed his face and looked around, eyes shut to help him see. "I ran into it on the way back in," he said.

They all went still. He told them what had happened. "The blue in your pocket?"

They considered his story in silence. No one understood it.

No one spoke of Hester. Oliver found he couldn't. She had been his friend. To live without that gaunt crow's voice....

Sometime later the side door slid up, and they hurried into the barn to eat. The chickens squawked as they took the eggs, the cows mooed as they milked them. The stove plates turned the slightest bit luminous—redblack, again—and by their light his three eyes saw all. Solly cracked and fried eggs. Oliver went to work on his vats of cheese, pulled out a round of it that was ready. Jakob sat at the rear of one cow and laughed as it turned to butt his knee. *Splish splish! Splish splish!* When he was done he picked up the cow and put it down in front of its hay, where it chomped happily. Animal stink of them all, the many fine smells of food cutting through it. Jakob laughed at his cow, which butted his knee again as if objecting to the ridicule. "Little pig of a cow, little piglet. Mexican cows. They bred for this size, you know. On Earth the ordinary cow is as tall as Oliver, and about as big as this whole pen."

They laughed at the idea, not believing him. The buzzer cut them off, and the meal was over. Back into their pen, to lay their bodies down.

Still no talk of Hester, and Oliver found his skin crawling again as he recalled his encounter with whatever it was that sniffed through the mines. Jakob came over and asked him about it, sounding puzzled. Then he handed Oliver a rock. "Imagine this is a perfect sphere, like a baseball."

"Baseball?"

"Like a ball bearing, perfectly round and smooth you know."

Ah yes. Spherical geometry again. Trigonometry too. Oliver groaned, resisting the work. Then Jakob got him interested despite himself, in the intricacy of it all, the way it all fell together in a complex but comprehensible pattern. Sine and cosine, so clear! And the clearer it got the more he could see: the mesh of the bullpen, the network of shafts and tunnels and caverns piercing the jumbled fabric of the moon's body... all clear lines of redblack on black, like the metal of the stove plate as it just came visible, and all from Jakob's clear, patiently fingered, perfectly balanced equations. He could see through rock.

"Good work," Jakob said when Oliver got tired. They lay there among the others, shifting around to find hollows for their hips.

Silence of the off-shift. Muffled clanks downshaft, floor trembling at a detonation miles of rock away; ears popped as air smashed into the dead end of their tunnel, compressed to something nearly liquid for just an instant. Must have been a Boesman. Ringing silence again.

"So what is it, Jakob?" Solly asked when they could hear each other again.

"It's an element," Jakob said sleepily. "A strange kind of element, nothing else like it. Promethium. Number 61 on the periodic table. A rare earth, a lanthanide, an inner transition metal. We're finding it in veins of an ore called monazite, and in pure grains and nuggets scattered in the ore."

Impatient, almost pleading: "But what makes it so special?"

For a long time Jakob didn't answer. They could hear him thinking. Then he said, "Atoms have a nucleus, made of protons and neutrons bound together. Around this nucleus shells of electrons spin, and each shell is either full or trying to get full, to balance with the number of protons—to balance the positive and negative charges. An atom is like a human heart, you see.

"Now promethium is radioactive, which means it's out of balance, and parts of it are breaking free. But promethium never reaches its balance, because it radiates in a manner that increases its instability rather than the reverse. Promethium atoms release energy in the form of positrons, flying free when neutrons are hit by electrons. But during that impact more neutrons appear in the nucleus. Seems they're coming from nowhere. So each atom of the blue is a power loop in itself, giving off energy perpetually. Some people say that they're little white holes, every single atom of them. Burning forever at nine hundred and forty curies per gram. Bringing energy into our universe from somewhere else. Little gateways."

Solly's sigh filled the black, expressing incomprehension for all of them. "So it's poisonous?"

"It's dangerous, sure, because the positrons breaking away from it fly right through flesh like ours. Mostly they never touch a thing in us, because that's how close to phantoms we are—mostly blood, which is almost light. That's why we can see each other so well. But sometimes a beta particle will hit something small on its way through. Could mean nothing or it could kill you on the spot. Eventually it'll get us all."

Oliver fell asleep dreaming of threads of light like concentrations of the foremen's fierce flashes, passing right through him. Shifts passed in their timeless round. They ached when they woke on the warm basalt floor, they ached when they finished the long work shifts. They were hungry and often injured. None of them could say how long they had been there. None of them could say how old they were. Sometimes they lived without light other than the robots' lasers and the stove plates. Sometimes the foremen visited with their scorching lighthouse beams every off-shift, shouting questions and beating them. Apparently cows were disappearing, cylinders of air and oxygen, supplies of all sorts. None of it mattered to Oliver but the spherical geometry. He knew where he was, he could see it. The three-dimensional map in his head grew more extensive every shift. But everything else was fading away....

"So it's the most powerful substance in the world," Solly said. "But why us? Why are we here?"

"You don't know?" Jakob said.

"They blanked us, remember? All that's gone."

But because of Jakob, they knew what was up there: the domed palaces on the lunar surface, the fantastic luxuries of Earth… when he spoke of it, in fact, a lot of Earth came back to them, and they babbled and chattered at the unexpected upwellings. Memories that deep couldn't be blanked without killing, Jakob said. And so they prevailed after all, in a way.

But there was much that had been burnt forever. And so Jakob sighed. "Yeah yeah, I remember. I just thought—well. We're here for different reasons. Some were criminals. Some complained."

"Like Hester!" They laughed.

"Yeah, I suppose that's what got her here. But a lot of us were just in the wrong place at the wrong time. Wrong politics or skin or whatever. Wrong look on your face."

"That was me, I bet," Solly said, and the others laughed at him. "Well I got a funny face, I know I do! I can feel it."

Jakob was silent for a long time. "What about you?" Oliver asked. More silence. The rumble of a distant detonation, like muted thunder.

"I wish I knew. But I'm like you in that. I don't remember the actual arrest. They must have hit me on the head. Given me a concussion. I must have said something against the mines, I guess. And the wrong people heard me."

"Bad luck."

"Yeah. Bad luck."

More shifts passed. Oliver rigged a timepiece with two rocks, a length of detonation cord and a set of pulleys, and confirmed over time what he had come to suspect; the work shifts were getting longer. It was more and more difficult to get all the way through one, harder to stay awake for the meals and the geometry lessons during the off-shifts. The foremen came every off-shift now, blasting in with their searchlights and shouts and kicks, leaving in a swirl of afterimages and pain. Solly went out one shift cursing them under his breath, and never came back. Disappeared. The foremen beat them for it and Oliver shouted with rage. "It's not our fault! There's something out there, I saw it! It's killing us!"

Then next shift his little tendril of a vein bloomed, he couldn't find any rock around the blue: a big bole. He would have to tell the foremen, start working in a crew. He dismantled his clock.

On the way back he heard the footsteps again, shuffling along slowly behind him. This time he was at the entrance to the last tunnel, the pens close behind him. He turned to stare into the darkness with his third eye, willing himself to see the thing. Whoosh of air, a sniff, a footfall on the rail…. Far across the thin wedge of air a beam of light flashed, making a long narrow cone of white talc. Steel tracks gleamed where the wheels of the car burnished them. Pupils shrinking like a snail's antennae, he stared back at the footsteps, saw nothing. Then, just barely, two points of red: retinas, reflecting the distant lance of light. They blinked. He bolted and ran again, reached the foremen at the checkpoint in seconds. They blinded him as he panted, passed him through and into the bullpen.

After the meal on that shift Oliver lay trembling on the floor of the bullpen and told Jakob about it. "I'm scared, Jakob. Solly, Hester, Freeman, mute Lije, Naomi—they're all gone. Everyone I know here is gone but us."

"Free at last," Jakob said shortly. "Here, let's do your problems for tonight."

"I don't care about them."

"You have to care about them. Nothing matters unless you do. That blue is the mind of the moon being torn away, and the moon knows it. If we learn what the network says in its shapes, then the moon knows that too, and we're suffered to live."

"Not if that thing finds us!"

"You don't know. Anyway nothing to be done about it. Come on, let's do the lesson. We need it."

So they worked on equations in the dark. Both were distracted and the work went slowly; they fell asleep in the middle of it, right there on their faces.

Shifts passed. Oliver pulled a muscle in his back, and excavating the bole he had found was an agony of discomfort. When the bole was cleared it left a space like the interior of an egg, ivory and black and quite smooth, punctuated only by the bluish spots of other tendrils of monazite extending away through the basalt. They left a catwalk across the central space, with decks cut into the rock on each side, and ramps leading to each of the veins of blue; and began drilling on their own again, one man and robot team to each vein. At each shift's end Oliver rushed to get to the egg-chamber at the same time as all the others, so that he could return the rest of the way to the bullpen in a crowd. This worked well until one shift came to an end with the hoist chock-full of the ore. It took him some time to dump it into the ore car and shut down.

So he had to cross the catwalk alone, and he would be alone all the way back to the pens. Surely it was past time to move the pens closer to the shaft heads! He didn't want to do this….

Halfway across the catwalk he heard a faint noise ahead of him. *Scrick;*

scriiiiiik. He jerked to a stop, held the rail hard. Couldn't reach the ceiling here. Back stabbing its protest, he started to climb over the railing. He could hang from the underside.

He was right on the top of the railing when he was seized up by a number of strong cold hands. He opened his mouth to scream and his mouth was filled with wet clay. The blue. His head was held steady and his ears filled with the same stuff, so that the sounds of his own terrified sharp nasal exhalations were suddenly cut off. Promethium; it would kill him. It hurt his back to struggle on. He was being carried horizontally, ankles whipped, arms tied against his body. Then plugs of the clay were shoved up his nose and in the middle of a final paroxysm of resistance his mind fell away into the black.

The lowest whisper in the world said, "Oliver Pen Twelve." He heard the voice with his stomach. He was astonished to be alive.

"You will never be given anything again. Do you accept the charge?"

He struggled to nod. I never wanted anything! he tried to say. I only wanted a life like anyone else.

"You will have to fight for every scrap of food, every swallow of water, every breath of air. Do you accept the charge?"

I accept the charge. I welcome it.

"In the eternal night you will steal from the foremen, kill the foremen, oppose their work in every way. Do you accept the charge?" I welcome it.

"You will live free in the mind of the moon. Will you take up this charge?"

He sat up. His mouth was clear, filled only with the sharp electric aftertaste of the blue. He saw the shapes around him: there were five of them, five people there. And suddenly he understood. Joy ballooned in him and he said, "I will. Oh, I will!"

A light appeared. Accustomed as he was either to no light or to intense blasts of it, Oliver at first didn't comprehend. He thought his third eye was rapidly gaining power. As perhaps it was. But there was also a laser drill from one of the A robots, shot at low power through a cylindrical ceramic electronic element, in a way that made the cylinder glow yellow. Blind like a fish, open-mouthed, weak eyes gaping and watering floods, he saw around him Solly, Hester, Freeman, mute Elijah, Naomi. "Yes," he said, and tried to embrace them all at once. "Oh, yes."

They were in one of the long-abandoned caverns, a flat-bottomed bole with only three tendrils extending away from it. The chamber was filled with objects Oliver was more used to identifying by feel or sound or smell: pens of cows and hens, a stack of air cylinders and suits, three ore cars, two

B robots, an A robot, a pile of tracks and miscellaneous gear. He walked through it all slowly, Hester at his side. She was gaunt as ever, her skin as dark as the shadows; it sucked up the weak light from the ceramic tube and gave it back only in little points and lines. "Why didn't you tell me?"

"It was the same for all of us. This is the way."

"And Naomi?"

"The same for her too; but when she agreed to it, she found herself alone."

Then it was Jakob, he thought suddenly. "Where's Jakob?"

Rasped: "He's coming, we think."

Oliver nodded, thought about it. "Was it you, then, following me those times? Why didn't you speak?"

"That wasn't us," Hester said when he explained what had happened. She cawed a laugh. "That was something else, still out there...."

Then Jakob stood before them, making them both jump. They shouted and the others all came running, pressed into a mass together. Jakob laughed. "All here now," he said. "Turn that light off. We don't need it."

And they didn't. Laser shut down, ceramic cooled, they could still see: they could see right into each other, red shapes in the black, radiating joy. Everything in the little chamber was quite distinct, quite *visible*.

"We are the mind of the moon."

Without shifts to mark the passage of time Oliver found he could not judge it at all. They worked hard, and they were constantly on the move: always up, through level after level of the mine. "Like shells of the atom, and we're that particle, busted loose and on its way out." They ate when they were famished, slept when they had to. Most of the time they worked, either bringing down shafts behind them, or dismantling depots and stealing everything Jakob designated theirs. A few times they ambushed gangs of foremen, killing them with laser cutters and stripping them of valuables; but on Jakob's orders they avoided contact with foremen when they could. He wanted only material. After a long time—twenty sleeps at least—they had six ore cars of it, all trailing an A robot up long-abandoned and empty shafts, where they had to lay the track ahead of them and pull it out behind, as fast as they could move. Among other items Jakob had an insatiable hunger for explosives; he couldn't get enough of them.

It got harder to avoid the foremen, who were now heavily armed, and on their guard. Perhaps even searching for them, it was hard to tell. But they searched with their lighthouse beams on full power, to stay out of ambush: it was easy to see them at a distance, draw them off, lose them in dead ends, detonate mines under them. All the while the little band moved up, rising by infinitely long detours toward the front side of the moon. The rock around them cooled. The air circulated more strongly, until it was a constant wind. Through the seismometers they could hear from far below the rumbling of cars, heavy machinery, detonations. "Oh they're after us all right," Jakob said. "They're running scared."

He was happy with the booty they had accumulated, which included a great number of cylinders of compressed air and pure oxygen. Also vacuum suits for all of them, and a lot more explosives, including ten Boesmans, which were much too big for any ordinary mining. "We're getting close," Jakob said as they ate and drank, then tended the cows and hens. As they lay down to sleep by the cars he would talk to them about their work. Each of them had various jobs: mute Elijah was in charge of their supplies, Solly of the robot, Hester of the seismography. Naomi and Freeman were learning demolition, and were in some undefined sense Jakob's lieutenants. Oliver kept working at his navigation. They had found charts of the tunnel systems in their area, and Oliver was memorizing them, so that he would know at each moment exactly where they were. He found he could do it remarkably well; each time they ventured on he knew where the forks would come, where they would lead. Always upward.

But the pursuit was getting hotter. It seemed there were foremen everywhere, patrolling the shafts in search of them. "Soon they'll mine some passages and try to drive us into them," Jakob said. "It's about time we left."

"Left?" Oliver repeated.

"Left the system. Struck out on our own."

"Dig our own tunnel," Naomi said happily.

"Yes."

"To where?" Hester croaked.

Then they were rocked by an explosion that almost broke their eardrums, and the air rushed away. The rock around them trembled, creaked, groaned, cracked, and down the tunnel the ceiling collapsed, shoving dust toward them in a roaring *whoosh!* "A Boesman!" Solly cried.

Jakob laughed out loud. They were all scrambling into their vacuum suits as fast as they could. "Time to leave!" he cried, maneuvering their A robot against the side of the chamber. He put one of their Boesmans against the wall and set the timer. "Okay," he said over the suit's intercom. "Now we got to mine like we never mined before. To the surface!"

The first task was to get far enough away from the Boesman that they wouldn't be killed when it went off. They were now drilling a narrow tunnel and moving the loosened rock behind them to fill up the hole as they passed through it; this loose fill would fly like bullets down a rifle barrel when the Boesman went off. So they made three abrupt turns at acute angles to stop the fill's movement, and then drilled away from the area as fast as they could. Naomi and Jakob were confident that the explosion of the Boesman would shatter the surrounding rock to such an extent that it would never be possible for anyone to locate the starting point for their tunnel.

"Hopefully they'll think we did ourselves in," Naomi said, "either on purpose or by accident." Oliver enjoyed hearing her light laugh, her clear voice that was so pure and musical compared to Hester's croaking. He had never known Naomi well before, but now he admired her grace and power, her pulsing energy; she worked harder than Jakob, even. Harder than any of them.

A few shifts into their new life Naomi checked the detonator timer she kept on a cord around her neck. "It should be going off soon. Someone go try and keep the cows and chickens calmed down." But Solly had just reached the cows' pen when the Boesman went off. They were all sledgehammered by the blast, which was louder than a mere explosion, something more basic and fundamental: the violent smash of a whole world shutting the door on them. Deafened, bruised, they staggered up and checked each other for serious injuries, then pacified the cows, whose terrified moos they felt in their hands rather than actually heard. The structural integrity of their tunnel seemed okay; they were in an old flow of the mantle's convection current, now cooled to stasis, and it was plastic enough to take such a blast without shattering. Perfect miners' rock, protecting them like a mother. They lifted up the cows and set them upright on the bottom of the ore car that had been made into the barn. Freeman hurried back down the tunnel to see how the rear of it looked. When he came back their hearing was returning, and through the ringing that would persist for several shifts he shouted, "It's walled off good! Fused!"

So they were in a little tunnel of their own. They fell together in a clump, hugging each other and shouting. "Free at last!" Jakob roared, booming out a laugh louder than anything Oliver had ever heard from him. Then they settled down to the task of turning on an air cylinder and recycler, and regulating their gas exchange.

They soon settled into a routine that moved their tunnel forward as quickly and quietly as possible. One of them operated the robot, digging as narrow a shaft as they could possibly work in. This person used only laser drills unless confronted with extremely hard rock, when it was judged worth the risk to set off small explosions, timed by seismometer to follow closely other detonations back in the mines; Jakob and Naomi hoped that the complex interior of the moon would prevent any listeners from noticing that their explosion was anything more than an echo of the mining blast.

Three of them dealt with the rock freed by the robot's drilling, moving it from the front of the tunnel to its rear, and at intervals pulling up the cars' tracks and bringing them forward. The placement of the loose rock was a serious matter, because if it displaced much more volume than it had at the front of the tunnel, they would eventually fill in all the open space they had; this was the classic problem of the "creeping worm" tunnel. It was necessary to pack the blocks into the space at the rear with an absolute minimum of gaps, in exactly the way they had been cut, like pieces of a puzzle; they all got very good at the craft of this, losing only a few inches of open space in every mile they dug. This work was the hardest both physically and mentally, and each shift of it left Oliver more tired than he had ever been while mining. Because the truth was all of them were working at full speed, and for the middle team it meant almost running, back and forth, back and forth, back and forth.... Their little bit of open tunnel was only some sixty yards long, but after a while on the midshift it seemed like five hundred.

The three people not working on the rock tended the air and the livestock, ate, helped out with large blocks and the like, and snatched some sleep. They rotated one at a time through the three stations, and worked one shift (timed by detonator timer) at each post. It made for a routine so mesmerizing in its exhaustiveness that Oliver found it very hard to do his calculations of their position in his shift off. "You've got to keep at it," Jakob told him as he ran back from the robot to help the calculating. "It's not just anywhere we want to come up, but right under the domed city of Selene, next to the rocket rails. To do that we'll need some good navigation. We get that and we'll come up right in the middle of the masters who have gotten rich from selling the blue to Earth, and that will be a very gratifying thing I assure you."

So Oliver would work on it until he slept. Actually it was relatively easy; he knew where they had been in the moon when they struck out on their own, and Jakob had given him the surface coordinates for Selene: so it was just a matter of dead reckoning.

It was even possible to calculate their average speed, and therefore when they could expect to reach the surface. That could be checked against the rate of depletion of their fixed resources—air, water lost in the recycler, and food for the livestock. It took a few shifts of consultation with mute Elijah to determine all the factors reliably, and after that it was a simple matter of arithmetic.

When Oliver and Elijah completed these calculations they called Jakob over and explained what they had done.

"Good work," Jakob said. "I should have thought of that."

"But look," Oliver said, "we've got enough air and water, and the robot's power pack is ten times what we'll need—same with explosives—it's only food is a problem. I don't know if we've got enough hay for the cows."

Jakob nodded as he looked over Oliver's shoulder and examined their figures. "We'll have to kill and eat the cows one by one. That'll feed us and cut down on the amount of hay we need, at the same time."

"Eat the cows?" Oliver was stunned.

"Sure! They're meat! People on Earth eat them all the time!"

"Well...." Oliver was doubtful, but under the lash of Hester's bitter laughter he didn't say any more.

Still, Jakob and Freeman and Naomi decided it would be best if they stepped up the pace a little bit, to provide them with more of a margin for error. They shifted two people to the shaft face and supplemented the robot's continuous drilling with hand drill work around the sides of the tunnel, and ate on the run while moving blocks to the back, and slept as little as they could. They were making miles on every shift.

The rock they wormed through began to change in character. The hard, dark, unbroken basalt gave way to lighter rock that was sometimes dangerously fractured. "Anorthosite," Jakob said. "We're reaching the crust." After that every shift brought them through a new zone of rock. Once they tunneled through great layers of calcium feldspar striped with basalt intrusions, so that it looked like badly made brick. Another time they blasted their way through a wall of jasper as hard as steel. Only once did they pass through a vein of the blue; when they did it occurred to Oliver that his whole conception of the moon's composition had been warped by their mining. He had thought the moon was bursting with promethium, but as they dug across the narrow vein he realized it was uncommon, a loose net of threads in the great lunar body.

As they left the vein behind, Solly picked up a piece of the ore and stared at it curiously, lower eyes shut, face contorted as he struggled to focus his third eye. Suddenly he dashed the chunk to the ground, turned and marched to the head of their tunnel, attacked it with a drill. "I've given my whole life to the blue," he said, voice thick. "And what is it but a Goddamned rock."

Jakob laughed shortly. They tunneled on, away from the precious metal that now represented to them only a softer material to dig through. "Pick up the pace!" Jakob cried, slapping Solly on the back and leaping over the blocks beside the robot. "This rock has melted and melted again, changing over eons to the stones we see. Metamorphosis," he chanted, stretching the word out, lingering on the syllable *mor* until the word became a kind of song. "Metamorphosis. Meta-*mor*-pho-sis." Naomi and Hester took up the chant, and mute Elijah tapped his drill against the robot in double time. Jakob chanted over it. "Soon we will come to the city of the masters, the domes of Xanadu with their glass and fruit and steaming pools, and their vases and sports and their fine aged wines. And then there will be a—"

"Meta*mor*phosis."

And they tunneled ever faster.

Sitting in the sleeping car, chewing on a cheese, Oliver regarded the bulk of Jakob lying beside him. Jakob breathed deeply, very tired, almost asleep. "How do you know about the domes?" Oliver asked him softly. "How do you know all the things that you know?"

"Don't know," Jakob muttered. "Everyone knows. Less they burn your brain. Put you in a hole to live out your life. I don't know much, boy. Make most of it up. Love of a moon. Whatever we need...." And he slept.

They came up through a layer of marble—white marble all laced with quartz, so that it gleamed and sparkled in their lightless sight, and made them feel as though they dug through stone made of their cows' good milk, mixed with water like diamonds. This went on for a long time, until it filled them up and they became intoxicated with its smooth muscly texture, with the sparks of light lazing out of it. "I remember once we went to see a jazz band," Jakob said to all of them. Puffing as he ran the white rock along the cars to the rear, stacked it ever so carefully. "It was in Richmond among all the docks and refineries and giant oil tanks and we were so drunk we kept getting lost. But finally we found it—huh!—and it was just this broken-down trumpeter and a back line. He played sitting in a chair and you could just see in his face that his life had been a tough scuffle. His hat covered his whole household. And trumpet is a young man's instrument, too, it tears your lip to tatters. So we sat down to drink not expecting a thing, and they started up the last song of a set. 'Bucket's Got a Hole in It.' Four bar blues, as simple as a song can get."

"Meta*mor*phosis," rasped Hester.

"Yeah! Like that. And this trumpeter started to play it. And they went through it over and over and over. Huh! They must have done it a hundred times. Two hundred times. And sure enough this trumpeter was playing low and half the time in his hat, using all the tricks a broken-down trumpeter uses to save his lip, to hide the fact that it went west thirty years before. But after a while that didn't matter, because he was playing. He was playing! Everything he had learned in all his life, all the music and all the sorry rest of it, all that was jammed into the poor old 'Bucket' and by God it was mind over matter time, because that old song began to *roll*. And still on the run he broke into it:

"Oh the buck-et's got a hole in it
Yeah the buck-et's got a hole in it
Say the buck-et's got a hole in it.
Can't buy no beer!"

And over again. Oliver, Solly, Freeman, Hester, Naomi—they couldn't help laughing. What Jakob came up with out of his unburnt past! Mute Elijah banged a car wall happily, then squeezed the udder of a cow between one verse and the next— "Can't buy no beer!—*Moo!*"

They all joined in, breathing or singing it. It fit the pace of their work perfectly: fast but not too fast, regular, repetitive, simple, endless. All the syllables got the same length, a bit syncopated, except "hole," which was stretched out, and "can't buy no beer," which was high and all stretched out, stretched into a great shout of triumph, which was crazy since what it was saying was bad news, or should have been. But the song made it a cry of joy, and every time it rolled around they sang it louder, more stretched out. Jakob scatted up and down and around the tune, and Hester found all kinds of higher harmonics in a voice like a saw cutting steel, and the old tune rocked over and over and over and over and over and over and over and over and over and over, in a great passacaglia, in the crucible where all poverty is wrenched to delight: the blues. Metamorphosis. They sang it continuously for two shifts running, until they were all completely hypnotized by it; and then frequently, for long spells, for the rest of their time together.

It was sheer bad luck that they broke into a shaft from below, and that the shaft was filled with armed foremen; and worse luck that Jakob was working the robot, so that he was the first to leap out firing his hand drill like a weapon, and the only one to get struck by return fire before Naomi threw a knotchopper past him and blew the foremen to shreds. They got him on a car and rolled the robot back and pulled up the track and cut off in a new direction, leaving another Boesman behind to destroy evidence of their passing.

So they were all racing around with the blood and stuff still covering them and the cows mooing in distress and Jakob breathing through clenched teeth in double time, and only Hester and Oliver could sit in the car with him and try to tend him, ripping away the pants from a leg that was all cut up. Hester took a hand drill to cauterize the wounds that were bleeding hard, but Jakob shook his head at her, neck muscles bulging out. "Got the big artery inside of the thigh," he said through his teeth.

Hester hissed. "Come here," she croaked at Solly and the rest. "Stop that and come here!"

They were in a mass of broken quartz, the fractured clear crystals all pink with oxidation. The robot continued drilling away, the air cylinder hissed, the cows mooed. Jakob's breathing was harsh and somehow all of them were also breathing in the same way, irregularly, too fast; so that as his breathing slowed and calmed, theirs did too. He was lying back in the sleeping car, on a bed of hay, staring up at the fractured sparkling quartz ceiling of their tunnel, as if he could see far into it. "All these different kinds of rock," he said, his voice filled with wonder and pain. "You see, the moon itself was the world, once upon a time, and the Earth its moon; but there was an impact, and everything changed."

They cut a small side passage in the quartz and left Jakob there, so that when they filled in their tunnel as they moved on he was left behind, in his own deep crypt. And from then on the moon for them was only his big tomb, rolling through space till the sun itself died, as he had said it someday would.

Oliver got them back on a course, feeling radically uncertain of his navigational calculations now that Jakob was not there to nod over his shoulder to approve them. Dully he gave Naomi and Freeman the coordinates for Selene. "But what will we do when we get there?" Jakob had never actually made that clear. Find the leaders of the city, demand justice for the miners? Kill them? Get to the rockets of the great magnetic rail accelerators, and hijack one to Earth? Try to slip unnoticed into the populace?

"You leave that to us," Naomi said. "Just get us there." And he saw a light in Naomi's and Freeman's eyes that hadn't been there before. It reminded him of the thing that had chased him in the dark, the thing that even Jakob hadn't been able to explain; it frightened him.

So he set the course and they tunneled on as fast as they ever had. They never sang and they rarely talked; they threw themselves at the rock, hurt themselves in the effort, returned to attack it more fiercely than before. When he could not stave off sleep Oliver lay down on Jakob's dried blood, and bitterness filled him like a block of the anorthosite they wrestled with.

They were running out of hay. They killed a cow, ate its roasted flesh. The water recycler's filters were clogging, and their water smelled of urine. Hester listened to the seismometer as often as she could now, and she thought they were being pursued. But she also thought they were approaching Selene's underside.

Naomi laughed, but it wasn't like her old laugh. "You got us there, Oliver. Good work."

Oliver bit back a cry.

"Is it big?" Solly asked.

Hester shook her head. "Doesn't sound like it. Maybe twice the diameter of the Great Bole, not more."

"Good," Freeman said, looking at Naomi.

"But what will we do?" Oliver said.

Hester and Naomi and Freeman and Solly all turned to look at him, eyes blazing like twelve chunks of pure promethium. "We've got eight Boesmans left," Freeman said in a low voice. "All the rest of the explosives add up to a couple more. I'm going to set them just right. It'll be my best work ever, my masterpiece. And we'll blow Selene right off into space."

It took them ten shifts to get all the Boesmans placed to Freeman's and Naomi's satisfaction, and then another three to get far enough down and to one side to be protected from the shock of the blast, which luckily for them was directly upward against something that would give, and therefore would have less recoil.

Finally they were set, and they sat in the sleeping car in a circle of six, around the pile of components that sat under the master detonator. For a long time they just sat there cross-legged, breathing slowly and staring at it. Staring at each other, in the dark, in perfect redblack clarity. Then Naomi put both arms out, placed her hands carefully on the detonator's button. Mute Elijah put his hands on hers—then Freeman, Hester, Solly, finally Oliver—just in the order that Jakob had taken them. Oliver hesitated, feeling the flesh and bone under his hands, the warmth of his companions. He felt they should say something but he didn't know what it was.

"Seven," Hester croaked suddenly.

"Six," Freeman said.

Elijah blew air through his teeth, hard.

"Four," said Naomi.

"Three!" Solly cried.

"Two," Oliver said.

And they all waited a beat, swallowing hard, waiting for the moon and the man in the moon to speak to them. Then they pressed down on the button. They smashed at it with their fists, hit it so violently they scarcely felt the shock of the explosion.

They had put on vacuum suits and were breathing pure oxygen as they came up the last tunnel, clearing it of rubble. A great number of other shafts were revealed as they moved into the huge conical cavity left by the

Boesmans; tunnels snaked away from the cavity in all directions, so that they had sudden long vistas of blasted tubes extending off into the depths of the moon they had come out of. And at the top of the cavity, struggling over its broken edge, over the rounded wall of a new crater....

It was black. It was not like rock. Spread across it was a spill of white points, some bright, some so faint that they disappeared into the black if you looked straight at them. There were thousands of these white points, scattered over a black dome that was not a dome.... And there in the middle, almost directly overhead: a blue and white ball. Big, bright, blue, distant, rounded; half of it bright as a foreman's flash, the other half just a shadow.... It was clearly round, a big ball in the... sky. In the sky.

Wordlessly they stood on the great pile of rubble ringing the edge of their hole. Half buried in the broken anorthosite were shards of clear plastic, steel struts, patches of green grass, fragments of metal, an arm, broken branches, a bit of orange ceramic. Heads back to stare at the ball in the sky, at the astonishing fact of the void, they scarcely noticed these things.

A long time passed, and none of them moved except to look around. Past the jumble of dark trash that had mostly been thrown off in a single direction, the surface of the moon was an immense expanse of white hills, as strange and glorious as the stars above. The size of it all! Oliver had never dreamed that everything could be so big.

"The blue must be promethium," Solly said, pointing up at the Earth. "They've covered the whole Earth with the blue we mined."

Their mouths hung open as they stared at it. "How far away is it?" Freeman asked. No one answered.

"There they all are," Solly said. He laughed harshly. "I wish I could blow up the Earth too!"

He walked in circles on the rubble of the crater's rim. The rocket rails, Oliver thought suddenly, must have been in the direction Freeman had sent the debris. Bad luck. The final upward sweep of them poked up out of the dark dirt and glass. Solly pointed at them. His voice was loud in Oliver's ears, it strained the intercom: "Too bad we can't fly to the Earth, and blow it up too! I wish we could!"

And mute Elijah took a few steps, leaped off the mound into the sky, took a swipe with one hand at the blue ball. They laughed at him. "Almost got it, didn't you!" Freeman and Solly tried themselves, and then they all did: taking quick runs, leaping, flying slowly up through space, for five or six or seven seconds, making a grab at the sky overhead, floating back down as if in a dream, to land in a tumble, and try it again.... It felt wonderful to hang up there at the top of the leap, free in the vacuum, free of gravity and everything else, for just that instant.

After a while they sat down on the new crater's rim, covered with white dust and black dirt. Oliver sat on the very edge of the crater, legs over the edge, so that he could see back down into their sublunar world, at the same time that he looked up into the sky. Three eyes were not enough to judge such immensities. His heart pounded, he felt too intoxicated to move anymore. Tired, drunk. The intercom rasped with the sounds of their breathing, which slowly calmed, fell into a rhythm together. Hester buzzed one phrase of "Bucket" and they laughed softly. They lay back on the rubble, all but Oliver, and stared up into the dizzy reaches of the universe, the velvet black of infinity. Oliver sat with elbows on knees, watched the white hills glowing under the black sky. They were lit by earthlight—earthlight and starlight. The white mountains on the horizon were as sharp-edged as the shards of dome glass sticking out of the rock. And all the time the Earth looked down at him. It was all too fantastic to believe. He drank it in like oxygen, felt it filling him up, expanding in his chest.

"What do you think they'll do with us when they get here?" Solly asked.

"Kill us," Hester croaked.

"Or put us back to work," Naomi added.

Oliver laughed. Whatever happened, it was impossible in that moment to care. For above them a milky spill of stars lay thrown across the infinite black sky, lighting a million better worlds; while just over their heads the Earth glowed like a fine blue lamp; and under their feet rolled the white hills of the happy moon, holed like a great cheese.

ZÜRICH

When we were getting ready to leave Zürich I decided to try to leave our apartment as clean as it had been when we moved into it two years before. An employee of the Federal Institute of Technology, owners of the building, would be coming by to inspect the place, and these inspections were legendary among the foreign residents living in the building: they were tough. I wanted to be the first *Aüslander* to make an impression on the inspector.

Certainly this wasn't going to be easy; the apartment's walls were white, the tables were white, the bookcases and wardrobes and bed-tables and dressers and bedframes were white. The sheets and towels and dishes were white. In short practically every surface in the place was white, except for the floors, which were a fine blond hardwood. But I was getting good at cleaning the apartment, and having lived in Switzerland for two years, I had a general idea what to expect from the inspection. I knew the standard that would be applied. My soul rose to the challenge, and defiantly I swore that I was going to leave the place *immaculate*.

Soon I realized how difficult this was going to be. Every scuff from a muddy shoe, every drip of coffee, every sweaty palm, every exhalation of breath had left its mark. Lisa and I had lived here in our marvelous domestic chaos, and the damage proved it. We had put up pictures and there were holes in the walls. We had never dusted under the beds. The previous tenant had gotten away with things, having moved out in a hurry. It was going to be difficult.

Immediately it was obvious to me that the oven was going to be the crux of the problem. You see, once we went over to some American friends to have a home-like barbeque, and the grill was out on the balcony up on the fifth floor in the town of Dübendorf, looking out at all the other apartment blocks, the fine smell of barbequed chicken and hamburger spiralling out into the humid summer sky—when there was the howl of sirens below, and a whole fleet of fire engines docked and scores of firemen leaped out—all to combat our barbeque. One of the neighbors had called the police to report a fire on our balcony. We explained to the firemen and they nodded, staring coldly at the clouds of thick smoke filling the sky, and suddenly it seemed to us all that a barbeque was a very messy thing indeed.

So I never bought a grill for the balcony of our apartment. Instead I broiled our teriyaki shish-kebob in the oven, and it tasted all right. We use a fine teriyaki sauce, my mother got the recipe out of a magazine years ago; but it calls for brown sugar, and this was the source of the problem. When heated, the liquefied brown sugar caramelizes, as Lisa and her chemist colleagues are wont to say; and so on every interior surface of the oven there were little brown dots that refused to come off. They laughed at Easy Off, they laughed at Johnson & Johnson's Force. I began to understand that caramelization is a process somewhat like ceramic bonding. I needed a laser, and only had steel wool. So I began to rub.

It was a race between the flesh of my fingertips and the brown ceramic dots; which would the steel wool remove first? Flesh, of course; but it grows back, while the dots didn't. Only the miracle of regeneration allowed me to win this titanic battle. Over the course of the next two days (and imagine spending fifteen hours staring into a two-foot cube!) I muscled off every single dot, hour by hour becoming more and more enraged at the stubbornness of my foe.

Eventually the victory was mine; the oven was clean, a sparkling box of gray-black metal. It would pass the inspection. I stalked through the apartment in an ecstasy of rage, promising similar treatment for every other surface in the place.

I attacked the rest of the kitchen. Food had suffused into every nook and cranny, it was true; but none of it had caramelized. Stains disappeared with a single wipe, I was Mr. Clean, my soul was pure and my hands all-powerful. I put Beethoven on the stereo, those parts of his work that represent the mad blind energy of the universe: the *Grosse Fugue,* the second movement of the Ninth, the finale of the Seventh, and of the *Hammerklavier.* I was another manifestation of this mad blind energy, cleaning in a dance, propelled also by the complex and frenetic music of Charlie Parker, of Yes, "Salt Peanuts" and "Perpetual Change." And soon enough the kitchen gleamed like a factory display model. It would pass the inspection.

The other rooms offered feeble resistance. Dust, what was it to me now? "I am the mad blind energy of the universe, I vacuum under the beds!" Cleaning lint from the vacuum I sliced the very tip of my right forefinger off, and for a while it was hard not to get blood on the walls. But that was the most resistance these rooms could offer. Soon they shone with a burnished glow.

Now, inspired, I decided to get *really* thorough. It was time for details. I had been going to leave the floors alone, as they appeared clean enough to pass; but now with everything else so clean I noticed that there were little dark marks around the doorways, little dips in the grain of the wood where dirt had managed to insinuate itself. I bought some wood polish and went to work on the floors, and when I was done it was like walking on ice.

I dusted off the tops of the bookcases, up near the ceiling. I put spackle in the nail holes in the walls. When I was done the walls were all smooth, but it seemed to me that I could see a little discoloration where the spackle had gone. A few moments' pacing and inspiration struck: I got some typewriter Wite-Out from our boxes, and used it as touch-up paint. It really worked well. Nicks in doorways, a place where the wall was scraped by a chair back; typewriter Wite-Out, perfect.

In the evenings during this week of cleaning frenzy, I sat with friends, drinking and feeling my hands throb. One night I overheard by chance an Israeli friend tell a story about a Swiss friend of hers who had unscrewed the frames on her double-paned windows, to clean the inside surfaces. I shot up in my chair, mouth hanging open; I had noticed dust on the inner sides of our double-paned windows that very afternoon, and figured it was something I wouldn't be able to do anything about. It never would have occurred to me to unscrew the frames! But the Swiss know about these things. The next day I got out a screwdriver, and unscrewed and polished until my wrists were liked cooked spaghetti. And the windows sparkled from all four surfaces. They would pass the inspection.

On the morning of Inspection Day I walked through the big rooms of the apartment, with their tan leather chairs and couches, and the white walls and bookcases, and the sun streamed in and I stood there transfixed as if in the dream of a cognac advertisement, in air like mineral water.

Glancing at the long mirror in the foyer something caught my eye; I frowned; I walked up to it, feeling uneasy as I often do around mirrors, and looked at it closely. Sure enough, some dust. I had forgotten to clean the mirror. As I went to work on it I marvelled: you can see the difference between a dusty mirror and a clean one, even when—staring at the paper towel in my hand—there is only enough dust to make a thin short line, like a faint pencil mark. So little dust, distributed over such a large surface—and yet we still can see it. The eye is that powerful. If we can see that, I thought, why not ourselves? Why not everything?

So I strode around the cognac advertisement in a state of rapture; until I remembered the sheets, down in the washing machine. All would have been well, if not for the sheets. All through the week I had been washing those sheets, downstairs in the basement. Red plastic laundry basket filled with linen: we had seven bottom sheets, seven pillow cases, seven big duvet cases. The duvets were fine, as white as cotton. But the bottom sheets, the pillow cases.... Well. They were yellowed. Stained. Alarming evidence of our bodies, our physical existence: oils, fluids, minuscule scraps of us rubbed into the cloth like butter, ineradicably.

Certainly, I thought, the Swiss must have methods for dealing with evidence as serious as this. So I had gone out and bought bleaches. Recalling the bleach ads from back home, I trustfully assumed that the stained linen would emerge from one trip through the wash gleaming like lightning. But it wasn't so. Wash after wash did nothing to change their color. I went out and bought a different kind of bleach, then another. Two powders, one liquid. I upped the doses on each of them. Nothing worked.

And now it was the morning of Inspection Day, and I had recalled the sheets in the basement, and my rapture was shattered. I hurried down stairs, walked down the long concrete underground hallway to the laundry room. I saw that the building would stand for a thousand years. It would resist ten megatons. The washing machine was trilingual and as big as a truck. I brought it online, gave it its pre-run check-off for the final attempt, set my array of bleaches on top of the machine. It was the fourteenth time I had run things through this week, and I had the procedure streamlined; but this time I stopped to think. I looked at the three different kinds of bleach on top of the dryer, and I had an idea. I took the largest cap and turned it open end up, then poured in liquid bleach until the cup was half full. Then I poured in some of both of the powders.

Synergy, right? Singing a little tune in praise of the mysterious force of synergy, I took the pencil from the sign-in book and stirred the mix in the cap vigorously. It began to bubble a little, then to foam.

Only at that point did I remember my wife, the chemist, yelling at me for mixing two cleansers together in an attempt to get a bathtub clean. "If you had mixed ammonia and Ajax it would have made chloramine gas and killed you!" she had said. "*Never* mix stuff like that together!"

So I left the cap of bleaches on the dryer and ran out of the room. From the concrete hall I stared back in, sniffing carefully. Glancing down I noticed the pencil, still clenched in my hand; and the bottom half of it, the part that had stirred the bleaches, was as white as a stick of chalk. "Ho!" I exclaimed, and retreated farther up the hall. Synergy can be a powerful thing.

After some thought, and a closer inspection of the pencil, which now had a pure white eraser, I returned to the washroom. The air seemed okay. I was committed at this point, I had to meet the Swiss challenge. So I tipped the capful of bleaches carefully into the plastic opening on top of the washer, and I stuffed our yellowy bottom sheets and pillow cases inside, and I closed up the washer and punched the buttons for the hottest water available, ninety degrees centigrade. Walking back upstairs I noticed that the very tip of my left forefinger had a white patch on it. Back in the apartment I found it wouldn't wash off. "Bleached my flesh!" I exclaimed. "That stuff is finally working the way it's supposed to."

An hour later I returned to the washroom apprehensively, hoping that the sheets had not been eaten to shreds or the like. On the contrary; when I opened the washer door there was a glare as if several camera flashes had gone off right in my face, just like in the ads; and there were the sheets, as white as new snow.

I hooted for glee, and stuffed them in the dryer. And by the time the Inspector rang the bell below, they were dried and ironed and folded and neatly stacked in the linen drawers of the bedroom wardrobe, looking like great hunks of Ivory soap.

I hummed cheerfully as I let the Inspector in. He was a young man, perhaps younger than myself. His English was excellent. He was apologetic, defensive; it was a boring task for both of us, he said, but necessary. No problem, I replied, and showed him around the place. He nodded, frowning slightly. "I must count the various items in the kitchen," he said, brandishing an inventory.

That took a long time. When he was done he shook his head disapprovingly. "There are four glasses missing, and one spoon, and the top off the tea kettle."

"That's right," I said happily. "We broke the glasses and lost the spoon, and I think we broke the tea kettle, though I can't remember." These things didn't matter, they didn't have to do with the essential challenge, which concerned not number but order; not quantity, but quality; not inventory, but cleanliness.

And the Inspector understood this too; after listening to my admission, he shook his head seriously and said, "Fine, fine; however, what about *this?*" And with a satisfied look he reached up into the back of the top shelf of the broom closet, and held out before me a short stack of grimy kitchen towels.

In that moment I understood that the Inspector wanted dirtiness, in the same way that a policeman wants crime; it's the only thing that can make the job interesting. I stared at the kitchen towels, which I had completely forgotten. "What about them?" I said. "We never used those, I forgot they were up there." I shrugged. "The previous tenant must have done that to them."

He stared at me disbelievingly. "How did you dry your dishes?"

"We stood them in the drainer and let them dry on their own."

He shook his head, not believing that anyone would rely on such a method. I recalled the Swiss friend of ours who dried her bathtub with a towel after showering. I shrugged stubbornly; the Inspector shook his head stubbornly. He turned to look in the broom closet again, to see if there were any other forgotten treasures. Without forethought I quickly reached behind him and touched the stained kitchen towels with my bleached forefinger.

They turned white.

When the young inspector was done searching the broom closet, I said casually, "But they're not that bad, are they?" He looked at the kitchen towels and his eyebrows shot up. He regarded me suspiciously; I just shrugged, and left the kitchen. "Are you about done?" I asked. "I have to go downtown."

He prepared to leave. "We will have to see about the missing glasses," he said, voice heavy with dissatisfaction.

"And the spoon," I said. "And the tea kettle top."

He left.

I danced through the sparkling air of the empty apartment. My work was done, I had passed the inspection, my soul was pure, I was in a state of grace. Weak sunlight lanced between low clouds, and out on the balcony the air was frigid. I put on my down jacket to go into the city center, to see my Zürich one last time.

Down the old overgrown steps and through the wintry garden of the ETH, past the big building housing the Chinese graduate students. Down the steep walkway to Voltastrasse, past the Japanese fire maple and the interior design store. I touched one red rose and was not particularly surprised to see it turn white. My whole fingertip looked like paraffin now.

Down at the Voltastrasse tram stop, in the wind. Across the street the haunted house stood, a pinkish wreck with big cracks in its walls; Lisa and I had always marvelled at it, there was nothing even remotely as derelict as it anywhere in Zürich. It was an anomaly, an exile like we were, and we loved it. "I'll never touch you," I said to it.

A Number Six tram hummed down the hill from Kirche Fluntern and squealed to a halt before me. You have to touch a button to get the doors to open, so I did that and the whole tram car turned white. Usually they are blue, but there are a few trams painted different colors to advertise the city museums, and there are some painted white to advertise the Oriental museum in Rietliberg, so I assumed that this car would now be taken for one of those; and I climbed aboard.

We slid off down the hill toward Platte, ETH and Central. I sat in the back of the tram and watched the Swiss in front of me, getting on and off. Many of them were old. None of them ever sat in seats beside each other until all the seats had been filled by single parties. If single seats were vacated at a stop, people sitting next to strangers in double seats would get up and move to the single seat. No one talked, though they did look at each other a little. Mostly they looked out the windows. The windows were clean. These trams on the Number Six line had been built in 1952, but they were still in factory perfect condition; they had passed the inspection.

Looking down, I suddenly noticed that each pair of shoes on the tram was flawless. Then I noticed that each head of hair was perfectly coifed. Even the two punks on the tram had their hair perfectly done, in their own style. Shoes and hair, I thought, these will reveal the wealth of a nation. These extremes reveal the soul.

At the ETH stop a Latin American man got on the tram. He was dressed in a colorful serape, and thin black cotton pants, and he looked miserably cold. He was carrying an odd thing that looked like a bow; it was painted crudely, in many colors, and there was a small painted gourd attached to it, where you would hold the bow if it were meant to shoot arrows. The man had long lanky black hair that fell loosely over his shoulders and down the back of the serape, and his face was big and broad-cheeked; he looked like a *mestizo*, or perhaps a purebred Indian from Bolivia or Peru or Ecuador. There were quite a few of them living in Zürich, Lisa and I often saw groups of them on Bahnhofstrasse, playing music for change. Pan pipes, guitars, drums, gourds filled with beans: street music performed right through the winter, with the players and audience alike shivering in the snowy air.

When the tram started to move again, this Latino walked to the front of the car and turned around to face us all. He said something loudly in Spanish, and then began to play the bow and gourd instrument, plucking it rapidly. Moving one thumb up and down the metal bowstring changed the pitch of the sound, which reverberated in the gourd, making a kind of loud twang. The resulting sound was awful: loud, unmelodic, impossible to ignore.

The Swiss stared resentfully at this intrusion. This was not done; I had never seen it before, and neither had the others aboard, it was clear. And the sound of the primitive instrument was so insistent, so weird. The disapproval in the car was as palpable as the sound, the two vibrations battling each other in tense air.

The tram stopped at Haldenegg, and several people got off, more than would usually; clearly some were just escaping the musician, and would get on the next tram to come along. Newcomers, unpleasantly surprised, stared at the man as he twanged away. The tram doors closed and we moved off again, down the hill to Central. The captive audience stared at the musician, as belligerent as cows eyeing a passing car.

Then he broke into song. It was one of those Bolivian or Peruvian hill ballads, a sad tale dramatically told, and the man sang it over the twanging of his absurd instrument in a hoarse wild voice, expressing all the anguish of the exile, lost in a cold land. What a voice the man had! Suddenly the ridiculous twanging made sense, it all fell together; this voice in a foreign language cut through all the barriers and spoke to us, to each and every person on the tram. That kind of singing is impossible to ignore or deny—we knew exactly what he was feeling, and so for that moment we were a little community. And all without understanding a word. What power the voice has to express what really matters! People shifted in their seats, they sat up, they watched the singer intently, they smiled. When he walked up and down the tram, holding out a black felt hat, they dug deep in their pockets and purses and dropped change in, smiling at him and saying things in Swiss German, or even in High German so he might perhaps understand. When the doors hissed open at Central, they were surprised; no one aboard had noticed our arrival.

The Swiss! I had to laugh. So closed in, so generous….

Then as each person touched the white parts of my white tram, they went white themselves. Chairback or railing or overhead support, it didn't matter; they touched the tram and left it as white as porcelain figures of themselves. And no one at Central paid any attention.

As we left the tram together, I touched the musician on the shoulder, in a sort of greeting, or an experiment. He only looked at me, eyes black as obsidian; and it seemed to me that the vivid colored thread sewn riotously into his serape actually grew more brilliant, more intensely colorful: little rainbow crosshatchings, scarlet and saffron and green and violet and pink and sky blue, glowing in crude brown woolen cloth. Without a glance back the musician walked off into the Niederdorf, Zürich's medieval town.

I crossed the bridge looking down at the white swans in the gray Limmat, feeling the wind rush through me, buoyant with the memory of his music and my apartment's purity. I walked down Bahnhofstrasse seeing it all again, seeing it fully for the first time in a long while and the last time in who knew how long, perhaps forever, and my heart filled and I said, "Ah handsome Züri my town, my town, I too am one of your exiled sons," and I caressed the granite blocks of the stolid elegant buildings and they turned white as wedding cakes under my hand, with a keening sound like violins taped and played backwards. When would I ever see it again like this, with its low pearl gray sky rushing overhead in the cold wind, with the Alps at the end of the Zürichsee standing up like cardboard cutout mountains, steeper than mountains could ever be? I touched the tram tracks and they turned to white gold, in a wide street of glazed sugar. And I walked down this white street looking in the sparkling window displays of the rich merchants, the jewelry and clothing and watches all perfect and gleaming, and, as I traced my fingers over the window glass, as white as white opals.

In among the narrow alleyways of the medieval town I wandered, touching every massive building until it seemed I walked in a silent world of milk and baking soda, saying good-bye with every touch. To consciously be doing something you loved, for the last time! Past St. Peter's church which was already alabaster before I touched it, past Fraumünster and across the river to Grossmünster with its painfully spare interior, like a tall empty warehouse made entirely of white marble.... Then back across the river again, on a paper bridge. And looking down the gray Limmat I saw that much of Zürich had turned white, bleached by my touch.

I came to the lakefront at Burkliplatz, touched the steps and suddenly the fine little park and the boat docks gleamed like soap carvings. The beautiful statue of Ganymede and the eagle looked like they had been molded out of white ceramic, and in Ganymede's outstretched arms it seemed to me a whole world was being embraced, a rushing world of gray sky and gray water where everything passed by so fast that you never got the chance to hold it, to touch it, to make it yours. Can't we keep anything? These years of our life, we were happy, we were here, and now it was all white and clean and still, turning to marble under the touch of my hand. So that in the pure rapture of final things I walked down the white concrete ramp to the lapping lake water and crouched down and touched it; and before me I saw the whole long lake go still and turn white, as if it were an immense tub of white chocolate; and in the distance the magnificent Alps were white; and overhead the rushing clouds pulsed white and glowed like spun glass. I turned around and saw that the city's transformation was complete: it was a still and silent Zürich of snow and white marble, white chocolate, white ceramic, milk, salt, cream.

But from a distant street I could still hear that twanging.

VINLAND THE DREAM

Abstract. It was sunset at L'Anse aux Meadows. The water of the bay was still, the boggy beach was dark in the shadows. Flat arms of land pointed to flat islands offshore; beyond these a taller island stood like a loaf of stone in the sea, catching the last of the day's light. A stream gurgled gently as it cut through the beach bog. Above the bog, on a narrow grassy terrace, one could just make out a pattern of low mounds, all that remained of sod walls. Next to them were three or four sod buildings, and beyond the buildings, a number of tents.

A group of people—archaeologists, graduate students, volunteer laborers, visitors—moved together onto a rocky ridge overlooking the site. Some of them worked at starting a campfire in a ring of blackened stones; others began to unpack bags of food, and cases of beer. Far across the water lay the dark bulk of Labrador. Kindling caught and their fire burned, a spark of yellow in the dusk's gloom.

Hot dogs and beer, around a campfire by the sea; and yet it was strangely quiet. Voices were subdued. The people on the hill glanced down often at the site, where the head of their dig, a lanky man in his early fifties, was giving a brief tour to their distinguished guest. The distinguished guest did not appear pleased.

Introduction. The head of the dig, an archeology professor from McGill University, was looking at the distinguished guest with the expression he wore when confronted by an aggressive undergraduate. The distinguished guest, Canada's Minister of Culture, was asking question after question. As she did, the professor took her to look for herself, at the forge, and the slag pit, and the little midden beside Building E. New trenches were cut across the mounds and depressions, perfect rectangular cuts in the black peat; they could tell the minister nothing of what they had revealed. But she had insisted on seeing them, and now she was asking questions that got right to the point, although they could have been asked and answered just as well in Ottawa. Yes, the professor explained, the fuel for the forge was wood charcoal, the temperature had gotten to around twelve hundred degrees Celsius, the process was direct reduction of bog ore, obtaining about one kilogram of iron for every five kilograms of slag. All was as it was in other Norse forges—except that the limonites in the bog ore had now been precisely identified by spectroscopic analysis; and that analysis had revealed that the bog iron smelted here had come from northern Quebec, near Chicoutimi. The Norse explorers, who had supposedly smelted the bog ore, could not have obtained it.

There was a similar situation in the midden; rust migrated in peat at a known rate, and so it could be determined that the many iron rivets in the midden had only been there a hundred and forty years, plus or minus fifty.

"So," the minister said, in English with a Francophone lilt. "You have proved your case, it appears?"

The professor nodded wordlessly. The minister watched him, and he couldn't help feeling that despite the nature of the news he was giving her, she was somewhat amused. By him? By his scientific terminology? By his obvious (and growing) depression? He couldn't tell.

The minister raised her eyebrows. "L'Anse aux Meadows, a hoax. Parcs Canada will not like it at all."

"No one will like it," the professor croaked.

"No," the minister said, looking at him. "I suppose not. Particularly as this is part of a larger pattern, yes?"

The professor did not reply.

"The entire concept of Vinland," she said. "A hoax!" The professor nodded glumly.

"I would not have believed it possible."

"No," the professor said. "But—" He waved a hand at the low mounds around them—"So it appears." He shrugged. "The story has always rested on a very small body of evidence. Three sagas, this site, a few references in Scandinavian records, a few coins, a few cairns..." He shook his head. "Not much." He picked up a chunk of dried peat from the ground, crumbled it in his fingers.

Suddenly the minister laughed at him, then put her hand to his upper arm. Her fingers were warm. "You must remember it is not your fault."

He smiled wanly. "I suppose not." He liked the look on her face; sympathetic as well as amused. She was about his age, perhaps a bit older. An attractive and sophisticated Quebecoise. "I need a drink," he confessed.

"There's beer on the hill."

"Something stronger. I have a bottle of cognac I haven't opened yet…"

"Let's get it and take it up there with us."

Experimental Methods. The graduate students and volunteer laborers were gathered around the fire, and the smell of roasting hot dogs filled the air. It was nearly eleven, the sun a half-hour gone, and the last light of the summer dusk slowly leaked from the sky. The fire burned like a beacon. Beer had been flowing freely, and the party was beginning to get a little more boisterous.

The minister and the professor stood near the fire, drinking cognac out of plastic cups.

"How did you come to suspect the story of Vinland?" the minister asked as they watched the students cook hot dogs.

A couple of the volunteer laborers, who had paid good money to spend their summer digging trenches in a bog, heard the question and moved closer.

The professor shrugged. "I can't quite remember." He tried to laugh. "Here I am an archaeologist, and I can't remember my own past."

The minister nodded as if that made sense. "I suppose it was a long time ago?"

"Yes." He concentrated. "Now what was it. Someone was following up the story of the Vinland map, to try and figure out who had done it. The map showed up in a bookstore in New Haven in the 1950s—as you may know?"

"No," the minister said. "I hardly know a thing about Vinland, I assure you. Just the basics that anyone in my position would have to know."

"Well, there was a map found in the 1950s called the Vinland map, and it was shown to be a hoax soon after its discovery. But when this investigator traced the map's history, she found that the book it had been in was accounted for all the way back to the 1820s, map and all. It meant the hoaxer had lived longer ago than I had expected." He refilled his cup of cognac, then the minister's. "There were a lot of Viking hoaxes in the nineteenth century, but this one was so early. It surprised me. It's generally thought that the whole phenomenon was stimulated by a book that a Danish scholar published in 1837, containing translations of the Vinland sagas and related material. The book was very popular among the Scandinavian settlers in America, and after that, you know… a kind of twisted patriotism, or the response of an ethnic group that had been made fun of too often… So we got the Kensington stone, the halberds, the mooring holes, the coins. But if a hoax predated *Antiquitates Americanae…* it made me wonder."

"If the book itself were somehow involved?"

"Exactly," the professor said, regarding the minister with pleasure. "I wondered if the book might not incorporate, or have been inspired by, hoaxed material. Then one day I was reading a description of the field work here, and it occurred to me that this site was a bit too pristine. As if it had been built but never lived in. Best estimates for its occupation were as low as one summer, because they couldn't find any trash middens to speak of, or graves."

"It could have been occupied very briefly," the minister pointed out.

"Yes, I know. That's what I thought at the time. But then I heard from a colleague in Bergen that the *Gronlendinga Saga* was apparently a forgery, at least in the parts referring to the discovery of Vinland. Pages had been inserted that dated back to the 1820s. And after that, I had a doubt that wouldn't go away."

"But there are more Vinland stories than that one, yes?"

"Yes. There are three main sources. The *Gronlendinga Saga, The Saga of Erik the Red,* and the part of *The Hauksbók* that tells about Thorfinn Karlsefni's expedition. But with one of those questioned, I began to doubt them all. And the story itself. Everything having to do with the idea of Vinland."

"Is that when you went to Bergen?" a graduate student asked.

The professor nodded. He drained his plastic cup, felt the alcohol rushing through him. "I joined Nielsen there and we went over *Erik the Red* and *The Hauksbók,* and damned if the pages in those concerning Vinland weren't forgeries too. The ink gave it away—not its composition, which was about right, but merely how long it had been on that paper. Which was thirteenth century paper, I might add! The forger had done a super job. But the sagas had been tampered with sometime in the early nineteenth century."

"But those are masterpieces of world literature," a volunteer laborer exclaimed, round-eyed; the ads for volunteer labor had not included a description of the primary investigator's hypothesis.

"I know," the professor said irritably, and shrugged.

He saw a chunk of peat on the ground, picked it up and threw it on the blaze. After a bit it flared up.

"It's like watching dirt burn," he said absently, staring into the flames.

Discussion. The burnt garbage smell of peat wafted downwind, and offshore the calm water of the bay was riffled by the same gentle breeze. The minister warmed her hands at the blaze for a moment, then gestured at the bay. "It's hard to believe they were never here at all."

"I know," the professor said. "It looks like a Viking site, I'll give him that."

"Him," the minister repeated.

"I know, I know. This whole thing forces you to imagine a man in the eighteen twenties and thirties, traveling all over—Norway, Iceland, Canada, New England, Rome, Stockholm, Denmark, Greenland…. Crisscrossing the North Atlantic, to bury all these signs." He shook his head. "It's incredible."

He retrieved the cognac bottle and refilled. He was, he had to admit, beginning to feel drunk. "And so many parts of the hoax were well hidden! You can't assume we've found them all. This place had two butternuts buried in the midden, and butternuts only grow down below the St. Lawrence, so who's to say they aren't clues, indicating another site down there? That's where grapevines actually grow, which would justify the name Vinland. I tell you, the more I know about this hoaxer, the more certain I am that other sites exist. The tower in Newport, Rhode Island, for instance—the hoaxer didn't build that, because it's been around since the seventeenth century—but a little work out there at night, in the early nineteenth century… I bet if it were excavated completely, you'd find a few Norse artifacts."

"Buried in all the right places," the minister said.

"Exactly." The professor nodded. "And up the coast of Labrador, at Cape Porcupine where the sagas say they repaired a ship. There too. Stuff scattered everywhere, left to be discovered or not."

The minister waved her plastic cup. "But surely this site must have been his masterpiece. He couldn't have done too many as extensive as this."

"I shouldn't think so." The professor drank deeply, smacked his numbed lips. "Maybe one more like this, down in New Brunswick. That's my guess. But this was surely one of his biggest projects."

"It was a time for that kind of thing," the volunteer laborer offered. "Atlantis, Mu, Lemuria…."

The minister nodded. "It fulfills a certain desire."

"Theosophy, most of that," the professor muttered. "This was different."

The volunteer wandered off. The professor and the minister looked into the fire for a while.

"You are *sure?*" the minister asked.

The professor nodded. "Trace elements show the ore came from upper Quebec. Chemical changes in the peat weren't right. And nuclear resonance dating methods show that the bronze pin they found hadn't been buried long enough. Little things like that. Nothing obvious. He was amazingly meticulous, he really thought it out. But the nature of things tripped him up. Nothing more than that."

"But the effort!" the minister said. "This is what I find hard to believe. Surely it must have been more than one man! Burying these objects, building the walls—surely he would have been noticed!"

The professor stopped another swallow, nodded at her as he choked once or twice. A broad wave of the hand, a gasping recovery of breath:

"Fishing village, kilometer north of here. Boarding house in the early nineteenth century. A crew of ten rented rooms in the summer of 1842. Bills paid by a Mr. Carlsson."

The minister raised her eyebrows. "Ah."

One of the graduate students got out a guitar and began to play. The other students and the volunteers gathered around her.

"So," the minister said, "Mr. Carlsson. Does he show up elsewhere?"

"There was a Professor Ohman in Bergen. A Dr. Bergen in Reykjavik. In the right years, studying the sagas. I presume they were all him, but I don't know for sure."

"What do you know about him?"

"Nothing. No one paid much attention to him. I've got him on a couple transatlantic crossings, I think, but he used aliases, so I've probably missed most of them. A Scandinavian-American, apparently Norwegian by birth. Someone with some money—someone with patriotic feelings of some kind—someone with a grudge against a university—who knows? All I have are a few signatures, of aliases at that. A flowery handwriting. Nothing more. That's the most remarkable thing about him! You see, most hoaxers leave clues to their identities, because a part of them wants to be caught. So their cleverness can be admired, or the ones who fell for it embarrassed, or whatever. But this guy didn't want to be discovered. And in those days, if you wanted to stay off the record...." He shook his head.

"A man of mystery."

"Yeah. But I don't know how to find out anything more about him."

The professor's face was glum in the firelight as he reflected on this. He polished off another cup of cognac. The minister watched him drink, then said kindly, "There is nothing to be done about it, really. That is the nature of the past."

"I know."

Conclusions. They threw the last big logs on the fire, and flames roared up, yellow licks breaking free among the stars. The professor felt numb all over, his heart was cold, the firelit faces were smeary primitive masks, dancing in the light. The songs were harsh and raucous, he couldn't understand the words. The wind was chilling, and the hot skin of his arms and neck goosepimpled uncomfortably. He felt sick with alcohol, and knew it would be a while before his body could overmaster it.

The minister led him away from the fire, then up the rocky ridge. Getting him away from the students and laborers, no doubt, so he wouldn't embarrass himself. Starlight illuminated the heather and broken granite under their feet. He stumbled. He tried to explain to her what it meant, to be an archaeologist whose most important work was the discovery that a bit of their past was a falsehood.

"It's like a mosaic," he said, drunkenly trying to follow the fugitive thought. "A puzzle with most of the pieces gone. A tapestry. And if you pull a thread out… it's ruined. So little lasts! We need every bit we can find!"

She seemed to understand. In her student days, she told him, she had waitressed at a café in Montreal. Years later she had gone down the street to have a look, just for nostalgia's sake. The café was gone. The street was completely different. And she couldn't remember the names of any of the people she had worked with. "This was my own past, not all that many years ago!"

The professor nodded. Cognac was rushing through his veins, and as he looked at the minister, so beautiful in the starlight, she seemed to him a kind of muse, a spirit sent to comfort him, or frighten him, he couldn't tell which. Clio, he thought. The muse of history. Someone he could talk to.

She laughed softly. "Sometimes it seems our lives are much longer than we usually think. So that we live through incarnations, and looking back later we have nothing but…." She waved a hand.

"Bronze pins," the professor said. "Iron rivets."

"Yes." She looked at him. Her eyes were bright in the starlight. "We need an archeology for our own lives."

Acknowledgments. Later he walked her back to the fire, now reduced to banked red coals. She put her hand to his upper arm as they walked, steadying herself, and he felt in the touch some kind of portent; but couldn't understand it. He had drunk so much! Why be so upset about it, why? It was his job to find the truth; having found it, he should be happy! Why had no one told him what he would feel?

The minister said goodnight. She was off to bed; she suggested he do likewise. Her look was compassionate, her voice firm.

When she was gone he hunted down the bottle of cognac, and drank the rest of it. The fire was dying, the students and workers scattered—in the tents, or out in the night, in couples.

He walked by himself back down to the site.

Low mounds, of walls that had never been. Beyond the actual site were rounded buildings, models built by the park service, to show tourists what the "real" buildings had looked like. When Vikings had camped on the edge of the new world. Repairing their boats. Finding food. Fighting among themselves, mad with epic jealousies. Fighting the dangerous Indians. Getting killed, and then driven away from this land, so much lusher than Greenland.

A creak in the brush and he jumped, startled. It would have been like that: death in the night, creeping up on you—he turned with a jerk, and every starlit shadow bounced with hidden skraelings, their bows drawn taut, their arrows aimed at his heart. He quivered, hunched over.

But no. It hadn't been like that. Not at all. Instead, a man with spectacles and a bag full of old junk, directing some unemployed sailors as they dug. Nondescript, taciturn, nameless; one night he would have wandered back there into the forest, perhaps fallen or had a heart attack—become a skeleton wearing leathers and sword-belt, with spectacles over the skull's eyesockets, the anachronism that gave him away at last.... The professor staggered over the low mounds toward the trees, intent on finding that inadvertent grave....

But no. It wouldn't be there. The taciturn figure hadn't been like that. He would have been far away when he died, nothing to show what he had spent years of his life doing. A man in a hospital for the poor, the bronze pin in his pocket overlooked by the doctor, stolen by an undertaker's assistant. An anonymous figure, to the grave and beyond. The creator of Vinland. Never to be found.

The professor looked around, confused and sick. There was a waist-high rock, a glacial erratic. He sat on it. Put his head on his hands. Really quite unprofessional. All those books he had read as a child. What would the minister think! Grant money. No reason to feel so bad!

At that latitude midsummer nights are short, and the party had lasted late. The sky to the east was already gray. He could see down onto the site, and its long sod roofs. On the beach, a trio of long narrow high-ended ships. Small figures in furs emerged from the longhouses and went down to the water, and he walked among them and heard their speech, a sort of dialect of Norwegian that he could mostly understand. They would leave that day, it was time to load the ships. They were going to take everything with them, they didn't plan to return. Too many skraelings in the forest, too many quick arrow deaths. He walked among them, helping them load stores. Then a little man in a black coat scurried behind the forge, and he roared and took off after him, scooping up a rock on the way, ready to deal out a skraeling death to that black intruder.

The minister woke him with a touch of her hand. He almost fell off the rock. He shook his head; he was still drunk. The hangover wouldn't begin for a couple more hours, though the sun was already up.

"I should have known all along," he said to her angrily. "They were stretched to the limit in Greenland, and the climate was worsening. It was amazing they got that far. Vinland"—he waved a hand at the site—"was just some dreamer's story."

Regarding him calmly, the minister said, "I am not sure it matters."

He looked up at her. "What do you mean?"

"History is made of stories people tell. And fictions, dreams, hoaxes—they also are made of stories people tell. True or false, it's the stories that matter to us. Certain qualities in the stories themselves make them true or false."

He shook his head. "Some things really happened in the past. And some things didn't."

"But how can you know for sure which is which? You can't go back and see for yourself. Maybe Vinland was the invention of this mysterious stranger of yours; maybe the Vikings came here after all, and landed somewhere else. Either way it can never be anything more than a story to us."

"But..." He swallowed. "Surely it matters whether it is a true story or not!"

She paced before him. "A friend of mine once told me something he had read in a book," she said. "It was by a man who sailed the Red Sea, long ago. He told of a servant boy on one of the dhows, who could not remember ever having been cared for. The boy had become a sailor at age three—before that, he had been a beachcomber." She stopped pacing and looked at the beach below them. "Often I imagined that little boy's life. Surviving alone on a beach, at that age—it astonished me. It made me... happy."

She turned to look at him. "But later I told this story to an expert in child development, and he just shook his head. 'It probably wasn't true,' he said. Not a lie, exactly, but a...."

"A stretcher," the professor suggested.

"A stretcher, exactly. He supposed that the boy had been somewhat older, or had had some help. You know."

The professor nodded.

"But in the end," the minister said, "I found this judgment did not matter to me. In my mind I still saw that toddler, searching the tidepools for his daily food. And so for me the story lives. And that is all that matters. We judge all the stories from history like that—we value them according to how much they spur our imaginations."

The professor stared at her. He rubbed his jaw, looked around. Things had the sharp-edged clarity they sometimes get after a sleepless night, as if glowing with internal light. He said, "Someone with opinions like yours probably shouldn't have the job that you do."

"I didn't know I had them," the minister said. "I only just came upon them in the last couple hours, thinking about it."

The professor was surprised. "You didn't sleep?"

She shook her head. "Who could sleep on a night like this?"

"My feeling exactly!" He almost smiled. "So. A *nuit blanche,* you call it?"

"Yes," she said. "A *nuit blanche* for two." And she looked down at him with that amused glance of hers, as if... as if she understood him.

She extended her arms toward him, grasped his hands, helped pull him to his feet. They began to walk back toward the tents, across the site of L'Anse aux Meadows. The grass was wet with dew, and very green.

"I still think," he said as they walked together, "that we want more than stories from the past. We want something not easily found—something, in fact, that the past doesn't have. Something secret, some secret meaning... something that will give our lives a kind of sense."

She slipped a hand under his arm. "We want the Atlantis of childhood. But, failing that...." She laughed and kicked at a clump of grass; a spray of dew flashed ahead of them, containing, for just one moment, a bright little rainbow.

"A HISTORY OF THE TWENTIETH CENTURY, WITH ILLUSTRATIONS"

*"If truth is not to be found on the shelves of the British Museum, where,
I asked myself, picking up a notebook and a pencil, is truth?"*
—*Virginia Woolf*

Daily doses of bright light markedly improve the mood of people suffering from depression, so every day at eight in the evening Frank Churchill went to the clinic on Park Avenue, and sat for three hours in a room illuminated with sixteen hundred watts of white light. This was not exactly like having the sun in the room, but it was bright, about the same as if sixteen bare lightbulbs hung from the ceiling. In this case the bulbs were probably long tubes, and they were hidden behind a sheet of white plastic, so it was the whole ceiling that glowed.

He sat at a table and doodled with a purple pen on a pad of pink paper. And then it was eleven and he was out on the windy streets, blinking as traffic lights swam in the gloom. He walked home to a hotel room in the west Eighties. He would return to the clinic at five the next morning for a predawn treatment, but now it was time to sleep. He looked forward to that. He'd been on the treatment for three weeks, and he was tired. Though the treatment did seem to be working—as far as he could tell; improvement was supposed to average twenty percent a week, and he wasn't sure what that would feel like.

In his room the answering machine was blinking. There was a message from his agent, asking him to call immediately. It was now nearly midnight, but he pushbuttoned the number and his agent answered on the first ring.

"You have DSPS," Frank said to him.

"What? What?"

"Delayed sleep phase syndrome. I know how to get rid of it."

"Frank! Look, Frank, I've got a good offer for you."

"Do you have a lot of lights on?"

"What? Oh, yeah, say, how's that going?"

"I'm probably sixty percent better."

"Good, good. Keep at it. Listen, I've got something should help you a hundred percent. A publisher in London wants you to go over there and write a book on the twentieth century."

"What kind of book?"

"Your usual thing, Frank, but this time putting together the big picture. Reflecting on all the rest of your books, so to speak. They want to bring it out in time for the turn of the century, and go oversize, use lots of illustrations, big print run—"

"A coffee table book?"

"People'll want it on their coffee tables, sure, but it's not—"

"I don't want to write a coffee table book."

"Frank—"

"What do they want, ten thousand words?"

"They want thirty thousand words, Frank. And they'll pay a hundred-thousand-pound advance."

That gave him pause.

"Why so much?"

"They're new to publishing, they come from computers and this is the kind of numbers they're used to. It's a different scale."

"That's for sure. I still don't want to do it."

"Frank, come on, you're the one for this! The only successor to Barbara Tuchman!" That was a blurb found on paperback editions of his work. "They want you in particular—I mean, Churchill on the twentieth century, ha ha. It's a natural."

"I don't want to do it."

"Come on, Frank. You could use the money, I thought you were having trouble with the payments—"

"Yeah yeah." Time for a different tack. "I'll think it over."

"They're in a hurry, Frank."

"I thought you said turn of the century!"

"I did, but there's going to be a lot of this kind of book then, and they want to beat the rush. Set the standard and then keep it in print for a few years. It'll be great."

"It'll be remaindered within a year. Remaindered before it even comes out, if I know coffee table books."

His agent sighed. "Come on, Frank. You can use the money. As for the book, it'll be as good as you make it, right? You've been working on this stuff your whole career, and here's your chance to sum up. And you've got a lot of readers, people will listen to you." Concern made him shrill: "Don't let what's happened get you so down that you miss an opportunity like this! Work is the best cure for depression anyway. And this is your chance to influence how we think about what's happened!"

"With a coffee table book?"

"God damn it, don't think of it that way!"

"How should I think of it."

His agent took a deep breath, let it out, spoke very slowly. "Think of it as a hundred thousand pounds, Frank."

His agent did not understand.

Nevertheless, the next morning as he sat under the bright white ceiling, doodling with a green pen on yellow paper, he decided to go to England. He didn't want to sit in that room anymore; it scared him, because he suspected it might not be working. He was not sixty percent better. And he didn't want to shift to drug therapy. They had found nothing wrong with his brain, no physical problems at all, and though that meant little, it did make him resistant to the idea of drugs. He had his reasons and he wanted his feelings!

The light room technician thought that this attitude was a good sign in itself. "Your serotonin level is normal, right? So it's not that bad. Besides London's a lot farther north than New York, so you'll pick up the light you lose here. And if you need more you can always head north again, right?"

He called Charles and Rya Dowland to ask if he could stay with them. It turned out they were leaving for Florida the next day, but they invited him to stay anyway; they liked having their flat occupied while they were gone. Frank had done that before, he still had the key on his key-ring. "Thanks," he said. It would be better this way, actually. He didn't feel like talking.

So he packed his backpack, including camping gear with the clothes, and the next morning flew to London. It was strange how one traveled these days: he got into a moving chamber outside his hotel, then shifted from one chamber to the next for several hours, only stepping outdoors again when he emerged from the Camden tube station, some hundred yards from Charles and Rya's flat.

The ghost of his old pleasure brushed him as he crossed Camden High Street and walked by the cinema, listening to London's voices. This had been his method for years: come to London, stay with Charles and Rya until he found digs, do his research and writing at the British Museum, visit the used bookstores at Charing Cross, spend the evenings at Charles and Rya's, watching TV and talking. It had been that way for four books, over the course of twenty years.

The flat was located above a butcher shop. Every wall in it was covered with stuffed bookshelves, and there were shelves nailed up over the toilet, the bath, and the head of the guest bed. In the unlikely event of an earthquake the guest would be buried in a hundred histories of London.

Frank threw his pack on the guest bed and went past the English poets downstairs. The living room was nearly filled by a table stacked with papers and books. The side street below was an open-air produce market, and he could hear the voices of the vendors as they packed up for the day. The sun hadn't set, though it was past nine; these late May days were already long. It was almost like still being in therapy.

He went downstairs and bought vegetables and rice, then went back up and cooked them. The kitchen windows were the color of sunset, and the little flat glowed, evoking its owners so strongly that it was almost as if they were there. Suddenly he wished they were.

After eating he turned on the CD player and put on some Handel. He opened the living room drapes and settled into Charles's armchair, a glass of Bulgarian wine in his hand, an open notebook on his knee. He watched salmon light leak out of the clouds to the north, and tried to think about the causes of the First World War.

In the morning he woke to the dull *thump thump thump* of frozen slabs of meat being rendered by an axe. He went downstairs and ate cereal while leafing through the *Guardian,* then took the tube to Tottenham Court Road and walked to the British Museum.

Because of *The Belle Époque* he had already done his research on the pre-war period, but writing in the British Library was a ritual he didn't want to break; it made him part of a tradition, back to Marx and beyond. He showed his still-valid reader's ticket to a librarian and then found an empty seat in his usual row; in fact he had written much of *Entre Deux Guerres* in that very carrel, under the frontal lobes of the great skull dome. He opened a notebook and stared at the page. Slowly he wrote, *1900 to 1914.* Then he stared at the page.

His earlier book had tended to focus on the sumptuous excesses of the pre-war European ruling class, as a young and clearly leftist reviewer in the *Guardian* had rather sharply pointed out. To the extent that he had delved into the causes of the Great War, he had subscribed to the usual theory; that it had been the result of rising nationalism, diplomatic brinksman-ship, and several deceptive precedents in the previous two decades. The

Spanish-American War, the Russo-Japanese War, and the two Balkan wars had all remained localized and non-catastrophic; and there had been several "incidents," the Moroccan affair and the like, that had brought the two great alliances to the brink, but not toppled them over. So when Austria-Hungary made impossible demands to Serbia after the assassination of Ferdinand, no one could have known that the situation would domino into the trenches and their slaughter.

History as accident. Well, no doubt there was a lot of truth in that. But now he found himself thinking of the crowds in the streets of all the major cities, cheering the news of the war's outbreak; of the disappearance of pacifism, which had seemed such a force; of, in short, the apparently unanimous support for war among the prosperous citizens of the European powers. Support for a war that had no real reason to be!

There was something irreducibly mysterious about that, and this time he decided he would admit it, and discuss it. That would require a consideration of the preceding century, the *Pax Europeana;* which in fact had been a century of bloody subjugation, the high point of imperialism, with most of the world falling to the great powers. These powers had prospered at the expense of their colonies, who had suffered in abject misery. Then the powers had spent their profits building weapons, and used the weapons on each other, and destroyed themselves. There was something weirdly just about that development, as when a mass murderer finally turns the gun on himself. Punishment, an end to guilt, an end to pain. Could that really explain it? While staying in Washington with his dying father, Frank had visited the Lincoln Memorial, and there on the right hand wall had been Lincoln's Second Inaugural Address, carved in capital letters with the commas omitted, an oddity which somehow added to the speech's Biblical massiveness, as when it spoke of the ongoing war: "YET IF GOD WILLS THAT IT CONTINUE UNTIL ALL THE WEALTH PILED BY THE BONDSMAN'S TWO HUNDRED AND FIFTY YEARS OF UNREQUITED TOIL SHALL BE SUNK AND UNTIL EVERY DROP OF BLOOD DRAWN WITH THE LASH SHALL BE PAID BY ANOTHER DRAWN WITH THE SWORD AS WAS SAID THREE THOUSAND YEARS AGO SO STILL IT MUST BE SAID 'THE JUDGMENTS OF THE LORD ARE TRUE AND RIGHTEOUS ALTOGETHER.'"

A frightening thought, from that dark part of Lincoln that was never far from the surface. But as a theory of the Great War's origin it still struck him as inadequate. It was possible to believe it of the kings and presidents, the generals and diplomats, the imperial officers around the world; they had known what they were doing, and so might have been impelled by unconscious guilt to mass suicide. But the common citizen at home, ecstatic in the streets at the outbreak of general war? That seemed more likely to be just another manifestation of the hatred of the other. All my problems are your fault! He and Andrea had said that to each other a lot. Everyone did.

And yet… it still seemed to him that the causes were eluding him, as they had everyone else. Perhaps it was a simple pleasure in destruction. What is the primal response to an edifice? Knock it down. What is the primal response to a stranger? Attack him.

But he was losing his drift, falling away into the metaphysics of "human nature." That would be a constant problem in an essay of this length. And whatever the causes, there stood the year 1914, irreducible, inexplicable, unchangeable. "AND THE WAR CAME."

In his previous books he had never written about the wars. He was among those who believed that real history occurred in peacetime, and that in war you might as well roll dice or skip ahead to the peace treaty. For anyone but a military historian, what was interesting would begin again only when the war ended.

Now he wasn't so sure. Current views of the Belle Époque were distorted because one only saw it through the lens of the war that ended it; which meant that the Great War was somehow more powerful than the Belle Époque, or at least more powerful than he had thought. It seemed he would have to write about it, this time, to make sense of the century. And so he would have to research it.

He walked up to the central catalogue tables. The room darkened as the sun went behind clouds, and he felt a chill.

For a long time the numbers alone staggered him. To overwhelm trench defenses, artillery bombardments of the most astonishing size were brought to bear: on the Somme the British put a gun every twenty yards along a fourteen-mile front, and fired a million and a half shells. In April 1917 the French fired six million shells. The Germans' Big Bertha shot shells seventy-five miles high, essentially into space. Verdun was a "battle" that lasted ten months, and killed almost a million men.

The British section of the front was ninety miles long. Every day of the war, about seven thousand men along that front were killed or wounded—not in any battle in particular, but just as the result of incidental sniper fire or bombardment. It was called "wastage."

Frank stopped reading, his mind suddenly filled with the image of the Vietnam Memorial. He had visited it right after leaving the Lincoln Memorial, and the sight of all those names engraved on the black granite plates had powerfully affected him. For a moment it had seemed possible to imagine all those people, a little white line for each.

But at the end of every month or two of the Great War, the British had had a whole Vietnam Memorial's worth of dead. Every month or two, for fifty-one months.

He filled out book request slips and gave them to the librarians in the central ring of desks, then picked up the books he had requested the day before, and took them back to his carrel. He skimmed the books and took notes, mostly writing down figures and statistics. British factories produced two hundred and fifty million shells. The major battles all killed a half million or more. About ten million men died on the field of battle, ten million more by revolution, disease, and starvation.

Occasionally he would stop reading and try to write; but he never got far. Once he wrote several pages on the economy of the war. The organization of agriculture and business, especially in Germany under Rathenau and England under Lloyd George, reminded him very strongly of the postmodern economy now running things. One could trace the roots of late capitalism to Great War innovations found in Rathenau's *Kriegsrohstoffabteilung* (the "War Raw Stuff Department"), or in his *Zentral Einkaufs-Gesellschaft.* All business had been organized to fight the enemy; but when the war was over and the enemy vanquished, the organization remained. People continued to sacrifice the fruits of their work, but now they did it for the corporations that had taken the wartime governments' positions in the system.

So much of the twentieth century, there already in the Great War. And then the Armistice was signed, at eleven A.M. on November 11th, 1918. That morning at the front the two sides exchanged bombardments as usual, so that by eleven A.M. many people had died.

That evening Frank hurried home, just beating a thundershower. The air was as dark as smoky glass.

And the war never ended.

This idea, that the two world wars were actually one, was not original to him. Winston Churchill said it at the time, as did the Nazi Alfred Rosenberg. They saw the twenties and thirties as an interregnum, a pause to regroup in the middle of a two-part conflict. The eye of a hurricane.

Nine o'clock one morning and Frank was still at the Dowlands', lingering over cereal and paging through the *Guardian,* and then through his notebooks. Every morning he seemed to get a later start, and although it was May, the days didn't seem to be getting any longer. Rather the reverse.

There were arguments against the view that it was a single war. The twenties did not seem very ominous, at least after the Treaty of Locarno in 1925: Germany had survived its financial collapse, and everywhere economic recovery seemed strong. But the thirties showed the real state of things: the depression, the new democracies falling to fascism, the brutal Spanish Civil War; the starvation of the kulaks; the terrible sense of fatality in the air. The sense of slipping on a slope, falling helplessly back into war.

But this time it was different. *Total War.* German military strategists had coined the phrase in the 1890s, while analyzing Sherman's campaign in Georgia. And they felt they were waging total war when they torpedoed neutral ships in 1915. But they were wrong; the Great War was not total war. In 1914 the rumor that German soldiers had killed eight Belgian nuns was enough to shock all civilization, and later when the *Lusitania* was sunk, objections were so fierce that the Germans agreed to leave passenger ships alone. This could only happen in a world where people still held the notion that in war armies fought armies and soldiers killed soldiers, while civilians suffered privation and perhaps got killed accidentally, but were never deliberately targeted. This was how European wars had been fought for centuries: diplomacy by other means.

In 1939, this changed. Perhaps it changed only because the capability for total war had emerged from the technological base, in the form of mass long-range aerial bombardment. Perhaps on the other hand it was a matter of learning the lessons of the Great War, digesting its implications. Stalin's murder of the kulaks, for instance: five million Ukrainian peasants, killed because Stalin wanted to collectivize agriculture. Food was deliberately shipped out of that breadbasket region, emergency supplies withheld, hidden stockpiles destroyed; and several thousand villages disappeared as all their occupants starved. This was total war.

Every morning Frank leafed around in the big catalogue volumes, as if he might find some other twentieth century. He filled out his slips, picked up the books requested the previous day, took them back to his carrel. He spent more time reading than writing. The days were cloudy, and it was dim under the great dome. His notes were getting scrambled. He had stopped working in chronological order, and kept returning compulsively to the Great War, even though the front wave of his reading was well into World War Two.

Twenty million had died in the first war, fifty million in the second. Civilian deaths made the bulk of the difference. Near the end of the war, thousands of bombs were dropped on cities in the hope of starting fire-storms, in which the atmosphere itself was in effect ignited, as in Dresden,

Berlin, Tokyo. Civilians were the target now, and strategic bombing made them easy to hit. Hiroshima and Nagasaki were in that sense a kind of exclamation point, at the end of a sentence which the war had been saying all along: we will kill your families at home. War is war, as Sherman said; if you want peace, surrender! And they did.

After two bombs. Nagasaki was bombed three days after Hiroshima, before the Japanese had time to understand the damage and respond. Dropping the bomb on Hiroshima was endlessly debated in the literature, but Frank found few who even attempted a defense of Nagasaki. Truman and his advisors did it, people said, to a) show Stalin they had more than one bomb, and b) show Stalin that they would use the bomb even as a threat or warning only, as Nagasaki demonstrated. A Vietnam Memorial's worth of civilians in an instantaneous flash, just so Stalin would take Truman seriously. Which he did.

When the crew of the *Enola Gay* landed, they celebrated with a barbeque.

In the evenings Frank sat in the Dowland flat in silence. He did not read, but watched the evening summer light leak out of the sky to the north. The days were getting shorter. He needed the therapy, he could feel it. More light! Someone had said that on their deathbed—Newton, Galileo, Spinoza, someone like that. No doubt they had been depressed at the time.

He missed Charles and Rya. He would feel better, he was sure, if he had them there to talk with. That was the thing about friends, after all: they lasted and you could talk. That was the definition of friendship.

But Charles and Rya were in Florida. And in the dusk he saw that the walls of books in the flat functioned like lead lining in a radioactive environment, all those recorded thoughts forming a kind of shield against poisonous reality. The best shield available, perhaps. But now it was failing, at least for him; the books appeared to be nothing more than their spines.

And then one evening in a premature blue sunset it seemed that the whole flat had gone transparent, and that he was sitting in an armchair, suspended over a vast and shadowy city.

The Holocaust, like Hiroshima and Nagasaki, had precedents. Russians with Ukrainians, Turks with Armenians, white settlers with Native Americans. But the mechanized efficiency of the Germans' murder of the Jews was something new and horrible. There was a book in his stack on the designers of the death camps, the architects, engineers, builders. Were these functionaries less or more obscene than the mad doctors, the sadistic guards? He couldn't decide.

And then there was the sheer number of them, the six million. It was hard to comprehend it. He read that there was a library in Jerusalem where they had taken on the task of recording all they could find about every one of the six million. Walking up Charing Cross Road that afternoon he thought of that and stopped short. All those names in one library, another transparent room, another memorial. For a second he caught a glimpse of how many people that was, a whole London's worth. Then it faded and he was left on a street corner, looking both ways to make sure he didn't get run over.

As he continued walking he tried to calculate how many Vietnam Memorials it would take to list the six million. Roughly two per hundred thousand; thus twenty per million. So, one hundred and twenty. Count them one by one, step by step.

He took to hanging out through the evenings in pubs. The Wellington was as good as any, and was frequented occasionally by some acquaintances he had met through Charles and Rya. He sat with them and listened to them talk, but often he found himself distracted by his day's reading. So the conversations tumbled along without him, and the Brits, slightly more tolerant than Americans of eccentricity, did not make him feel unwelcome.

The pubs were noisy and filled with light. Scores of people moved about in them, talking, smoking, drinking. A different kind of lead-lined room. He didn't drink beer, and so at first remained sober; but then he discovered the hard cider that pubs carried. He liked it and drank it like the others drank their beer, and got quite drunk. After that he sometimes became very talkative, telling the rest things about the twentieth century that they already knew, and they would nod and contribute some other bit of information, to be polite, then change the subject back to whatever they had been discussing before, gently and without snubbing him.

But most of the time when he drank he only got more remote from their talk, which jumped about faster than he could follow. And each morning after, he would wake late and slow, head pounding, the day already there and a lot of the morning light missed in sleep. Depressives were not supposed to drink at all. So finally he quit going to the Wellington, and instead ate at the pubs closest to the Dowlands'. One was called The Halfway House, the other World's End, a poor choice as far as names were concerned, but he ate at World's End anyway, and afterwards would sit at a corner table and nurse a whisky and stare at page after page of notes, chewing the end of a pen to plastic shrapnel.

The Fighting Never Stopped, as one book's title put it. But the atomic bomb meant that the second half of the century looked different than the first. Some, Americans for the most part, called it the *Pax Americana*. But most called it the Cold War, 1945–1989. And not that cold, either. Under the umbrella of the superpower stalemate local conflicts flared everywhere, wars which compared to the two big ones looked small; but there had been over a hundred of them all told, killing about 350,000 people a year, for a total of around fifteen million, some said twenty; it was hard to count. Most occurred in the big ten: the two Vietnam wars, the two Indo-Pakistan wars, the Korean war, the Algerian war, the civil war in Sudan, the massacres in Indonesia in 1965, the Biafran war, and the Iran-Iraq war. Then another ten million civilians had been starved by deliberate military action; so that the total for the period was about the equal of the Great War itself. Though it had taken ten times as long to compile. Improvement of a sort.

And thus perhaps the rise of atrocity war, as if the horror of individualized murders could compensate for the lack of sheer number. And maybe it could; because now his research consisted of a succession of accounts and color photos of rape, dismemberment, torture—bodies of individual people, in their own clothes, scattered on the ground in pools of blood. Vietnamese villages, erupting in napalm. Cambodia, Uganda, Tibet—Tibet was genocide again, paced to escape the world's notice, a few villages destroyed every year in a process called *thamzing*, or reeducation: the villages seized by the Chinese and the villagers killed by a variety of methods, "burying alive, hanging, beheading, disemboweling, scalding, crucifixion, quartering, stoning, small children forced to shoot their parents; pregnant women given forced abortions, the fetuses piled in mounds on the village squares."

Meanwhile power on the planet continued to shift into fewer hands. The Second World War had been the only thing to successfully end the Depression, a fact leaders remembered; so the economic consolidation begun in the First War continued through the Second War and the Cold War, yoking the whole world into a war economy.

At first 1989 had looked like a break away from that. But now, just seven years later, the Cold War losers all looked like Germany in 1922, their money worthless, their shelves empty, their democracies crumbling to juntas. Except this time the juntas had corporate sponsors; multinational banks ran the old Soviet bloc just as they did the Third World, with "austerity measures" enforced in the name of "the free market," meaning half the world went to sleep hungry every night to pay off debts to millionaires. While temperatures still rose, populations still soared, "local conflicts" still burned in twenty different places.

One morning Frank lingered over cereal, reluctant to leave the flat. He opened the *Guardian* and read that the year's defense budgets worldwide would total around a trillion dollars. "More light," he said, swallowing hard. It was a dark, rainy day. He could feel his pupils enlarging, making the effort. The days were surely getting shorter, even though it was May; and the air was getting darker, as if London's Victorian fogs had returned, coal smoke in the fabric of reality.

He flipped the page and started an article on the conflict in Sri Lanka. Singhalese and Tamils had been fighting for a generation now, and some time in the previous week, a husband and wife had emerged from their house in the morning to find the heads of their six sons arranged on their lawn. He threw the paper aside and walked through soot down the streets.

He got to the British Museum on automatic pilot. Waiting for him at the top of the stack was a book containing estimates of total war deaths for the century. About a hundred million people.

He found himself on the dark streets of London again, thinking of numbers. All day he walked, unable to gather his thoughts. And that night as he fell asleep the calculations returned, in a dream or a hypnogogic vision: it would take two thousand Vietnam Memorials to list the century's war dead. From above he saw himself walking the Mall in Washington, D.C., and the whole park from the Capitol to the Lincoln Memorial was dotted with the black Vs of Vietnam Memorials, as if a flock of giant stealth birds had landed on it. All night he walked past black wing walls, moving west toward the white tomb on the river.

The next day the first book on the stack concerned the war between China and Japan, 1931–1945. Like most of Asian history this war was poorly remembered in the West, but it had been huge. The whole Korean nation became in effect a slave labor camp in the Japanese war effort, and the Japanese concentration camps in Manchuria had killed as many Chinese as the Germans had killed Jews. These deaths included thousands in the style of Mengele and the Nazi doctors, caused by "scientific" medical torture. Japanese experimenters had for instance performed transfusions in which they drained Chinese prisoners of their blood and replaced it with horses' blood, to see how long the prisoners would live. Survival rates varied from twenty minutes to six hours, with the subjects in agony throughout.

Frank closed that book and put it down. He picked the next one out of the gloom and peered at it. A heavy old thing, bound in dark green leather, with a dull gold pattern inlaid on the spine and boards. A *History of the Nineteenth Century, with Illustrations*—the latter tinted photos, their colors faded and dim. Published in 1902 by George Newnes Ltd; last century's equivalent of his own project, apparently. Curiosity about that had caused him to request the title. He opened it and thumbed through, and on the last page the text caught his eye: "I believe that Man is good. I believe that we stand at the dawn of a century that will be more peaceful and prosperous than any in history."

He put down the book and left the British Museum. In a red phone box he located the nearest car rental agency, an Avis outlet near Westminster. He took the Tube and walked to this agency, and there he rented a blue Ford Sierra station wagon. The steering wheel was on the right, of course. Frank had never driven in Great Britain before, and he sat behind the wheel trying to hide his uneasiness from the agent. The clutch, brake, and gas pedal were left-to-right as usual, thank God. And the gear shift was arranged the same, though one did have to operate it with the left hand.

Awkwardly he shoved the gearshift into first and drove out of the garage, turning left and driving down the left side of the street. It was weird. But the oddity of sitting on the right insured that he wouldn't forget the necessity of driving on the left. He pulled to the curb and perused the Avis street map of London, plotted a course, got back in traffic, and drove to Camden High Street. He parked below the Dowlands' and went upstairs and packed, then took his backpack down to the car. He returned to leave a note: *Gone to the land of the midnight sun.* Then he went down to the car and drove north, onto the highways and out of London.

It was a wet day, and low full clouds brushed over the land, dropping here a black broom of rain, there a Blakean shaft of sunlight. The hills were green, and the fields yellow or brown or lighter green. At first there were a lot of hills, a lot of fields. Then the highway swung by Birmingham and Manchester, and he drove by fields of rowhouses, line after line after line of them, on narrow treeless streets—all orderly and neat, and yet still among the bleakest human landscapes he had ever seen. Streets like trenches. Certainly the world was being overrun. Population densities must be near the levels set in those experiments on rats which had caused the rats to go insane. It was as good an explanation as any. Mostly males affected, in both cases: territorial hunters, bred to kill for food, now trapped in little boxes. They had gone mad. "I believe that Man is this or that," the Edwardian author had written, and why not; it couldn't be denied that it was mostly men's doing. The planning, the diplomacy, the fighting, the raping, the killing.

The obvious thing to do was to give the running of the world over to women. There was Thatcher in the Falklands and Indira Gandhi in Bangladesh, it was true; but still it would be worth trying, it could hardly get worse! And given the maternal instinct, it would probably be better. Give every first lady her husband's job. Perhaps every woman her man's job. Let the men care for the children, for five thousand years or fifty thousand, one for every year of murderous patriarchy.

North of Manchester he passed giant radio towers, and something that looked like nuclear reactor stacks. Fighter jets zoomed overhead. The twentieth century. Why hadn't that Edwardian author been able to see it coming? Perhaps the future was simply unimaginable, then and always. Or perhaps things hadn't looked so bad in 1902. The Edwardian, looking forward in a time of prosperity, saw more of the same; instead there had followed a century of horrors. Now one looked forward from a time of horrors; so that by analogy, what was implied for the next century was grim beyond measure. And with the new technologies of destruction, practically anything was possible: chemical warfare, nuclear terrorism, biological holocaust; victims killed by nano-assassins flying through them, or by viruses in their drinking supply, or by a particular ringing of their telephone; or reduced to zombies by drugs or brain implants, torture or nerve gas; or simply dispatched with bullets, or starved; hi tech, low tech, the methods were endless. And the motivations would be stronger than ever; with populations rising and resources depleted, people were going to be fighting not to rule, but to survive. Some little country threatened with defeat could unleash an epidemic against its rival and accidentally kill off a continent, or everyone, it was entirely possible. The twenty-first century might make the twentieth look like nothing at all.

He would come to after reveries like that and realize that twenty or thirty or even sixty miles had passed without him seeing a thing of the outside world. Automatic pilot, on roads that were reversed! He tried to concentrate.

He was somewhere above Carlisle. The map showed two possible routes to Edinburgh: one left the highway just below Glasgow, while a smaller road left sooner and was much more direct. He chose the direct route and took an exit into a roundabout and onto the A702, a two-lane road heading northeast. Its black asphalt was wet with rain, and the clouds rushing overhead were dark. After several miles he passed a sign that said "Scenic Route," which suggested he had chosen the wrong road, but he was unwilling to backtrack. It was probably as fast to go this way by now, just more work: frequent roundabouts, villages with traffic lights, and narrow stretches where the road was hemmed by hedges or walls. Sunset was near, he had been driving for hours; he was tired, and when black trucks rushed at him out of the spray and shadows it looked like they were going to collide with him head-on. It became an effort to stay to the left rather than the right where his instincts shrieked he should be. Right and left had to be reversed on that level, but kept the same at foot level—reversed concerning which hand went on the gearshift, but not reversed for what the gearshift did—and it all began to blur and mix, until finally a huge lorry rushed head first at him and he veered left, but hit the gas rather than the brakes. At the unexpected lurch forward he swerved farther left to be safe, and that ran his left wheels off the asphalt and into a muddy gutter, causing the car to bounce back onto the road. He hit the brakes hard and the lorry roared by his ear. The car skidded over the wet asphalt to a halt.

He pulled over and turned on the emergency blinker. As he got out of the car he saw that the driver's side mirror was gone. There was nothing there but a rectangular depression in the metal, four rivet holes slightly flared to the rear, and one larger hole for the mirror adjustment mechanism, missing as well.

He went to the other side of the car to remind himself what the Sierra's side mirrors looked like. A solid metal and plastic mounting. He walked a hundred yards back down the road, looking through the dusk for the missing one, but he couldn't find it anywhere. The mirror was gone.

Outside Edinburgh he stopped and called Alec, a friend from years past.

"What? Frank Churchill? Hello! You're here? Come on by, then."

Frank followed his directions into the city center, past the train station to a neighborhood of narrow streets. Reversed parallel parking was almost too much for him; it took four tries to get the car next to the curb. The Sierra bumped over paving stones to a halt. He killed the engine and got out of the car, but his whole body continued to vibrate, a big tuning fork humming in the twilight. Shops threw their illumination over passing cars. Butcher, baker, Indian deli.

Alec lived on the third floor. "Come in, man, come in." He looked harried. "I thought you were in America! What brings you here?"

"I don't know."

Alec glanced sharply at him, then led him into the flat's kitchen and living area. The window had a view across rooftops to the castle. Alec stood in the kitchen, uncharacteristically silent. Frank put down his backpack and walked over to look out at the castle, feeling awkward. In the old days he and Andrea had trained up several times to visit Alec and Suzanne, a primatologist. At that time those two had lived in a huge three-storied flat in the New Town, and when Frank and Andrea had arrived the four of them would stay up late into the night, drinking brandy and talking in a high-ceilinged Georgian living room. During one stay they had all driven into the Highlands, and another time Frank and Andrea had stayed through a festival week, the four attending as many plays as they could. But now Suzanne and Alec had gone their ways, and Frank and Andrea were divorced, and Alec lived in a different flat; and that whole life had disappeared.

"Did I come at a bad time?"

"No, actually." A clatter of dishes as Alec worked at the sink. "I'm off to dinner with some friends, you'll join us—you haven't eaten?"

"No. I won't be—"

"No. You've met Peg and Rog before, I think. And we can use the distraction, I'm sure. We've all been to a funeral this morning. Friends of ours, their kid died. Crib death, you know."

"Jesus. You mean it just…"

"Sudden infant death syndrome, yeah. Dropped him off at day care and he went off during his nap. Five months old."

"Jesus."

"Yeah." Alec went to the kitchen table and filled a glass from a bottle of Laphroaig. "Want a whisky?"

"Yes, please."

Alec poured another glass, drank his down. "I suppose the idea these days is that a proper funeral helps the parents deal with it. So Tom and Elyse came in carrying the coffin, and it was about this big." He held his hands a foot apart.

"No."

"Yeah. Never seen anything like it."

They drank in silence.

The restaurant was a fashionably bohemian seafood place, set above a pub. There Frank and Alec joined Peg and Rog, another couple, and a woman named Karen. All animal behaviorists, and all headed out to Africa in the next couple of weeks—Rog and Peg to Tanzania, the rest to Rwanda. Despite their morning's event the talk was quick, spirited, wide-ranging; Frank drank wine and listened as they discussed African politics, the problems of filming primates, rock music. Only once did the subject of the funeral come up, and then they shook their heads; there wasn't much to say. Stiff upper lip.

Frank said, "I suppose it's better it happened now than when the kid was three or four."

They stared at him. "Oh no," Peg said. "I don't think so."

Acutely aware that he had said something stupid, Frank tried to recover: "I mean, you know, they've more time to…." He shook his head, foundering.

"It's rather comparing absolutes, isn't it," Rog said gently.

"True," he said. "It is." And he drank his wine. He wanted to go on: True, he wanted to say, any death is an absolute disaster, even that of an infant too young to know what was happening; but what if you had spent your life raising six such children and then went out one morning and found their heads on your lawn? Isn't the one more absolute than the other? He was drunk, his head hurt, his body still vibrated with the day's drive, and the shock of the brush with the lorry; and it seemed likely that the dyslexia of exhaustion had invaded all his thinking, including his moral sense, making everything backward. So he clamped his teeth together and concentrated on the wine, his fork humming in his hand, his glass chattering against his teeth. The room was dark.

Afterwards Alec stopped at the door to his building and shook his head. "Not ready for that yet," he said. "Let's try Preservation Hall, it's your kind of thing on Wednesday nights. Traditional jazz."

Frank and Andrea had been fans of traditional jazz. "Any good?"

"Good enough for tonight, eh?"

The pub was within walking distance, down a wide cobblestone promenade called the Grassmarket, then up Victoria Street. At the door of the pub they were stopped; there was a cover charge, the usual band had been replaced by a buffet dinner and concert, featuring several different bands. Proceeds to go to the family of a Glasgow musician, recently killed in a car crash. "Jesus Christ," Frank exclaimed, feeling like a curse. He turned to go.

"Might as well try it," Alec said, and pulled out his wallet. "I'll pay."

"But we've already eaten."

Alec ignored him and gave the man twenty pounds. "Come on."

Inside, a very large pub was jammed with people, and an enormous buffet table stacked with meats, breads, salads, seafood dishes. They got drinks from the bar and sat at the end of a crowded picnic table. It was noisy, the Scots accents so thick that Frank understood less than half of what he heard. A succession of local acts took the stage: the traditional jazz band that usually played, a stand-up comedian, a singer of Forties' music hall songs, a country-western group. Alec and Frank took turns going to the bar to get refills. Frank watched the bands and the crowd. All ages and types were represented. Each band said something about the late musician, who apparently had been well-known, a young rocker and quite a hellion from the sound of it. Crashed driving home drunk after a gig, and no one a bit surprised.

About midnight an obese young man seated at their table, who had been stealing food from all the plates around him, rose whalelike and surged to the stage. People cheered as he joined the band setting up. He picked up a guitar, leaned into the mike, and proceeded to rip into a selection of r&b and early rock and roll. He and his band were the best group yet, and the pub went wild. Most of the crowd got to their feet and danced in place. Next to Frank a young punk had to lean over the table to answer a gray-haired lady's questions about how he kept his hair spiked. A Celtic wake, Frank thought, and downed his cider and howled with the rest as the fat man started up Chuck Berry's "Rock and Roll Music."

So he was feeling no pain when the band finished its last encore and he and Alec staggered off into the night, and made their way home. But it had gotten a lot colder while they were inside, and the streets were dark and empty. Preservation Hall was no more than a small wooden box of light, buried in a cold stone city. Frank looked back in its direction and saw that a streetlight reflected off the black cobblestones of the Grassmarket in such a way that there were thousands of brief white squiggles underfoot, looking like names engraved on black granite, as if the whole surface of the earth were paved by a single memorial.

The next day he drove north again, across the Forth Bridge and then west along the shores of a loch to Fort William, and north from there through the Highlands. Above Ullapool steep ridges burst like fins out of boggy treeless hillsides. There was water everywhere, from puddles to lochs, with the Atlantic itself visible from most high points. Out to sea the tall islands of the Inner Hebrides were just visible.

He continued north. He had his sleeping bag and foam pad with him, and so he parked in a scenic overlook, and cooked soup on his Bluet stove, and slept in the back of the car. He woke with the dawn and drove north. He talked to nobody.

Eventually he reached the northwest tip of Scotland and was forced to turn east, on a road bordering the North Sea. Early that evening he arrived in Scrabster, at the northeast tip of Scotland. He drove to the docks, and found that a ferry was scheduled to leave for the Orkney Islands the next day at noon. He decided to take it.

There was no secluded place to park, so he took a room in a hotel. He had dinner in the restaurant next door, fresh shrimp in mayonnaise with chips, and went to his room and slept. At six the next morning the ancient crone who ran the hotel knocked on his door and told him an unscheduled ferry was leaving in forty minutes: did he want to go? He said he did. He got up and dressed, then felt too exhausted to continue. He decided to take the regular ferry after all, took off his clothes and returned to bed. Then he realized that exhausted or not, he wasn't going to be able to fall back asleep. Cursing, almost crying, he got up and put his clothes back on. Downstairs the old woman had fried bacon and made him two thick bacon sandwiches, as he was going to miss her regular breakfast. He ate the sandwiches sitting in the Sierra, waiting to get the car into the ferry. Once in the hold he locked the car and went up to the warm stuffy passenger cabin, and lay on padded vinyl seating and fell back asleep.

He woke when they docked in Stromness. For a moment he didn't remember getting on the ferry, and he couldn't understand why he wasn't in his hotel bed in Scrabster. He stared through salt-stained windows at fishing boats, amazed, and then it came to him. He was in the Orkneys.

Driving along the southern coast of the main island, he found that his mental image of the Orkneys had been entirely wrong. He had expected an extension of the Highlands; instead it was like eastern Scotland, low, rounded, and green. Most of it was cultivated or used for pasture. Green fields, fences, farmhouses. He was a bit disappointed.

Then in the island's big town of Kirkwall he drove past a Gothic cathedral—a very little Gothic cathedral, a kind of pocket cathedral. Frank had never seen anything like it. He stopped and got out to have a look. Cathedral of St. Magnus, begun in 1137. So early, and this far north! No wonder it was so small. Building it would have required craftsmen from the continent, shipped up here to a rude fishing village of drywall and turf roofs; a strange influx it must have been, a kind of cultural revolution. The finished building must have stood out like something from another planet.

But as he walked around the bishop's palace next door, and then a little museum, he learned that it might not have been such a shock for Kirkwall after all. In those days the Orkneys had been a crossroads of a sort, where Norse and Scots and English and Irish had met, infusing an indigenous culture that went right back to the Stone Age. The fields and pastures he had driven by had been worked, some of them, for five thousand years!

And such faces walking the streets, so intent and vivid. His image of the local culture had been as wrong as his image of the land. He had thought he would find decrepit fishing villages, dwindling to nothing as people moved south to the cities. But it wasn't like that in Kirkwall, where teenagers roamed in self-absorbed talky gangs, and restaurants open to the street were packed for lunch. In the bookstores he found big sections on local topics: nature guides, archaeological guides, histories, sea tales, novels. Several writers, obviously popular, had as their entire subject the islands. To the locals, he realized, the Orkneys were the center of the world.

He bought a guidebook and drove north, up the east coast of Mainland to the Broch of Gurness, a ruined fort and village that had been occupied from the time of Christ to the Norse era. The broch itself was a round stone tower about twenty feet tall. Its wall was at least ten feet thick, and was made of flat slabs, stacked so carefully that you couldn't have stuck a dime in the cracks. The walls in the surrounding village were much thinner; if attacked, the villagers would have retired into the broch. Frank nodded at the explanatory sentence in the guidebook, reminded that the twentieth century had had no monopoly on atrocities. Some had happened right here, no doubt. Unless the broch had functioned as a deterrent.

Gurness overlooked a narrow channel between Mainland and the smaller island of Rousay. Looking out at the channel, Frank noticed white ripples in its blue water; waves and foam were pouring past. It was a tidal race, apparently, and at the moment the entire contents of the channel were rushing north, as fast as any river he had ever seen.

Following suggestions in the guidebook, he drove across the island to the Neolithic site of Brodgar, Stenness, and Maes Howe. Brodgar and Stenness were two rings of standing stones; Maes Howe was a nearby chambered tomb.

The Ring of Brodgar was a big one, three hundred and forty feet across. Over half of the original sixty stones were still standing, each one a block of roughly dressed sandstone, weathered over the millennia into shapes of great individuality and charisma, like Rodin figures. Following the arc they made, he watched the sunlight break on them. It was beautiful.

Stenness was less impressive, as there were only four stones left, each tremendously tall. It roused more curiosity than awe: how had they stood those monsters on end? No one knew for sure.

From the road, Maes Howe was just a conical grass mound. To see the inside he had to wait for a guided tour, happily scheduled to start in fifteen minutes.

He was still the only person waiting when a short stout woman drove up in a pickup truck. She was about twenty-five, and wore Levi's and a red windbreaker. She greeted him and unlocked a gate in the fence surrounding the mound, then led him up a gravel path to the entrance on the southwest slope. There they had to get on their knees and crawl, down a tunnel three feet high and some thirty feet long. Midwinter sunsets shone directly down this entryway, the woman looked over her shoulder to tell him. Her Levi's were new.

The main chamber of the tomb was quite tall. "Wow," he said, standing up and looking around.

"It's big isn't it," the guide said. She told him about it in a casual way. The walls were made of the ubiquitous sandstone slabs, with some monster monoliths bracketing the entryway. And something unexpected: a group of Norse sailors had broken into the tomb in the twelfth century (four thousand years after the tomb's construction!) and taken shelter in it through a three-day storm. This was known because they had passed the time carving runes on the walls, which told their story. The woman pointed to lines and translated: "'Happy is he who finds the great treasure.' And over here: 'Ingrid is the most beautiful woman in the world.'"

"You're kidding."

"That's what it says. And look here, you'll see they did some drawing as well."

She pointed out three graceful line figures, cut presumably with axe blades: a walrus, a narwhale, and a dragon. He had seen all three in the shops of Kirkwall, reproduced in silver for earrings and pendants. "They're beautiful," he said.

"A good eye, that Viking."

He looked at them for a long time, then walked around the chamber to look at the runes again. It was a suggestive alphabet, harsh and angular. The guide seemed in no hurry, she answered his questions at length. She was a guide in the summer, and sewed sweaters and quilts in the winter. Yes, the winters were dark. But not very cold. Average temperature around thirty.

"That warm?"

"Aye it's the Gulf Stream you see. It's why Britain is so warm, and Norway too for that matter."

Britain so warm. "I see," he said carefully.

Back outside he stood and blinked in the strong afternoon light. He had just emerged from a five-thousand-year-old tomb. Down by the loch the standing stones were visible, both rings. Ingrid is the most beautiful woman in the world. He looked at Brodgar, a circle of black dots next to a silver sheen of water. It was a memorial too, although what it was supposed to make its viewers remember was no longer clear. A great chief; the death of one year, birth of the next; the planets, moon and sun in their courses. Or something else, something simpler. *Here we are.*

It was still midafternoon judging by the sun, so he was surprised to look at his watch and see it was six o'clock. Amazing. It was going to be just like his therapy! Only better because outdoors, in the sunlight and the wind. Spend summer in the Orkneys, winter in the Falklands, which were said to be very similar.... He drove back to Kirkwall and had dinner in a hotel restaurant. The waitress was tall, attractive, about forty. She asked him where he was from, and he asked her when it would get busy (July), what the population of Kirkwall was (about ten thousand, she guessed) and what she did in the winter (accounting). He had broiled scallops and a glass of white wine. Afterward he sat in the Sierra and looked at his map. He wanted to sleep in the car, but hadn't yet seen a good place to park for the night.

The northwest tip of Mainland looked promising, so he drove across the middle of the island again, passing Stenness and Brodgar once more. The stones of Brodgar stood silhouetted against a western sky banded orange and pink and white and red.

At the very northwest tip of the island, the Point of Buckquoy, there was a small parking lot, empty this late in the evening. Perfect. Extending west from the point was a tidal causeway, now covered by the sea; a few hundred yards across the water was a small island called the Brough of Birsay, a flat loaf of sandstone tilted up to the west, so that one could see the whole grass top of it. There were ruins and a museum at the near end, a small lighthouse on the west point. Clearly something to check out the next day.

South of the point, the western shore of the island curved back in a broad, open bay. Behind its beach stood the well-preserved ruins of a sixteenth-century palace. The bay ended in a tall sea cliff called Marwick Head, which had a tower on its top that looked like another broch, but was, he discovered in his guidebook, the Kitchener Memorial. Offshore in 1916 the HMS *Hampshire* had hit a mine and sunk, and six hundred men, including Kitchener, had drowned.

Odd, to see that. A couple of weeks ago (it felt like years) he had read that when the German front lines had been informed of Kitchener's death, they had started ringing bells and banging pots and pans in celebration; the noisemaking had spread up and down the German trenches, from the Belgian coast to the Swiss frontier.

He spread out his sleeping bag and foam pad in the back of the station wagon, and lay down. He had a candle for reading, but he did not want to read. The sound of the waves was loud. There was still a bit of light in the air, these northern summer twilights were really long. The sun had seemed to slide off to the right rather than descend, and suddenly he understood what it would be like to be above the Arctic Circle in midsummer: the sun would just keep sliding off to the right until it brushed the northern horizon, and then it would slide up again into the sky. He needed to live in Ultima Thule.

The car rocked slightly on a gust of wind. It had been windy all day;

apparently it was windy all the time here, the main reason the islands were treeless. He lay back and looked at the roof of the car. A car made a good tent: flat floor, no leaks.... As he fell asleep he thought, it was a party a mile wide and a thousand miles long.

He woke at dawn, which came just before five A.M. His shadow and the car's shadow were flung out toward the brough, which was an island still, as the tidal bar was covered again. Exposed for only two hours each side of low tide, apparently.

He ate breakfast by the car, and then rather than wait for the causeway to clear he drove south, around the Bay of Birsay and behind Marwick Head, to the Bay of Skaill. It was a quiet morning, he had the one-lane track to himself. It cut through green pastures. Smoke rose from farmhouse chimneys and flattened out to the east. The farmhouses were white, with slate roofs and two white chimneys, one at each end of the house. Ruins of farmhouses built to the same design stood nearby, or in back pastures.

He came to another parking lot, containing five or six cars. A path had been cut through tall grass just behind the bay beach, and he followed it south. It ran nearly a mile around the curve of the bay, past a big nineteenth-century manor house, apparently still occupied. Near the south point of the bay stretched a low concrete seawall and a small modern building, and some interruptions in the turf above the beach. Holes, it looked like. The pace of his walk picked up. A few people were bunched around a man in a tweed coat. Another guide?

Yes. It was Skara Brae.

The holes in the ground were the missing roofs of Stone Age houses buried in the sand; their floors were about twelve feet below the turf. The interior walls were made of the same slab as everything else on the island, stacked with the same precision. Stone hearths, stone bedframes, stone dressers: because of the islands' lack of wood, the guide was saying, and the ready availability of the slabs, most of the houses' furniture had been made of stone. And so it had endured.

Stacks of slabs held up longer ones, making shelves in standard college student bricks-and-boards style. Cupboards were inset in the walls. There was a kind of stone kitchen cabinet, with mortar and pestle beneath. It was instantly obvious what everything was for; everything looked deeply familiar.

Narrow passageways ran between houses. These too had been covered; apparently driftwood or whale rib beams had supported turf roofs over the entire village, so that during bad storms they need never go out. The first mall, Frank thought. The driftwood had included pieces of spruce, which had to have come from North America. The Gulf Stream again.

Frank stood at the back of a group of seven, listening to the guide as he looked down into the homes. The guide was bearded, stocky, fiftyish. Like the Maes Howe guide he was good at his work, wandering about with no obvious plan, sharing what he knew without memorized speeches. The village had been occupied for about six hundred years, beginning around 3000 B.C. Brodgar and Maes Howe had been built during those years, so probably people from here had helped in their construction. The bay had likely been a fresh-water lagoon at that time, with a beach separating it from the sea. Population about fifty or sixty. A heavy dependence on cattle and sheep, with lots of seafood as well. Sand filled in the homes when the village was abandoned, and turf grew over it. In 1850 a big storm tore the turf off and exposed the homes, completely intact except for the roofs....

Water seepage had rounded away every edge, so that each slab looked sculpted, and caught at the light. Each house a luminous work of art. And five thousand years old, yet *so* familiar: the same needs, the same thinking, the same solutions.... A shudder ran through him, and he noticed that he was literally slack-jawed. He closed his mouth and almost laughed aloud. Open-mouthed astonishment could be so natural sometimes, so physical, unconscious, genuine.

When the other tourists left, he continued to wander around. The guide, sensing another enthusiast, joined him.

"It's like the Flintstones," Frank said, and laughed.

"The what?"

"You expect to see stone TVs and the like."

"Oh aye. It's very contemporary, isn't it."

"It's marvelous."

Frank walked from house to house, and the guide followed, and they talked. "Why is this one called the chief's house?"

"It's just a guess, actually. Everything in it is a bit bigger and better, that's all. In our world a chief would have it."

Frank nodded. "Do you live out here?"

"Aye." The guide pointed at the little building beyond the site. He had owned a hotel in Kirkwall, but sold it; Kirkwall had been too hectic for him. He had gotten the job here and moved out, and was very happy with it. He was getting a degree in archaeology by correspondence. The more he learned, the more amazed he was to be here; it was one of the most important archaeological sites in the world, after all. There wasn't a better one. No need to imagine furnishings and implements, "and to see so clearly how much they thought like we do."

Exactly. "Why did they leave, in the end?"

"No one knows."

"Ah."

They walked on.

"No sign of a fight, anyway."

"Good."

The guide asked Frank where he was staying, and Frank told him about the Sierra.

"I see!" the man said. "Well, if you need the use of a bathroom, there's one here at the back of the building. For a shave, perhaps. You look like you haven't had the chance in a while."

Frank rubbed a hand over his stubble, blushing. In fact he hadn't thought of shaving since well before leaving London. "Thanks," he said. "Maybe I'll take you up on that."

They talked about the ruins a while longer, and then the guide walked out to the seawall, and let Frank wander in peace.

He looked down in the rooms, which still glowed as if lit from within. Six hundred years of long summer days, long winter nights. Perhaps they had set sail for the Falklands. Five thousand years ago.

He called good-bye to the guide, who waved. On the way back to the car park he stopped once to look back. Under a carpet of cloud the wind was thrashing the tall beach grass, every waving stalk distinct, the clouds' underside visibly scalloped; and all of it touched with a silvery edge of light.

He ate lunch in Stromness, down by the docks, watching the fishing boats ride at anchor. A very practical-looking fleet, of metal and rubber and bright plastic buoys. In the afternoon he drove the Sierra around Scapa Flow and over a bridge at the east channel, the one Winston had ordered blocked with sunken ships. The smaller island to the south was covered with green fields and white farmhouses.

Late in the afternoon he drove slowly back to the Point of Buckquoy, stopping for a look in the nearby ruins of the sixteenth-century earl's palace. Boys were playing soccer in the roofless main room.

The tide was out, revealing a concrete walkway set on a split bed of wet brown sandstone. He parked and walked over in the face of a stiff wind, onto the Brough of Birsay.

Viking ruins began immediately, as erosion had dropped part of the old settlement into the sea. He climbed steps into a tight network of knee-high walls. Compared to Skara Brae, it was a big town. In the middle of all the low foundations rose the shoulder-high walls of a church. Twelfth century, ambitious Romanesque design: and yet only fifty feet long, and twenty wide! Now this was a pocket cathedral. It had had a monastery connected to it, however; and some of the men who worshipped in it had traveled to Rome, Moscow, Newfoundland.

Picts had lived here before that; a few of their ruins lay below the Norse. Apparently they had left before the Norse arrived, though the record wasn't clear. What was clear was that people had been living here for a long, long time.

After a leisurely exploration of the site Frank walked west, up the slope of the island. It was only a few hundred yards to the lighthouse on the cliff, a modern white building with a short fat tower.

Beyond it was the edge of the island. He walked toward it and emerged from the wind shelter the island provided; a torrent of gusts almost knocked him back. He reached the edge and looked down.

At last something that looked like he thought it would! It was a long way to the water, perhaps a hundred and fifty feet. The cliff was breaking off in great stacks, which stood free and tilted out precariously, as if they were going to fall at any moment. Great stone cliffs, with the sun glaring directly out from them, and the surf crashing to smithereens on the rocks below: it was so obviously, grandiloquently the End of Europe that he had to laugh. A place made to cast oneself from. End the pain and fear, do a Hart Crane off the stern of Europe… except this looked like the bow, actually. The bow of a very big ship, crashing westward through the waves; yes, he could feel it in the soles of his feet. And foundering, he could feel that too, the shudders, the rolls, the last sluggish list. So jumping overboard would be redundant at best. The end would come, one way or another. Leaning out against the gale, feeling like a Pict or Viking, he knew he stood at the end—end of a continent, end of a century; end of a culture.

And yet there was a boat, coming around Marwick Head from the south, a little fishing tub from Stromness, rolling horribly in the swell. Heading northwest, out to—out to where? There were no more islands out there, not until Iceland anyway, or Greenland, Spitsbergen… where was it going at this time of day, near sunset and the west wind tearing in?

He stared at the trawler for a long time, rapt at the sight, until it was nothing but a black dot near the horizon. Whitecaps covered the sea, and the wind was still rising, gusting really hard. Gulls skated around on the blasts, landing on the cliffs below. The sun was very near the water, sliding off to the north, the boat no more than flotsam: and then he remembered the causeway and the tide.

He ran down the island and his heart leaped when he saw the concrete walkway washed by white water, surging up from the right. Stuck here, forced to break into the museum or huddle in a corner of the church… but no; the concrete stood clear again. If he ran—

He pounded down the steps and ran over the rough concrete. There were scores of parallel sandstone ridges still exposed to the left, but the right side was submerged already, and as he ran a broken wave rolled up onto the walkway and drenched him to the knees, filling his shoes with seawater and scaring him much more than was reasonable. He ran on cursing.

Onto the rocks and up five steps. At his car he stopped, gasping for breath. He got in the passenger side and took off his boots, socks, and pants. Put on dry pants, socks, and running shoes.

He got back out of the car.

The wind was now a constant gale, ripping over the car and the point and the ocean all around. It was going to be tough to cook dinner on his stove; the car made a poor windbreak, wind rushing under it right at stove level.

He got out the foam pad, and propped it with his boots against the lee side of the car. The pad and the car's bulk gave him just enough wind shelter to keep the little Bluet's gas flame alive. He sat on the asphalt behind the stove, watching the flames and the sea. The wind was tremendous, the Bay of Birsay riven by whitecaps, more white than blue. The car rocked on its shock absorbers. The sun had finally slid sideways into the sea, but clearly it was going to be a long blue dusk.

When the water was boiling he poured in a dried Knorr's soup and stirred it, put it back on the flame for a few more minutes, then killed the flame and ate, spooning split pea soup straight from the steaming pot into his mouth. Soup, bit of cheese, bit of salami, red wine from a tin cup, more soup. It was absurdly satisfying to make a meal in these conditions: the wind was in a fury!

When he was done eating he opened the car door and put away his dinner gear, then got out his windbreaker and rain pants and put them on. He walked around the carpark, and then up and down the low cliffy edges of the point of Buckquoy, watching the North Atlantic get torn by a full force gale. People had done this for thousands of years. The rich twilight blue looked like it would last forever.

Eventually he went to the car and got his notebooks. He returned to the very tip of the point, feeling the wind like slaps on the ear. He sat with his legs hanging over the drop, the ocean on three sides of him, the wind pouring across him, left to right. The horizon was a line where purest blue met bluest black. He kicked his heels against the rock. He could see just well enough to tell which pages in the notebooks had writing on them; he tore these from the wire spirals, and bunched them into balls and threw them away. They flew off to the right and disappeared immediately in the murk and whitecaps. When he had disposed of all the pages he had written on he cleared the long torn shreds of paper out of the wire rings, and tossed them after the rest.

It was getting cold, and the wind was a constant kinetic assault. He went back to the car and sat in the passenger seat. His notebooks lay on the driver's seat. The western horizon was a deep blue, now. Must be eleven at least.

After a time he lit the candle and set it on the dash. The car was still rocking in the wind, and the candle flame danced and trembled on its wick. All the black shadows in the car shivered too, synchronized perfectly with the flame.

He picked up a notebook and opened it. There were a few pages left between damp cardboard covers. He found a pen in his daypack. He rested his hand on the page, the pen in position to write, its tip in the quivering shadow of his hand. He wrote, "I believe that man is good. I believe we stand at the dawn of a century that will be more peaceful and prosperous than any in history." Outside it was dark, and the wind howled.

MUIR ON SHASTA

"Your goodness must have an edge to it," Emerson had said to him, as if a single week's acquaintanceship in euphoric Yosemite could reveal any of the edges in a man. Still it had been valuable advice, for Muir's edges lay buried under sunny meadows and brook babble, and it could be that the old philosopher had only meant to say, You should let your edges show, or It is all right to have edges. A valuable lesson indeed.

Shasta was an Emersonian mountain, it occurred to Muir as he sat on its summit pinnacle. In its youth it had leaped toward heaven, rising ten thousand feet above the surrounding plains; now it was ancient, glacier-cloaked, its broad peak rounded and craterless, its creative fires banked. And yet there were still sharp outcroppings of lava on the ridges, and enough fire rising from the depths to boil a muddy spring near the summit; and there was in the end the massive snowy fact of the mountain itself, isolate, powerful, brooding, godlike. Emerson had been just like that.

Muir hefted a brass barometer. He and an acquaintance, Jerome Bixby, had ascended Shasta that morning to take readings, although really the readings were no more than an excuse to climb the mountain and have a look around. From the peak, one saw mountains everywhere—the Coast Range, the Siskiyous, the Trinity Alps, the northern Sierra, snowy flat-topped Lassen—mountains to every point of the compass, a wild tangle of ridges and peaks.

As he sat and watched, clouds rose out of the valleys and over the ridges, until everything except Shasta was submerged. He stood on a snow island in an ocean of cloud. To the west a thunderhead billowed up, its bright lobes as solid as marble. He gazed at it with a connoisseur's eye, feeling the wind yank his beard, feeling it rake through the weave of his coat, rapt with his usual peak exaltation—

But there was Bixby, plodding across the white summit plain, looking like a black ant. He had been waiting below the ultimate peak, but now he huffed up the small remnant of the crater wall that was the mountain's highest point, and once at Muir's side said, "We should go down—a storm is coming!"

"One more reading," Muir said, irritated. He didn't care about the reading, but he didn't want to descend.

So they stayed on the peak, and the wind freshened, and then the clear air overhead was suddenly marred by streams of mist like carded wool. Just as he completed the last reading they were enveloped in cloud, and the wind grew stronger; and as he followed Bixby down the knob and onto the summit plain, six-faceted hailstones clattered onto the tortured red rock, and thumped into the packed snow, and onto their backs.

Then as they forced their way west, past the hissing fumaroles of the hot spring and over big chunks of black lava, snow began to fall in waves so thick that at times they were unable to see even their own feet. Blasts of wind slapped them on the ear, snow crystals stung their faces, and it got so cold so fast that Muir became curious, and stopped to read his thermometer; the temperature had dropped twenty-two degrees in ten minutes, and was now below zero.

Lightning flicked, dim in the clouds, and thunder began to bang around them, in explosions so violent that they vibrated one's whole body. "Wow!" Muir shouted, inaudible in the barrage. He was grinning. The truth was, he loved storms in the mountains. He had been in them so many times that he was confident no storm could harm him, if he continued to walk in it; the heat engendered by exertion was always enough to counter even the wildest assaults. And so he struggled on through the crashing, howling vortex of snow and wind and thunder, head down, thrusting forward as if wrestling some herculean elder brother, whooping at the storm's high drama and spectacle, its brute strength and godlike grandeur—laughing at its sheer excess—

But he had entirely forgotten to think of Bixby. Who, in fact, had fallen behind, and was out of sight. Muir crouched in the shelter of a giant lava block that marked the route along their ridge, and waited. After a while Bixby appeared out of the snow, and one look made it clear that he was not having the same sort of fun that Muir was.

The two men huddled together in the lee of the block. Weird light illuminated them in flashes, and it was almost too noisy to hold a conversation. "We can't go on!" Bixby shouted.

"What?" Muir said, astonished.

"We can't go on!"

"But we must! We have no choice!"

"We'll be killed!"

"No, no—we'll stay on the ridge, I know the way!"

"It's too exposed!"

This was the very reason that they must take the ridge. The slopes to either side would be swept by avalanches, and even if they escaped these, they would be likely to wander onto a glacier. The ridge, on the other hand, would be blown clear of snow, providing a rocky road down to safety. It would be windy, but no wind could blow a man from a rock; if gusts threatened to do so, one could always lie flat till they were over.

Irritably he tried to explain this, but Bixby would have none of it. He just shook his head and shouted again, "We can't go down!" He looked the same as always, face calm, his shouts in a reasonable tone of voice; but there was a stubbornness in him, and when Muir shouted, "I memorized the way down the ridge," he stared at Muir as if confronted with a madman. And the thunder crashed, and the hurtling air roared across the ridge, catching on a million jagged lava teeth and shrieking, keening, howling, drowning out mere human voices.

"We must go down!" Muir shouted again. "We have no choice!"

"We can't go down! It's impossible! We'll be killed!"

"It's stopping will kill us!" Muir replied, getting angry. Stupid man, did he think this block's feeble shelter would be enough to protect them? "We have no choice!" he repeated.

Bixby shook his head. For an instant he looked like Muir's father, insisting on a point of Bible doctrine. "I won't go on!"

"We must go on!"

"I won't go on!"

And that was that. There is a stubbornness in fear that will balk at even the most perfect logic. Muir tugged furiously at his beard. "What do you propose to do!" he shouted.

Bixby wiped the snow from his face and looked around, blinking cowlike. "The fumaroles are warm," he said.

"The fumaroles are *boiling!*" Muir shouted. Anger spiked through him, he wanted to grab the man by the coat and shake his courage back into him. "Superheated poison gas!"

But Bixby was trudging back toward the fumaroles, hunched into the wind, staggering as gusts shoved him from side to side. "Fool!" Muir cried, and cursed him roundly.

He stayed by the block, searching the clouds for a break that he could use as argument to convince Bixby to continue. But none came; the storm raged on; and suddenly he realized that his anger at Bixby was a transitive expression of his own fear. He could not leave his companion behind; and so now they were both in very great danger.

The fumaroles near the peak were among the last small vestiges of Shasta's volcanic glory. Superheated gases rose through cracks in the long throat, and emerged in a small depression on the western side of the summit, where they heated a mixture of snowmelt, volcanic ash, and sand, creating a patch of boiling black mud.

Muir approached it. In the storm's cold air the patch steamed heavily, making it look like the clouds were pouring out of the mountain as well as rushing over it: an eerie sight. Bixby was already crouched at the mud's edge. Muir stomped to his side.

Bixby looked up. "This will keep us safe from frost!"

"Oh yes, safe from frost!" Muir said sarcastically. "But how will we keep from scalding ourselves? And how will we protect our lungs from the acid gases? And how will we get off the mountain once we soak our clothes? Storm or clear, we'll freeze on our way down! We'll have to stay until morning, and who knows what kind of day it will be!"

Bixby shivered miserably.

Muir held his breath, let out a long sigh. There was nothing for it. They were there. He crouched and looked over the roiling snow-rimmed pit. Wind whipped any warmth coming off the mud directly away; their zone of safety was about a quarter of an acre in extent, but only an eighth of an inch thick. Scylla and Charybdis, embracing.

Muir sighed again and tromped into the mud, sinking immediately to his knees and feeling the heat burn his legs. Jetting bubbles of gas made the mud look like molten lava. But on the windward side of the pool they would probably be safe from the gas. As long as the wind held steady. And it seemed it would; it roared out of the west, cutting through clothing; they couldn't stand in it long. Growling, Muir finished sitting in the shallows of the pool. Hot water seeped out of the mud into his pants, then his shirt and coat. He lay back, his head against the windward snowbank, his body outstretched in the mud. Spindrift ran across his face. His nose, which had no feeling to it, still conveyed to him the stench of sulphur. The warmth of the mud burned his skin, but he had to admit it was a relief from the fierce wind. A laugh burst from him like gas from the mud; then a jet of rising bubbles scalded his back and he yelped, rolled hastily to the side. He elbowed a snow and mud poultice over the hot spot, dizzy with the carbonic stink. Now he was covered with mud, his coat and trousers completely soaked. Bixby was the same. Standing up would have turned them into ice statues of themselves. They were committed.

It was necessary to shift position frequently, to immerse an exposed limb, or expose a boiled one. The passage of time was marked by pain. The storm continued unabated, and the two men lay isolated by the shrieking wind, so that each might have been there alone except that occasionally Muir would raise his head and cry out, and Bixby would shout something back, and both would subside into solitude again. Snow fell so thickly that they breathed it. It settled on the exposed parts of them, and packed to a rime so hard that they crackled when they shifted.

The sun had apparently set, and it was dark. Muir could see nothing but blackness. At times the mud seemed blacker than the sky; then the sky would seem blacker than the mud. As black as the world had been during his episode of blindness, so many years before. He saw the file leaping into his eye, the aqueous humor draining into his hand, the swift darkening in his sight on the wounded side, and then, that night as he lay trembling in a strange bed, the relentless darkening on the other. Until he was left in total darkness. That fear had been the worst of his life; this was nothing to it, a natural darkness, a storm in its fury to be watched and loved. I will lift up mine eyes unto the hills, and *see*. He had been blind for three weeks, three full weeks of doctor's assurances and secret terror; and when his sight had returned he had walked out of his life and never returned, never looked back, tossing away the destiny that his father and country had thought proper for him, farming, inventing machinery, all that; he abandoned all that and gave himself to the wilderness. So that, properly speaking, it was in fact a blessing to be here boiling in a volcano's caldera with a blizzard thick about his ears. Part of nature's bounty—

Groans from Bixby broke his thought. He saw the lump of the man, rolling to escape a fumarole, struggling to keep from sinking. In some places the mud was viscid clay, in others black tea, whistling in its pot. Lumps of something, perhaps soaked pumice, floated under the surface, and he tried arranging a bed of the lumps under him to protect him from rising gas jets, but they kept slipping away. The wind still howled, but the clouds were thinning; the snow blowing across their bodies must have been spindrift, for he saw a star. If you can see one star, press on! as the saying had it. But not tonight.

Soon the clouds scudded off east, and starlight bathed the scene. The familiar patterns sparked the night sky, drawing around him all the other nights he had lain out in the world. The eye is a flower that sees the stars. If they had continued their descent, they would now be down on the snow slopes, where starlight would have made darkness visible, and guided them home. Instead, soaked as they were, and with a mile of wind-ripped ridge to negotiate, they were going to have to spend the night. But he said nothing. It was done. And his fault really, for staying on the peak so long. Besides, the sight of the stars brought it to him that whatever the discomfort, they were likely to survive; so it did not signify. He had spent many a cold night on a mountain. It could even be said that the boiling mud made this night less miserable than some, though—the skin of his back suddenly flaring—none other had been so purely painful. Still, he was used to pain, accustomed to it. He had grown up with it, working a hardscrabble farm for his father, a mean, small-minded man, a lesson in how not to be a Christian, all those days spent studying the Bible while his boys worked to get his bread, and then beating them with switch, belt—

His leg was on fire. He pulled his knee up into the icy wind, and for an instant smelled the gas. Once his father had set him to digging wells, and seventy feet down seeping gas had overwhelmed him, he had swooned and had only just come to, only just dragged himself far enough up the rope ladder to breathe good air, and live. He lifted his head and shouted at Bixby. "Still there, Jerome?"

A croak. Something about the cold. Still there. Muir settled back into the mud. Forget that whole world, that whole life, the way it could make his stomach knot. Look at the stars. The eye is a flower that sees the stars, immersed in primal cold and heat. His left foot squelched in its boot, propped on the snowbank. Wiggle the toes against wet leather, make sure they were still there. No. They were cold past feeling, only a certain vague numbness; while his right foot burned, scalded so that he nearly shouted, and certainly groaned. Leg yanked up; the wind wrapped the wet trouser to his leg and froze his thigh, while the foot still throbbed with the pain of the burn.

"Are you suffering much?" Bixby called.

"Yes!" Fool, what did he think? "Frozen and burned! But never mind, it won't kill us!" As long as they weren't overcome by gas. A jet of bubbles pushed at his backbone, he rolled and shoved mud over the scalding spot, hitting at it furiously with a fist gone numb with frostbite.

Each hour was a year. The stars were in the same places they had been when they first became visible; so not many years could have passed. Concentrating on the stars near the horizon, he tried to see them creep west. That one, nearly occluded by a low wall of lava: focus on it, watch it, watch it, watch it... had it moved? No. Time had stopped. They had continued the descent, perhaps, and died in the attempt, and now they lay in some well-bottom hell of his father's stripe, or in a circle of Dante's inferno, in which heat and cold mingled without moderating the other, creating a pain unfamiliar to those in the simpler circles. He could hear their moans—

Ah, that star was occluded. Half an hour had jumped past all at once. As if time were a matter of instantaneous jumps, from one eternal moment to the next—which in fact it often seemed to him to be, as during those sunny warm afternoons when he would lie in a Sierra meadow by a chuckling stream and watch the clouds, dreaming of nothing, until with a jerk he would return to the meadow and the shadows would be stretching twice as long as before, over perfectly sculpted patches of meadow grass, the larks singing "wé-ero, spé-ero, wé-eo, wé-erlo, wé-it."

Drifting in and out. A call to Bixby got a feeble response. Still alive if nothing else. A bubble burst, splashed hot mud over his face, and he spluttered and wiped his nose clear. He couldn't feel his left arm, or make it move; he wasn't sure when that had happened. That was his windward side, so presumably it was benumbed in the onslaught of air. He tried to dip the arm further under the mud, to bury it. Not a process one would want to carry too far, descending limb by limb into black muck. Now the arm seemed to be burning; was that a fumarole bubbling up? No. In fact he had accidentally plunged the arm into the snowbank; his right hand confirmed it. But how the skin burned!

Then a gas bubble lifted his knee, and the back of his leg felt like glacier melt had been poured over it; it ached with cold, the knee joint creaked with it! He groaned. Cold now scalded and heat froze, and he didn't know which was which!

Perhaps it didn't matter. Caught between cold reason and hot passion, ignorant flesh always paid the price. One could never tell which was which. Outrageous pain! Better to leave all that behind.

A solution occurred to him. He stood up. He looked back down and saw his body lying there, stretched out in the mud, mostly submerged. A sponge, soaked in immortality. A mass of eternal atoms, bound together in just that particular way, to witness the beauty of the universe.

Yes: he stood there gazing down at his boiled and frozen body. Somewhat bemused, he tried a few steps; circled the mud patch; then took off across the windswept snow, toward an exposed rock outcropping. There was a building there, a small square cabin, white in the starlight. As he approached he saw that its walls were made of pure white quartz. Its door and windows were edged with quartz crystals. The door and the roof were made of slate, all dotted with lichen. The windows were thin smooth sheets of water.

He opened the door and walked in. The table was a slab of glacier-polished granite. The benches around it were fallen logs. The bed was made of spruce boughs. The carpet was green moss.

It was his home. He sat on one of the logs, and put his hand on the table.

His hand sank into the granite. His body sank into the log, and then into the moss, and then into the quartz.

He felt himself dissolving out into the great mass of the mountain, tumbling slowly down through the rock. He had melted into Shasta. The mountain mumbled in his ear "I am." With a puff of its cheeks it blew him aloft, threw his atoms out into the sky. They tumbled off on the wind and dispersed to every point of the compass, then fell and steeped into the fabric of the land, one atom in every rock, in every grain of sand and soil, like gas in mud, or water in sponge, until his body and California were contiguous, united, one. Only his vision remained separate, his precious sight, the landscape's consciousness soaring like a hawk over the long sand beaches, the great valley, the primeval sequoias, the range of light—but the mountains were different—blinding glaciers covered all but the highest peaks, fingered down through the hills, and cut Yosemite's walls. Then they retreated, dried up and ran away.

He tumbled, soared west. It was night, now, and below lay the bay like a sparkling black map, the black water crisscrossed with bridges of light, the surrounding hills dotted with millions of white points like stars, defining towers, roadways, docks, arenas, monuments; a bay-circling city, impossibly beautiful. But so many people! It had to be thousands of years in the future, as glaciers were thousands of years in the past. He was soaring through time, out of the knife-edge present, back to glaciers and forward to supercities, perhaps ten thousand years each way. An eyeblink in the life of stones, and the Sierra would stand throughout; but chewed at by the future city as much as by the ancient glaciers, perhaps. Sheep cropped meadows to dust in a single summer; and the shepherds were worse. And if so many came to live by the bay....

Curious, fearful, he tilted in his flight, soared east over the great valley, through the gold-choked foothills, up among the peaks. He rose in a gyre and stared down at starlit granite. There a valley had been drowned, a shocking sight. Wheel, turn, soar, take heart: for all was dark. Not a light to be seen, the whole length of the range. The backbone of California, gleaming in moonlight.

This much beauty would always be in danger, there was no avoiding that. Its animals must defend it. All its animals. He soared over the highest peaks, and then looked back; a full moon bathed the great eastern escarpment with white light. Death Valley burned, Whitney froze—

His ankle was in a fumarole, his head in the muddy snowbank. He shifted, saw that the wheel of stars had turned nearly a quarter turn. He took several long deep breaths. His vision cleared with the cold air, he returned to the moment and his bed in the mud. He could feel his lungs and his mind; beyond that, he and the mountain still seemed one undifferentiated mass, which he felt only in a distant, seismic way. But now he knew where he was. For a while he had soared on a great wind through time, but now he was just John again, flat on his back, and numb with cold.

Still, he remembered the vision perfectly. That was quite a voyage great Shasta had sent him on! Perhaps visions like that were why the Indians worshipped it.

As for what he had seen… well, the habitable zone was never thick. Caught between the past and future, we squirm in a dangerous eighth of an inch. Perhaps it was like that always. The atmosphere, for instance, was frighteningly thin; hike for a day and you could ascend the larger part of it, as when climbing Shasta itself. The landscape was tightly wrapped in a thin skin of gas. And the earth itself rolled in a thin temperate sphere around the sun, a zone of heat that neither boiled the seas nor allowed them to freeze solid; that shell might only be a few feet thick, or an eighth of an inch, who knew? It was a miracle the earth rolled within that sphere! Delicate, precious dewdrop of a world, hung in the light with the nicest precision, like every dewdrop in every morning's spider-web….

The wheel of stars had turned again. Bixby was shifting, muttering as in a dream. The sky in the east was the black nearest blue. And then the blue nearest black. Light seeped into the world as if vision were a new faculty, a sense born instant by instant, to creatures formerly blind. The stars began to slip away; he watched a dim one grow fainter and then wink out of visibility, a strange moment. The eyes are flowers that see the stars.

Bixby croaked something about leaving. But they were on the western side of the peak, and it would be hours before the sun appeared. Meanwhile it was cold beyond movement. When they shifted, their coats crackled as if made of thin glass.

The sky, though cloudless, was a dull and frosty blue. He could see nothing of the earth but their mud patch, and the snow and lava bordering it. He still felt part of the mountain, with no discernable break between his skin and the mud. As the morning light blossomed it seemed to fill him, pouring through his eyes and down into the rock; he felt himself a conduit in a vast interconnected totality, an organism pulsing with its own universal breath. The heat at his core caught and burned, so that he was warm enough to melt his coat's sheath of ice; that was heat displaced from the volcano, which was heat displaced from the sun; which was heat displaced from the heart of the Milky Way; which was heat displaced from the heart of the universe, from that original heart's diastolic expansion. No dualism was significant in the face of this essential unity: he was an atom of God's great body, and he knew it. The landscape and his mind were two expressions of the same miracle.

On the lonely peak of a nearly extinct volcano, two black specks of consciousness observed the morning light.

The time came at last to try a descent. Imagination over reason, action over contemplation; thus he had always believed, and never more than now! It was time to think two thoughts down the mountain.

Spindrift sparked overhead like chips of mica, and then the sun cracked the mountaintop. They stood like golems new-made of clay, ice shattering from their chests, mud sluicing off their backs. They slapped their arms together and the world burned in their fingertips. Nature was the greatest teacher, for those who listened; and Muir had learned long ago that there was a reserve of energy at the end of any long period of suffering. It was something mountaineers often had the chance to discover.

They staggered crazy-legged over the long ridge. They reached the snow slopes and descended more rapidly, swimming through drifts, glissading at the top of little avalanches, falling on their faces; but all downward, and so of use, their weakness only speeding the descent.

Then the clean smell of pinesap cut through the sulphur stench in their hair, and they were at treeline. Bixby sat against a tree and rested, while Muir went on, in search of their host Sisson. Godlike he strode through a meadow, its wildflowers exploding in his sight, dot after dot of pure drenched color. And then he saw Sisson's horses through the trees, and smelled his coffee on the fire. Smoke rose through slanting sunbeams. He was home; and now he was home.

SEXUAL DIMORPHISM

The potential for hallucination in paleogenomics was high. There was not only the omnipresent role of instrumentation in the envisioning of the ultramicroscopic fossil material, but also the metamorphosis over time of the material itself, both the DNA and its matrices, so that the data were invariably incomplete, and often shattered. Thus the possibility of psychological projection of patterns onto the *rorschacherie* of what in the end might be purely mineral processes had to be admitted.

Dr. Andrew Smith was as aware of these possibilities as anyone. Indeed it constituted one of the central problems of his field—convincingly to sort the traces of DNA in the fossil record, distinguishing them from an array of possible pseudofossils. Pseudofossils littered the history of the discipline, from the earliest false nautiloids to the famous Martian pseudonanobacteria. Nothing progressed in paleogenomics unless you could show that you really were talking about what you said you were talking about. So Dr. Smith did not get too excited, at first, about what he was finding in the junk DNA of an early dolphin fossil.

In any case there were quite a few distractions to his work at that time. He was living on the south shore of the Amazonian Sea, that deep southerly bay of the world-ringing ocean, east of Elysium, near the equator. In the summers, even the cool summers they had been having lately, the extensive inshore shallows of the sea grew as warm as blood, and dolphins—adapted from Terran river dolphins like the baiji from China, or the boto from the Amazon, or the susu from the Ganges, or the bhulan from the Indus—sported just off the beach. Morning sunlight lanced through the waves and picked out their flashing silhouettes, sometimes groups of eight or ten of them, all playing in the same wave.

The marine laboratory he worked at, located on the seafront of the harbour town of Eumenides Point, was associated with the Acheron labs, farther up the coast to the west. The work at Eumenides had mostly to do with the shifting ecologies of a sea that was getting saltier. Dr. Smith's current project dealing with this issue involved investigating the various adaptations of extinct cetaceans that had lived when the Earth's sea had exhibited different levels of salt. He had in his lab some fossil material, sent to the lab from Earth for study, as well as the voluminous literature on the subject including the full genomes of all the living descendants of these creatures. The transfer of fossils from Earth introduced the matter of cosmic-ray contamination to all the other problems involved in the study of ancient DNA, but most people dismissed these effects as minor and inconsequential, which was why fossils were shipped across at all. And of course with the recent deployment of fusion-powered rapid vehicles, the amount of exposure to cosmic rays had been markedly reduced. Smith was therefore able to do research on mammal salt-tolerance both ancient and modern, thus helping to illuminate the current situation on Mars, also joining the debates ongoing concerning the paleohalocycles of the two planets, now one of the hot research areas in comparative planetology and bioengineering.

Nevertheless, it was a field of research so arcane that if you were not involved in it, you tended not to believe in it. It was an offshoot, a mix of two difficult fields, its ultimate usefulness a long shot, especially compared to most of the enquiries being conducted at the Eumenides Point Labs. Smith found himself fighting a feeling of marginalization in the various lab meetings and informal gatherings, in coffee lounges, cocktail parties, beach luncheons, boating excursions. At all of these he was the odd man out, with only his colleague Frank Drumm, who worked on reproduction in the dolphins currently living offshore, expressing any great interest in his work and its applications. Worse yet, his work appeared to be becoming less and less important to his advisor and employer, Vlad Taneev, who as one of the First Hundred, and the co-founder of the Acheron labs, was ostensibly the most powerful scientific mentor one could have on Mars; but who in practice turned out to be nearly impossible to access, and rumoured to be in failing health, so that it was like having no boss at all, and therefore no access to the lab's technical staff and so forth. A bitter disappointment.

And then of course there was Selena, his—his partner, roommate, girl-friend, significant other, lover—there were many words for this relationship, though none was quite right. The woman with whom he lived, with whom he had gone through graduate school and two post-docs, with whom he had moved to Eumenides Point, taking a small apartment near the beach, near the terminus of the coastal tram, where when one looked back east the point itself just heaved over the horizon, like a dorsal fin seen far out to sea. Selena was making great progress in her own field, genetically engineering salt grasses; a subject of great importance here, where they were trying to stabilize a thousand-kilometer coastline of low dunes and quicksand swamps. Scientific and bioengineering progress; important achievements, relevant to the situation; all things were coming to her professionally, including of course offers to team up in any number of exciting public/co-op collaborations.

And all things were coming to her privately as well. Smith had always thought her beautiful, and now he saw that with her success, other men were coming to the same realization. It took only a little attention to see it; an ability to look past shabby lab coats and a generally unkempt style to the sleekly curving body and the intense, almost ferocious intelligence. No—his Selena looked much like all the rest of the lab rats when in the lab, but in the summers when the group went down in the evening to the warm tawny beach to swim, she walked out the long expanse of the shallows like a goddess in a bathing suit, like Venus returning to the sea. Everyone in these parties pretended not to notice, but you couldn't help it.

All very well; except that she was losing interest in him. This was a process that Smith feared was irreversible; or, to be more precise, that if it had got to the point where he could notice it, it was too late to stop it. So now he watched her, furtive and helpless, as they went through their domestic routines; there was a goddess in his bathroom, showering, drying off, dressing, each moment like a dance.

But she didn't chat anymore. She was absorbed in her thoughts, and tended to keep her back to him. No—it was all going away.

They had met in an adult swimming club in Mangala, while they were both graduate students at the university there. Now, as if to re-invoke that time, Smith took up Frank's suggestion and joined him at an equivalent club in Eumenides Point, and began to swim regularly again. He went from the tram down to the big fifty-meter pool, set on a terrace overlooking the ocean, and swam so hard in the mornings that the whole rest of the day he buzzed along in a flow of beta endorphins, scarcely aware of his work problems or the situation at home. After work he took the tram home feeling his appetite kick in, and banged around the kitchen throwing together a meal and eating much of it as he cooked it, irritated (if she was there at all) with Selena's poor cooking and her cheery talk about her work, irritated also probably just from hunger, and dread at the situation hanging over them; at this pretence that they were still in a normal life. But if he snapped at her during this fragile hour she would go silent for the rest of the evening; it happened fairly often; so he tried to contain his temper and make the meal and quickly eat his part of it, to get his blood sugar level back up.

Either way she fell asleep abruptly around nine, and he was left to read into the timeslip, or even slip out and take a walk on the night beach a few hundred yards away from their apartment. One night, walking west, he saw Pseudophobos pop up into the sky like a distress flare down the coast, and when he came back into the apartment she was awake and talking happily on the phone; she was startled to see him, and cut the call short, thinking about what to say, and then said, "That was Mark, we've got tamarisk three fifty-nine to take repetitions of the third salt flusher gene!"

"That's good," he said, moving into the dark kitchen so she wouldn't see his face.

This annoyed her. "You really don't care how my work goes, do you?"

"Of course I do. That's good, I said."

She dismissed that with a noise.

Then one day he got home and Mark was there with her, in the living room, and at a single glance he could see they had been laughing about something; had been sitting closer together than when he started opening the door. He ignored that and was as pleasant as he could be.

The next day as he swam at the morning workout, he watched the women swimming with him in his lane. All three of them had swum all their lives, their freestyle stroke perfected beyond the perfection of any dance move ever made on land, the millions of repetitions making their movement as unconscious as that of any fish in the sea. Under the surface he saw their bodies flowing forward, revealing their sleek lines—classic swimmer lines, like Selena's—rangy shoulders tucking up against their ears one after the other, ribcages smoothed over by powerful lats, breasts flatly merged into big pecs or else bobbing left then right, as the case might be; bellies meeting high hipbones accentuated by the high cut of their swimsuits, backs curving up to bottoms rounded and compact, curving to powerful thighs then long calves, and feet outstretched like ballerinas'. Dance was a weak analogy for such beautiful movement. And it all went on for stroke after stroke, lap after lap, until he was mesmerized beyond further thought or observation; it was just one aspect of a sensually saturated environment.

Their current lane leader was pregnant, yet swimming stronger than any of the rest of them, not even huffing and puffing during their rest intervals, when Smith often had to suck air—instead she laughed and shook her head, exclaiming, "Every time I do a flip turn he keeps kicking me!" She was seven months along, round in the middle like a little whale, but still she fired down the pool at a rate none of the other three in the lane could match. The strongest swimmers in the club were simply amazing. Soon after getting into the sport, Smith had worked hard to swim a hundred-meter freestyle in less than a minute, a goal appropriate to him, and finally he had done it once at a meet and been pleased; then later he heard about the local college women's team's workout, which consisted of a hundred hundred-meter freestyle swims, *all on a minute interval.* He understood then that although all humans looked roughly the same, some were stupendously stronger than others. Their pregnant leader was in the lower echelon of these strong swimmers, and regarded the swim she was making today as a light stretching-out, though it was beyond anything her lane mates could do with their best effort. You couldn't help watching her when passing by in the other direction, because despite her speed she was supremely smooth and effortless, she took fewer strokes per lap than the rest of them, and yet still made substantially better time. It was like magic. And that sweet blue curve of the new child carried inside.

Back at home things continued to degenerate. Selena often worked late, and talked to him less than ever.

"I love you," he said. "Selena, I love you."

"I know."

He tried to throw himself into his work. They were at the same lab, they could go home late together. Talk as they used to about their work, which though not the same, was still genomics in both cases; how much closer could two sciences be? Surely it would help to bring them back together.

But genomics was a very big field. It was possible to occupy different parts of it, no doubt about that. They were proving it. Smith persevered, however, using a new and more powerful tracking microscope, seeing things atom by atom, and he began to make some headway in unravelling the patterns in his fossilized DNA.

It looked as if what had been preserved in the samples he had been given was almost entirely what used to be called the junk DNA of the creature. In times past this would have been bad luck, but the Kohl labs in Acheron had recently been making great strides in unravelling the various purposes of junk DNA, which proved not to be useless after all, as might have been guessed. Their breakthrough consisted of characterizing very short and scrambled repetitive sequences within junk DNA that could be demonstrated to code instructions for higher hierarchical operations than they were used to seeing at the gene level—cell differentiation, information order sequencing, apoptosis and the like.

Using this new understanding to unravel any clues in partially degraded fossil junk DNA would be hard, of course. But the nucleotide sequences were there in his images—or, to be more precise, the characteristic mineral replacements for the adenine-thymine and cytosine-guanine couplets, replacements well-established in the literature, were there to be clearly identified. Nanofossils, in effect; but legible to those who could read them. And once read, it was then possible to brew identical sequences of living nucleotides, matching the originals of the fossil creature. In theory one could re-create the creature itself, though in practice nothing like the entire genome was ever there, making it impossible. Not that there weren't people trying anyway with simpler fossil organisms, either going for the whole thing or using hybrid DNA techniques to graft expressions they could decipher onto living templates, mostly descendants of the earlier creature.

With this particular ancient dolphin, almost certainly a freshwater dolphin (though most of these were fairly salt-tolerant, living in river-mouths as they did), complete resuscitation would be impossible. It wasn't what Smith was trying to do anyway. What would be interesting would be to find fragments that did not seem to have a match in the living descendants' genome, then hopefully synthesize living in-vitro fragments, clip them into contemporary strands, and see how these experimental animals did in hybridization tests and in various environments. Look for differences in function.

He was also doing mitochondrial tests when he could, which if successful would permit tighter dating for the species' divergence from precursor species.

He might be able to give it a specific slot on the marine mammal family tree, which during the early Pliocene was very complicated.

Both avenues of investigation were labour-intensive, time-consuming, almost thoughtless work—perfect, in other words. He worked for hours and hours every day, for weeks, then months. Sometimes he managed to go home on the tram with Selena; more often he didn't. She was writing up her latest results with her collaborators, mostly with Mark. Her hours were irregular. When he was working he didn't have to think about this; so he worked all the time. It was not a solution, not even a very good strategy—it seemed to be making things worse—and he had to attempt it against an ever-growing sense of despair and loss; but he did it nevertheless.

"What do you think of this Acheron work?" he asked Frank one day at work, pointing to the latest print-out from the Kohl lab, lying heavily annotated on his desk.

"It's very interesting! It makes it look as if we're finally getting past the genes to the whole instruction manual."

"If there is such a thing."

"Has to be, right? Though I'm not sure the Kohl labs' values for the rate at which adaptive mutants will be fixed are high enough. Ohta and Kimura suggested ten percent as the upper limit, and that fits with what I've seen."

Smith nodded, pleased. "They're probably just being conservative."

"No doubt, but you have to go with the data."

"So—in that context—you think it makes sense for me to pursue this fossil junk DNA?"

"Well, sure. What do you mean? It's sure to tell us interesting things."

"It's incredibly slow."

"Why don't you read off a long sequence, brew it up and venter it, and see what you get?"

Smith shrugged. Whole-genome shotgun-sequencing struck him as slipshod, but it was certainly faster. Reading small bits of single-stranded DNA, called expressed sequence tags, had quickly identified most of the genes on the human genome; but it had missed some, and it ignored even the regulatory DNA sequences controlling the protein-coding portion of the genes, not to mention the junk DNA itself, filling long stretches between the more clearly meaningful sequences.

Smith expressed these doubts to Frank, who nodded, but said, "It isn't the same now that the mapping is so complete. You've got so many reference points you can't get confused where your bits are on the big sequence. Just plug what you've got into the Lander-Waterman, then do the finishing with the Kohl variations, and even if there are massive repetitions, you'll still be okay. And with the bits you've got, well they're almost like ESTs anyway, they're so degraded. So you might as well give it a try."

Smith nodded.

That night he and Selena trammed home together. "What do you think of the possibility of shotgun-sequencing in-vitro copies of what I've got?" he asked her shyly.

"Sloppy," she said. "Double jeopardy."

A new schedule evolved. He worked, swam, took the tram home. Usually Selena wasn't there. Often their answering machine held messages for her from Mark, talking about their work. Or messages from her to Smith, telling him that she would be home late. As it was happening so often, he sometimes went out for dinner with Frank and other lane-mates, after the evening workouts. Once at a beach restaurant they ordered several pitchers of beer, and then went out for a walk on the beach, and ended up running out into the shallows of the bay and swimming around in the warm dark water, so different from their pool, splashing each other and laughing hard.

It was a good time.

But when he got home that night, there was another message on the answering machine from Selena, saying that she and Mark were working on their paper after getting a bite to eat, and that she would be home extra late.

She wasn't kidding; at two o'clock in the morning she was still out. In the long minutes following the timeslip Smith realized that no one stayed out this late working on a paper without calling home. This was therefore a message of a different kind.

Pain and anger swept through him, first one then the other. The indirectness of it struck him as cowardly. He deserved at least a revelation—a confession—a scene. As the long minutes passed he got angrier and angrier; then frightened for a moment, that she might have been hurt or something. But she hadn't. She was out there somewhere fooling around. Suddenly he was furious.

He pulled cardboard boxes out of their closet and yanked open her drawers, and threw all her clothes in heaps in the boxes, crushing them in so they would fit. But they gave off their characteristic scent of laundry soap and her, and smelling it he cried out and sat down on the bed, knees weak. If he carried through with this he would never again see her putting on and taking off these clothes, and just as an animal he groaned at the thought.

But men are not animals. He finished throwing her things into boxes, took them outside the front door and dropped them there.

She came back at three. He heard her kick into the boxes and make some muffled exclamation.

He hurled open the door and stepped out.

"What's this?" She had been startled out of whatever scenario she had planned, and now was getting angry. Her, angry! It made him furious all over again.

"You know what it is."

"What!"

"You and Mark."

She eyed him.

"Now you notice," she said at last. "A year after it started. And this is your first response." Gesturing down at the boxes.

He hit her in the face.

Immediately he crouched at her side and helped her sit up, saying, "Oh God Selena I'm sorry, I'm sorry, I didn't mean to," he had only thought to slap her for her contempt, contempt that he had not noticed her betrayal earlier, "I can't believe I—"

"Get away!"—striking him off with wild blows, crying and shouting—"get away, get away!"—frightened—"you bastard, you miserable bastard, what do you, don't you *dare* hit me!" in a near-shriek, though she kept her voice down too, aware still of the apartment complex around them. Hands held to her face.

"I'm sorry Selena. I'm very very sorry, I was angry at what you said but I know that isn't, that doesn't… I'm sorry." Now he was as angry at himself as he had been at her—what could he have been thinking, why had he given her the moral high ground like this, it was she who had broken their bond, it was she who should be in the wrong! She who was now sobbing—turning away—suddenly walking off into the night. Lights went on in a couple of windows nearby. Smith stood staring down at the boxes of her lovely clothes, his right knuckles throbbing.

That life was over. He lived on alone in the apartment by the beach, and kept going into work, but he was shunned there by the others, who all knew what had happened. Selena did not come in to work again until the bruises were gone, and after that she did not press charges, or speak to him about that night, but she did move in with Mark, and avoided him at work when she could. As who wouldn't? Occasionally she dropped by his nook to ask in a neutral voice about some logistical aspect of their breakup. He could not meet her eye. Nor could he meet the eye of anyone else at work, not properly. It was strange how one could have a conversation with people and appear to be meeting their gaze during it, when all the time they were not really quite looking at you and you were not really quite looking at them. Primate subtleties, honed over millions of years on the savannah.

He lost appetite, lost energy. In the morning he would wake up and wonder why he should get out of bed. Then looking at the blank walls of the bedroom, where Selena's prints had hung, he would sometimes get so angry at her that his pulse hammered uncomfortably in his neck and forehead. This got him out of bed, but then there was nowhere to go, except work. And there everyone knew he was a wife-beater, a domestic abuser, an asshole. Martian society did not tolerate such people.

Shame or anger; anger or shame. Grief or humiliation. Resentment or regret. Lost love. Omnidirectional rage.

Mostly he didn't swim anymore. The sight of the women swimmers was too painful now, though they were as friendly as always; they knew nothing of the lab except him and Frank, and Frank had not said anything to them about what had happened. It made no difference. He was cut off from them. He knew he ought to swim more, and he swam less. Whenever he resolved to turn things around he would swim two or three days in a row, then let it fall away again.

Once at the end of an early evening workout he had forced himself to attend—and now he felt better, as usual—while they were standing in the lane steaming, his three most constant lane-mates made quick plans to go to a nearby trattoria after showering. One looked at him. "Pizza at Rico's?"

He shook his head. "Hamburger at home," he said sadly.

They laughed at this. "Ah come on. It'll keep another night."

"Come on, Andy," Frank said from the next lane. "I'll go too, if that's okay."

"Sure," the women said. Frank often swam in their lane too.

"Well…" Smith roused himself. "Okay."

He sat with them and listened to their chatter around the restaurant table. They still seemed to be slightly steaming, their hair wet and wisping away from their foreheads. The three women were young. It was interesting; away from the pool they looked ordinary and undistinguished: skinny, mousy, plump, maladroit, whatever. With their clothes on you could not guess at their fantastically powerful shoulders and lats, their compact smooth musculatures. Like seals dressed up in clown suits, waddling around a stage.

"Are you okay?" one asked him when he had been silent too long.

"Oh yeah, yeah." He hesitated, glanced at Frank. "Broke up with my girlfriend."

"Ah ha! I *knew* it was something!" Hand to his arm (they all bumped into each other all the time in the pool): "You haven't been your usual self lately."

"No." He smiled ruefully. "It's been hard."

He could never tell them about what had happened. And Frank wouldn't either. But without that none of the rest of his story made any sense. So he couldn't talk about any of it.

They sensed this and shifted in their seats, preparatory to changing the topic. "Oh well," Frank said, helping them. "Lots more fish in the sea."

"In the pool," one of the women joked, elbowing him.

He nodded, tried to smile.

They looked at each other. One asked the waiter for the bill, and another said to Smith and Frank, "Come with us over to my place, we're going to get in the hot tub and soak our aches away."

She rented a room in a little house with an enclosed courtyard, and all the rest of the residents were away. They followed her through the dark house into the courtyard, and took the cover off the hot tub and turned it on, then took their clothes off and got in the steaming water. Smith joined them, feeling shy. People on the beaches of Mars sunbathed without clothes all the time, it was no big deal really. Frank seemed not to notice, he was perfectly relaxed. But they didn't swim at the pool like this.

They all sighed at the water's heat. The woman from the house went inside and brought out some beer and cups. Light from the kitchen fell on her as she put down the carton of beer and passed out the cups. Smith already knew her body perfectly well from their many hours together in the pool; nevertheless he was shocked seeing the whole of her. Frank ignored the sight, filling the cups from the carton.

They drank beer, made small talk. Two were vets; their lane leader, the one who had been pregnant, was a bit older, a chemist in a pharmaceutical lab near the pool. Her baby was being watched by her co-op that night. They all looked up to her, Smith saw, even here. These days she brought the baby to the pool and swam just as powerfully as ever, parking the babycarrier just beyond the splash line. Smith's muscles melted in the hot water, he sipped his beer, listening to them.

One of the women looked down at her breasts in the water and laughed. "They float like pool buoys."

Smith had already noticed this.

"No wonder women swim better than men."

"As long as they aren't so big they interfere with the hydrodynamics."

Their leader looked down through her fogged glasses, pink-faced, hair tied up, misted, demure. "I wonder if mine float less because I'm nursing."

"But all that milk."

"Yes but the water in the milk is neutral density, it's the fat that floats. It could be that empty breasts float even more than full ones."

"Whichever has more fat, yuck."

"I could run an experiment, nurse him from just one side and then get in and see—" But they were laughing too hard for her to complete this scenario. "It would work! Why are you laughing!"

They only laughed more. Frank was cracking up, looking blissed, blessed. These women friends trusted them. But Smith still felt set apart. He looked at their lane leader: a pink bespectacled goddess, serenely vague and unaware; the scientist as heroine; the first full human being.

But later when he tried to explain this feeling to Frank, or even just to describe it, Frank shook his head. "It's a bad mistake to worship women," he warned. "A category error. Women and men are so much the same it isn't worth discussing the difference. The genes are almost entirely identical, you know that. A couple hormonal expressions and that's it. So they're just like you and me."

"More than a couple."

"Not much more. We all start out female, right? So you're better off thinking that nothing major ever really changes that. Penis just an oversized clitoris. Men are women. Women are men. Two parts of a reproductive system, completely equivalent."

Smith stared at him. "You're kidding."

"What do you mean?"

"Well—I've never seen a man swell up and give birth to a new human being, let me put it that way."

"So what? It happens, it's a specialized function. You never see women ejaculating either. But we all go back to being the same afterward. Details of reproduction only matter a tiny fraction of the time. No, we're all the same. We're all in it together. There are no differences."

Smith shook his head. It would be comforting to think so. But the data did not support the hypothesis. Ninety-five percent of all the murders in history had been committed by men. This was a difference.

He said as much, but Frank was not impressed. The murder ratio was becoming more nearly equal on Mars, he replied, and much less frequent for everybody, thus demonstrating very nicely that the matter was culturally conditioned, an artefact of Terran patriarchy no longer relevant on Mars. Nurture rather than nature. Although it was a false dichotomy. Nature could prove anything you wanted, Frank insisted. Female hyenas were vicious killers, male bonobos and muriquis were gentle co-operators. It meant nothing, Frank said. It told them nothing.

But Frank had not hit a woman in the face without ever planning to.

Patterns in the fossil DNA data sets became clearer and clearer. Stochastic-resonance programs highlighted what had been preserved.

"Look here," Smith said to Frank one afternoon when Frank leaned in to say good-bye for the day. He pointed at his computer screen. "Here's a sequence from my boto, part of the GX three-oh-four, near the juncture, see?"

"You've got a female then?"

"I don't know. I think this here means I do. But look, see how it matches with this part of the human genome. It's in Hillis 8050…"

Frank came into his nook and stared at the screen. "Comparing junk to junk… I don't know…"

"But it's a match for more than a hundred units in a row, see? Leading right into the gene for progesterone initiation."

Frank squinted at the screen. "Um, well." He glanced quickly at Smith.

Smith said, "I'm wondering if there's some really long-term persistence in junk DNA, all the way back to earlier mammal precursors to both these."

"But dolphins are not our ancestors," Frank said.

"There's a common ancestor back there somewhere."

"Is there?" Frank straightened up. "Well, whatever. I'm not so sure about the pattern congruence itself. It's sort of similar, but, you know."

"What do you mean, don't you see that? Look right there!"

Frank glanced down at him, startled, then noncommittal. Seeing this Smith became inexplicably frightened.

"Sort of," Frank said. "Sort of. You should run hybridization tests, maybe, see how good the fit really is. Or check with Acheron about repeats in non-gene DNA."

"But the congruence is perfect! It goes on for hundreds of pairs, how could that be a coincidence?"

Frank looked even more noncommittal than before. He glanced out of the door of the nook. Finally he said, "I don't see it that congruent. Sorry, I just don't see it. Look, Andy. You've been working awfully hard for a long time. And you've been depressed too, right? Since Selena left?"

Smith nodded, feeling his stomach tighten. He had admitted as much a few months before. Frank was one of the very few people these days who would look him in the eye.

"Well, you know. Depression has chemical impacts in the brain, you know that. Sometimes it means you begin seeing patterns that others can't see as well. It doesn't mean they aren't there, no doubt they are there. But whether they mean anything significant, whether they're more than just a kind of analogy, or similarity—" He looked down at Smith and stopped. "Look, it's not my field. You should show this to Amos, or go up to Acheron and talk to the old man."

"Uh huh. Thanks, Frank."

"Oh no, no, no need. Sorry, Andy. I probably shouldn't have said anything. It's just, you know. You've been spending a hell of a lot of time here."

"Yeah."

Frank left.

Sometimes he fell asleep at his desk. He got some of his work done in dreams. Sometimes he found he could sleep down on the beach, wrapped in a greatcoat on the fine sand, lulled by the sound of the waves rolling in. At work he stared at the lined dots and letters on the screens, constructing the schematics of the sequences, nucleotide by nucleotide. Most were completely unambiguous. The correlation between the two main schematics was excellent, far beyond the possibility of chance. X chromosomes in humans clearly exhibited non-gene DNA traces of a distant aquatic ancestor, a kind of dolphin. Y chromosomes in humans lacked these passages, and they also matched with chimpanzees more completely than X chromosomes did. Y chromosomes were quite stable. Frank had appeared not to believe it, but there it was, right on the screen. But how could it be? What did it mean? Where did any of them get what they were? They had natures from birth. Just under five million years ago, chimps and humans separated out as two different species from a common ancestor, a woodland ape. The *Inis geoffrensis* fossil Smith was working on had been precisely dated to about 5.1 million years old. About half of all orangutan sexual encounters are rape.

One night after finishing work alone in the lab, he took a tram in the wrong direction, downtown, without ever admitting to himself what he was doing, until he was standing outside Mark's apartment complex, under the steep rise of the dorsum ridge. Walking up a staircased alleyway ascending the ridge gave him a view right into Mark's windows. And there was Selena, washing dishes at the kitchen window and looking back over her shoulder to talk with someone. The tendon in her neck stood out in the light. She laughed.

Smith walked home. It took an hour. Many trams passed him.

He couldn't sleep that night. He went down to the beach and lay rolled in his greatcoat. Finally he fell asleep.

He had a dream. A small hairy bipedal primate, chimp-faced, walked like a hunchback down a beach in east Africa, in the late afternoon sun. The warm water of the shallows lay greenish and translucent. Dolphins rode inside the waves. The ape waded out into the shallows. Long powerful arms, evolved for hitting; a quick grab and he had one by the tail, by the dorsal fin. Surely it could escape, but it didn't try. Female; the ape turned her over, mated with her, released her. He left and came back to find the dolphin in the shallows, giving birth to twins—one male, one female. The ape's troop swarmed into the shallows, killed and ate them both. Farther offshore the dolphin birthed two more.

The dawn woke Smith. He stood and walked out into the shallows. He saw dolphins inside the transparent indigo waves. He waded out into the surf. The water was only a little colder than the workout pool. The dawn sun was low. The dolphins were only a little longer than he was, small and lithe. He bodysurfed with them. They were faster than him in the waves, but flowed around him when they had to. One leapt over him and splashed back into the curl of the wave ahead of him. Then one flashed under him, and on an impulse he grabbed at its dorsal fin and caught it, and was suddenly moving faster in the wave, as it rose with both of them inside it—by far the greatest bodysurfing ride of his life. He held on. The dolphin and all the rest of its pod turned and swam out to sea, and still he held on. This is it, he thought. Then he remembered that they were air-breathers too. It was going to be all right.

DISCOVERING LIFE

The final approach to the Jet Propulsion Laboratory, a narrow road running up the flank of the ugly brown mountains overlooking Los Angeles, is an adequate road in ordinary circumstances, but when something newsworthy occurs it is inadequate to handle the influx of media visitors. On this morning the line of cars and trailers extended down from the security gate almost to the freeway off-ramp, and Bill Dawkins watched the temperature gauge of his old Ford Escort rise as he inched forward, all the vehicles adding to the smog already making the air a tangible gray mist. Eventually he passed the security guards and drove up to the employee parking lot, then walked down past the guest parking lot, overflowing with TV trailers topped by satellite dishes. Surely every language and nation in the world was represented, all bringing their own equipment, of course.

Inside the entry building Bill turned right and looked in the press-conference room, also jammed to overflowing. A row of Bill's colleagues sat up on the stage behind a long table crowded with mikes, facing the cameras and lights and reporters. Bill's friend Mike Collinsworth was answering a question about contamination, trying to look like he was enjoying himself. But very few scientists like other scientists listening in on them when they are explaining things to nonscientists, because then there is someone there to witness just how gross their gross simplifications are; so an affair like this was in its very nature embarrassing. And to complicate the situation this press corps was a very mixed crowd, ranging from experts who in some senses (social context, historical background) knew more than the scientists themselves, all the way to TV faces who could barely read their prompters. That plus the emotional load of the subject matter, amounting almost to hysteria, gave the event an excruciating quality that Bill found perversely fascinating to watch.

A telegenic young woman got the nod from John and took the radio mike being passed around. "What does this discovery mean to you?" she said. "What do you think the meaning of this discovery will be?"

The seven men on stage looked at one another, and the crowd laughed. John said, "Mike?" and Mike made a face that got another laugh. But John knew his crew; Mike was a smart ass in real life, indeed Bill could imagine some of his characteristic answers scorching the air: It means I have to answer stupid questions in front of billions of people, it means I can stop working eighty-hour weeks and see what a real life is like again; but Mike was also good at the PR stuff, and with a straight face he answered the second of the questions, which Bill would have thought was the harder of the two.

"Well, the meaning of it depends, to some extent, on what the exobiologists find out when they investigate the organisms more fully. If the organisms follow the same biochemical principles as life on Earth, then it's possible they are a kind of cousin to Terran life, bounced on meteorites from Mars to here, or here to Mars. If that's the case, then it's possible that DNA analysis will even be able to determine about when the two families parted company, and which planet has the older population. We may find out that we're all Martians originally."

He waited for the obligatory laugh. "On the other hand, the investigation may show a completely alien biochemistry, indicating a separate origin. That's a very different scenario." Now Mike paused, realizing he was at the edge of his soundbite envelope, also of deep waters. He decided to cut it short: "Either way that turns out, we'll know that life is very adaptable, and that it can either cross space between planets, or begin twice in the same solar system, so either way we'll be safer in assuming that life is fairly widespread in the universe."

Bill smiled. Mike was good; the answer provided a quick summary of the situation, bullet points, potential headlines: "Life on Mars Proves Life Is Common in the Universe." Which wasn't exactly true, but there was no winning the soundbite game.

Bill left the room and crossed the little plaza, then entered the big building forming the north flank of the compound. Upstairs the little offices and cubicles all had their doors open and portable TVs on, all tuned to the press conference just a hundred yards away; there was a holiday atmosphere, including streamers and balloons, but Bill couldn't feel it somehow. There on the screens under the CNN logo his friends were being played up as heroes, Young Devoted Rocket Scientists replacing astronauts, as the exploration of Mars proceeded robotically—silly, but very much preferable to the situation when things went wrong, when they were portrayed as Harried

Geek Rocket Scientists not quite up to the task, the extremely important (though underfunded) task of teleoperating the exploration of the cosmos from their desks. They had played both roles several times at JPL, and had come to understand that for the media and perhaps the public there was no middle ground, no recognition that they were just people doing their jobs, difficult but interesting jobs in difficult but not intolerable circumstances. No, for the world they were a biannual nine-hours' wonder, either nerdy heroes or nerdy goats, and the next day forgotten.

That was just the way it was, and not what was bothering Bill. He felt at loose ends. Mission accomplished, his TO DO list almost empty; it left him feeling somewhat empty; but that was not it either. He still had phone and e-mail media questions waiting, and he worked through those on automatic pilot, his answers honed by the previous week's work. The lander had drilled down and secured a soil sample from under the sands at the mouth of Shalbatana Vallis, where thermal sensors had detected heat from a volcanic vent, which meant the permafrost ice in that region had liquid percolations in it. The sample had been placed in a metal sphere which had been hermetically sealed and boosted to Martian orbit. After a rendezvous with an orbiter it had been flown back to Earth and been released in such a manner that it had dropped into Earth's atmosphere without orbiting at all, and slammed into Utah's Dugway Proving Grounds a mere ten yards from its target. An artificial meteorite, yes. No, the ball could not have broken on impact, it had been engineered for that impact, indeed could have withstood striking a sidewalk or a wall of steel, and had been recovered intact in the little crater it had made—recovered by robot and flown robotically to Johnson Space Center in Houston, where it had been placed inside hermetically sealed chambers in sealed labs in sealed buildings before being opened, everything having been designed for just this purpose. No, they did not need to sterilize Dugway, or all of Utah, they did not need to nuke Houston (not to kill Martian bacteria anyway), and all was well; the alien life was safely locked away and could not get out. People were safe.

Bill answered many such questions, feeling that there were far too many people who badly needed a better education in risk assessment. They got in their cars and drove on freeways, smoking cigarettes and holding high-energy radio transmitters against their heads, in order to get to newsrooms where they were greatly concerned to find out if they were in danger from microbacteria locked away behind triple hermetic seals in Houston. By the time Bill broke for lunch he was feeling more depressed than irritated. People were ignorant, short-sighted, poorly educated, fearful, superstitious; deeply meshed in magical thinking of all kinds. And yet that too was not really what was bothering him.

Mike was in the cafeteria, hungrily downing his lunchtime array of flavonoids and antioxidants, and Bill joined him, feeling cheered. Mike was giving a low-voiced recap of the morning's press conference (many journalists were in the JPL cafeteria on guest passes). "What is the meaning of life?" Mike whispered urgently, "it means metabolism, it means hunger at lunchtime, please *God* let us eat, that's what it means." Then the TVs overhead began to show the press conference from Houston, and like everyone else they watched and listened to the tiny figures on the screen. The exobiologists at Johnson Space Center were making their initial report: the Martian bacteria were around one hundred nanometers long, bigger than the fossil nanobacteria tentatively identified in ALH 84001, but smaller than most Terran bacteria; they were single-celled, they contained proteins, ribosomes, DNA strands composed of base pairs of adenine, thymine, guanine, and cytosine.

"Cousins," Mike declared.

The DNA resembled certain Terran organisms like the Columbia Basement Archaea *Methanospirillum jacobii*, thus possibly they were the descendant of a common ancestor.

"Cousins!"

Very possibly mitochondrial DNA analysis would reveal when the split had happened. "Separated at birth," one of the Johnson scientists offered, to laughter. They were just like the JPL scientists in their on-screen performances. Spontaneous generation versus panspermia, frequent transpermia between Earth and Mars; all these concepts poured out in a half-digested rush, and people would still be calling for the nuclear destruction of Houston and Utah in order to save the world from alien infection, from andromeda strains, from fictional infections—infictions, as Mike said with a grin.

The Johnson scientists nattered on solemnly, happy still to be in the limelight; it had been an oddity of NASA policy to place the Mars effort so entirely at JPL, in effect concentrating one of the major endeavors of human history into one small university lab, with many competing labs out there like baby birds in the federal nest, ready to peck JPL's eyes out if given the chance. Now the exobiology teams at Johnson and Ames were finally involved, and it was no longer just JPL's show, although they were still headquarters and had engineered the sample-return operation just as they had all the previous Martian landers. The diffusion of the project was a relief of course, but could also be seen as a disappointment—the end of an era. But now, watching the TV, Bill could tell that wasn't what was bothering him either.

Mike returned with Bill and Nassim to their offices, and they continued to watch the Johnson press conference on a desk TV. Apparently the sample contained more than one species, perhaps as many as five, maybe more. They just didn't know yet. They thought they could keep them all alive in Mars jars, but weren't sure. They were sure that they had the organisms contained, and that there was no danger.

Someone asked about ramifications for the human exploration of Mars, and the answers were scattered. "Very severely problematized," someone said; it would be a matter for discussion at the very highest levels, NASA of course but also NSF, the National Academy of Sciences, the International Astronomical Union, various UN bodies—in short, the scientific government of the world.

Mike laughed. "The human mission people must be freaking out."

Nassim nodded. "The Ad Martem Club has already declared that these things are only bacteria, like bathroom scum, we kill billions of them every day, they're no impediment to us conquering Mars."

"They can't be serious."

"They are serious, but crazy. We won't be setting foot there for a very long time. If ever."

Suddenly Bill understood. "That would be sad," he said. "I'm a humans-to-Mars guy myself."

Mike grinned and shook his head. "You better not be in too much of a hurry."

Bill went back into his office. He cleaned up a little, then called Eleanor's office, wanting to talk to her, wanting to say, We did it, the mission is a success and the dream has therefore been shattered, but she wasn't in. He left a message that he would be home around the usual time, then concentrated on his TODO list, no longer adding things to the bottom faster than he took them off at the top, trying to occupy his mind but failing. The realization was sinking in that he had always thought that their work was about going to Mars, about making a better world there; this was how he had justified everything about his life, the killing hours of the job, the looks on his family's faces, Eleanor's fully sympathetic but disappointed, frustrated that it had turned out this way, the two of them caught despite their best efforts in a kind of 1950s marriage, the husband gone all day every day—except of course that Eleanor worked long hours too, so that their kids had always been daycare and after-school care kids, all day every weekday. Once Bill had dropped Joe, their younger one, off at daycare on a Monday morning, and looking back in through the window he had seen an expression on the boy's face of abandonment and stoic solitude, of facing another ten hours at the same old place, to be gotten through somehow like everyone else, a look which on the face of a three-year-old had pierced Bill to the heart. And all that, all he had done, all the time he had put in, all those days and years, had been so that one day humans would inhabit Mars and make a decent civilization at last; his whole life burned in a cubicle because the start of this great project was so tenuous, because so few people believed or understood, so that it was down to them, one little lab trying its best to execute the "faster better cheaper" plan which contained within it (as they often pointed out) a contradiction of the second law of thermodynamics among other problems, a plan that they knew could only really achieve two out of the three qualities in any real-world combination, but making the attempt anyway, finding that the only true "cheaper" involved was the cost of their own labor and the quality of their own lives, rocket scientists running like squirrels in cages to make the inhabitation of Mars a reality—a project which only the future Martians of some distant century would truly appreciate and honor. Except now there weren't going to be any future Martians.

Then it was after six, and he was out in the late summer haze with Mike and Nassim, carpooling home. They got on the 210 freeway and rolled along quite nicely until the carpool lane stalled with all the rest, because of the intersection of 210 and 110; and then they were into stop-and-go like everyone else, the long lines of cars brake-lighting forward in that accordion pattern of acceleration and deceleration so familiar to them all. The average speed on the L.A. freeway system was now eleven miles per hour, low enough to make them and many other Angelenos try the surface streets instead, but Nassim's computer modeling and their empirical trials had made it clear that for any drive over five miles long the clogged freeways were still faster than the clogged streets.

"Well, another red letter day," Mike announced, and pulled a bottle of Scotch from his daypack. He snapped open the cap and took a swig, then passed the bottle to Bill and Nassim. This was something he did on ceremonial occasions, after all the great JPL successes or disasters, and though both Bill and Nassim found it alarming, they did not refuse quick pulls. Mike took another one before twisting the cap very tightly on the bottle and stuffing it back inside his daypack, actions which appeared to give him the feeling he had retuned the bottle to a legally sealed state. Bill and Nassim had mocked him for this belief before, and now Nassim said, "Why don't you just carry a little soldering iron with you so you can reseal it properly."

"Ha ha."

"Or adopt the NASA solution," Bill said, "take your swigs and then throw the bottle overboard."

"Ha ha, now don't be biting the hand that feeds you."

"That's the hand people always bite."

Mike stared at him. "You're not happy about this big discovery, are you, Bill."

"No!" Bill said, sitting there with his foot on the brake. "No! I always thought we were the, the bringing of the inhabitation of Mars. I thought that people would go on to live there, and terraform the planet, you know, red green and blue—establish a whole *world* there, a second strand of history, and we would always be back at the start of it all. And now these damn bacteria are there already, and we may never land there at all. We'll stay here and leave Mars to the Martians, the bacterial Martians."

"The little red natives."

"And so we're at the start of nothing! We're the start of a dead end."

"Balderdash," Mike said. And Bill's spirits rose a bit; he felt a glow like the Scotch running through him; he may have slaved away in a cubicle burning ten years of his life on the start of a dead-end project, a project that would never be enacted, but at least he had been able to work on it with people like these, people like brothers to him now after all the years, brilliant weird guys who would use the word "balderdash" in conversation in all seriousness; Mike who read Victorian boys' literature for his entertainment, who was as funny as they got; who had not even in the slightest way appeared on TV while playing the Earnest Rocket Scientist, playing a stupid role created by the media's questions and expectations, all them playing their stupid roles in precisely the stupid soap opera that Bill had dreamed they were going to escape someday, What does life *mean* to you, Dr. Labcoat, what does this discovery *mean*, Well, it means we have burned up our lives on a dead-end project. "What do you mean balderdash!" Bill exclaimed. "They'll make Mars a nature preserve, a bacterial nature preserve, for God's sake! No one will risk even *landing* there, much less terraforming the place!"

"Sure they will," Mike said. "People will go there. Eventually. They'll settle, they'll terraform—just like you've been dreaming. It might take longer than you were thinking, but you were never going to be one of the ones going anyway, so what's the rush? It'll happen."

"I don't think so," Bill said darkly.

"Sure it will. Whichever way it happens it'll happen."

"Oh thank you! Thank you very much! Whichever way it happens it'll happen? That's so very helpful!"

"Not your most testable hypothesis," Nassim noted.

Mike grinned. "You don't have to test it, it's that good."

Bill laughed harshly. "Too bad you didn't tell the reporter that! Whatever happens will happen! This discovery means whatever it means!" and then they were all cackling, "This discovery means that there's life on Mars!" "This discovery means whatever you want it to mean!" "That's how meaning always means!"

Their mirth subsided. They were still stuck in stop-and-go traffic, in the rows of red blinks on the vast viaduct slashing through the city, under a sour-milk sky.

"Well, shit," Mike said, waving at the view. "We'll just have to terraform Earth instead."

PROMETHEUS UNBOUND, AT LAST

Please append your report here

This novel postulates that science is an ongoing utopian proto-political experiment poorly theorized as such and lacking a paradigm within which to exert power in human affairs commensurate with its actual productive capacity and life-maintenance criticality. Scientists are first seen marginalized from macro-decision-making in a backstory (written in the style of a Cold War thriller) in which agents sequester science by convincing Truman *et al.* that science's metastasizing wartime ability to create new technologies crucial to victory (radar, penicillin, atom bomb, etc.) might constitute a threat to postwar civilian-corporate control of society.

Scientists, subsequently inoperative in surplus value investment and allocation decisions, produce goods and services unconscious of themselves as a group and individually willing to work within the existing hierarchical extractive non-sustainable system for $100,000\pm50,000$ annually plus pension, stock options and a light teaching load. (This chapter is in the form of a zombie novel, highly amusing.)

Then the scientifically augmented human population catastrophically overshoots the long-term carrying capacity of the planet. Scientists in their various toothless non-decision-making organizations conclude that the anthropogenically initiated climate change, and mass extinction event associated with it, probably threatens their descendants' welfare, and thus scientists' own evolutionary fitness. The sleepers awake.

Meanwhile a certain proportion of humanity makes a cost-benefit analysis comparing fifteen years' work learning a science with saying "I believe" and through group political action controlling more calories per capita than scientists do, also more power over funding and rather more offspring. Many conclude faith-based parasitism on science less costly to the individual, so more adaptive. (Vampires living off zombies, guns brandished, chases by night: the novel gets pretty lurid at this point.)

Then at a modelling conference a discussion springs up concerning Hamilton's rule, which states that altruism should evolve whenever the cost to the giver, C, is less than the fitness benefits, B, obtained by helping another individual who is related by r, with r being calculated as the proportion of genes these two individuals share by common descent (as in Hrdy, 1999): $C \leq Br$.

A geneticist at the conference points out that as humans share 60% of their genes with fruitflies, and all eukaryotes share 938 core genes, r is probably always higher than heretofore calculated. An ecologist mentions the famous *Nature* article in which the benefits provided by the biosphere to humans were estimated at $33 trillion a year (R. Costanza *et al. Nature* 387, 253–260; 1997). An economist suggests that the cost for individual scientists wanting to maintain these benefits could be conceptualized in the form of a mutual hedge fund, with initial investment set for the sake of discussion at $1,000 per scientist.

Comic scene here as modellers debate the numbers, with a biologist pointing out that the benefit of life to every living organism could justifiably be defined as infinity, considerably altering equation's results. (Shouting, fights, saloon demolished in Wild West manner.)

Conference attendees conclude altruism is probably warranted, and hedge fund is established. (Readers of novel wishing to pre-invest are directed to a website http://www.sciencemutual.net.) Participating scientists then vote to establish a board; a model constitution for all governments to adopt; a policy-research institute tasked with forming a political platform; and a lobbying firm. All scientific organizations are urged to join the fund. Fund's legal team goes to World Court to claim compensation for all future biospheric damage, to be paid into the fund by those wreaking the damage and the governments allowing it.

Many meetings follow, no doubt explaining the presence in this chapter of most of the novel's sex scenes. Author seemingly familiar with and perhaps overfond of the bonobo literature. Strenuous attempts to maximize reproductive success in Davos, Santa Fe, Las Vegas, etc.

Novel's style shifts to amalgam of legal thriller and tolkienesque high fantasy as scientists take power from corporate military-industrial global élite. A spinradian strategic opacity here obscures the actual mechanism that would allow this to work in the real world, said opacity created by deployment of complicated syntax, phrases low in semantic content ("information cascade"), especially active stage business (man runs through with hair on fire), explosions, car chases, and reinvocation of Very Big Numbers—in this case Science Mutual's potential assets if World Court returns positive judgment, after which subsequent chapter (with toll-free number as epigraph!) emerges in newly utopian space, looking plausible to those still suspended in coleridgean willed non-disbelief.

Speed of narration accelerates. Science Mutual arranges winners in all elections everywhere. Hedge fund continues to grow. Scientific organizations form international supra-organization. Black helicopters proliferate. Entire population decides to follow new scientific guidelines indicating that reproductive fitness is maximal the closer behaviour conforms to palaeolithic norms, this being the lifestyle that tripled brain size in only 1.2 million years. Widespread uptake of this behavioural set augmented by appropriate technology (especially dentistry) reduces global resource demand by an order of magnitude despite demographic surge to UN-predicted mid-range peak of ten billion humans. A rationally balanced positive feedback loop into maximized universal fitness obtains. (Novel ends with standard finale, singing, dancing, reproducing. All Terran organisms live optimally ever after.)

Please give your recommendation

Reader recommends acceptance for publication, but suggests that the apparent size of the text's strategic opacity be reduced to three seconds of arc or less. Publisher should take steps to secure domain name sciencemutual. com. (Also, more car chases.)

THE TIMPANIST OF THE BERLIN PHILHARMONIC, 1942

First movement: Allegro ma non troppo, un poco maestoso
The first movement is about death. It begins with a little joke, that's Beethoven for you—the most terrifying music ever, yet he begins by making it sound like the horn players are warming up their lips and mouthpieces, the strings tuning their note against the oboe, the flashier ones throwing in a fifth below as if to test even the harmonics—and then the whole thing falls over a cliff into something urgent and loud, jagged and dark. The timpanist got to hammer this sudden fall home with the most violent entrance of his life. The stroke of doom, the bad news—he hit his D and A drums like the sledgehammer of Death, killing everything. A complete Götterdämmerung in sixteen notes; the perfect music for the evening, in other words. Because they were all doomed.

Furtwängler knew it of course, none better; he had marched up to the podium as if to the gallows, and begun conducting the instant he got there, as he always did now—but this time it was different, the grim look on his face unprecedented and frightening. Behind him, out among the packed audience filling the big hall of the Philharmonie, the timpanist could see any number of uniformed men with eyepatches, arms in slings, bandaged noses, missing legs. In his peripheral vision he could see the giant swastikas draped to each side of the stage, and there was another one above and behind them. The Nazi officials sat in the front row, Goebbels chewing his underlip like a rabbit. It was best not to look at them. During the short rests between his assaults, and throughout the second theme, as the counter-tune kept trying to tiptoe out of the room, the timpanist locked his gaze on their conductor; nevertheless he still saw the bandaged men, also a scattering of soberly dressed women, their faces twisted with pity, dread, longing, regret. When the return of the first theme caught them all he brought his sticks down harder than ever, pounding out their doom.

Not that this music was only about death. The first movement of Beethoven's Ninth was an entire world in itself, one relearned this every time one traversed it; its seventeen or eighteen minutes expanded into a Greek tragedy that felt like it filled years. There were shifts, respites, restless searches, kindly moments... In certain bars the woodwinds followed a pause with a little cantabile, a pulse of life, and the strings carried it away in a nervous interrogation, asking Can this sweetness exist? Can we get away with such delicate play? Can we leave all the rest of the world behind? Only to be answered NO, the little tune smashed down in another flood of doom, the dark plunge, the knell in the heart of the first theme, its falling thirds and fifths like tripping down cliffs at the edge of an abyss. Struggle away as hard as they could, they kept falling back. This was not like the famous first theme of the Fifth, which was a very different call, a matter of adversity defied, Fate heraldic, its eight notes quickly elaborated, woven together, lifted up in a shout that was ultimately heroic; yes, the Fifth's first movement was heroic; while the Ninth's was simply death, arriving without any possibility of denial, right there in the great hall of the Philharmonie. April 19, 1942.

And everyone there knew it, everyone who was not a fool, anyway, and in such fundamental things there were very few fools. Perhaps Goebbels was a fool, if he was not a calculating opportunist, or simply mad. But most of the people in the hall knew very well. They had heard the bombers at night, had descended into the Untergrund when the air raid sirens howled, had stood in the dark listening as the whole world above them became a throbbing band of kettle drums. They saw the maimed boys sitting among them. They read the newspapers, they listened to the radio, they talked in kitchens late at night with friends they trusted. They were Berliners, they knew.

Recently the timpanist had discovered that in the extremity of the violent passages throughout the middle minutes of the first movement, the long rolls Beethoven had given him to play could be made to sound precisely like the bombers at night overhead, and different kinds of bombers at that, depending on how close to the rim he hit and how fast, so that he could imitate the low grumble of Heinkels struggling for take-off, or the high staccato of de Havillands, or the creamy thrum of Lancasters rushing by on a massed run. These engine rolls were punctuated by explosive hits mid-drumhead, like anti-aircraft fire; it was amazingly like. From within his prophetic solitude the deaf old man had apparently heard the deadly future reverberating back to him, had translated it into *x*'s and *tr*'s and *sf*'s and *fff*'s, and the diagonal crosses through the notes that meant *bomber*.

Now back to the fateful hammering of the first theme. Here he re-created the sounds of the big guns of the last war. He had fought in that war and heard each kind of gun innumerable times, sometimes in the very rhythms Beethoven now required, sometimes for hours on end. Fifty kilometers of Big Berthas, going off all night long: useful knowledge in this moment. Happily he pounded as hard as he could get away with, or harder. Every person in the hall surely recognized what he was doing.

Of course outside the music they rarely discussed the war, you couldn't. The timpanist was as careful as anyone when he was in the building, and never said anything around Rammelt or Kleber in the cellos, or Bucholz, Schuldes, Woywoth—these five were the really obnoxious party members. Just five of them, and yet that was enough to poison the whole ensemble. Once he had seen Woywoth tell Hans Bastiaan, a mild little violinist, "You have to say Heil Hitler when you greet someone now," and Bastiaan had replied, "Ah but it's also nice to simply wish a good morning, isn't it?" and Woywoth had glared at him until Bastiaan had scurried away like a mouse.

But very few of them were like that. They were like children when it came to politics, they didn't know what to say about it and didn't want to know. Most of them hadn't fought in the first war; most lived their whole lives inside music. Although sometimes a few of them gathered in a rehearsal room, and someone would look over someone's shoulder at a newspaper and mutter things, Oh dear this latest victory in Russia seems to be only half as far along as the one before, it's a Zeno's paradox of a front. Or tough talk under the breath, ha ha ja sure, a mode common to everyone since the Twenties at least. The latest word was that hundreds of British bombers had destroyed Hamburg in a single night, burned it to the ground. Berlin was sure to follow, no one could doubt it. And yet no one could say it, not with Nazis in their midst, sanctimonious petty assholes that they were. The Berlin Philharmonic used to belong to its players, they had owned it, each player a share, but Goebbels had forced them to sell, had seized them. They were birds in a cage now, and had to be fearful of traitors. Around the midnight tables a few of the most disgusted had even discussed the situation and what they would do the moment the war was over: they would immediately dismiss Rammelt, Kleber, Bucholz, Schuldes, and Woywoth, and then they would open their first postwar concert with an overture by Mendelssohn. That was the plan, that was what they would do, they told each other drunkenly, when it was all over—at which point they could only wince and nod when Erich Hartmann added his usual coda to any such talk: *When we're all dead.*

Now, glancing helplessly through the glare of the lights at the audience, the timpanist could see in the little faces out there that they had all heard a Hartmann, one way or another. The knowledge filled them like an iron bell in the chest: in a year or two, only a few here would be alive. Less than half? A tenth? None at all? None could tell, and yet all knew; indeed the music *insisted* that they know, and the timpanist's mallets drove it into their skulls. That repetitive little dirge in the basses that announced the coda, the phrase that had given Berlioz the shivers, convinced him that the old man had known madness full well: it filled them now, vibrated their guts, they could not escape it. Six notes down, two notes up, over and over and over. Never had they played the first movement like this before, it was their knowledge playing it. The final massive D-minor falling fourths, implacable, unavoidable, dragging them down, pushing them off the cliff into the abyss—hit every note:

Bah bum! bah bum, bah bum, bah bummmmmm,
bah bum bum bah! bah! bah! bah! bum.

Second movement: Scherzo molto vivace

The scherzo is best regarded as a concerto for timpani and orchestra, especially if you are the timpanist. The solo timpani notes called for in the fifth bar are part of the tune, simply an octave apart, Ds both, repeating and thereafter anchoring the syncopated dactylic theme, and often banging it solo in the resonant pause of all the others. Soloist and orchestra. You had to love Beethoven for thinking of it.

The timpanist thumped his great three notes home and then off they went, rollicking inside a juggernaut that stopped for nothing. *Molto vivace,* sure, but alive with some kind of thoughtless life, something insectile or germlike which shrugged off all obstruction. A life manic and onrushing, a life that killed. The mad blind energy of the universe.

Furtwängler conducted this relentless engine in his usual spastic style, urging the group along by mysterious movements. Jerky, uncoordinated, enigmatic: the timpanist like all the rest of them had long since learned that the actual beat Furtwängler wanted could be best read in the movements of his upper arms, or in his shoulders more generally. Nothing else about him was reliable as to tempo; his other shudderings meant God knew what. One could only conclude they referred to some qualities beyond physical expression which he nevertheless tried to convey, qualities which Furtwängler himself was at a loss to define, even in rehearsal. He was a little bit crazy. He spoke in bursts, after pauses, and could be amazingly inarticulate when talking about what he wanted in a piece. He would pause at questions, tap the score, cluck in exasperation: Just look at the music, he would say in the end. Just play what's there.

And so they would. Ultimately it became a matter of group telepathy.

This was always partly true, but under Furtwängler's baton, completely the case. There was nothing else for it; they had to make it up themselves. The sudden responsibility of this, the imposed task, was startling, worrisome, sometimes electrifying. And it was in keeping with Furtwängler's slippery resistance to the Nazis. Just as he would not let them dictate to him, he would not dictate to his players, even though as conductor this could be said to be his job. The surprising thing was how often he made it work—how watching him flail up there, seeing him out of tempo and yet believing in him, they so often played as one organism, one mind. It was the best feeling in the world.

Naturally they would have loved him just for that alone. Some of the other conductors were martinets, like Knappertsbusch, or idiots, like Krauss, and of course there was always the icy ugliness of the maestro's great enemy von Karajan. No—a good conductor was always appreciated, a great conductor often loved.

But with Furtwängler it was so much more. The timpanist had felt like that for more than half his life; he had been a bass player as a young man, won his place in the Berlin Philharmonic right beside Erich Hartmann himself, but had gone to the front in the first war and fallen in no-man's land during an attack, broken his left arm and leg and for the following eleven days been caught there under fire from both sides, eating dead men's provisions and trying to hide or crawl back to the German side, which seemed to retreat before him. A night patrol had finally brought him in, but he had never afterward been the same, not in mind nor body, and often could not suppress a small quiver in his left hand. It had looked to be the end of his musical career, but Furtwängler had watched him play, then suggested to him that his tremor would go away if he hit the drums, that it would only make him "quicker." It made a way to go forward.

That was big; but now scattered among the orchestra there were many other men who were only there, and perhaps only alive, because of Furtwängler. Bottermund, Zimolong, Leuschner, and Bruno Stenzel were half-Jews; several others, including their concertmaster Hugo Kolberg, were married to Jewish women. She's always been that way, Kolberg would explain plaintively, I regret it but there it is, what can I do. Nothing; but Furtwängler did something. The full Jews in the orchestra had been driven into exile in the Thirties, to the maestro's great distress and over his objections; but after that he insisted he had to have his people, that they and their wives were to be left alone. Naturally this made Goebbels intent to break him, and the maestro had had to sacrifice his career to hold the line; had quit as the musical director of the Philharmonic, and of the Staat Opere, quit all his official positions until now he conducted only as a guest, accepting invitations on an individual basis, and never in the conquered countries. And he never gave the Nazi salute, not even when Hitler was there, always marching to the podium baton in hand and beginning the moment he got there, in a way he never had in the past. Everyone knew it was a defiance.

Now he was far away, deep in Beethoven, the greatest German of all. Light on his feet. It was easy to think of Beethoven as a kind of god, his music as natural as sunlight or the ocean, but he had been a deaf old man too, scribbling day after day, a hard worker. Furtwängler somehow made that clear, made the music new again, an improvisation only written down by chance and will. The players saw him struggling to convey this to them. Fighting for them, in so many ways: talking about it in empty cafés, late at night among the most trusted friends, the ones who were also in trouble, they had figured there were about a hundred people the maestro was protecting from the Nazis. Not counting the hundred in the orchestra itself, all balanced precariously on his jerky shoulders.

So of course they loved him. The timpanist would have died for him, and he was not alone in this. And in performance they were forced by his indirection to follow him into that mysterious other land, and do what they could to bring it back into the hall. The timpani part in the second movement allowed the timpanist many little solos reiterating its syncopated theme, a theme so mechanically regular that its effect was ultimately terrible, as if the wild finale of the Seventh had somehow been punched onto the roll of a player piano: blind energy, relentless, remorseless. Again the kettle drums sounded like artillery, even a brief return of the bombers overhead. Furtwängler nodded grimly as he heard this. He had been hauled back from Vienna for this one, Hitler's birthday again, a predictable occasion and so he had been out of town as usual, in Vienna where the city's Gauleiter would have to give permission for him to leave, and von Schirach hated Hitler and presumably would refuse any such permission, making it a safe haven. But the word going round was that Goebbels had gotten von Schirach on the telephone and threatened him so effectively that Furtwängler had been sent back. Now here they were between the swastikas, playing for the Führer's birthday with the cameras rolling and the tapes recording, so that the performance would be seen by all the world, saved for all eternity. So all the maestro's efforts to keep his distance had come to naught, and now his body was clenched, his baton flew about spasmodically, the abstracted but pained set of his face twisted often into something like rage. Everything about him made it clear to his men that this was a bad occasion, a disaster, a defeat to be suffered. People in times to come would hear the tapes and see the film, and judge them. They would not understand. Only if the orchestra played well enough might people take pause, feel confused—recall the crimes of their own countries, recall how they had turned their heads and hoped it was just a bad time that would go away—recall how they too had failed to resist. Then they might hear the pain of being caught when the bad time didn't go away, when the thugs took over and there was nothing you could do. Or nothing you did. And if they imagined they would do something different, he thought with a sudden forte smash, they lied! They lied!

But if they heard they would understand. So there was nothing for it but to play as if possessed, to live inside Beethoven and throw it in the teeth of their captors, inhabit their music like a fortress and defy the Nazis from inside it. The whole band understood this, their traitors notwithstanding; these first two movements showed it, they were playing in a fury, never had they ridden these old warhorses as hard as this! Feeling the effort all through his body, striking as if his mallets were clubs, the timpanist hit the final notes of the scherzo so hard that the head of his D drum split right across.

Third movement: Adagio molto e cantabile

Normally when the third movement began, he would sit on his stool with about eight minutes of rest, and there were other rests later; he rested more than played. So he would listen to the sweet flow of the strings, and think over his life in a particular order, as if fingering a rosary: first his mother, then his father, then his childhood and youth, lastly his music.

This time however he had to sit on the floor behind the drums and as quietly as possible pull a new head from the head folder, then unscrew the broken drumhead, unhoop it, and get the new one on, all in time for the drum to make its appearance. Possibly he could play the adagio's first timpani part on the other drums, then continue the repair between his first and second entries. It would take almost twenty minutes for the maestro to traverse this longest of adagios. At the worst he should be ready in time for the finale. But it would be better if he could do it right, so he went to work as fast as he could, given the requirement of utter silence and invisibility. Jürgen, one of the percussionists, noticed his predicament and crawled over to help him. "Günther!" he whispered in his ear. "What have you done!"

"Never mind that," the timpanist replied. "Just help me."

They went to it, sitting on the floor and reaching up to the rims of the copper kettle. As they worked, a part of his mind still took in the music. The adagio was one of his favorite parts. People had a tendency to dismiss the Ninth's adagio a little bit, he had noticed, at least in comparison to the other three movements, each in their different ways so monumental. But that was a mistake; the adagio too was a marvel. Indeed if any one movement of the Ninth were to be singled out as being less astonishing than the rest, it would probably have to be the second, much though a timpanist should never say so, of course. Really it was best just to listen and accept: the whole symphony was great. The adagio was a blessing from God.

Furtwängler routinely played it as if pouring syrup, and on this night he took it slower than ever. The stately melody wound through its series of variations, meandering more each time, with a richness of elaboration reminiscent of Bruckner. Simply put, a very beautiful song. It steadied his hand as he untightened the screws, ignoring the anxious face staring up from inside the copper.

Then there was a shift, a second theme that interrupted the song, coming as if from far away: trumpets speaking briefly. It might have been a call, a rally to return to town; but it was for others; and the song resumed, carried them downstream and away. Furtwängler's dreamy pace never lost a nice line; they flowed in a way that revealed the deep currents beneath. This was what the maestro was listening for in his own world, it was obvious. All around the timpanist the strings were following that line.

It was a hopeless task to change the drumhead in complete silence, and at one point there was a metallic clank as the loosened hoop hit the edge of a music stand. The maestro's sound technician, Friedrich Schnapp, glared up from his cockpit to the side; he had heard it. Now he saw their situation and grimaced at them fiercely. His gaze darted back and forth between his monitors and them. He looked desperate for a cigarette, he always was, but the Führer didn't like smoking and the maestro neither, so there was no chance of that until the whole thing was over. Schnapp chewed his moustache instead, and Günther and Jürgen pulled the new head over the drum, then placed the hoop over it, after which they screwed it down in careful half turns, moving around the drum opposite each other. He would have to tune the new head while playing, alas, unless he could risk tapping away sotto voce before his part began. He had done that before once or twice when the piece itself called him to do it. The maestro had heard these little additions to the score and tipped his head to the side as if considering whether such a thing was permissible; and then more than once had *conducted* the transgression, the tip of his baton making little gestures as if to say, If you are going to be so bold, I am not necessarily opposed in theory; but you must be conducted. So he could tune the drum that way on this misbegotten Walpurgisnacht, and the maestro would understand—or not, in which case he could explain the situation to him later.

Despite his focus on their silent handiwork, some inner part of him was also persisting with his rosary; apparently this music now triggered it in him no matter what else was happening. So, his mother. How he missed her. How hard she had worked. A baker who had raised her son in her bakery, while her husband was out on the road or in the bars. The main impression of her that remained with him was how hard she had worked. Even as a child he had been impressed by that; even now, remembering it, awe filled him. No one he had ever known since had worked as hard. Now she had been dead twenty-eight years.

Then his father, his crazy father, who had been too old even for the first war, and yet nevertheless was now working as a truck mechanic on the eastern front. Recently he had been in Berlin on a leave and taken his son out drinking, and regaled him with stories of what it was like to be the only mechanic on truck convoys numbering in the scores of vehicles, with just him and a road engineer named Matthias to keep things moving. Every trip is the fucking *Iliad* and *Odyssey* combined, boy, the roads have been destroyed and we're always axle deep, and last time out Matthias wasn't along and trucks were sliding into ditches and canals, jack-knifing, you name it, and we'd drive up and get out and they would look at me! And I would look at the mess and think, Please, Matthias, *speak* to me now, *be* with me now, what would you *do* with this ridiculous mess—and I swear to you, Günther, I swear to God, I swear by your mother, that Matthias *would* speak to me! And I would tell everyone what he was saying, tell them to do things I had never seen or heard of! It was Matthias inside me, speaking through me. We would fix the mess and on we would go. We're all inside each other, boy. We can call mind to mind, you can hear it if you listen.

I know, the timpanist had said. It's like that when we play.

But he could see that his father believed it literally. It was funny to think that the fate of the entire Russian campaign, in other words of the war itself, rested on the shoulders of a sixty-year-old mechanic who heard voices in his head.

Furtwängler flowed on. He was indeed taking the adagio slower than usual, no doubt as a rebuke to Goebbels and his gang. You people are here for the fire and glory of the other movements, Furtwängler's tempo said, but I'm not going to hurry for you. Now you're the captives, caught by Beethoven, and the music that we bathe in is precisely the world that you have taken away from us. This is the meadow in the forest, this is Sunday at dawn in the clean washed street. This is the flow of slow time, the empty hour, contemplation itself. These are the things you have taken from us with your vicious stupidity. Listen and remember, if you can. If you ever knew.

The theme was very like a hymn, and they played it that way, sure. They were praying now, they were singing a devotional. But the devotional that you sing when you are twenty-three and have just been hired as a double bass player in the Berlin Philharmonic, is very different from the devotional that you hum in the Untergrund when the Lancasters growl overhead. It was the latter they sang now, both rebuke and consolation, the mix ultimately some kind of deep ache for the world they had lost. It would never come back.

Plucked emphases from the basses formed a perfect cover for him to tap the D drum around the rim and check the tuning. It seemed all right. As a totality it was perhaps a bit sharp, but it was consistent, and he could pedal it down and all would be well.

Now he came to the similar light taps that were actually written in the score. How Beethoven had loved pulse, no composer before him and few since had ever thought to use the timpani in this way. Schnapp still glared at them from his cockpit; they definitely had made some noise during their operation, but as there were people in the audience coughing from time to time in helpless little explosions, it did not seem to the timpanist that it could matter much. He focused on his part, the gentle tapping in time with the tune. When else did he ever get to sing like this? It was such a sweet and peaceful thing.

But then, a light bang: the end was nigh. Slower than ever, as the coda declared itself; even there he got to tap along, gently gently. Then the solid thumps at the end; but not the end (another little joke); but then the end.

Fourth movement: Presto Ode to Joy

From the first shot of the finale they were cast immediately back into the violence of the first and second movements. His big copper drums were fully involved in that, simply *smashing* people back into reality and the war. The brief recollections of the first three movements made their truncated appearances each in turn, but each then mutated back into the war. The conflict swirled, thundered, sucked them all back down. All this dark re-announcement of the world was soon to be broken by the sound of the human voice, the hoarse shout of a man. But for the moment darkness was all.

Then the famous theme, the raw material they would be wrestling with for the next half hour, came into the world as a kind of feeling in the stomach, a mere whispering from the basses. The maestro liked this very pianissimo, and as usual he had arranged for the choir to come onto the stage during this first enunciation, so that the singers' little coughs and the unavoidable creaks of their feet on the risers were almost as loud as the basses, which made Schnapp glower; but the maestro liked it that way. The first time through, he would say, it's supposed to ghost into you.

So the Bruno Kittel choir shuffled in, as quietly as they could; and as they did (it took a while) the strings picked up the great tune and carried it and its most basic descant up into consciousness, rising then like a wave to break into the brasses. Now standing all around and behind the timpanist was a crowd of people, men and women ranked on risers. Easily a hundred women there to his right, in their white blouses and perfect hair—their presence palpable, their scent a mix of shampoo and sweat that smelled to him like bread. Now the whole nation was the band.

The quartet of soloists stood up together, down there to Furtwängler's right. *Not these tones!* the bass singer bellowed, and they began the immense and unstable mix of vocal and orchestral that would surge thereafter around the stage. Meanings ricocheted out of the strange lyrics: something better *had* to exist, they seemed to say, or they would make it out of nothing; this is how he interpreted it, and the phrases often matched that feeling. Then the whole choir jumped in with the bass, saying the same lines: and they were well launched on the tumultuous ride of the great finale.

The structure of the movement made for many moments and passages complete in themselves, each section a kind of continent they were to traverse. It was not quite a tone poem, but rather a set of variations so various that they were hardly recognizable as such; still the great tune lay inside each one of them, concealed within inversions, reversals, textural changes, tempo changes—every kind of change deployed, every kind of magnificence revealed. Keeping the order and flow between the sections was part of the maestro's job, and one aspect of his genius.

Among other things, he had taught them that when the quartet of soloists sang, the players had to dampen their sound to make the four audible to the listeners in the hall. He was very insistent on this dynamic modulation, and they had learned to play in a mode that might be called *piano furioso,* an intense mode which kept the music and the players on fire without overwhelming the soloists' sound. The orchestra was better at this than the Kittel choir, or so it sounded to the timpanist; when choir and soloists were both singing, the soloists could not possibly be heard over their massed ensemble. Maybe it didn't matter. They were all singing the solos in their heads anyway, hearing them the way his dad heard Matthias.

Surely there could be no one happier than a timpanist in the midst of this finale. He was asked to bang, thump, grumble, pound, tap, roar. He drove the music, punctuated it, played in it; it was as if Beethoven had been concerned to make him joyful. The so-called Turkish variation, with the tenor's solo in it, went off with jaunty gaiety, his fellow percussionists clanging away like drunken Ottomans. And the tenor was very fine. Every quartet had its best member, and this time it appeared to be the tenor, one Helge Roswange, whose voice had a friendly and even noble tone. Unfortunately his solo's final flourish, his leap to the sky, was completely overwhelmed by the choir.

One had to hear it like Beethoven had heard it.

This led to the solemn chords of the passage in which the choir sang very slowly. *Over— the— stars*, and so on. That too went well. Again a prayer. The women's voices were an unearthly sound, there was no instrument that could match that sound for sheer beauty.

On they moved, as if through rooms in heaven; and as each part of the symphony had gone so well, as well as any of them had ever heard it, the stakes were somehow raised, their spirits were raised; they became exhilarated. He could hear very clearly that the choir was as caught up by this as the instrumentalists: their voices, my Lord! All were caught together in something tremendous, flying up into it; and Furtwängler was alive to it, he was pulling it together for them to hear and sing. On his face they saw: if they made it beautiful enough, they might leave the planet altogether. Oh they were culpable, yes, but they had not intended it. Suffering had driven them to it. They had gone mad, but in their madness made this. What if the worst culture made the most beautiful thing, what then? Wasn't it then more complicated than people thought? It would at least be a conundrum forever, people would look at the film and listen to the tapes and hear this music and take pause, see birds in a cage, hear that not everyone had been suborned, that some had had to stay and fight from within as best they could, with whatever they had, even if it was just to make a music that would remind people hunched by their radio that there was a better world.

Then there came the timpanist's favorite part in the entire symphony: the big fugue marked *Allegro energico, sempre ben marcato*—a braided fugue in which different parts of the choir split first into two parts, then moved on to other melodies while new voices took up the original pair, after which the orchestra also broke into sections and joined either one vocal part or another, while violins and basses also tossed back and forth a rapid obbligato, above or below, or both at once. Large groups of people therefore were simultaneously belting out tunes entirely distinct and different from the rest— *Joy, beautiful divine spark, we are intoxicated with fire as we enter your sanctuary— All men become brothers wherever your gentle wing reposes— Do you have a presentiment of the eternal, O world? Seek it above the starry tent! Over the stars it must dwell!* —all these phrases overlapping in the same time and space, and yet the weaving lines made something massive and right, a polyphony with so many interlocking melodies that the timpanist could not believe that Beethoven in his deafness could really have imagined what it would sound like, he must only have seen it as a pattern on the page, a hope in him, a hope now filling the hall, a magnificent chaos that was not chaos—he got to emphasize this on his drums—out of *chaos* emerged *order*, out of *chaos* emerged *beauty*, a beauty so complex it could not be comprehended. This must be the passage, Günther thought, as he always thought when playing it, where Beethoven had gotten confused during the premiere performance. The old man had sat on the stage next to the conductor, trying to help with tempi, but had lost his place, and the conductor had forged on without him; and when it was all over and the audience clapped and cheered, Beethoven had sat there still facing the orchestra, his back to the audience, deaf and unaware, perhaps disconsolate at losing his place; and so the soprano, Fraulein Unger, had gone to him and taken his hand and turned him around so he could see the audience, who then began leaping in the air to show him how they felt. *This* was his country, *these* were his people, the nation of musicians, sovereign even in chains. *Wherever your gentle wing reposes. Whoever has become a friend of a friend.* He pounded this feeling home at the fugue's end, just as Beethoven required of him.

Now their faces were all flushed. Red-faced, bright-eyed, they kept their gazes fixed on the maestro or their sheet music, as if to look around might reveal something unbearable. Intently the choir whispered the tip-toe section that followed, rocking back and forth, the whispered staccato *seek it—above—the star—ry tent* before the sudden shouts, *Brothers! Brothers!* Back and forth, whisper shout, whisper shout, such fun to do, all now shouting together as loudly as they could. Two hundred strong—he had never heard music this loud in his life. The performance just kept on getting better, they all heard it, it seized them up and carried them off!

The final quartet of the soloists came at last, sign of the approaching end: a curious gnarled thing to the timpanist's ear, like four lines of wool all kinked in knots; but with the gorgeous high turn of the soprano at the climax, that downward bend on the word *wing— Where your gentle wiiiing alights.* Where grace comes down and touches our soul.

The moment the soprano finished her last words, *dein sanfter Flügel weilt*, Furtwängler rushed them through the complex coda, he *drove* them. First very fast, in a real hurry—then the final ritard, for the toppling off the cliff of the voices, the falling fifths again—at the bottom of which he redoubled the pace to something quite inhuman. Always he did it this way, "go like a bat out of hell," he would say, but never so fast as on this night of nights. Even at his usual tempo the piccolo player was forced to play with supernatural speed and volume, but on this night Frans had to simply throw his hat to the wind and skreel like a maniac, and the timpanist had to strike every note of it with him, and he did!

Then they stood there, still inside the reverberations of the final chord, still ringing with it. The timpanist listened, quivering, his eyes fixed on Furtwängler's face. In the silence certain to follow, everything that so horribly portended would come to pass, all that hung over this night like a sword—their ongoing crime, the inevitable judgment, death itself—none of it mattered. They were gone.

AFTERWORD

Thanks

First: thank you, readers of my fiction; I appreciate your giving it your time and thought, which brings it to life.

This is also a good place to thank all the editors who helped me with these stories. Damon Knight was my first editor and one of my most important teachers. I miss him. Same for my second editor, Terry Carr. Thank you also to Ed Ferman, Beth Meacham, Lou Aronica, Shawna McCarthy, Ellen Datlow, Gardner Dozois, Robert Silverberg and Karen Haber, Dean Wesley Smith and Kristine Kathryn Rusch, Gregory Benford, Jan O'Nale, David Pringle, Henry Gee, and Jane Johnson. Many of the stories in this book exist because of requests from these friends and colleagues.

In this book particularly, it is a pleasure to thank Jonathan Strahan, whose idea the book was, and who selected and arranged the stories in a way I really like, but could not have figured out myself.

My writing teachers were also important to most of these stories, and I remain grateful to them: Donald Wesling, Fredric Jameson, Samuel R. Delany, Gene Wolfe, Roger Zelazny, Joe Haldeman, Kate Wilhelm, Ursula K. Le Guin, and Gary Snyder.

Science fiction is, among other things, a community—something like a small town, scattered (as if by some cosmic accident) across space and time. I wrote these stories as a resident of that town, in conversation with that community. Some of my friends had a particularly strong effect on my short fiction, either by comment or example, and I'd like to thank in particular my Clarion classmates; also Carter Scholz, Lucius Shepard, James Patrick Kelly, John Kessel, John Clute, Terry Bisson, Paul Park, and Karen Fowler. I am lucky to know these people.

The Stories

I don't have much to say about these stories in the aggregate. I can see that there are differences and similarities among them, but this is not a deep insight. I also see some shifts in my methods over the years, as well as some enduring concerns and habits; again, not a remarkable observation. I think I will do better by speaking about the stories individually, as almost all of them spark a few memories or observations in me, which may be of interest. So let's do it that way.

"Venice Drowned"

In the summer of 1977 I traveled through Europe with friends, and on the way to Trieste our train pulled into the Venice train station to transfer our car to another train. I had just enough time to walk out the main entry of the station, see that its broad stairs dropped into a canal, and then hurry back to our train.

That glimpse stuck with me, and after some reading about Venice (Shelley's poem "Julian and Maddalo" told me about the island asylum), I wrote this story. It was my first sale to Terry Carr, and the start of a too-short friendship with him. What a beautiful guy.

After the story was published, in December of 1985, my wife Lisa and I came into Venice on the ferry from Athens, and only then did I really see the city and its lagoon, including the nearly deserted island of Torcello, and its church's great mosaic of the Virgin Mary—the one the tourists in my story are trying to take away. Last year I visited Venice again, and found giant posters of the Torcello Mary plastered all over town, as if to tell me: still here.

The rise in sea level described in the story is pretty stupendous, and yet in a century or two we may have done it.

"Ridge Running"

I started this story at the end of the Clarion I attended, in the summer of 1975, then worked on it again for Ursula Le Guin's writing class at UC San Diego, in the spring of 1977. Final efforts were made in 1983, when Ed Ferman bought it for *The Magazine of Fantasy & Science Fiction*.

This was the first published story of mine about being in the mountains, so I was really pleased when readers put it on the Hugo ballot—a generous gesture that has been a permanent encouragement to me.

"Before I Wake"

I kept a dream journal from 1975 to about 1980, and found that the ability to remember dreams is like a muscle: the more you work it, the stronger it gets. While recording my dreams I was often amazed at their surreality, and wished I could be so bold in my waking fiction. Then one morning I woke with the idea for this story. It would necessarily be a disaster story, but it would be a new kind of disaster—something to add to the Ballardian list of ways to wreck the world. I used some of my dreams' images in the story, so this one was truly "writing unconscious."

"Black Air"

I wrote this one in early 1982, soon after moving in with Lisa in Davis. I don't remember the idea coming to me; seems like one day I was writing it, and it already knew what it was. A mysterious visitor.

It was given the World Fantasy Award for best novella, and that was the occasion for a fun trip to Ottawa to receive the award. While there I visited Canada's national art gallery, and went to the Europe floor and was really unimpressed. I was in the elevator leaving the building, thinking Poor Canada, so culturally deprived, they have even managed to acquire five bad van Goghs, maybe the five worst van Goghs of all—when the elevator doors opened on the Canadian floor, revealing several giant canvases of the Group of Seven. I got out there and had one of the most visually stunning hours of my life. I learned that Canada does not need van Goghs.

"The Lucky Strike"

One day in 1983, when we were living in our little place in downtown Davis, the image came to me of the *Enola Gay*, flying toward Japan but then tipping over and falling into the sea. That was a story for sure, but what? After a few weeks of reading I wrote it out pretty quickly.

"A Sensitive Dependence on Initial Conditions"

After I wrote "The Lucky Strike," I began to have second thoughts about the postwar alternative history described at the end of that story. Back in DC after our Swiss adventure, I was reading all the new stuff about chaos theory, and some historiography in preparation for the Mars books, and it seemed to me human history might be regarded as a kind of chaotic system. This story was the result. It had a strange form, but it did what I wanted; and "form follows function" is one of the great rules.

"Arthur Sternbach Brings the Curveball to Mars"

This one I wrote in 1998, but the inspiration for it came from our two years in Zürich (1986–87), when I was a member of the baseball team Züri 85. My teammates were great guys, who made us feel more at home in Switzerland.

Arthur Sternbach also makes an appearance in my climbing story from 1983, "Green Mars."

"The Blind Geometer"

We first lived in Washington, DC, when Lisa was doing a summer internship for the EPA, in 1985. I was amazed by the thunderstorms that hit almost daily, storms far beyond any I had seen in California.

Right before moving to DC, I had decided that writing first-person from the point of view of a blind man could be my way to do an "alien story." Our Davis friend Ward Newmeyer introduced me to his friend Jim Gammon, who walked me around the UC Berkeley campus and told me a lot about the experience of being blind.

Carter Scholz taught me about the music Carlos listens to.

The story first appeared as a slim book. Gardner Dozois helped it a great deal when he edited it for its appearance in *Asimov's*. At that time I was experimenting with having the first and last words of stories be binary pairs that meant something to the story; thus "The Lucky Strike" starts with *war* and ends with *peace*, and *The Memory of Whiteness* starts with *now* and ends with *forever*. I had done the same in this story, starting with *point* and ending with *infinity*, but Gardner pointed out to me that while arranging this trick I had missed a much better last line located just a couple paragraphs earlier. We changed the ending, the story was much improved (thanks, Gardner!), and I stopped playing that first-and-last word game.

"Our Town"

I wrote this one in the autumn of 1985, as Lisa and I were taking the long way around in our move from Washington, DC, to Switzerland. The first half was written on a night train from Bangkok to Kosamui, the second half on a night train from Cairo to Luxor.

"Escape From Kathmandu"

When Lisa and I moved to Switzerland in the fall of 1985, we took the long way around, visiting Thailand, Nepal, Egypt, and Greece. The heart of the trip was our trek in Nepal. From the end of the road at Jiri to Everest Base camp and back, it was certainly one of the most beautiful months of our lives. Kathmandu was also beautiful, and it had a goofy cheerful quality I hoped to capture in a story. We had run into Jimmy and Rosalynn Carter and their group in Namche Bazaar, and even while we were still in our room at the Hotel Star, I was thinking "that should be used."

"Remaking History"

Greg Benford asked me for a contribution to the series of alternative history anthologies he was editing, and I sent him this. It is one of five stories in this volume written in 1987. I guess that was my Year of the Short Story.

"The Translator"

Robert Silverberg and Karen Haber asked me for a story for their *Universe* anthology, and this was the result. Lisa and I were taking German classes, and we would often laugh as we consulted our yellow German-English dictionary and found it less than helpful. Some of the multiple definitions in this story were taken directly from that dictionary, and the rest were inspired by it.

Being in Zürich, I was reading Joyce's *Ulysses* for the first time, and during my runs visiting the statue of him at his grave on the hill above us (see my introduction to *The Planet on the Table* for more about that). I think that a little of the style and character of Joyce's Leopold Bloom seeped into my translator.

"Glacier"

Another one from 1987. I had recently done some hiking on glaciers, a new and powerful experience for me. This story mixed that experience with my Boston year of 1974–75, and the time in Davis we cared for the cat Stella. I was also reading the magazine *Chinese Literature*, which published translated contemporary Chinese short stories, often beautiful examples of socialist realism.

The song from Gilbert and Sullivan that the mom sings is "Sorry Her Lot (who loves too well)," and it is actually from *H.M.S. Pinafore*; but it was included in the Linda Ronstadt production of *The Pirates of Penzance*, so I was fooled about its origin. I've kept the mistake in this story because I want *Pirates* to be the music in the family's listening repertoire; so one must assume they too owned the Ronstadt recording.

While writing this one I listened to Paul Winter's album *Sun Singer* over and over, and I think it would serve very well as a soundtrack for the story—it sure did for me. I can still hear it, and still see the view from my desk out our apartment window, with its linden trees, stately old buildings, and the rooftops of Zürich. For me this story has all those things too.

"The Lunatics"

If I recall right, this one came after spotting the element "promethium" in a periodic table lying around a friend's kitchen. (We were hanging with chemists.) I had had no idea there was any such element, and it made me laugh.

It's also true that a South African student I had taught at UCSD named Thabo Moeti, and his stories, and the plays of Athol Fugard that he introduced me to, and my travels in Asia, and my time in DC, had all made me think about things in new ways. This story fits with "Down and Out in the Year 2000," "Our Town," and "A Transect," in a little strand of stories I thought of as my South Africa strand. All of them owed much to Thabo's appearance in my life.

As I was working on this story, Beth Meacham asked me to contribute to an anthology she was assembling as a memorial to Terry Carr, who had recently died. This one felt right for that purpose, and I dedicated it to his memory. Then I remembered that the jazz trumpeter described in the story was one Terry himself had taken Lisa and me to see, back in the early eighties—driving us all over Richmond, California, before finding the right little dive. After that it seemed even more appropriate. "Now the bucket's got a hole in it—"

"Zürich"

It happened just like this. How we loved those years.

From Washington, DC, I sent this story to our German teacher, Oskar Pfenninger, who had lived in Japan. When he wrote back he told me that in Japan and Korea, white is the color for grief.

"Vinland the Dream"

When I was a kid I loved the stories of the Vikings in North America, including the story of the Kensington Stone, which revealed that Vikings had made it all the way to Minnesota. When that find was demonstrated to be a hoax (the fact that all its rune lines were multiples of one inch was the real clincher for me), I was shocked. Then later, reading about the questionable nature of the famous Vinland map at Yale, I began to wonder: two parts of the story were hoaxes, and the remaining evidence consisted of the L'Anse aux Meadows site and three Icelandic sagas. So what if….

Around the time I wrote the story, Lisa and I stopped at the little stone tower in Newport, Rhode Island, which has also been called a Viking artifact. It did look unusual.

"'A History of the Twentieth Century, with Illustrations'"

I drove around Scotland and the Orkneys by myself in 1987, starting the trip at the Clutes' flat in London, where I got the news that Terry Carr had died. I wrote the story in 1988, in Washington, DC, and I believe it was the last story I wrote before starting *Red Mars*. It would be about a decade before I got back to short fiction.

"Muir on Shasta"

This story is a companion piece to John Muir's own account of his Shasta climb, called "A Perilous Night on Mount Shasta," which is available in many collections of his work, including *Steep Trails* and *The Wild Muir*. Muir's Victorian-polite account of the crucial disagreement with his climbing partner made me laugh, and I thought it might be fun to portray what it must have really been like, while also using their adventure to make a brief homage to Muir. If you read the two pieces together you will see I have used a few phrases of his that were too good not to use; and for his visionary spirit voyage I took several images from his early journals, including the little house made of natural mountain materials. Muir's early writing, in many ways his best, can be found in *To Yosemite and Beyond*.

"Sexual Dimorphism"

This is from *The Martians*, written in Davis in 1998. Most of the stories in *The Martians* were written that year, joining two older stories, "Exploring Fossil Canyon" and "Green Mars." To that pair I added one more Roger and Eileen story, several about characters from the Mars trilogy, and then some like this one, about characters who weren't in the trilogy or the Roger and Eileen sequence. The thrust of my Mars books was mostly utopian, but even in utopia things can go wrong.

"Discovering Life"

Jane Johnson, my friend and editor at HarperCollins UK, asked me for a story for a private volume celebrating the fifth anniversary of her imprint Harper Voyager. I had visited JPL in Pasadena a few times in the previous years, and the recent claim by NASA scientists in Houston, that they had found signs of fossil bacteria in a Martian meteorite, had surprised everyone. The story was then included in the American paperback edition of *The Martians*, in 2000.

I wouldn't be surprised if one day this one came to pass. Seasonal appearances of methane on Mars seem to suggest life may be there.

"Prometheus Unbound At Last"

Henry Gee at *Nature* asked me for an 800-word story, to join his "last page of *Nature*" science fiction series, which ran weekly for over a year. It seemed to me that 800 words was awfully short, and I decided on the form of a publisher's reader report in order to cram in as much as possible. This one still makes me laugh, although it also contains my "prediction" for the twenty-first century that I think is most likely to come true—or hope is most likely. It's either that or big trouble.

"The Timpanist of the Berlin Philharmonic, 1942"
Last fall I was running with my iPod, listening to the Berlin Philharmonic's March 1942 recording of Beethoven's Ninth, when it seemed to me that the timpanist was imitating the sound of bombers. The story came from that impression, and from what I learned when I researched the situation.

You can see the last five minutes of the performance described in this story on YouTube. It's a German newsreel clip, which turns Hitler's birthday concert into Nazi propaganda. Only the footage used in the newsreel survives, so I pretended the complete recording of the symphony from March 22–24 (the one I had been listening to on my run) was of April 19, for the sake of imagining the story. Surviving evidence suggests the two performances were quite similar.

That I was looking for a short story to write at this time, I owe to the encouragement of Jonathan Strahan, the inspiration of my Clarion students of 2009, and the example of my friend Karen Fowler. My thanks to them; and again, to all my readers.

—Kim Stanley Robinson
January 2010

FIRST PUBLICATIONS:

"Venice Drowned," *Universe 11*, ed. Terry Carr, 1981.

"Ridge Running," *The Magazine of Fantasy & Science Fiction*, January 1984.

"Before I Wake," *Interzone #27*, January 1989.

"Black Air," *The Magazine of Fantasy & Science Fiction*, March 1983.

"The Lucky Strike," *Universe 14*, ed. Terry Carr, 1984.

"A Sensitive Dependence on Initial Conditions," *Author's Choice Monthly #20: A Sensitive Dependence on Initial Conditions*, 1990.

"Arthur Sternbach Brings the Curveball to Mars," *The Martians*, 1999.

"The Blind Geometer," Cheap Street Press, 1986.

"Our Town," *Omni*, November 1986.

"Escape from Kathmandu," *Isaac Asimov's Science Fiction Magazine*, September 1986.

"Remaking History," *Other Edens II*, ed. Christopher Evans & Robert Holdstock, 1988.

"The Translator," *Universe 1*, ed. Robert Silverberg and Karen Haber, 1990.

"Glacier," *Isaac Asimov's Science Fiction Magazine*, September 1988.

"The Lunatics," *Terry's Universe*, ed. Beth Meacham, 1988.

"Zürich," *The Magazine of Fantasy & Science Fiction*, March 1990.

"Vinland the Dream," *Isaac Asimov's Science Fiction Magazine*, November 1991.

"'A History of the Twentieth Century, with Illustrations,'" *Isaac Asimov's Science Fiction Magazine*, April 1991.

"Muir on Shasta," *Author's Choice Monthly #20: A Sensitive Dependence on Initial Conditions*, 1990.

"Sexual Dimorphism," *The Martians*, 1999.

"Discovering Life," *Voyager 5: Collector's Edition*, ed. 2000.

"Prometheus Unbound, At Last," *Nature*, August 11, 2005.

"The Timpanist of the Berlin Philharmonic, 1942" is original to this volume.